When Angels Rejoice

When Angels Rejoice
Guardians of the Saints, Book 3
©2023 by MaryLu Tyndall

ISBN: 978-1-7344420-9-0
E-Version ISBN: 978-1-7344420-8-3

Library of Congress Cataloging-in-Publication Data is on file at the Library of Congress, Washington, D.C.

This book is a work of fiction. Names, characters, places, incidents, and dialogues are either products of the author's imagination or used fictitiously. Any similarity to actual people, organizations, and/or events is purely coincidental.

Unless otherwise indicated, all Scripture quotations are taken from the King James Version of the Bible. Scripture quotations marked NKJV are taken from the New King James Version®. Copyright © 1982 by Thomas Nelson, Inc. Used by permission. All rights reserved.

Cover Design by Ravven
Editor: Louise M. Gouge

RANS🜨M
PRESS

Foreword

Dear readers, this book is not meant to be a study in theology. It is a work of fiction, an adventurous story that I hope will both entertain and enlighten you. Based on many years of personal research into the Scriptures and end-times prophecies, I have presented one possible scenario of what the future might look like. I realize there are a variety of opinions and theories regarding these important times. I also realize there are different viewpoints on predestination, free will, the gifts of the Holy Spirit, eternal salvation, and the Book of Revelation. However, the Word of God that is quoted and emulated by the characters is an expression of the truths found in the Bible. If you have questions or even objections, I encourage you to search the Scriptures for yourself and ask God to reveal His truth to you personally. In addition, no one really knows what the seven-year Tribulation will look like, nor the timing of the Seals, Trumpets, and Bowls of Revelation. I have offered one possible timeline based on my studies, along with descriptions of what life might be like during the most harrowing time ever known on Earth. It is not a pretty picture, but my hope in this series is for the reader to see how close we are to the Rapture and the Tribulation and therefore submit their lives to the only One who can save them—Jesus! Having said all that, if you're ready for an intense spiritual ride, then turn the page and let's get started!

Check out my When Angels Rejoice Pinterest Board as you read.

Dedication

To the magnificent saints who endure the Tribulation and
are willing to die for their Savior

And they overcame him by the blood of the Lamb, and by the word of their testimony; and they loved not their lives unto the death.

Revelation 12:11

But the wicked are like the troubled sea,
When it cannot rest,
Whose waters cast up mire and dirt.
"There is no peace,"
Says my God, "for the wicked."
Isaiah 57:20-21

Chapter 1

St. Augustine, Florida. Three- and one-half years into the Tribulation

Thomas Benton poured himself a healthy shot of his favorite Glenfiddich single malt and plopped onto his sofa with a sigh. "Play Daniel," he said, and instantly a hologram appeared before him, a scene as clear as the day he'd witnessed it and one he'd seen countless times since.

He took a sip of his drink, but as Daniel was led into the execution room, Thomas tossed the entire shot to the back of his throat. The pungent liquid seared a path to his belly, where it fanned out to numb his senses. Apparently not numb enough as words were exchanged between Daniel and his executioner—words Thomas had long since memorized—and a bundle of emotions spun a wicked web around his heart. A restricting, choking web.

The executioner had tried one last time to save Daniel's life, to get him to denounce Jesus, the fake Son of God so many fools had lost their lives over. But the stubborn idiot refused. Yet it wasn't so much Daniel's words, but the look on his face that confused Thomas. It was a look of complete and utter peace—something that had eluded Thomas his entire life.

Then, with a smile on his face, Daniel willingly put his neck onto the guillotine block and said, "Jesus, please receive me. I'm coming home."

And down went the blade.

Thomas looked away. Gripping the whiskey bottle, he poured another shot, but before he lifted it to his lips, he pitched it into the hologram and uttered a foul curse.

The scene disappeared. The glass struck the wall and shattered. Whiskey puddled on the floor.

Rising, he grabbed another glass, poured another drink, and made his way out the back sliding doors onto his immaculate lawn, complete with pool, hot tub, waterfall and so many lush tropical flowers, it smelled like a perfume factory. Tonight, it might as well smell like sewage for all he cared. Shoving past it all, he dropped onto the sand of his private beach and stared at a hazy moon rising over a dark sea.

Daniel had been dead for six months, so why couldn't Thomas get the man out of his head? Sure, they'd been friends, best friends since high school. They'd gone to seminary together. In fact, Thomas had been the one who got Daniel *into* seminary in the first place. Not only that, he'd risked everything to help Daniel succced, and together they'd started one of the largest and most successful churches in South Florida. Daniel had been well on his way to becoming the spiritual adviser to the US President, and Thomas would have been right there beside him.

Until Angelica Smoke came back into Daniel's life.

The fool! Giving all that up for a silly woman.

A humid breeze sifted through the hair at Thomas's collar, bringing with it the barest hint of the salty sea, rare these days when so much of it was polluted.

He sipped his drink. Thomas had given up everything for Daniel—time, money, his own preferences. He'd lied and cheated and even been willing to kill for him. But Daniel betrayed him in the end. Just like everyone else.

And for what? Some lie from the Bible? Some fictitious *messiah*. Or worse, a God who was evil, who punished, who ruled like a tyrant.

Daniel had chosen the wrong side.

Then why had he looked so peaceful, so happy at the end?

Arithem stood, feet spread, arms crossed over his mighty chest, shifting his gaze over the surroundings, alert to any incoming danger. His eyes landed back on Thomas, and he groaned at the sight.

"What ails you, my friend?" Zarall appeared beside him, following his gaze to the forlorn human.

"I have followed this son of Adam for three and thirty earth years, and he seems farther from the light than he's ever been."

"Ah, 'tis often darkest before the dawn, Arithem." Zarall, much shorter than Arithem, stared up at his friend.

Arithem snorted. "If that were the case, I should have seen many dawns before now."

Zarall chuckled. "Have faith, my friend. The Commander would not keep you with this son of Adam were there no hope."

Wind tossed Arithem's long black hair, stirring the sand at his feet. "I fear my hope has much diminished. Yet I still find myself determined to do all I can for him. See how he drinks that foul liquid? It robs him of his wits. He thinks it dulls his pain, but only our Lord can give such comfort."

"True. 'Tis unfortunate we cannot simply appear to these humans and tell them the truth, prove to them the Father is real and good."

"He wishes them to make up their own minds. But alas, their minds are so corrupted! So susceptible to deception. I could not bear it should this man end up in eternal fire."

Zarall laid a hand on Arithem's arm. "Never fear. 'Tis why I have come. The Commander has informed me our assignments have intertwined. We shall be working together."

"I don't understand. Your ward is a believer, a child of the Most High. Fortunate for you." He grumbled.

"Aye, and her path and this son of Adam's path are about to meet."

Thomas's phone chirped in his ear. He tapped it. "Benton."

"Regent Landry has a prisoner he needs you to interrogate, sir."

Thomas frowned. It was his assistant, Rodney's voice. "Now? I'm off for the night."

"Yeah. He says now. Sorry, sir."

"On my way." Thomas tapped the phone off before Rodney could answer. Growling, he rose, powered down the rest of his drink, and dragged himself back to his house. Before entering, he brushed off the sand and ran a hand through his hair. He hadn't even had time to get out of his business suit.

He'd wanted to be alone tonight. More than anything. He needed to think, to stare at the ocean, to get so drunk he'd pass out and maybe get some much-needed sleep. He could have attended the many parties thrown tonight to celebrate the death of those two crazy old Jewish men in Jerusalem, but he'd already gone to several the past few days. In truth, he found most parties dull.

After stopping to check himself in the mirror, he rushed out the door, waved his hand over it and commanded it to "lock and arm," then leapt into his electric Mercedes, whose door had automatically opened as he approached.

Within minutes, he stopped at the security gate of the New World Faith Reformation Headquarters, waited to be scanned by two robot security guards, then drove in and parked in his Vice Regent spot. He smiled as he got out of his car and approached the building. *Vice Regent.* Just one step below Regent Landry, the faith leader of the entire North American Region and one of ten spiritual regents who reported directly to His Excellency Gabriel Wolfe, Master Immu Aali's spiritual guide. Which meant Thomas was only two steps below the most powerful and influential religious leader in the world.

"Take that, Daniel Cain!" he snapped under his breath, as he passed his hand over the front door scanner and entered the building. He had made it. He had become even more successful and more powerful than Daniel could ever have dreamed of becoming.

Down the long, sterile hall and into the main operations room, Thomas marched with the authority of his station. Immediately upon entering, his assistant Rodney Barnes and the three other men in the room stood at attention.

Screens in all shapes and sizes lined the back wall, filled with views from the many cameras placed throughout all the reformation camps in the North American Region. Hooked to some of the fastest quantum computers, these systems kept track of every prison, prisoner, and guard. They knew every movement, everything they ate, even when they relieved themselves. Thomas often wondered if the computers could read their thoughts as well. He nodded at the technicians who ran the programs, lowly technicians doing their menial work, work that he would never have to do again.

No, Thomas was a spiritual guide, a New World Faith leader whose job it was to convert the masses to worship the one true god. Part of that job was to interrogate prisoners and recondition the brainwashing they'd received from democratic Christian ideas.

"Who is this prisoner?" Thomas took the folder from Rodney containing the prisoner's information and quickly scanned it. "A woman?"

"Yes, sir." Rodney tilted his head and shrugged. Dressed in the New World Faith uniform skirt and blouse, complete with heels, the only indication Rodney was a biological male was the shadow of a beard on his chin, though he tried to cover it up with makeup. Who was Thomas to judge? Since the Neflam arrived, it was a new, more inclusive world. Whatever Rodney identified as, he had been a great assistant, and that's all that mattered.

"Must be pretty important to be housed here at headquarters," Thomas said, "*and* for me to be called in so late."

"All I know, sir, is she's a high-level Deviant caught six months ago. Regent Landry says she knows a lot about the Deviants' plans, their meeting locations, and possibly even the location of their biggest hideout."

"Let me guess. She's not talking." Which was why Thomas had been brought in. Landry always assigned him the tough cases.

"Nope." Rodney quirked his red painted lips. "And she won't say a word to anyone but you."

"Me?" Shocked, Thomas glanced over the name. Victoria Williams. "Don't know her." He blew out a sigh. "And it couldn't wait until morning?"

"Not according to Regent Landry. He says if you can't break her, he wants her executed immediately, not put back into her cell where"—he raised a manicured brow—"apparently, she's been converting others with her lies."

Great. Another Deviant nutjob. Thomas glanced at the screen showing the celebrations in Jerusalem. The camera focused on the dead Jewish men lying on the ground before the newly erected temple. Crowds of cheering people danced and guzzled drinks around them. He was just as happy as everyone to see these two lunatics dead—thanks to Master Aali—but why leave their bodies to rot in the street? They must stink by now.

"Sorry to have to drag you away from your celebrations, sir."

"Naw. Went home. Which is where I'm heading again when I finish with this woman." He attempted a smile. "Where is she?"

"Room 5. Want me have a guard come with you?"

Thomas laughed. "For a woman? No. I'll be fine."

Turning, he headed down another hall to the left. Two uniformed men bowed their heads slightly as they passed him. *Respect.* Yes, he had well earned such respect.

The guard standing before Room 5 stood at attention at his approach and then opened the door.

Thomas walked in, slamming the door behind him, then sat in the chair across a table from the Deviant. Without looking up, he slapped her folder on the table, flipped it open, and briefly browsed her crimes, history, and psychological profile. Typical stuff. He'd done a thousand such interrogations before. Then leaning back in the chair, he raised his gaze to hers.

And nearly fell out of his chair.

There before him sat the one girl he had once loved more than any other. His high school sweetheart. "Tori. Tori Griffin."

*And I will give power unto my two witnesses, and they
shall prophesy a thousand two hundred and threescore days,
clothed in sackcloth. These are the two olive trees, and the two
candlesticks standing before the God of the earth.*
*And if any man will hurt them, fire proceedeth out of their
mouth, and devoureth their enemies: and if any man will hurt
them, he must in this manner be killed.*
*These have power to shut heaven, that it rain not in the
days of their prophecy: and have power over waters to turn
them to blood, and to smite the earth with all plagues, as often
as they will.*
*And when they shall have finished their testimony, the
beast that ascendeth out of the bottomless pit shall make war
against them, and shall overcome them, and kill them.*
*And their dead bodies shall lie in the street of the great
city, which spiritually is called Sodom and Egypt, where also
our Lord was crucified.*
*And they of the people and kindreds and tongues and
nations shall see their dead bodies three days and an half, and
shall not suffer their dead bodies to be put in graves.*
*And they that dwell upon the earth shall rejoice over them,
and make merry, and shall send gifts one to another; because
these two prophets tormented them that dwelt on the earth.*
Revelation 11:3-10

Chapter 2

Tori smiled at the shock in Thomas's eyes. Man, he
looked good. Tall, still boyishly handsome, but no
longer the thin, scrawny teenager she'd known. No, this man
was fit, powerfully built, with an air of authority about him. Or
was it arrogance? An expensive dark blue suit fitted nicely on
his muscular frame, complete with pins and various badges

displayed across his chest and rows of multi-colored stripes and banners lining the upper shoulders—an odd mix of religious and military emblems—all meant to show his position and power and to render fear and respect in those around him. His blond hair was perfectly slicked back and lay neatly at his collar, and not an ounce of stubble shadowed his stern jaw. He'd always been meticulous about his appearance, but this man before her could sway a crowd just by walking on stage. The eyes were the same, however, still a striking blue, blinking as if he could make her vanish.

"Tori?" His brows scrunched together.

"You remember me." She smiled again. "Wasn't sure you would after fifteen years."

"What are you doing here?" His expression remained twisted.

"You tell me. You're the interrogator."

He closed his eyes and snorted. "You're a Deviant? I don't get it, Tori. What? How?"

Tori cocked her head as a whiff of his expensive cologne enveloped her, not the cheap stuff he'd worn as a teen. "You've never been at a loss for words. Well, except when you were eighteen and you deserted me."

His jaw instantly stiffened. "*You* deserted me." He stared down at her file for several minutes, obviously trying to regain his composure. Same old Thomas, never wanting to show emotion, always wanting to be in control.

Shaking his head, he sat back in his chair, returning his gaze to hers. But this time, gone was the shock and confusion, replaced by a sheen of steel. Not only hard and impervious but clouded with hundreds of dark shadows flitting back and forth. *Demons.* Tori had plenty of personal experience with the heinous beings to spot them instantly.

"This says you were caught proselytizing Christianity, handing out illegal food, running an unsanctioned orphanage, defacing government property with Christian symbols, and causing distress and chaos among the citizens."

Laughter bubbled up in Tori's throat, but she did her best to subdue it. Still, a tiny smile escaped.

"You find this amusing?" Thomas's stern voice ricocheted over the white-washed walls of the room no bigger than a prison cell. He leaned forward. "Do you realize I could have you executed within minutes?"

So she'd been informed by her last interrogator. "Would you?"

Pushing his chair out, Thomas stood, his fists clenching and unclenching. "This isn't high school anymore, Tori. I am Vice Regent of the North American Region. I only interrogate prisoners no one else can break. Your life is in my hands."

Tori studied him. Past all the pomp, power, and pride, she could still see the insecure boy she had fallen in love with so long ago. "My life is in my Father's hands."

"You don't have a father," he spat back. "He left your mother twenty years ago."

"I'm speaking of my Heavenly Father."

Thomas shook his head, that confused look returning. "What happened to you, Tori? You were the last person in the world who would have fallen for these lies."

Tori nodded, thinking back to those years so long ago. She hardly recognized that young girl anymore or the woman she'd become afterward. "Let's just say I found the truth."

Thomas leaned his knuckles on the table. "The truth is that your God is an evil, controlling bully. Why do you follow Him? Why risk everything for Him?"

Tori's heart shriveled, not only at his words, but at the darkness pulsating in his eyes. She had heard Thomas and Daniel had started a successful church. When she'd finally got saved, she hoped Thomas had also. She'd prayed for him, in fact, even though she'd heard he'd been left behind when the Rapture occurred. But this? This complete denial and defilement of the true God?

"What happened to *you*, Thomas?" she shot back. "You, of all people, know the truth."

Thomas pushed from the table. "Bunch of lies. Lies that lead to death."

She fingered the course fabric of her gray prison jumpsuit before gazing up at him. "Jesus is the one true and living God, Thomas. It is you who have been deceived."

Horror filled his eyes as he shifted them to a camera perched in the top right corner, then back to her. "You shouldn't say such things, Tori. You could be executed on sight."

"And that's a bad thing?" Being freed from this horrible world and going home to her Savior? She hated being in prison, locked up where she couldn't do any good, couldn't help people, couldn't try to open people's eyes before it was too late. She lifted an unspoken prayer. *Either bring me home, Father, or set me free so I can serve You.*

"Don't be a fool!" Thomas shouted, bringing her attention back to him. "Listen, I can have the file deleted, if you will only cooperate with me." His voice softened, making her pity him, pity the darkness covering his mind and heart, pity the tough position she was putting him in.

Tori ran a hand through her messy black hair. "What is it you want?"

Retaking his seat, Thomas leaned closer to her. "Just two little things. Two things, and I can set you free."

She waited, all the while knowing whatever he asked, she could not comply. The smell of alcohol stung her nose. "You're drunk."

He frowned. "Not yet. But I plan on it soon."

"You never used to drink."

"Do you want to hear my demands or not?"

She shrugged. "Go ahead."

"One, you deny this Jesus, this God of the Bible, and two, you give me the location or locations of any illegal churches you are aware of."

"No can do, Thomas. Sorry." No hesitation. No need to ponder her answer.

His jaw stiffened again, and he emitted a low growl. "You don't have to actually believe it. Just say it," he whispered. "*And just give me one location. Something I can take to the Regent to prove your value.*"

Tori searched his eyes for any glimpse of her old friend. That he was willing to compromise his position to help her meant part of the old Thomas was still in there. But she could not meet him. Not even halfway. "You just don't get it, do you?"

"Get what?" He reached a hand toward her across the table, but instantly pulled back. "That you're throwing your life away and putting me in an impossible position."

"Okay, how about this then? If you order my execution, I forgive you and absolve you of all guilt." She smiled. "And as far as throwing my life away, that's what you don't get. I've found my life, eternal life, real life in Jesus. I would never give that up. Ever. So, you might as well close that file, stamp it with "Unable to reprogram. Recommend Execution," and be on your way."

Tori smiled at the shock in Thomas's eyes. Man, he looked good. Tall, still boyishly handsome, but no longer the thin, scrawny teenager she'd known. No, this man was fit, powerfully built, with an air of authority about him. Or was it arrogance? An expensive dark blue suit fitted nicely on his muscular frame, complete with pins and various badges displayed across his chest and rows of multi-colored stripes and banners lining the upper shoulders—an odd mix of religious and military emblems—all meant to show his position and power and to render fear and respect in those around him. His blond hair was perfectly slicked back and lay neatly at his collar, and not an ounce of stubble shadowed his stern jaw. He'd always been meticulous about his appearance, but this man before her could sway a crowd just by walking on stage. The eyes were the same, however, still a striking blue, blinking as if he could make her vanish.

"Tori?" His brows scrunched together.

"You remember me." She smiled again. "Wasn't sure you would after fifteen years."

"What are you doing here?" His expression remained twisted.

"You tell me. You're the interrogator."

He closed his eyes and snorted. "You're a Deviant? I don't get it, Tori. What? How?"

Tori cocked her head as a whiff of his expensive cologne enveloped her, not the cheap stuff he'd worn as a teen. "You've never been at a loss for words. Well, except when you were eighteen and you deserted me."

His jaw instantly stiffened. "*You* deserted me." He stared down at her file for several minutes, obviously trying to regain his composure. Same old Thomas, never wanting to show emotion, always wanting to be in control.

Shaking his head, he sat back in his chair, returning his gaze to hers. But this time, gone was the shock and confusion, replaced by a sheen of steel. Not only hard and impervious but clouded with hundreds of dark shadows flitting back and forth. *Demons.* Tori had plenty of personal experience with the heinous beings to spot them instantly.

"This says you were caught proselytizing Christianity, handing out illegal food, running an unsanctioned orphanage, defacing government property with Christian symbols, and causing distress and chaos among the citizens."

Laughter bubbled up in Tori's throat, but she did her best to subdue it. Still, a tiny smile escaped.

"You find this amusing?" Thomas's stern voice ricocheted over the white-washed walls of the room no bigger than a prison cell. He leaned forward. "Do you realize I could have you executed within minutes?"

So she'd been informed by her last interrogator. "Would you?"

Pushing his chair out, Thomas stood, his fists clenching and unclenching. "This isn't high school anymore, Tori. I am Vice

Regent of the North American Region. I only interrogate prisoners no one else can break. Your life is in my hands."

Tori studied him. Past all the pomp, power, and pride, she could still see the insecure boy she had fallen in love with so long ago. "My life is in my Father's hands."

"You don't have a father," he spat back. "He left your mother twenty years ago."

"I'm speaking of my Heavenly Father."

Thomas shook his head, that confused look returning. "What happened to you, Tori? You were the last person in the world who would have fallen for these lies."

Tori nodded, thinking back to those years so long ago. She hardly recognized that young girl anymore or the woman she'd become afterward. "Let's just say I found the truth."

Thomas leaned his knuckles on the table. "The truth is that your God is an evil, controlling bully. Why do you follow Him? Why risk everything for Him?"

Tori's heart shriveled, not only at his words, but at the darkness pulsating in his eyes. She had heard Thomas and Daniel had started a successful church. When she'd finally got saved, she hoped Thomas had also. She'd prayed for him, in fact, even though she'd heard he'd been left behind when the Rapture occurred. But this? This complete denial and defilement of the true God?

"What happened to *you*, Thomas?" she shot back. "You, of all people, know the truth."

Thomas pushed from the table. "Bunch of lies. Lies that lead to death."

She fingered the course fabric of her gray prison jumpsuit before gazing up at him. "Jesus is the one true and living God, Thomas. It is you who have been deceived."

Horror filled his eyes as he shifted them to a camera perched in the top right corner, then back to her. "You shouldn't say such things, Tori. You could be executed on sight."

"And that's a bad thing?" Being freed from this horrible world and going home to her Savior? She hated being in prison, locked up where she couldn't do any good, couldn't help people, couldn't try to open people's eyes before it was too late. She lifted an unspoken prayer. *Either bring me home, Father, or set me free so I can serve You.*

"Don't be a fool!" Thomas shouted, bringing her attention back to him. "Listen, I can have the file deleted, if you will only cooperate with me." His voice softened, making her pity him, pity the darkness covering his mind and heart, pity the tough position she was putting him in.

Tori ran a hand through her messy black hair. "What is it you want?"

Retaking his seat, Thomas leaned closer to her. "Just two little things. Two things, and I can set you free."

She waited, all the while knowing whatever he asked, she could not comply. The smell of alcohol stung her nose. "You're drunk."

He frowned. "Not yet. But I plan on it soon."

"You never used to drink."

"Do you want to hear my demands or not?"

She shrugged. "Go ahead."

"One, you deny this Jesus, this God of the Bible, and two, you give me the location or locations of any illegal churches you are aware of."

"No can do, Thomas. Sorry." No hesitation. No need to ponder her answer.

His jaw stiffened again, and he emitted a low growl. "You don't have to actually believe it. Just say it," he whispered. "*And* just give me one location. Something I can take to the Regent to prove your value."

Tori searched his eyes for any glimpse of her old friend. That he was willing to compromise his position to help her meant part of the old Thomas was still in there. But she could not meet him. Not even halfway. "You just don't get it, do you?"

"Get what?" He reached a hand toward her across the table, but instantly pulled back. "That you're throwing your life away and putting me in an impossible position."

"Okay, how about this then? If you order my execution, I forgive you and absolve you of all guilt." She smiled. "And as far as throwing my life away, that's what you don't get. I've found my life, eternal life, real life in Jesus. I would never give that up. Ever. So, you might as well, close that file, stamp it with "Unable to reprogram. Recommend Execution," and be on your way."

And after three days and an half, the spirit of life from God entered into them, and they stood upon their feet; and great fear fell upon them which saw them.
And they heard a great voice from heaven saying unto them, Come up hither. And they ascended up to heaven in a cloud; and their enemies beheld them.
Revelation 11:11-12

Thomas studied the woman he had once loved with all his heart. Instead of robbing her of her beauty, fifteen years had only enhanced it. Not even the stained prison jumpsuit detracted from her charm. Or was it charm? Or even beauty? There was something else that went beyond both, something in her eyes—a wisdom, a purity, a confidence—he'd not seen before.

What *had* remained the same was her hair, a wild mess of black silk, and those eyes—green, mesmerizing. Another thing that had remained was his reaction to her, the leap of his heart, the warmth surging through every inch of his body. It made no sense. He'd been with so many women after her, he was sure he was over her.

Obviously, he'd been wrong.

Then how could he send her to her death, no matter her beliefs?

Steeling his expression, he lowered his gaze and pretended to study her file again. She was the enemy, the enemy of everything he believed, the enemy of all humanity. He must remember that. He must put aside his emotions, shove them down, and lock them up in a forgotten chamber of his heart with all the others.

Gathering his resolve, he lifted his eyes to her again. Only then did he notice a small tattoo of a boot crushing a snake just below her right ear. Odd. Another small tat marked the left side of her neck, an eagle in flight. She'd always told him she wanted to fly away from her family, her childhood, her life. She'd begged him to come with her. But he'd had other plans.

Shaking off the memories, he searched for strength, for the familiar unfeeling resolve he'd acquired since taking this position. He'd ordered so many Deviants to their deaths. If it were anyone else, he'd have already stormed out of the room, already called the guard and given the order for her immediate execution.

But it wasn't anyone else. It was Tori.

"Tori, I beg you." He leaned forward, whispering again. "I'm asking one more time, just say a phrase, a simple phrase for the camera and then give me a location. Just one. None of the other interrogators would be so generous."

Her green eyes flitted between his, searching, yearning. Not a speck of fear appeared within them. Instead, something he never expected to see.

Pity.

His heart crumbled. His anger rose. No one looked at him with pity. Not anymore. Ever.

"I'm sorry, Thomas." Her lips flattened. "The Jewish men will rise."

"What?" He shook his head, confusion upping his irritation "Why are you talking about them?"

"I just want you to know before you have me killed that the God I serve is the real God. The Jewish men will rise, and Aali will be wounded in the head, but he will recover."

Thomas snorted. He seemed to remember some prophecy in the Bible about that, but he wasn't well-versed on such things. They'd never taught eschatology in seminary, and Daniel had never given a sermon on it.

"Don't you dare proselytize me. I am a mere two steps from Master Aali's spiritual adviser."

"Exactly why I need to tell you the truth."

Fury surged, tightening his nerves.

A knock sounded on the door.

Growling, Thomas rose and opened it. "No one disturbs me—"

"Apologies, sir, but you gotta come see this." If not for the look of fear on Rodney's face, Thomas would have chewed him out for the interruption. Instead, after one last glance at Tori, he shut the door and followed him to the control room.

Rodney pointed to the largest screen against the wall where a GNN reporter, her face a mask of shock, turned to stare behind her at the empty square in front of the Jewish temple in Jerusalem. A crowd of people stood around the edges of the square murmuring among themselves.

"They're gone," she said, turning back to face the camera. "Got up, raised their hands to the heavens, and flew into the sky." She pressed her ear where obviously someone was directing her. "We have a clip now."

The scene switched, filling the screen with the two old Jewish men who'd been a constant plague on mankind for nearly four years. Messengers of the God of the Bible, they'd said, and they'd proven it by preaching His false doctrines and threatening the world with disasters. Why would anyone follow a God who was so angry that He threatened His own children with pain and suffering? Whether or not the string of catastrophes—asteroids, meteors, poison seas and poison water, famines, volcanoes, droughts, and quakes—were a result of the Jewish men's threats or just coincidences, no one knew. But one thing was sure. No one could kill them. No one could remove them. No one could even get close to them, or fire came out of their mouth, devouring them.

Not until Master Immu Aali had finally shot them himself and thus had rid the world of their constant lies and threats.

Thomas sighed, impatiently watching the scene where the dead Jewish men lay in the same spot where Aali had killed them, the same place he'd seen them before he went into the interrogation room. Music, laughter and celebrations could be heard all around them when…suddenly, they moved. Slowly at first. Just a twitch of a hand, an arm lifting, a foot jerking. Then, they sat up, looked around, glanced at each other and smiled. *Smiled?* Rising to their feet, they lifted arms toward the sky, and Thomas could have sworn he heard a voice say, "Come up here." Then slowly they started to rise off the ground. The camera panned upward, following their movements, until they disappeared into a bank of white clouds.

Gasps and screams filled the air as the crowd surrounding them—people who'd been celebrating just moments before—covered their mouths and collapsed to the ground in fear.

Rodney eased onto a chair beside Thomas, so unlike him to sit in his presence, but Thomas would allow it for now. "Did you see that, sir?"

Yes, Thomas had. But he refused to believe it. "It's just a trick, Rodney. A hologram, some Project Blue Beam thing their God performed." Why? Because no one could raise the dead, and especially not after three days.

The scene switched back to the GNN reporter, who pressed her ear again. "Wait. We have a word from Master Aali."

The Grand Master himself appeared on the screen, walking down a long corridor, flanked by bodyguards on either side. Following close behind was His Excellency Gabriel Wolfe.

A reporter strode beside him. "Master Aali, what do you make of the two Jewish men who you killed suddenly rising from the dead?"

Exiting the building into the bright sunlight, Master Aali *tsked* but continued walking. "Surely you don't believe that? It was just a trick. I assure you, their dead bodies have only been moved out of our sight. Our enemy merely attempts to deceive us."

"That would be some trick," the reporter continued. "Are you sure? I mean, we all saw them rise with our own eyes."

Thomas cringed. Rarely did anyone question Master Aali's statements.

"A trick, I said!" Stopping, Aali glared at the poor reporter, who instantly backed away. But it was the look in Aali's eyes that sent ice down Thomas's back. Odd. He'd met the Premier more than once and never seen such a negative reaction.

"Now, if you please." Instantly, the hatred in Aali's eyes disappeared and his charming smile returned. "I must address the world." Dismissing the reporter with a wave, he mounted a set of stairs leading to a small stage before a crowd of reporters and citizens. Thomas could not place the exact location, but it had to be somewhere in D.C., where the Premier had been meeting with world leaders regarding food shortages.

Gabriel Wolfe took a seat behind him as Master Aali raised his hands to quiet the crowd.

"Citizens of the world, I can assure you—"

Crack! The air echoed with the sharp blast of a gunshot.

A red blotch appeared on Master Aali's head, and the leader of the world collapsed to the stage.

And I saw one of his heads as it were wounded to death;
and his deadly wound was healed: and all the world wondered
after the beast.
Revelation 13:3

Chapter 3

The world's only hope had been shot, the leader who had single-handedly brought peace to a war-torn, climate-stricken planet, who had given everyone a guaranteed income, free medicines, and provided food and shelter to those in need. The only leader who'd been able to dissolve the restrictions of nationalism and unite all countries into World Regions beneath a banner of peace and prosperity for all. The only man with the ideas, the technical expertise at his fingertips, to change weather patterns, increase crop production, and stop global warming. The only one through whom the Neflams spoke, giving him their wisdom and direction.

Thomas felt as though he'd been the one shot. Panic turned into pandemonium around the fallen leader. Screams and cries of agony blared from the TV screen as he was quickly put on a gurney and escorted to the nearest hospital. Would he live or die, they did not know, and the not knowing left the world without hope.

One of the guards in the room began to sob as others stared at the screen in shock and horror. Rodney kept repeating, "Oh no, oh no, oh no," until finally Thomas gripped his arm and gave it a squeeze. He stopped but didn't move. "Sorry, sir. I just can't…"

"I know." Suddenly fearful his own legs would give out, Thomas yanked a chair from another table and sat. Different reporters appeared on the screen, waiting for word about what had happened, who had shot Aali, and what his condition was. But it was too soon to know much of anything. No. Wait. The scene flashed to a man being dragged away in handcuffs. Blood oozed from fresh wounds on his face, where he'd no doubt been beaten.

"They found the shooter. A Deviant, it appears," one reporter said.

Of course. Only a Deviant would attempt such a thing. They hated Master Aali, hated everything he stood for, hated his reforms, even calling him the Antichrist.

As the officers dragged him away, other NWU police held back angry mobs as they spat on the man, uttering foul curses. Some even broke through and started slugging him. Finally, he was tossed into a black van and the door slammed shut. Thomas wouldn't want to be him right now. He faced nothing but years of endless torture and an excruciating death for what he'd done.

Scene after scene flashed across the screen—the ambulance racing through D.C., the hospital, the crowd screaming and crying. They wouldn't know anything of Aali's condition for quite some time.

Grabbing a remote, Thomas shut it off, flipping the screens back to scenes from the various reformation camps.

"We have work to do." He stood, glancing over the people in the room. "Now, more than ever, we have to do our jobs well. We have to rid the world of these Deviants and hold the New World Union together until Master Aali recovers." *If* he did.

Nodding and wiping tears from their faces, the guards and technicians went back to their duties.

Rodney stood. "What about your prisoner? What is your decision?"

Decision. Closing his eyes for a moment, Thomas rubbed them. He had no choice. He had to send the woman he'd once loved to the guillotine. She was a Deviant, and a Deviant had just shot the Global leader. All Deviants unable to be reformed must be executed. There was no other choice.

Yet…how could he?

Drawing a deep breath, he patted Rodney on the back. "I wasn't done with my interrogation. Afterward, I'll handle things. You are needed here more. Be strong for Aali's sake."

Wiping a tear from his eye, Rodney nodded and walked away.

Tori was not at all shocked to see the agitated look on Thomas's face when he rushed back into the interrogation room.

She crossed arms over her chest. "He was shot, wasn't he?"

"Yes," came his stern reply. Heaving a sigh of frustration, he rubbed the back of his neck. "How did you know?"

"God knew. It's written in the Bible."

"Bah. Lies!"

"Apparently not."

"Or"—placing his knuckles on the table, he leaned toward her, his eyes narrowing—"some crazy Deviant who knew the Bible wanted to make it happen."

Tori smiled. She had once believed that about Jesus and all the prophecies of His life in the Old Testament. That He knew what had been written about Him and simply performed it. But the more she studied His life, the more events she discovered that He, as an ordinary man, never could have controlled. "Maybe. But I'll tell you something else that's going to happen that no one but God can control."

Thomas gave her an annoyed look. "Listen, Tori. The only way I can save your life—"

"There's going to be a huge earthquake in Jerusalem within the hour. One-tenth of the city will be destroyed, and seven thousand people killed."

Thomas huffed and shook his head. "Give me a break, Tori. That's insane." He pushed from the table. "I'm giving you one more chance. Deny Jesus on camera and give me a verifiable location of one underground church, and I can spare your life. You'll go back to your cell and possibly even be released if you give us more locations. Otherwise, it's out of my hands, and you'll be killed tonight."

Tori's heart broke for the poor man. There was no peace about him, just a restlessness, an anxiety, and a deep sorrow. She leaned toward him, extending her hands, but he refused to grab them. "It's going to be okay, Thomas. Whatever happens, I don't fault you at all."

He growled, ran a hand through his perfect hair, messing it up, and turned his back to her.

"Sir!" A voice emanated from the intercom.

Thomas punched a button. "What!"

"Regent Landry is on the phone."

Without looking at her, Thomas slammed out the door, leaving Tori alone once again. Yet never alone. She felt the strong presence of her King, along with His mighty warriors. So, she did what she'd been doing for the past six months. She prayed. Only this time, she prayed for Thomas.

"You see what happened in D.C?" Regent Landry shouted over the phone so loudly, Thomas had to hold it away from his ear. Even in his office with the door shut, he worried everyone would hear the Regent's scolding. "This is all a result of Deviants. How is the interrogation of that Deviant witch going? I want the locations of these underground churches that plague me day and night! I want them located and every one of them shot on sight. No, I want their heads…or better, I want them crucified. Maybe that will stop this scourge of Christianity on our planet and the senseless murder of so many. Do you hear me, Thomas?"

"Yes, sir." He'd been waiting for an opportunity to speak. He'd learned long ago never to interrupt Landry when he was raging about something. "I have not been able to break the prisoner yet, sir."

"Well, you damn well better get it done tonight. Or better yet, we can have a public execution for all the world to see. That should appease some of the bloodlust over Master Aali's attempted assassination."

Everything inside Thomas knotted and coiled. Someone as high profile as Tori would make a great sacrifice for the world right now. But… "I promise you, sir. I'll either break her or turn her over to the executioners tonight." He nearly choked on the words.

"Keep me informed. I want to be there when she is executed. Call the press. I can hop on a plane and be there within two hours."

"Yes, sir." A huge, impenetrable lump swelled in Thomas's throat. Breaking Deviants or sending them to their deaths had been the main focus of his job the past two years. And he'd been good at it. He'd rid the world of hundreds of them, making it a safer place, a world of progress and peace. Yet they kept multiplying somehow. He could make no sense of it. What was the lure to follow a God with endless rules and regulations when it would only get you killed?

"You have an hour, Thomas. One hour. I want this finished quickly." The phone clicked off before Thomas had a chance to say anything else. Setting it down on his desk, he opened a drawer, grabbed his bottle of Five Malt Bourbon Whiskey and took a long drink.

Heat spread though him as he waited for the expected numbness to encase his heart. It never came. He took another sip and another and another. *Crap.* He felt no better. Certainly not calmer, nor able to make the horrible decision set before him.

Leaning back in his chair, he closed his eyes for a minute, suddenly wishing he had some higher power to pray to, someone who cared and could help. He laughed. No doubt the alcohol was affecting his reason.

Arithem folded arms across his powerful chest, watching his ward make one bad decision after another. 'Twas not like he wasn't used to disappointment when it came to this particular son of Adam, but he had to admit, he oft wondered why the Commander had him remain on task. There'd been no enemy attacks to ward off, no demons to battle, no messages to give, no sustenance to provide. Arithem felt useless, and he didn't like feeling that way. Especially when there was so much to do, so many worthy tasks to perform for the Kingdom of God.

Now, when faced with a pivotal decision, one that could affect his eternal soul, Thomas turned to alcohol, instead of to the only One who had all the answers. The liquor would only inhibit him from thinking clearly and rationally, from hearing from the Commander, and worse, it created openings for even more demonic beings to flood his already saturated body.

Still, Arithem could only stand by and watch as the dark shadows mocked him before they entered his ward. He'd grown accustomed to it with this one.

His one and only hope was that someday he would have a chance to battle these wicked spirits and thus wipe the grins from their evil lips. The Commander had told him such a battle would occur, though He'd withheld the outcome.

Regardless, Arithem must be ready. For there was much at stake—this son of Adam's eternal soul.

*I am crucified with Christ: nevertheless I live; yet not I,
but Christ liveth in me: and the life which I now live in the
flesh I live by the faith of the Son of God, who loved me, and
gave himself for me.*
Galatians 2:20

Chapter 4

Tori was not surprised when an hour later two guards
crashed into the interrogation room, unlocked her
shackles from the floor hooks, handcuffed her, and yanked her
to her feet. Neither was she surprised when they led her down a
narrow hall in the opposite direction from her cell. Thomas had
made his decision. She was to be executed. Rather than fear, all
she felt was pity…along with incredible sorrow for him. Her
heart had taken a blow seeing him again, but even more so
knowing that if he didn't repent and turn to Jesus, he'd spend
eternity in hell. Alternatively, in just a little while, she'd be
escorted to her heavenly home to see her Savior, her Prince, and
the One whom her soul loved more than anyone. She grew
excited with each step.

No doubt they'd make a spectacle of her and there might
even be some pain. A spark of fear tightened her nerves, but she
doused it with a simple prayer. "Not my will, but yours be done."
Wasn't that what Jesus had said in the garden of Gethsemane
before He was crucified? The pain and suffering He'd endured
for all mankind eclipsed any of man's pain since. And whatever
they threw at her, she could endure it because her Father was
with her.

The guard to her right released her and stopped to wave his
hand over a door. The lock clanked. He opened it, and Tori
stepped outside to the most gorgeous night she'd seen in a long
while. A half-moon smiled at her as if it were proud of the
splatter of twinkling diamonds spread across a black velvet sky.

A rare sight these days with all the smoke, pollution, and chemicals that often made things too hazy to see. So engrossed in the beauty, she tripped over a rock.

"Watch where you're going!" The guard to her left uttered a curse and wrenched her forward onto the courtyard where prisoners were allowed fifteen minutes a day. Fifteen minutes to see the sky, smell the air, feel the sun on their faces. Surrounding the compound, a tall fence, topped with electric barbwire reminded her she was a prisoner. Yet, in body only.

"Where are you taking me?" she asked.

One of the guards, a young burly man, spat to the side. "You're a special one, you are. You get the privilege of being crucified for all the world to see."

Tori gulped. Did Thomas hate her that much? Fear began to spearhead its way into her heart. Not the best way to die.

The other guard, gray haired with a hefty paunch, laughed. "Just like the God you worship. What an honor."

Oddly, the man's taunting words spread a blanket of peace over Tori, smothering her fear. Yes, it *was* an honor, a great honor to die as her Savior had. *Please give me strength, Lord.*

This is not to be your end.

The words filled her thoughts. She recognized that voice. It was her Savior's. "Thank you," she whispered into the night air.

"Did you hear that, Frank?" the first guard said. "She's thanking us for crucifying her. That's a first."

"Crazy Deviant," the other remarked, adding a vile string of more colorful adjectives.

They led her through another door, down a hallway, lit by blinking fluorescent lights, and then into another room, windowless, with one bench against the far wall. "You'll wait here until the Regent arrives. He wants to conduct your crucifixion." He shoved her onto the bench, locked her ankle shackles onto the floor hooks, and then promptly backhanded her across the cheek.

Pain radiated over her face and down her neck. Something warm trickled from her lips as the taste of blood filled her mouth.

The other guard laughed.

Tori slowly lifted her gaze to them both, knowing that what she said next would be rewarded by another blow, but she couldn't help it. "It's not too late for you. Repent, turn to Jesus. Worship the one true God, or you will be cast into the lake of fire."

At first, shock appeared on both their faces…for a brief moment…but then the expected hatred and fury twisted their expressions.

Bam! Another strike to her face, this time to her nose as more blood joined the drops from her mouth.

Cursing, both guards left. Tori glanced over the room, no bigger than a small bedroom. A tear rolled down her cheek, and she wiped it away, the handcuffs jangling on her wrists. A stench rose to join the acrid scent of blood in her nose—death and fear and sorrow. No doubt this was the execution waiting room. A camera perched in an upper corner watched every move she made.

The green light on top of it turned to red. Odd.

The lights went out. Nothing but thick blackness stretched before her. She moved her hands in front of her face. Nothing.

What's going on?

Thuds and groans sounded through the door. It squeaked open. A brilliant beam of light shone straight in her eyes. She blinked.

A person approached, knelt, removed a set of keys from his belt and unlocked her ankle chains. "Can you walk?"

"Thomas?" His aftershave surrounded her. "What are you doing?"

"Rescuing you, of course."

Arithem drew his blade. The spear of brilliant red light flashed as he took a stance over the fallen guards. "I am astonished he rescues her."

"I thank the Commander for it." Zarall, mighty ax in hand, emerged from the room where his ward had been imprisoned. "She did well, but human fear had begun to take its toll. The Commander has sent help at just the right time."

One of the guards attempted to rise, but Arithem put a foot on his head, keeping him on the floor. "You must be proud. She was ready to face a painful death for our Lord."

"Aye." Zarall glanced toward the room. "These humans speak boldly, but oft give in when faced with such excruciating pain. Not this daughter of Eve." Zarall smiled. "And you, my friend. Your ward rescues her. What an amazing miracle."

"I quite agree. Now we shall see where this leads."

"For now we must ensure their escape. This is our Commander's orders."

A slithering shadow flowed out of the burly guard, followed by another. Both created a cyclone around the human's head, whispering him back to consciousness. Gripping his ax, Zarall hefted it toward them, chopping them both in two. Agonized screams filled the air before they turned to dust and fell to the ground beside the guard.

Arithem nodded at his companion. Evil laughter rose from within the guards, along with the putrid odor of sulfur. He hated their smell most of all. A snake-like mist rose from the elder guard, swirling around Arithem's boots and circling up his leg. He attempted to shake it off, but 'twas strong, this one. The guard beneath his foot attempted to rise. Arithem looked to Zarall for help, but the warrior had retrieved his ax and battled two other demons.

In one swift move, Arithem sheathed his sword, grabbed his billhook and clipped the black snake, flinging it away from his legs. The repulsive demon flailed in mid-air but not for long. Drawing his light sword, Arithem severed off its head.

"Put on these clothes." Unlocking her handcuffs, Thomas handed Tori a guard uniform, the smallest he could find.

"What are you doing, Thomas?"

"You asked me that already. Hurry, we haven't much time." Still, her question made him wonder at his sanity. Honestly, he was acting on the only impulse permeating every inch of his heart—he could not watch the woman he once loved die, not without doing everything he could to deprogram her. He just needed more time! He shook his head. Perhaps the whiskey had given him more courage than sense. Either way, he was in too deep to quit now.

He turned his back while Tori undressed, calculating the time they had left before the power was restored and the guards returned from the small explosion he'd created in the generator room. The NWF Reformation Headquarters had its own power source in case of blackouts, which were frequent these days. They couldn't afford to have any of their high-profile prisoners escape, now could they? But that made it easy to sabotage from within. One strategically placed explosion had taken out both the main generator and the backup system.

Five minutes, he calculated. If all went well. Most likely they had only two.

Heart thundering, he shifted his flashlight to the guards he'd knocked out cold. One attempted to rise, but instantly fell back to the ground.

Shuffling sounded behind him. He clenched his jaw and glanced at his watch again. "We need to go. Now."

Tori dashed past him into the darkness. "Then what are you waiting for?"

Her tone carried no fear, but oddly a speck of humor. He ran to catch up with her, flashing his light in her direction. The uniform hung on her like old laundry on a line, and she had to hold up her pants to step over the fallen guards.

"Your doing?" She nodded toward the men and gave him a coy look over her shoulder.

Thankfully both of them were still unconscious. They'd have a fierce headache in the morning, but they'd survive. And they would have no clue how or why they'd passed out. Thomas had been sure of that. They would only remember passing a janitor with his cart of brooms and a distinct smell of mint in the air.

"Wait, Tori." He charged ahead, grabbed her arm, and halted her. "I'm rescuing *you*, remember?"

"It's not like I don't know my way around this place after six months," she said.

"No, but I take it since you are *still* here, you don't know how to get out." He raised a brow, his frustration growing beside his fear. But there was no time for either. "Follow me. Try to look normal. Like a guard."

Stuffing her hair up under her cap, she complied, falling in step beside him. But no matter what she did, there was no way she looked like any guard he'd met. She was far too petite, too curvy, and much too...well, at the risk of being labeled sexist...feminine.

Retrieving an arm band from his pocket, he passed it over the door lock, hoping, praying it would open. If not, all was lost. For security reasons, the doors and prison cell locks were on a separate power source from the main one that ran the complex, at least that's what he'd been told. Seconds passed like minutes. He waved the band over the lock again, his chest squeezed so tight, he thought it would implode.

Finally, the expected clank echoed through the room. Breathing a sigh of relief, he shoved it open, then charged down another pitch-black hallway. A left, a right, past two more locked doors, he led her through several stockrooms—the only rooms Thomas assumed would be empty at this hour.

In fact, so far, they'd not encountered a single person. A miracle, if he believed in them.

Also, the power—and the cameras—remained off, and the only sound Thomas heard was Tori breathing beside him. A sweet sound, if he weren't so petrified.

What the heck am I doing? Perhaps the whiskey was wearing off because he suddenly wondered if he'd lost his mind.

Along with his job *and* most likely his life if anyone found out he helped a high-profile prisoner escape.

Too late to go back.

Terror clawed up his spine as he adjusted his magnetic glove and used the armband to get through one last door.

A blast of humid night air that smelled of sewage and motor oil struck him. He gasped and tugged Tori beside him through the employee parking lot still blanketed in darkness. He had only seconds before the flood lights—and cameras—returned.

"Hurry!" Shining his flashlight ahead of them, he dashed for his car, weaving among the few cars still in the lot. Thankfully, Tori remained quiet beside him.

Why wasn't his door opening? Thomas charged toward the vehicle. Uttering a curse, he stripped off his glove. Instantly the door opened.

"Nice wheels." Tori started to get in, but he quickly moved his hand over the trunk.

"Sorry, babe. In here."

"The trunk? Really?"

"I know you hate enclosed spaces."

Tori bit her lip but quickly leapt inside…just as the parking lot flood lights turned night into day.

Another curse word shot from Thomas's mouth as he quickly shut the trunk, slid into the driver's seat, and started the engine. If he was lucky, the cameras hadn't had time to focus. Backing out of his spot, he forced down his rising nerves. He'd tried to think of everything, cover all his bases, but the one thing he couldn't have predicted was exactly how long it would take them to fix the power.

Tires screeching, he headed toward the exit. A guard stood at the security gate. A real human, not some robot or high-tech drone. Just what he'd hoped for. Stopping before the closed gate, he smiled at the guard.

"Oh, it's you, sir." The man instantly stiffened to attention.

"Yes," Thomas glanced at his name tag. "Officer Barnes, if you don't mind, I'd like to go home."

"Of course." Clearly flustered at meeting the Vice Regent, the man dropped his scanner onto the pavement. "Just a minute, sir." He fell from sight as he retrieved it. "They told me to check everyone." Rising, he dusted off his jacket.

"Is this really necessary?" Thomas glanced at the two large metallic scanners positioned high on the fence at his right and left. Red dots. Good. They had not yet come completely online. When they did, they would instantly detect Tori in the trunk, just as the guard's handheld scanner would do in moments.

"Yes, sir. I have my orders." He punched some buttons on his scanner and proceeded to scan the front part of Thomas's car.

Thomas stuck his head out the window. "You can't be serious! Do you know who I am?" He used his sternest tone, the one that sent his subordinates scrambling.

The guard instantly stiffened, halting his scan. "Yes, sir."

"Then I order you to open the gate immediately and let me pass!"

"Yes, sir. Sorry, sir. Wait." He pressed his ear where no doubt he received further instructions.

Sweat formed on Thomas's brow as he took a deep breath, trying to keep his focus. He revved his engine. The man held up a finger as he listened to the voice in his ear.

A voice that no doubt would put the seal on Thomas's fate.

Bless the Lord, ye his angels, that excel in strength, that
do his commandments, hearkening unto the voice of his word.
Psalm 103:20

Chapter 5

Z arall took the butt of his ax and struck the scanner in the guard's hand. It crashed to the ground. He hoped to damage the instrument, but the guard retrieved it, punched a few buttons, and it seemed to be working. He shook his head at Arithem.

"I shall attempt to cloak her." Arithem moved toward the trunk. A dozen demons scattered at his approach, shrieking and laughing. He ignored them. If the humans could not get past these scanners, as they called them, all would be lost. But losing was not an option. Not when the Commander had ordered them to ensure their escape. 'Twas possible for an angel to cloak a human from spiritual enemies, but from human electronics? Arithem was not sure. But what else could he do? Simply opening the gate—though Arithem could do so—would expose the attempted escape. In addition, they had no authority to harm this son of Adam, especially since a fellow warrior watched over him. The angel had acknowledged their presence but continued watching his ward with concern. Perhaps the innocent guard had a chance for redemption.

From within the car, Thomas shouted at the guard to let him go. He started to obey but then received a call.

Then the real battle began. A dozen of the enemy's fighters materialized out of the darkness and charged the three angels with weapons drawn. Arithem had his sword raised before they reached him. *Clank*! Their blades crossed, the sound reverberating into the night. Pushing the foul fallen one back, Arithem glanced at his friend, who was fending off two specters while also shouting in the guard's ear. Ah, brilliant! 'Twas a well-known tactic oft used by their enemy that if one caused enough noise in the spirit realm, the sons of Adam could not hear in the physical realm.

The guard's angel must have noticed as well for he fought off the hoard of demons trying to stop Zarall.

A putrid stench filled Arithem's nose, and he spun to find a short, squat demon charging him from behind. Gripping his blade, he slashed at the creature. The black mass let out a piercing shriek as the force of the blow flung him high in the air where he disappeared into the night.

Another more powerful spirit attacked Arithem from his left, catching him off guard. His light sword flung from his hand and landed on the ground, sending a shock wave through the pavement. Before he could grab another of his many weapons, the demon swung a mace at him clipping the armor on his chest. The evil spirit raised his weapon for another strike that would surely smash through Arithem's armor.

A whistle drew Arithem's gaze to his left, where Zarall tossed him a long knife. Catching it by the hilt, he swerved and drove the blade into the demon's belly.

The mace clattered to the ground. The demon screamed and turned to dust. Quickly retrieving his light sword, Arithem engaged two more advancing demons, dispatching both before rushing to help his friends.

A swoosh of night air blasted over Tori, along with the light of a moon and the dark silhouette of a man, hopefully Thomas. Yes, *Thomas*. His expensive aftershave filled her nose along with air, *precious* air. Her fear of small spaces was only surpassed by her fear of crucifixion, both of which she had faced tonight. Yet both times, the presence of the Lord had sustained her.

She took his outstretched hand, allowing him to pull her from the trunk. "Where are we?"

"My home. For now." His voice was tight, his tone unnerved. He took her arm and hurried her up a set of stairs to a beveled glass door that opened as they approached.

"Wait!" She jerked from his hand and halted at the threshold. "What's this about, Thomas? One minute I'm waiting to be crucified and the next I'm being escorted to your home."

"I'm trying to keep you alive," he ground out, clearly exasperated. Then grabbing her arm again, he attempted to pull her inside.

Struggling against his grip, she kicked him in the shin.

"Ouch." He released her and bent over to rub his leg. "What was that for?"

She crossed arms over her chest. "Alive for what? Brainwashing, torture? What are you up to?"

He sighed and stared at her. "Nothing nefarious, I assure you. Please, Tori. Will you trust me? At least come in the house before someone sees you."

"But you're one of them, a very high-powered one of them from what I can see." Her gaze took in his two-story mansion. "Why go against your own?"

"Please, Tori. I'll explain everything once we are inside."

He looked so pathetic standing there pleading with her like a lost boy who didn't know his way home.

Sighing, she turned and walked through the doorway.

Thomas followed and shut the door.

"Lights on," he said, and instantly an entryway appeared before them—a flash of sterile white from the marbled floor to the walls and up onto the ceilings. She blinked, her eyes adjusting as they landed on paintings on either side of her and a bronze statue of a dog guarding the way forward.

He moved into what must be a living room, though not like any she had seen. A long black and white checkered couch nearly filled the entire space except for a glass table that sat before it. To the right, a twist of stairs curved upward, framed by a wrought iron banister and to her left, a kitchen stretched on forever. All white. All pristine. Not a speck of dirt or grime anywhere.

"I thought we were done for back there." Thomas headed straight for a bar well stocked with bottles of alcohol neatly set in a row. "The guard got a call right before he opened the gate. I was sure his superior knew you'd escaped and was going to order him to search all cars, even mine."

"Why did he let us go?" Not that she already didn't know.

A sliding glass wall made up the entire back wall and beyond it, a swimming pool, lit with blue lights, rippled in the breeze. Thomas had done well for himself. But then again, he *was* a Vice Regent.

"Don't know." Thomas poured a drink and slammed it to the back of his throat. "He said he couldn't hear whoever it was on the other end, so he just passed us through. Odd. The power outage shouldn't have affected communications."

Tori lowered onto the edge of the large couch. She'd sensed a strong demonic presence around the car, knew they were being attacked, knew angels had defended them. Even now, she sensed God's mighty warriors in the room, though she couldn't see them. She'd had glimpses of them off and on when the Lord afforded her rare moments of spiritual sight, and the vision of such powerful beings usually brought her peace.

But she felt no such peace now. After six months in an eight-by-eight-foot cell, she'd had time to come to grips with her execution. With God's strength, she'd even resigned herself to a gruesome death. But now? Was she safe? Or was this merely another prison cell, albeit a more luxurious one?

"Want a drink?" Thomas glanced her way, but she shook her head. He poured another and took a seat across from her.

Tori glanced around the room, a bigger living space than the entirety of most homes.

He followed her gaze. "Pretty impressive, huh? Did you ever think I'd own a house like this?"

"House? More like a mansion," Tori said. "Do you spend any time here at all?"

"What do you mean?"

"It looks like no one lives here. Like a model home they use for tours or something."

He sipped his drink, clearly annoyed at her reaction. "I've worked hard for what I have."

She studied him. Darkness surrounded him in a mist of gloom and despair no amount of money could abolish.

"So, out with it. Why am I here?"

Breathing out a sigh, he stared at his empty glass. "I couldn't see you die. Not that way." He flattened his lips and finally raised his gaze to hers.

And beyond the alcoholic haze, she spotted the boy she'd once loved.

"If that's true, I'm grateful, but why risk everything for me? What is your plan?" Rising, she shifted her back against the itchy uniform.

"*If* that's true?" He slammed his glass on the table, his voice lowering to a primal growl. "You realize what I saved you from?"

Ignoring his angry outburst, Tori moved to the sliding glass wall and stared out. A shiver coursed through her as visions of crucifixions trampled her mind. She spun to face him, her own anger raging. "Do I realize that your people would have tortured me, nailed my feet and hands to a cross, and hung me up to die?" Forcing down her fury, she turned back around. "It would have been a privilege to die the same death as my Lord."

Thomas cursed, grabbed his glass and marched back to the bar. "Insane Deviant talk."

Tori's heart grew heavy. He was so lost, so deceived. *What do I do, Lord? What do I say?*

"What do you intend to do with me?"

"I'm going to help you see the truth."

"I already know the truth." Making her way to him, she laid a hand on his arm, stopping him from pouring another drink. "What will happen to you when they realize you helped me escape? Should we even be here now?"

Jerking from her touch, he huffed and continued pouring. "Don't worry, you're safe here, Tori."

"I'm not worried about myself."

Grabbing his glass, he stormed to the back windows. They slid open at his approach.

She followed him outside. "I don't care how powerful you are. I'm sure they tracked your movement...wait,"—Tori smiled—"you wore a glove."

He slid onto a chair by the pool. "And I used one of the temporary visitor arm bands. No one will know it was me."

"But won't they know who took the visitor band?" The black-bottomed pool looked so inviting, Tori longed to dive in. "They'll know it was an inside job."

"You underestimate me, Tori. I'm not the naive boy you knew. I have more power now than you can imagine." He finished his drink and set the glass down on the tiles beneath his seat. "No one will know it was me."

Relief swept over her, along with a breeze ripe with the scent of flowers and salt. The gentle crash of waves provided soothing music to the nerve-wracking events of the night. Of course, he would have beachfront property. Kicking off her shoes, Tori rolled up her baggy pant legs and sat, dangling her legs in the pool. "Still, you risked everything for me, and I'm grateful, Thomas." She looked up at him and caught him smiling at her before he glanced away.

With all the alcohol he'd just consumed, she wondered how he remained upright. "What I still don't understand is why. Despite our past, why risk everything for a Deviant?"

And the same hour was there a great earthquake, and the tenth part of the city fell, and in the earthquake were slain of men seven thousand: and the remnant were affrighted, and gave glory to the God of heaven.
Revelation 11:13

Tori's question whirled in Thomas's head, searching for a response, any response beside the one his heart was shouting. The star-lit sky above him spun uncontrollably, and he leaned back in his chair, doing his best to avoid looking at her, but unable to stop. Besides, she was far too cute in that baggy uniform, swinging her feet in the pool like a little girl, her hair a mass of dark waves, dirt smudged on her face, and her pointed questions that went straight to the heart of the matter. She'd really not changed all that much. Well, except for the Deviant brainwashing.

Why had he done it? Why had he risked everything he'd worked for?

"I needed more time with you," he blurted out.

She snapped her gaze to him. "I told you I'm not denying Jesus or giving you the information you want. No matter what you do for me. Or to me."

From the look in her eyes, she meant it.

"I could never hurt you," he murmured. With great effort, Thomas leaned forward on his knees. "You've been brainwashed. You are following the wrong god. I just couldn't stand by and let them kill you until I'd tried everything in my power to save you."

She laughed, swishing her legs through the water. "Save me? Thanks for your honesty, but you might as well just take me back to my cell now because I will never reject my God."

Thomas huffed. That's what many Deviants said before he'd cracked them. It was his job, one of many, and he'd been well trained. He would break her. He knew it. He just needed some time. "We'll see."

She drew a deep breath, then released it as wind whipped her hair. "So, am I your prisoner until you break me?"

"Just give me a week, Tori, okay? Promise you'll stay here a week and listen to me. Afterward, if you want to leave, you can." It's not like he could simply walk back into work and return her anyway.

She seemed to be pondering his offer….as if she had a choice. But that was the first step in breaking someone, making them believe they had choices.

"Deal," she finally said. "A week. But be careful"—she gave him a sly grin—"it might be you who breaks."

He laughed. He couldn't remember the last time he'd really laughed. It felt good.

"Why do you drink so much?" she asked.

"It relaxes me. Calms the voices in my head."

His phone chirped. Reaching in his pocket he pulled it out. "Benton."

"Sir," Rodney shouted from the other end. "That prisoner you interrogated. She escaped!"

"What?! Are you sure?" Pull it together Thomas. You don't sound very convincing.

"Yes. Somehow, she knocked out two guards. We have no idea how she got off the compound. Regent Landry just arrived and wanted me to call you."

Thomas rubbed his head. "Okay. Do you need me there?"

"No, sir. He says nothing you can do now. Just wanted to keep you informed. Sorry to disturb your sleep. Oh, sir, since you're awake now, turn on the TV. You aren't going to believe what's happening in Jerusalem."

"Will do, Rodney. See you in the morning."

"Was that about me?" Tori asked.

Thomas attempted to rise but fell back down. Maybe he'd overdone it a bit with the whiskey. Leaping to her feet, Tori headed toward him, but he raised a palm. "I'm okay. And yes, that was about you, and they don't suspect me." Standing, he got his bearings and stumbled back inside.

"TV on," he said and the wall beside the kitchen transformed into a giant screen.

A reporter, covered in dust, stood before a crumbled building as scenes flashed of ruptured streets, collapsed structures, and dead bodies. "Again, a major earthquake has just struck the city of Jerusalem. Scientists are saying it may have been well over a nine on the Richter scale."

Police sirens, along with screams and shouts could be heard in the background as the man continued. "Initial estimates are that at least ten percent of the city has been destroyed and thousands have been killed."

Shock speared through Thomas's veins, slicing away the effects of his drinks. He turned to find Tori standing beside him. "How did you know?"

Before she could answer, the scene switched to a woman standing in front of Walter Reed National Military Hospital in D.C. Tears streamed down the poor lady's face as she attempted to speak. Finally gathering herself, she took a deep breath. "Premier Immu Aali is dead."

*Because that which may be known of God is manifest in
them; for God hath shewed it unto them. For the invisible
things of him from the creation of the world are clearly seen,
being understood by the things that are made, even his eternal
power and Godhead; so that they are without excuse:*
Romans 1:19-20

Chapter 6

"Tom, this is Sergeant Kyle Cruz." Regent Landry entered
Thomas's office without knocking as usual, a young man
quick on his heels.

Gathering what remained of his brain behind the incessant
pounding, Thomas stood to attention. The quick action nearly
made him puke. Yes, he'd drunk too much. He knew that now
as much as he'd known it last night when Tori had yawned, said
goodnight, lay down on the couch, and promptly fallen asleep.
No amount of jostling or jiggling could rouse her so he could
show her to one of the bedrooms. How the woman could fall
asleep so quickly and so soundly after her terrifying night was
beyond him. But then again, she'd always been that way. Even
as kids, nothing stressed her out, at least not to the point of
missing sleep. Thomas, on the other hand, well, let's just say, he
couldn't be more different. Still, it had given him a chance to
watch her sleep while he powered down coffee that morning—
the rise and fall of her chest, her long lashes spread over her
cheeks, her light snoring, and the way she muttered and moved
her lips as if she were carrying on a conversation. Knowing Tori,
she probably was.

He'd hated to leave her, but he had to go to work, both to
dispel any suspicion and to help his colleagues deal with the loss
of one of the world's greatest leaders. Thomas still couldn't
believe that Aali had been assassinated. When things settled,
he'd no doubt accompany Regent Landry overseas to meetings

of the World Council where they would decide who would take Premier Aali's place. But for now, the world needed to mourn.

And Thomas needed to make sure no one suspected him of Tori's escape while he reversed her brainwashing.

"Tom!" Regent Landry barked. "Did you hear me?"

"Sorry, sir." He hated it when the man called him Tom. He especially hated that look of censure in his beady dark eyes whenever Thomas didn't live up to expectations. So much like his father—too much. With his outrageously expensive suit, slicked back salt and pepper hair, and perfectly trimmed beard, Landry always appeared ready for a photo shoot for Gray Foxes magazine—if there was such a thing. "I...I...Sorry, I'm a bit distracted today."

At first Landry frowned, but then he sighed and nodded. "I suppose we all are. Tragic. Just tragic what happened." He exchanged a glance with the young man, Kyle, was it? "Nevertheless," he continued, "I'm putting Sergeant Cruz in charge of the Tori Griffin debacle. Hard to believe that one of our own helped her escape, but there's no other explanation."

Thomas swallowed, studying the young man. Clean-shaven with a mop of black curly hair and a strong physique, the man couldn't be twenty-five. Maybe that was a good thing. *Inexperience.*

"Sergeant Cruz is an up-and-coming star in Global Reformation Security. In just three years, he's risen from a low-level guard to the head of security for all global reformation camps in the Florida region." Landry fingered his perfectly trimmed gray beard. "He's also become one of our best liaisons between the Tall Whites and our security forces."

A sour taste bubbled up in Thomas's throat. Tall Whites? Thomas had only seen the alien creatures twice, only spoken to one once, and that had been enough to send uncontrollable shivers—not entirely unpleasant—throughout his body. Yes, they had helped mankind immensely—arrived at just the right time before war hawks nuked the planet, slowed global warming, brought incredible new technology, and brokered a global peace. But in light of whatever spell they seemed to cast on others, Thomas wanted nothing to do with them. Still, they possessed great power, and that meant anyone connected with them had great power, perhaps even otherworldly power.

Landry patted Cruz on the back. "He's responsible for catching six escaped prisoners this past year alone. I have no doubt he'll get to the bottom of what happened and catch Ms. Griffin."

"You can bet on that, Regent Landry," the boy said with more authority than Thomas would have expected.

Six? Of course Thomas had heard about the escapes and that some wonder guard had captured them. But *this* kid?

He cleared the lump of dread in his throat, attempting a normal tone. "What is the secret to your success, sergeant?"

The boy's lips quirked to the side as a flash of pride beamed across his eyes. He shrugged. "Hard work and wits, sir. After my sister slipped through my hands, I became more determined than ever to make up for that mistake."

Sister? Brows raised, Thomas glanced between Cruz and Landry.

"You remember Nyla Cruz?" Landry asked.

Nyla Cruz, one of the most notorious Deviants! She'd been at the top of their wanted list for years. She and her husband were responsible for setting up multiple underground churches and deceiving many into committing treason against the New World Union. They were a festering cancer that must be eliminated, yet, for some reason, they always seemed to evade capture. And now, it was rumored they ran a hideout of Deviants somewhere in the Appalachian forests. "Yes, of course. I can see why you are so determined, sergeant."

"I will catch her one day, you can bet on that, sir. But for now, I will find Miss Griffin and discover who helped her escape."

Thomas gave a flat smile. "Of course. Let me know if I can be of any assistance."

"I've given Cruz complete authority here," Landry said. "Especially when you and I are absent, as we may well be. I expect us to be called overseas soon."

Thomas nodded, his usual excitement at being a part of such important global meetings squelched by the visitor hiding in his home. If he left town, she would most certainly leave. Who was he kidding? She might already be gone. Though her promise used to mean something, she might have taken the opportunity to flee for her life. Who wouldn't? The thought pierced him like a knife.

"I do hope you find whoever it was who helped the prisoner escape, sergeant." Thomas said. "Though it seems they covered their tracks pretty well."

"Don't worry, sir," Cruz lifted his chin slightly. "Everyone makes mistakes. Even the smartest and most cunning."

Tori never tired of the beauty of God's creation. Even after all the disasters—the meteors, asteroids, tsunamis, quakes, plagues, and volcanoes—had destroyed much of the land and sea, even after the NWU had manipulated weather patterns and most of the old farmland barely produced any crops, even after fires had destroyed parks and forests, and the skies remained a gloomy gray, even so, the original beauty of the planet couldn't help but shine through in rare moments. Moments like this morning when Tori rose, found paper and pencil, and headed out to the beach.

Lord, you are incredible. Even in the midst of the Tribulation, you display your beauty, delighting those of us who still notice. I praise You!

Digging her feet into the cool sand, she continued drawing while she prayed, thanking God for her rescue, for Thomas, for allowing her to stay to help save more souls, and praying for His strength and mercy.

A warm breeze eased over her as if God Himself were caressing her face. "Are you pleased with me, Lord?" she whispered into the wind, longing to hear an answer, longing to see a vision of the Lord Himself walking to her over the incoming waves. Rays from a golden sun scattered glitter upon foamy ripples as they lapped ashore. Birds with long skinny legs hopped about in the pools of water, no doubt seeking crabs or tiny sea creatures to eat. If there were any left. Much of the wildlife had died already. But she didn't want to think about that. She wanted to enjoy the gorgeous scenery and sing praises to her Father.

"I wish you'd appear to me, Lord, or maybe allow me to see one of your angels?" The ones she felt so strongly wherever she went. The ones people like Nyla saw so often. Tori glanced right, then left down the coast, still surprised no one else was enjoying the beach. But then again, these were private beaches belonging to the rich who could afford mansions like Thomas'.

No angels appeared. No visions of glory or heaven to keep her going, give her hope. Nothing. She sighed. She didn't deserve it anyway, not after the life she'd led. No, it seemed the only beings she ever saw were demons, and to be honest, she'd seen enough of those vile creatures to last a lifetime.

A bird squawked overhead as the first drip of perspiration slid down her back. She hurried to finish her drawing before the heat became oppressive. The Lord might not have given her the ability to see angels, but He had given her a prophetic gift, which she had used to help many people see the light.

"Thank you, Lord." She finished her drawing and set it aside, then leaned back on her arms and raised her face to the sun. "You have given me all I need to do Your work. Please help me to complete my job in these hardest of all last days. Give me a chance to make up for what I've done."

Instead of receiving an answer, a gust of hot wind struck her, firing sand into her face and sending her drawing teetering in the air. Leaping to her feet, she scrambled to get it just in time, then plopped back down into the sand and laughed. Placing the paper beneath a crusty shell, she laughed some more, unsure what was so funny. Certainly nothing in the world, nor anything in her life, but it felt good, and she fell back to lie in the sand. An odd thought flitted through her mind, and she swung out both arms and legs. A sand angel. *See, Lord, I can see angels*!

Thomas's heart shriveled as he walked through his house, calling Tori's name. She must have left, as he suspected, broken her promise like every other person he'd ever trusted. He couldn't really blame her, but somehow, he'd hoped…. hoped she would be different. He cursed. Hope was for fools. After pouring a shot of whiskey, he headed out to the pool, noticed the back gate open, and went to shut it when…

The most astounding, beautiful, yet *odd* vision appeared on the beach before him. Tori, lying on the sand, laughing and making a snow…no, a sand angel. Leaning against the gate, he stared at the spectacle, wondering if he was seeing things. Had she gotten into his alcohol? There was no other explanation.

But who cared? *She was still here*!

The leap of his heart nearly matched the confusion storming through his brain. She *was* here, but clearly the stress had driven her mad. Yet he found himself smiling, unable to tear his gaze away, unable to stay away at all.

Slowly, he made his way toward her, grumbling at the sand creeping into his Bontoni Italian shoes. He halted beside her, blocking the sun. "You're getting sand in your hair," was all he could think to say.

She stopped, opened one eye and squinted at him. "Join me. It's fun! And from the looks of you, you could use a little fun."

"I have plenty of fun," he returned sharply, thinking of all the parties he'd attended, all the drugs, alcohol, and women he'd had. Then why did this simple childish act of hers seem like more fun than all of those put together? He would ask what she was doing out here, but that much was obvious. Instead, his gaze landed on a paper flapping in the breeze beside her, and he moved to retrieve it.

It was an exquisite drawing of the sea, complete with foamy waves and sunlit sand and little birds hopping along the shore. Even though devoid of color, there was life to the drawing, as if it moved and danced in harmony with nature's song. Thomas knew she'd gone to art school, but he'd never actually seen her work.

"This is really good."

Sitting up, she squinted up at him. "Thanks."

Speckles of sand dotted her wind-swept hair as pink formed on the tip of her nose from the sun. And Thomas wanted nothing more than to take her in his arms and hold her until the ache in his soul went away.

"What are you doing home anyway?" she asked with a grin. "Checking on me?"

He longed to sit beside her but didn't want to soil his suit. Instead, he took his coat off and rubbed the sweat from the back of his neck. "I took a break…wanted to see how you were doing."

"Yeah, checking on me." She chuckled. "I promised you I'd stay for a week, didn't I?"

He held out his hand. "What say I order some food and we have lunch?"

"Sure." Gripping his fingers, she allowed him to pull her up, showering him in sand.

"Sorry," she said, giggling.

He attempted to brush off his shirt and pants. "By the way, what were you laughing at before?"

She glanced down at the perfectly formed angel and smiled. "Nothing in particular, I guess. Just enjoying a moment with God."

Thomas suppressed a gag. He certainly had his work cut out for him in the next week.

Back in the house, their food arrived, and if he were honest, he was having a wonderful time enjoying a meal with Tori. He didn't even mind that she'd dragged in sand everywhere, that her hair was a tangled mess, and she still wore that baggy guard uniform.

He'd missed her smile, her carefree attitude, and the way she erased all the problems of the world with her very presence. He'd have thought life would have hardened her by now, made her skeptical and cranky, but she seemed even more joyful than he remembered, if that were possible. She was a Deviant, on the run for her life, but she acted as if she were the one with the huge mansion and prestigious job and more money than she knew what to do with.

They talked about the fun times they'd had as teenagers, a little about her experiences at art school, but mostly about him. He'd forgotten how good a listener she was, how easy she was to talk to, and he found himself wanting to share everything with this woman. More than once, he had to remind himself that he was the interrogator, not her.

Finally, near the end of the meal, she blurted out, "Premier Aali will rise from the dead in three days. Well, two now, I guess."

The happy mood of moments ago fell to the floor in a heap. But it was a good reminder of his task here. To fix her. To reprogram her. "He's going to rise from the dead?" Standing, he dabbed the napkin over his mouth and tossed his paper plate in the garbage. "Come on, Tori, nobody rises from the dead, not even your Jesus. Even the Neflams can't do that. I know Aali was charismatic, kind and brilliant, but he was just a man."

"He won't be a man when he rises." She plopped a shrimp into her mouth. "You'll see."

He studied her, searching for insanity taunting him from her green eyes. Nothing but clarity and kindness returned his gaze.

"Okay. Let's talk about this tonight. In the meantime, you can use the third bedroom to your left. You'll probably find some clothes there that will fit you. And feel free to take a shower."

He hated to alert her to the fact that other women had stayed here, but it wasn't like he could order women's clothing without it being flagged by those searching for the person who helped her escape.

This Sergeant Cruz with his ties to the Tall Whites was not one to mess around with. Thomas must be extra careful not to make a single mistake. Or he had the feeling he'd be the one to be crucified.

*And there was war in heaven: Michael and his angels
fought against the dragon; and the dragon fought and his
angels, and prevailed not; neither was their place found any
more in heaven. And the great dragon was cast out, that old
serpent, called the Devil, and Satan, which deceiveth the whole
world: he was cast out into the earth, and his angels were cast
out with him. And I heard a loud voice saying in heaven, Now
is come salvation, and strength, and the kingdom of our God,
and the power of his Christ: for the accuser of our brethren is
cast down, which accused them before our God day and night.*
Revelation 12:7-10

Chapter 7

One more thing, sir, if you don't mind." Sergeant Cruz's pesky voice followed Thomas into his office.

Honestly, he *did* mind. After two days of annoyingly pointless questions by the young upstart, Thomas was developing a keen dislike of the man. Circling his desk, he took a seat and pretended to read a document laid out before him, hoping Cruz would take the hint and leave.

He didn't.

He merely stood at attention waiting for Thomas to look up. When he finally did, it was to a cocky grin that Thomas longed to punch off his face. Better yet, he'd love to send the lad packing to wherever he came from. Thomas had more power in his pinky than this boy could ever hope to achieve in a lifetime. Yet here he was having to endure being interrogated like some Deviant.

"Listen, Cruz. I know you have a job to do, but I've answered all your questions. Now, if you don't mind, I have a ton of work."

"Sir, of course. I'm sorry to bother you so much, but I still don't understand a few things." Cruz pulled out his phone and began typing. "For instance, how the perpetrator was able to get a visitor digital ID from Security without any record? And why all the sensors and cameras in that area were out for five minutes on the day of the escape?"

"And I've told you," Thomas ground out. "I have no idea."

Cruz looked up and sighed. "But that doesn't make sense, sir. You told me that very few people have access to Security or even the know-how to activate a digital badge."

Thomas returned his gaze to the document. "That's right."

"And that you are one of those few."

Thomas's gaze snapped to Cruz. "What are you saying, sergeant?" How dare he look at Thomas with such disrespect! How dare he even insinuate that Thomas was involved. "Do you know who you are talking to?" Slowly, he rose from his chair, hoping his six-foot-one height would intimate the boy.

It must have worked, for Cruz's Adam's apple slid to the bottom of his throat. But to his credit, his gaze never wavered from Thomas'.

"I'm not in any way implying you…"

Thomas blew out a snort. "Good." He waved him off. "Now, go question the others who had access and leave me to my work."

"I have questioned them, sir. But here's my problem."

Thomas remained standing, staring Cruz down, hoping he wouldn't have to throw him out. No doubt Landry would hear of it and there would be hell to pay.

Cruz shifted his feet, confusion twisting his expression. "You see, no one else *also* had access to the generator room. With your top clearance, only *you* could do both."

Fear clawed up Thomas's spine, agonizing, debilitating fear. Shoving it down, he circled his desk and stormed toward Cruz until he was inches from his face. "How dare you!? I could have you locked up for slanderous lies and insubordination!"

Cruz backed away, a spark of terror finally crossing his eyes. "I beg your pardon, sir. I wasn't insinuating…I mean, I wasn't implying you… I only meant to ask you if you could think of anyone else who had access to both places." He gulped again, his breath coming fast.

Good. At least Thomas was able to frighten the boy.

"No." Thomas remained in place, spearing an angry gaze at Cruz. "You are wasting your time here when you could be finding the true culprit. Better yet why aren't you focused on looking for Miss Griffin?"

The sergeant slipped his phone back in his pocket and attempted to compose himself. "I have people looking for her, sir, but the best way to find her is to discover who helped her and why. She is probably hiding out in that person's home right now."

Now, it was Thomas's turn to gulp. He spun around so Cruz wouldn't see. "Good. Then be about it." Resuming his seat, he began shuffling papers on his desk.

"Excellent, sir. I believe I'll go back over what little we have on video and see if I missed something."

Not until he heard Cruz walk out and shut the door did Thomas allow himself to breathe. Leaning back in his chair, he rubbed his temples where a headache brewed. One of many he'd had the past few days.

Cruz was smart, he'd give him that. *Too* smart. He was getting far too close. Damn his suspicions. Still, without definitive proof, such as a video or fingerprints, there was no way he could pin this on Thomas. Not unless... no, certainly during the split second the outside cameras turned back on, none of them were focused on him putting Tori in the trunk. No way. Thomas was in the clear.

Then why did his heart suddenly feel like a pincushion?

Opening a drawer, he pulled out his whiskey and took a long gulp. And another. Then putting it back, he tried to focus on the paperwork before him. He'd interrogated two Deviants this week. It had taken two long days and threats to butcher his children before the first one—a man in his thirties—finally denied Jesus and vowed his allegiance to the NWU. But not the second one. Thomas had tried every tactic he knew to break the sweet lady in her sixties. He stared at the paperwork that marked her as "Irredeemable," and recommending immediate execution. He hated this part of his job, hated it when he dealt with Deviants so far gone, there was no way to get them to see the truth. Hated that they had to be killed. But that rule came down from people above him. If they allowed these Deviants to live and spread their propaganda, the world would end up back where they started—with endless wars, poverty, destruction of the planet, and a society that could never advance to the global utopia it was destined for.

He quickly signed the paper and set it aside, his thoughts turning to Tori. The old lady had reminded him of her, stubborn yet kind, doomed, yet filled with joy.

Duties at work had stolen much of his time with her the past few days, but he hadn't made much progress anyway. A vision of last night filled his mind. After they ate, she'd insisted they go for a walk along the shore, and before he could agree, she tore off her shoes and darted out the back gate. Following her, he halted and watched as she ran to the waves, kicking up sand, and giggling like a child seeing the ocean for the first time. Of all the clothing left here by the various women who had spent the night, she'd found the most modest—white capris and a button up blouse that was a little too small for her figure. Not that he was complaining as he watched her bend over to pick up a shell.

Ashamed of the direction of his thoughts, he'd shaken them away and headed toward her. She'd not asked why he had women's clothing in his home, not that it would be too hard to figure out, but he wondered what she thought. *Who cares, Thomas? You're being an idiot.*

She dipped her toes in an incoming wavelet, watching the foam hop over her feet. "You are so blessed to live right by the ocean."

"I suppose." Yet now that he thought about it, he rarely walked down to the water, let alone strolled along the beach as they were doing now. He'd bought the house because it was what rich, powerful people did. They owned mansions on the beach. Didn't they?

Shielding her eyes from the setting sun, she smiled up at him. "Take off your shoes."

"No. I don't want to get tar on my feet." Or sand or seaweed or accidentally step on a jellyfish that would sting. It was bad enough he'd had to hike up his nice pants.

They walked in silence for several minutes, a comfortable silence Thomas rarely found with anyone. But Tori was not just anyone. She was someone special who brought life and color to a gray world. And for that reason, he needed to save her. But how? "Tori, promise you'll listen to me. I know you believe a certain way, but I want you to hear my beliefs too."

"Of course. I'll listen. As long as you promise to listen to me later on."

Wind blew strands of her black hair across her face, and she flung them away, staring out over the ocean with such a peaceful look on her face, he was envious.

"I'm not saying I don't believe in your God, the God of the Bible. I'm saying that He is not the good God. There is another god. You call him Lucifer, the light bearer. He is the true god. He is the good god, the one who truly loves mankind and who wants to create a utopia here on earth." Thomas stepped over an incoming wave, groaning when it saturated the hem of his pants. "Your Bible reverses their roles, makes Lucifer out to be the bad guy when he rebelled against God. But why did he rebel? Because your God is a bully. He's mean and wants to destroy people. He wants people to obey Him or else. Whereas Lucifer wants to free humanity to live life as we choose, no restrictions, complete freedom to do as we want."

She listened. He'd give her that. "Do as thou wilt," she said as she walked along. "The motto of the church of Satan."

"Yes. That's it, Tori. We live our lives as we wish. We are free. Whereas your God kills thousands of people just for not obeying Him. That's the definition of a tyrant. There are dozens of stories in your Bible where He did just that. You cannot deny it."

They continued on again in silence, giving Thomas hope that she was truly thinking about what he'd said. Another tool used to reverse brainwashing was to give them another choice, a better choice.

The sun sank farther behind the houses, drawing streams of shadows along with it over sea and sand. Somewhere a gull cried, people laughed, and the chink of glassware suggested a party. A gust of salty wind flapped his shirt and brought the scent of the sea, rotten fish, and something else unsavory to his nose. Another reason he didn't like to walk among the waves. So much of the water was polluted now.

Finally, she stopped and faced him. The last rays of an orange sun sparkled over her skin and flashed across her green eyes, so full of life and…spunk. Yes, she still had her spunk.

"Tell you what." She jabbed a finger on his chest. "Let's make a wager. Let's give ourselves, say, six months of spending time together. During which time I will try to convince you that my God is the true God, and you try and convince me that your god is the true god."

He couldn't help but chuckle.

"Ah, you can still laugh. I wondered about that."

Smiling, he eased a lock of hair from her face. *Six months*! He had never dreamed she'd want to stay here that long. He'd only given himself a week to break her, but now with this extra time, he was sure he could. "You're on."

Pleased, she looped her arm through his as they strolled to the house.

Back in his office, Thomas caught himself smiling at the memory. No, Tori was nothing like the older lady he'd just condemned to death. She would see reason, he was sure of it.

A knock on his door reignited his annoyance. "What?!" he snapped, thinking it was Cruz again.

Instead, Rodney's head popped through the opening. "I wouldn't bother you, sir, but you gotta see this."

"See what?" All Thomas wanted was to have another drink and head home for the day. Home to Tori.

"You aren't going to believe this, sir." Moisture filled Rodney's eyes as he blinked, fluttering his false eyelashes.

And for a split second, Thomas thought he'd been caught. "Out with it."

"It's Premier Aali. He's back."

Arithem stood, mighty arms crossed, watching the scene unfold on the huge flatscreen mounted on the wall. Scanon appeared beside him, eyes on his ward—one of the technicians—just as the son of Adam, called Rodney, dashed into the control room. Thomas followed close behind. Eyes wide and faces ashen, they, along with all the others, stared at the scene unfolding on the screen. No one said a word. Phones rang, but no one moved to answer them.

'Twas what the sons of Adam called shock, he supposed.

Arithem called what was happening blasphemy. Blasphemy against the Most High!

He returned his gaze back to the events unfolding in D.C., one of the many cities controlled by their enemy.

The reporter who'd been unable to speak for several minutes, finally settled herself and faced the camera. "I can't believe it!" Her breath came fast and hard, her eyes glistening with tears. "Premier Aali has risen from the dead!" She glanced over her shoulder to the Beast, himself, sitting up in the marble coffin in the center of the Washington National Cathedral where they'd held the funeral services the day before. The glass top of the coffin lay shattered in pieces on the floor.

Arithem's fingers ached to draw his sword, to fly to D.C. and put an end to this monster once and for all.

"So, it has finally happened," Scanon said with a stern frown.

"Aye." Arithem gripped the hilt of his sword, if only to ease his desire to do something…*anything* to stop what he knew must come. "Our enemy has entered him fully now."

"And all hell will soon be unleashed," Scanon added.

A small group of men formed around the Beast, helping him to his feet, while a crowd of onlookers circled the coffin, shouting, crying, some even swooning. The Beast raised his hands and smiled. "All is well. I am well! I have risen!"

The men surrounding him fell to their knees and the crowd followed suit.

Arithem growled. "He copies our Commander. Such blasphemy!"

Two people in the control room also fell to their knees. One of them was Scanon's ward, compelled by a dark spirit pushing him down. Scanon charged to his aid, quickly dispatching the demon with a blade to his gut. More demons swept into the area, stirred by the adoration rising in the hearts of the men and women as they watched with awe the deception of the Beast.

And though Arithem was itching for a fight, he had no authority to engage unless these humans belonged to the Commander and prayed for help. Unfortunately, none of them did, save Scanon's ward, who had not made a full commitment. At least the man had acknowledged the truth of the Gospel, which was far more than Thomas had done. Arithem glanced at his ward, frozen in place, staring at the screen along with everyone else. At least he had not bowed.

"He is risen!" the reporter exclaimed. "He is risen! The world is saved!"

A gurney pushed by men in doctors' uniforms rushed toward the Beast and seemed to be trying to get him to accompany them to a hospital.

"No need, my friends. No need." The Beast smiled. "I must go to Jerusalem right away."

Scanon returned to stand beside Arithem. "Of course he must."

Arithem snorted. "How I long to be a part of the warriors who protect God's chosen as they flee Jerusalem."

"Indeed, my friend. A privilege that!"

Finally, the doctors convinced the Beast to go to the hospital, and soon the cameras switched to a scene outside the Cathedral where thousands had gathered to wave at the ambulance as it took off down the street, sirens blaring.

Arithem watched as Thomas sank into a chair, his expression unreadable. "I fear for what must come to the humans remaining on Earth."

"I agree," Scanon sighed. "We now enter the worst time in human history."

...and that man of sin be revealed, the son of perdition;
Who opposeth and exalteth himself above all that is called
God, or that is worshipped; so that he as God sitteth in the
temple of God, shewing himself that he is God.
2 Thessalonians 2:3-4

Chapter 8

Thomas didn't go to work the next day. Or the day after that. He could hardly think clearly about much of anything. But he finally forced himself to answer his phone, especially when he saw it was Regent Landry calling.

"Are you well, Tom? I understand you haven't been to work in two days. I know the Premier's rising has us all out of sorts, but it doesn't mean we don't still have jobs to do. Besides, what a miracle, what a great thing for the world!"

"I know, sir. I'm actually feeling under the weather."

"Well, I suppose that explains why you've turned down all the parties celebrating Aali's return."

Thomas wondered how he knew about that, but then silently cursed Rodney, who had difficulty keeping his mouth shut.

"Yes, sir, I expect to be back tomorrow."

"Better yet, I'll meet you in Jerusalem. I'm leaving D.C. early in the morning. Catch the first flight you can get. Aali is on his way there, and he's going to make a major announcement."

A thrill spiraled through Thomas, immediately casting away the dark cloud of confusion that had consumed him these past days. He was still in the game! Still part of the global elite invited to important world events. Nothing had changed. No one knew what he had done. A wide grin stretched his lips. "I'd love to, sir. Thank you."

"See you there. And Tom? This might be your chance to speak to the Premier personally, so pull yourself together. Take some drugs or do whatever you need to do to get your head in the right space." His voice turned sinister. "Don't make a fool out of me, Tom, or you'll discover just how quickly I can demote you to prison guard. Do I make myself clear?"

The smile slipped from Thomas's face. "I won't let you down, Sir." Clicking off the phone, he set it down, an unsettling mix of elation and fear making him jittery.

"Something wrong?" Tori entered the room, a glass of juice in hand. The shorts and t-shirt she wore looked far better on her than…who was that other woman? He couldn't remember her name. And why did just thinking about it suddenly make him feel dirty?

In truth, he'd spent a lot of time feeling dirty the past few days with Tori. He couldn't figure out why. She'd been no saint. When they were teenagers, she'd been the bad influence on him, luring him into bed, introducing him to drugs. And when he'd decided to attend seminary, she'd thrown a fit, telling him he was tossing his life away on a book of myths. Why, then, was there now an aura of innocence and goodness about her?

"I've been invited to go to Jerusalem with the Regent."

"Oh." She sat cross-legged on the couch, staring at her juice.

"Don't worry. I'll come back."

Silence was her only response as her thoughts seemed elsewhere. Yet, when she raised her gaze to his, an odd sorrow filled her eyes. "The truth is you won't be going to Jerusalem."

Growling, Thomas headed toward the bar, but one glance at the clock told him it was only eleven AM. Instead, he uttered a curse and went to the kitchen, searching the cupboards for something to eat, and upon finding nothing, slammed them shut. "Why would you say that?"

"Listen, Thomas." She set her cup on the table. "I'm only telling you what I hear from God."

Blowing out a snort, he flattened his palms on the counter.

"I know a trip like that would mean the world to you," she said. "But I'm telling you, it's best you stay as far away from Aali as you can."

"Because he's the Antichrist, right?" Thomas laughed. "He's going to enter the Jewish temple and proclaim he is god, right?" He instantly regretted his harsh tone when Tori's expression fell.

Sure, he'd been shocked by Premier Aali's miraculous resurrection. Who wouldn't be? But he'd been more shocked by Tori predicting it days before. When he questioned her, she said it had been prophesied in the Bible. But of course he didn't possess a copy of the banned book, nor could anyone read it online. Regardless, whether it was in there or not, that was the second time she'd correctly foretold the future, which meant either she had some insider scoop with the powers that be— which no Deviant would have—or she was a fortuneteller. Not that he believed in such things. But what else could it be?

And now this—telling *his* future, a prediction he would dismiss outright if she hadn't been right before.

"I'm going to Jerusalem, Tori. It's my job. And when I get back, we'll continue our conversations on whose god is the real god."

One eyebrow quirked as she stared at him. "Since you've been doing such a good job already."

She made him smile, and he hated that. "I've been distracted these past few days." Too many thoughts of why and how and… What in the heck was going on? Not that he hadn't enjoyed her company. He had. Immensely. Everywhere he looked, he saw another exquisite example of her artwork lying about. Drawings of his house, his pool, the beach, the sunset, and even him. She'd captured him perfectly, though he'd argued about the sad look in his eyes. Regardless, he never knew how talented she was. Then there was her humming, beautiful and sweet, it filled every crevice of his house with a sense of joy. In fact, her very presence made the place more a home than it had ever been.

He moved to sit on the couch beside her, his body reacting to their closeness and the playfulness in her eyes. How many times in the past few days had he wanted to pull her into his arms, run his fingers through her hair, inhale her sweet scent, and kiss her deeply until they both became breathless. Just like the old days when they were young and madly in love.

But then he remembered the pain she had caused him when she'd broken things off and walked out of his life, leaving his heart so completely shattered, he'd never been able to love anyone since.

"What's up with the ink?" He gestured to her neck where the small tattoo of man's sandaled foot crushed the head of a snake.

She ran her fingers over it, her gaze far away. "Long story. But it represents good conquering the evil in my life."

"I don't get it."

"It's from Genesis in the Bible. Jesus's foot crushes the serpent or Satan."

Thomas grimaced. For some reason that name made his insides squirm. "Why does everything lead back to Him?"

She took his hand in hers, the gesture dissolving his anger. "Because it does. Everything does."

Pity replaced his anger. Then sorrow at how far gone she was.

"Listen, Thomas, I'm not kidding." Her tone drew his eyes to hers where he saw an unusual seriousness. "You will never go back to your job again."

Kyle had him. At last! He pounded his fist onto the table, startling the technician. They'd been poring over every millisecond of video from the night of the escape, searching for a sign of anything, a flash, a movement, anything that would expose the culprit. From the holding cell where Miss Griffin had been seated right before the generator blew to the minutes after the cameras came back online. There wasn't much to look at, and after several pass-throughs, Kyle had almost given up. But then. There it was! Just a second and not even that. A flash of a red Mercedes, a leg going into a trunk, and Vice Regent Thomas Benton slamming it shut.

"I knew it!" Kyle shot his fist in the air.

"I can't believe it," the technician murmured. "I never thought..."

Kyle patted him on the shoulder. "It's always the people we least suspect. Now keep this between us until I can formally arrest him."

"Yes, sir."

"And make me a copy of that video just in case someone tries to erase it."

Storming out of the room, Kyle felt like he walked on air. He'd gone from a drug-hazed, miserable, impoverished loser to a sergeant in the NWU Reformation Security Force, a friend of a Tall White—a rarity among humans. And now, he would catch the biggest fish of all, a traitor among the highest levels of global power, a man just two steps away from the Global Spiritual Leader. This would propel his career even higher and faster than expected. In addition, this victory would surely erase the stigma of his relationship to one of the most wanted Deviants in the region.

Marching into his temporary office, he remembered how the traitor had treated him like a bug to be squashed. He picked up the phone to call Regent Landry and grinned. "We'll see who's the bug now."

Tori peeked around the corner of the open door to Thomas's bedroom, a room she'd been avoiding the past three days for obvious reasons. The main one being she and Thomas had a past—a physical past—and she could not deny that her body reacted when he was near. How easy it would be to fall right back into old habits, old pleasures, old intimacies. She saw the way he looked at her, and she had a feeling he felt the same way.

But she was a new creature in Christ, and she would do nothing to harm her relationship with Jesus. Nothing would be worth that.

The room was as sterile and spotless as the rest of the house, with sharp modern furniture and very few personal items lying about to indicate the personality of the owner. Sad. On the king-sized bed lay two open leather suitcases into which Thomas placed ever-so-neatly his folded clothing, while laying out his suits inside a specialty suit holder.

Tori leaned against the door frame, watching him, his movements masculine and in command, a determined look on his handsome face. Long ago, she loved to watch him from afar, see him plunge into the surf with his board and catch a wave, admire him as he played varsity baseball at the high school they both attended, enjoy his laughter as they partied with friends, and melt at his smile when he picked her up for a date in his 1972 Camaro. Even now those memories stirred something within her—instantly squashed by the dark spirits that suddenly emerged from within him, snarling and grimacing at her. How she longed to cast them away using the one Name, the only Name, with the power to do so, but Thomas must want them gone.

He looked up at her then and grinned, and in that smile she saw the boy she'd once loved. But the demons spun harder and faster, and the light in his eyes faded. "I know. I know. I'm not going to Jerusalem." He returned to his packing.

She smiled. "Wasn't going to say that."

"Come to check out my bedroom then?" His tone was playful, but the look in his eyes heated her to her toes.

She made no reply, merely began staring at her shoes.

Thomas approached, slowly, methodically, like a panther on the prowl. Placing a finger beneath her chin, he raised her gaze to his. "Since when have you ever been shy?" He ran the back of his hand gently down her cheek just like he used to do.

She searched his eyes, the heat from his body radiating through every inch of her. The demons retreated, no doubt not wanting to distract her from the seduction. If they could get her to give into it, they would win a victory, not only over her, but over any chance for Thomas to come to the truth.

Zarall plucked his ax from his belt and took a battle stance against the multitude of dark forces hovering around Thomas, particularly those slithering toward his ward, Tori. "They tempt her. They use her weakness."

Arithem nodded, flinging an arm out to keep Zarall from charging. "We can do naught, my friend. We must wait." Still, he kept his grip on his blade. One word from the Commander or one command from this daughter of Eve, and they would be freed to battle these heinous entities.

The demons laughed at them, hissing displeasure at their presence.

Arithem narrowed his eyes, returning a gaze of his own that radiated with the power he held over them.

"'Tis the worst part of our assignments," Zarall said. "The waiting, watching our enemies lead humans astray and not being able to fight!" Aye, he knew his ward, knew her well, and he could tell she struggled against her fleshly passion. "She weakens." He pushed against Arithem's arm.

"Wait. She is strong, this one. She has gone through too much to fall for this temptation."

Zarall withdrew. "You are right. The Spirit is strong in her." Then why did she stand so close to the man and allow him to caress her cheek?

"I wish she would—"

Arithem raised a hand. "Hush, the Spirit speaks to her."

Lord, a little help here? Tori silently prayed as every ounce of her longed to fold into Thomas's embrace, to relive those happy, carefree moments of love and pleasure. But no! With every speck of strength within her, she took a step back. And that's when she heard *His* voice, a voice she'd come to recognize over the years, the voice of her Beloved.

Daughter, it is happening. Turn on the TV.

"Come, Thomas." She grabbed his hand and dragged him out the door.

"Wait. I need to finish packing. My flight is at 5:30 tomorrow morning."

"In a minute."

Down the circular stairs Tori led him, surprised when he complied so easily. But then again, he might be thinking she wanted to continue the seduction downstairs. If so, he would be sorely disappointed.

Grabbing the remote, she flipped on the screen and immediately it filled with scenes from Jerusalem.

"Hey, that's where I'll be tomorrow!" Thomas said. "You might even see me on this very screen."

His voice resonated with pride, a pride Tori knew would soon be crushed. She lifted up a prayer for God to open his eyes and prepare him for what was coming.

"Premier Immu Aali has just arrived in the City of the King," the announcer was saying as the camera panned to a black limousine making its way down the narrow streets, escorted by security cars with flashing lights. Crowds of cheering people lined both sides, held back by men in uniforms.

"His first appearance since his resurrection." Thomas, clearly in awe, took a seat on the couch and laughed. "I can't believe I just said that. It sounds so crazy."

Sliding onto the arm of the couch beside him, Tori watched in amazement as prophecy became reality, never tiring of seeing undeniable proof of the Divine inspiration of the Bible.

Aali's limousine, escorted by the IDF and Israeli Police, both in vehicles and on foot, finally came to a halt on Suq El Qatanin Street before the Temple Mount. Sunlight glistened off the white columns and gold decorations of the newly built temple, a product of a peace accord instituted by Aali himself. Another prophecy fulfilled.

The fiend exited the vehicle to the roar of thousands of people cheering and clapping. The camera spanned the enormous mob, zeroing in on some who were weeping with joy, others fainting, and still others with looks of awe and worship as if they were in the presence of God. Disgust bubbled in Tori's stomach.

Aali waved at the crowd as his spiritual leader, His Excellency Gabriel Wolfe emerged from the vehicle in his long flowing white robes and stood by his side. Together they were escorted into the court of Gentiles and then through another gate leading to the court of women. Tori only knew the names from her study of Scripture, but it was truly amazing to see it come to life on the screen. Jewish priests in ceremonial garb, complete with the breastplate containing the twelve jewels representing the tribes of Israel, lined the court and bowed their heads at his approach.

Tori felt like screaming.

Escorted by several security guards, Aali ascended a set of stairs and entered the Inner Court containing the brazen altar and the large bronze laver filled with water. Again, rows of priests stood to each side, bowing their heads before him. The chief priest approached and fell to his knees at Aali's feet.

"What the heck is going on?" Thomas asked, scooting to the edge of his seat.

"They are worshiping him. They think he is their long-awaited Messiah."

Thomas grew silent, and she knew his mind was spinning with her prophecy.

She had a general idea what would happen next, but she hadn't expected it to play out in such a gruesome way. She suspected Aali would most likely crash into the Holy of Holies and tear down the veil. She knew that a throne would be brought into the Holy Place where he would sit. What she hadn't expected was the human sacrifice placed upon the altar. The announcer, too, seemed shocked by the vision of the young woman who mounted the steps and willingly lay on the massive altar. But then he touched his earpiece and breathed a sigh of relief. "Oh, I'm told the woman is not human, but a robot. You know how realistic they look these days." Still, he could not hide the look of disgust on his face as he watched them light the fire and the woman burn.

Tori knew it was no robot, for Satan always demanded human blood. Unbeknown to many people, he had been sacrificing humans for years, mostly babies and children. But now that he had finally gained full power, he'd moved on to bigger prey. Nausea rose in her throat. No doubt they had drugged her or given her something that would kill her before the flames touched her flesh, because she neither screamed nor moved.

Tori tore her gaze away.

Thomas, however, continued to stare at the scene, both shock and despair wrinkling his face.

As the woman burned, Aali sat upon the throne. "I am god. I am your messiah and the savior of the World," he announced. "You will worship me."

Gabriel Wolfe, the false prophet, stood by his side and gestured for the priests, media, diplomats, and heads of states to bow.

Which they willingly did.

Deep sorrow settled in Tori's soul. She knew many of the Jews and most of the world would follow him, but seeing it actually happen broke her heart. She shifted her gaze to Thomas, hoping he saw through this evil man's charade.

He glanced her way, a stunned look in his eyes. "You told me this would happen."

"You cannot excuse what he did. Human sacrifices? You know where that comes from? Satan worship."

That stunned look turned to anger. "Insane! It's just a silly ceremony. Maybe he is god. I mean, we know the Neflams seeded Planet Earth. Maybe he is their leader, *their* creator." He jumped to his feet and charged toward his bar, pouring a drink. "He rose from the dead, for god's sakes."

Tori watched him rage, confusion, anger, and fear all jumbled together in his eyes.

"*Or* he is the Antichrist prophesied in the Bible," she said. "How else would I know he would do this?"

"I don't know, Tori. I don't know." He powered down his drink and started to pour another when his phone rang. Returning to yank it off the coffee table, he stared at the name, frowned, hesitated, then finally put it on speaker and set it down so he could finish pouring his drink. "Yes, Rodney."

"Sir. You must get out of there immediately." Hysteria rang in his assistant's voice.

Huffing, Thomas raked back his hair. "What are you talking about?"

"Sir." The voice returned more hushed, yet more serious. "They know. They know! They are coming for you now."

"They know what?"

No answer.

"They know what, Rodney?"

The phone went dead.

And the brother shall deliver up the brother to death, and the father the child: and the children shall rise up against their parents, and cause them to be put to death.
And ye shall be hated of all men for my name's sake: but he that endureth to the end shall be saved.
Matthew 10:21-22

Chapter 9

"We have to go," Tori said, leaping from the couch. "Now!"

Thomas couldn't move. Could barely breathe. Thoughts fired through his mind like laser beams in a light show, frying his reason and logic, along with anything else he could cling to for hope.

"We don't know what Rodney was talking about," he finally muttered, staring at the drink in his hand. He lifted it to his mouth, but Tori gripped him and removed the glass before he could take the sip he longed for—the sip that might ease the confusion and terror rampaging through him like a freight train.

She stared up at him, unblinking, more serious than he'd ever seen her. "We *do* know. And if we don't get out of here right now, we are both done for. Do you hear me? Now, come on!" Grabbing his hand, she headed for the door.

He tugged her to a halt. "What about my things? My phone, my clothes?"

"Don't need them." She pulled him harder, struggling to get him to move.

"I can't leave." Thomas shook his head, trying to dislodge the reality of what was happening. "I'm Vice Regent of the New World Faith North American Region. They can't...they won't..."

Tori released her grip. "They will." She studied him, sadness in her eyes, along with an unrelenting appeal. But how could he walk away from everything he'd accomplished? Everything he'd worked for?

"Stay, then, but I have to go." Turning, Tori rushed through the foyer and out the door.

And at that moment as he watched her dash away, his shock, his denial turned into fear. Rodney would never mislead him, and they would not be on their way to arrest him unless they had undeniable proof of how he'd helped Tori escape.

His life was over. Finished.

He rushed to catch up to Tori as she ran across his driveway, almost to the front gate. "Tori, we'll take my car. Get in." He moved his hand over the door, and it clicked open.

"Are you kidding me?" Tori shouted over her shoulder. "They'll use it to track you. Hurry. We need to run."

Thomas started toward her, then turned to look at his magnificent house, his Mercedes, symbols of his success and power, everything he'd worked to achieve these past three years. This couldn't be happening. Why was this happening?

Deep down, though, he knew why. He'd gone against the NWU, and at his level, that was treason and an automatic execution.

He gulped.

In the distance, sirens blared. For him? Or would they come stealthily to drag him from his home?

"Thomas!"

Spinning about, he did the only thing he could do. He ran. The gate opened automatically at his presence, and grabbing Tori's hand, they raced across the street and into a grove of bushy, shrubs just as five black NWU SUVs, sirens screaming and lights blaring, descended upon his house like vultures on a fresh kill.

"Check out back! I want every tree, bush, and rock searched! You two, follow me inside." The voice belonged to Sergeant Cruz.

Thomas didn't stay to hear the rest. Tori and he made a mad dash down the peninsula, making sure to stick to the foliage along the side of the road. They halted at the Matanzas River, breath heaving. Crossing on the two-lane bridge left them completely exposed, but what choice did they have? It was the quickest way to the mainland. Bolting after Tori, Thomas hoped they looked like two joggers out for a late afternoon run…a hard sell due to his designer pants and Italian leather loafers.

But no one stopped them. No sirens blared after them.

After that, everything became a blur of city streets covered in trash, boarded-up shops, people in rags pushing shopping carts filled with junk, and the most putrid odor Thomas had ever smelled. The sun sank behind the taller buildings, dragging with it only a pinch of the heat and humidity. Sweat beaded on his forehead and streamed down his back, soaking his shirt. His feet hurt. His legs ached. His heart raced. But most of all, his soul sank into a deep despair.

Yet all through this, Tori continued a jog-walk, always keeping to the back streets, hugging buildings, and avoiding groups of people milling about. Though she glanced his way occasionally, she said nothing.

Fear was not a familiar friend to Thomas. He had always sided with those in power, with those who had the numbers and the money. He'd decided long ago that was the best way to be successful and avoid punishment of any kind, avoid running for his life as he was doing now. He'd only been this afraid one time before, and that was the day he'd watched Angelica Smoke, "Smokes," as he'd called her, disappear before his eyes in a flash of lightning. The Rapture, Daniel had said, and that thought had scared Thomas most of all. Why? Because he'd been left behind. Or so he'd thought until the first Neflams appeared and explained things.

Slipping from an alleyway onto the sidewalk of a main street, Thomas followed Tori as she wove around piles of trash. Or was it trash? One of the piles moved. A hand reached out toward Thomas like a ghoul from the grave. He leapt aside, heart thumping.

"Food? A scrap of food?" the voice said.

Curling his nose, Thomas sped forward. He knew the city still had a homeless population. So many had suffered after the war and the economic collapse, but the NWU was doing much to improve people's lives. It just took time.

The purr of an engine reached his ears, an unusual sound with so few cars on the streets due to the carbon restrictions. He spun around just in time to see an NWU Black Hummer speed toward him.

"They found us!" Tori said. "Crud. I should have known."

What she should have known, Thomas didn't know or care as he grabbed her hand and crashed through the unlocked gate of a car impound lot to their right. Together they wove around the skeletons of old, broken cars, ducking and diving to avoid being seen. Then leaping on a chain-link fence, Thomas reached down to help Tori, and together they jumped to the pavement below and took off running once again.

Twenty minutes later, unable to go any further, he stopped and leaned his hands on his knees, breath heaving. "Guess I'm out of shape."

"Me too." Tori grabbed his shirt and yanked him beside a brick building, out of sight. "I've been sitting in your prison cell far too long."

He looked up at her, her black hair wild about her face, her chest rising and falling, her green eyes alert, scanning the area like a soldier at war. Even in the fading sunlight, she was beautiful, a wild cat prowling about the night. Yet instead of fear, there was a determination, a confidence in her expression.

Like running for her life was something she did every night.

Only then did he realize how difficult her life must have been as a hunted Deviant.

She peeked around the corner of the building, then jerked back. "Shoot! They found us again." She glared at him. "It's you! They are tracking you." Without giving him a chance to think or even respond, she yelled "Run!" and sprinted toward the back of the building, turning this way and that, weaving between overflowing garbage dumpsters, taking him deeper into narrow alleyways where no cars could drive.

She was right, of course. He cursed. If only he'd thought to grab his magnetic gloves. But that was the last thing on his mind as he dashed from his home, leaving everything he knew and loved behind. They would catch him. They could track his exact location. Unless he could get rid of his chip.

The stink of rotten food and sewage saturated his lungs. Gagging, he covered his mouth, forcing down a burst of nausea. He'd never been in this part of town, never really ventured outside his neighborhood except to drive to the airport, but what he'd seen so far made him wonder why Tori was taking him through the poorest slums of the city. People—if you could call them that—lay about the filthy pavement like discarded, broken toys, most too drunk or drugged to move. Wild dogs roamed in packs, seeking meat to devour. Thankfully, Thomas's size had deterred the few they'd run across. Music thumped from inside buildings. Agonizing screams accompanied sirens. Vacant eyes followed their movement from within broken windows. Up ahead, a group of people, including a small child, surrounded a barrel where a fire blazed. One of them glanced up as they passed, but otherwise paid them no mind.

It was a vision of hell, if there was such a place.

They darted right, slamming up against a brick building. The chink and chime of machines hummed from inside. A man leapt at them from the shadows, knife in hand. The crusty grime on his face made it hard to tell his age…or his race, but the evil intent in his eyes was unmistakable.

"Gimme your money, clothes, whatever you got!"

Tori backed up, hands raised, lips moving…*praying perhaps*? "We have nothing to give you." Her eyes lit as if she saw something beyond the man. Whatever it was, it must have given her courage, for she raised her chin. "All I have to offer is eternal life found only in the name of Jesus."

Thomas growled. Now was not the time for evangelizing! Pushing Tori behind him, he stepped toward the man. "Leave now, or I'll make you leave."

The sirens grew louder. Pounding footsteps echoed through the darkness. NWU troops had left the vehicles and were on foot. They hadn't much time.

The man laughed and lunged for Thomas.

Leaping backward, Thomas raised an arm against the advancing knife and kicked the man's legs out beneath him. He toppled to the ground. Stepping on his wrist, Thomas ground it into the road. The man released the knife. Grabbing it, Thomas backed away, only then feeling pain lance across his arm. Struggling to rise, the thief uttered a nonhuman growl and dashed into the darkness.

"Very impressive," Tori said.

Grabbing his injured arm, Thomas faced her. "Go, Tori. Run! Leave. They're tracking me. You can save yourself."

Commands fired through the air. Footsteps pounded closer. Soon they'd be surrounded.

She chuckled. "Duh. Why do you think I've been leading us through all these warehouses full of robotic machines." She started running, gesturing for him to follow. "I was hoping it would mask your signal." She glanced up at the murky dark sky. "At least they haven't released the drones yet."

Thomas had always been the smartest one in the room, but suddenly he felt like a little kid whose teacher had just embarrassed him in front of the class. Why had he not thought of the chip before, he couldn't say, except that in the past few years it had become a part of him—a part he rarely even thought about. No time to coddle his injured pride, he caught up to Tori and pulled her beside a stack of crates. A rat crawled over his shoe. Cringing, he withheld a squeal that would only add to his embarrassment. "It won't work," he finally said. "It's too strong a signal."

He couldn't make out her expression in the darkness, but he felt her looking at him, nonetheless. "I have something better." She started forward. "At my house."

"Wait." He tugged her back. "You go. They can't track you."

"But they'll catch you." Her voice broke—the first time he heard fear in her tone. "And, besides, you're in trouble because of me."

"Over here!" someone shouted, and a flurry of footsteps grew louder.

He swallowed. They would catch him. He knew that now. He'd known the risks when he'd helped her escape, but in all honesty, his pride had forbidden him to entertain the possibility of ever being caught. If it weren't for the puddles of sewage, rats, the stench, homeless and sirens screaming through the night, he'd think he was having a nightmare.

The worst kind of nightmare.

The kind you never wake up from.

Either way, they'd be on him in minutes. "Go!" He shouted, turning his back to her and walking away.

"No way." Her stern voice echoed behind him.

He faced her.

"You either come with me now, or I'll allow myself to be caught with you."

Her tone was enough to convince him she meant it.

A breeze eddied through the alleyway, spinning both trash *and* his thoughts into a cyclone.

No one had ever been willing to die for him.

"We'll never make it," he said.

"We will."

"Another one of your prophecies?"

"You could say that." A cloud moved, showering her in silver light as if she were an angel. A smile graced her lips. A smile? In the middle of this madness?

"Have I been wrong yet?" she said.

"He's close!" a voice blared.

"There's always a first time." Thomas grabbed her hand and started running. "I just hope this won't be it."

Tori turned down the familiar neighborhood street, too tired to run anymore. No doubt the NWU would be on them in minutes. That was, if God didn't intervene, which she'd been praying He would. The Tribulation was a different time. Scripture said God granted the Antichrist the power to overcome the saints. That meant a rescue wasn't always possible.

Darkness spilled over the rundown city like black sludge, and with very few streetlights functioning, she had difficulty finding her old house. Would it be safe? Not for long. But she prayed for enough time to get what she needed.

She glanced at Thomas, his breath coming hard and heavy beside her. She knew exactly what he was going through. His entire world had been stripped away from him in an instant. Not only his world, but his worldview, everything he believed. It was all starting to fizzle away like stale soda. She had to admit she was impressed with the way he was handling things. Although perhaps he was still in shock.

They had but minutes, seconds even, before the NWU found them again. Why they weren't already here, she could only attribute to God's intervention. When the man had attacked them in the alleyway, she'd seen the mighty angel standing guard behind him—a rare vision for her—and she knew God would protect them. What she hadn't known was that Thomas had fighting skills, something she would not have expected of the stylish man.

He said nothing as she led him past several empty homes with broken windows. Lights from the few houses where people still lived created an eerie glow on the sidewalk.

"Where'd everybody go?" he asked.

She wanted to laugh. "You don't know? They were rounded up and put in government housing downtown."

"Much better for them. They are closer to everything they need so they don't need cars."

"And the NWU income they were given isn't enough to pay for their bills. Hurry." She dove into her neighbor's yard and made her way to the back. Crouching, she looked through the hole in the fence. No men, no guards stationed in the backyard, and she'd not seen any out front. *Lord, please show me. Please protect us.* She rarely saw angels, but she felt their presence now, knew they were there because she saw no demons slithering about.

"Come on." Taking Thomas's hand, she led him through a gap in the fence and into the backyard.

"This is where you live?" he asked.

"Lived. Not anymore. It was my sister's home."

"What happened to her?"

"Rapture," she answered, not caring that he didn't believe. "Her, her husband, and my niece."

He huffed.

Fishing through the dirt of a potted plant on the back porch, she pulled out a key and unlocked the back door.

Before she could even open it, it swung and hit her in the face.

She fell backward into Thomas just as a man stepped onto the back porch, an AR-15 pointed straight at them.

*Verily I say unto you, Whatsoever ye shall bind on earth
shall be bound in heaven: and whatsoever ye shall loose on
earth shall be loosed in heaven.*
Matthew 18:18

Chapter 10

Groaning, Zarall took a stand beside his ward, Tori, and
leveled a threatening glare at the demons inhabiting
the human male. They'd fought off every vile spirit inside and
outside of the home before Tori and Thomas arrived, but they
had no authority over the ones inhabiting the damned human—
not until they came out of him and attacked.

Arithem drew his blade. "Hold steady, my friend."

"Come out, you cowards!" Zarall taunted the demons, the
number of which he could not determine, though he knew they
were many.

The main demon hissed. "What have we to do with you,
mighty warriors of the Most High? Leave us be. Our time has
not yet come."

"Aye, but it will come soon enough, dark one," Arithem
returned. "For now, touch not these holy saints."

The demon laughed. "We will make the man kill them
where they stand, and you can do naught to stop us."

Zarall hefted his ax in the air, but Arithem gripped his arm.
"Nay. He's right." He nodded toward Tori. "Only the daughter
of Eve can bind them. Without her permission, we can do
nothing."

The AR-15 waved before Tori's chest. Thomas started to
circle her, a protective gesture she appreciated, but she thrust out
her arm and held him back. "This is my home. Who are you?"

Snickering, the man stepped farther onto the porch, squinting his eyes at her. "So, it *is* you. Don't matter. This is my home now."

"Butch?" Tori stared up at the six-foot-three beast before her. "From across the street?" He had been such a great neighbor, friendly, kind, the type who took in your garbage cans when you weren't home and brought over extra fruit from the store. Aside from a few familiar physical features, the man who stood before her now looked more like a WWF wrestler filled with rage and fear.

"Get out now!" He gestured with his gun, his finger on the trigger. "No room for you here!"

"We will only be a minute, I promise."

"Tori, let's go," Thomas said from behind.

Lord, help.

That's when she saw them, dozens of black shadows crossing the man's eyes, back and forth, restless, angry spirits, unnerved by her presence.

Squaring her shoulders, she attempted to settle the beating of her heart. "You will let us inside. I bind and muzzle you in the name of Jesus."

"Excellent!" Zarall shouted, smiling at his ward. "I knew she could do it."

Both angels plucked ropes from their belt and went to work tying up every demon possessing the poor human. Arithem had been right. There were twenty of them. And though the foul spirits struggled a bit, they had to comply or face Arithem and Zarall in battle.

Zarall, happy to have something to do, worked steadily by Arithem's side until all the hellish creatures were bound. Then they strapped leather muzzles across each mouth and stood back to admire their work.

"How long will it hold?" Zarall asked.

"Long enough for our wards to escape."

"Praise be to the Commander!"

Thomas wouldn't have believed it if he hadn't seen it. Tori issued some command in Jesus' name, and the man she called Butch wilted like a flower before the hot sun. Confusion spun across eyes that now seemed vacant. He lowered his weapon.

"Yeah. I guess it's okay for you to come in, but only for a minute."

"Thanks, Butch. We won't be long." Tori pushed past him as if he were a friend asking her in for tea and not a man who had almost shot and killed her.

Thomas hesitated, eyeing the gun, still tight in the man's hands.

Sirens roared in the distance, reminding him they hadn't much time.

"Tori!" He eased past Butch, who stumbled forward and plopped down on a couch, staring into space as if he'd just awoke from a dream. White stuffing from inside the couch spilled around him like a cloud. The only other furniture in the room was a coffee table tipped on its side with three legs missing.

"In here!" Tori's voice echoed from down a hallway to the left.

Shattered glass from broken windows crunched beneath his shoes. A bookcase split in two lined the hallway. He picked up a framed picture lying on the floor and shook away the shattered glass. A woman who looked a lot like Tori, only older, stood beside a man. Both hugged a little girl around ten between them. He'd never seen such radiant smiles.

"Thomas!" Tori's shout accompanied the sirens, now closer.

What was he doing? Blinking away the fog of shock from his mind, he set down the picture and rushed into one of the bedrooms.

A broken-down bed had been shoved aside and several planks of wood flooring lay to the side of a hole from which Tori pulled a metal box. She inserted a key and opened it. "Come here."

The sirens grew louder as Thomas knelt beside her. "Tori, we don't have time for this. We have to go!"

She held up a small black object. "Show me your hand. The one with the chip."

"Why? What are you going to do? It's in so many pieces, there's no way to remove it surgically—"

A jolt of gut-wrenching pain shot through his hand, rippled up his arm, and seared through his body like a heated prong. Stunned, Thomas stumbled backward, unable to move or even right himself.

Tori caught him and leaned him against the wall.

"Sorry."

"What the heck, Tori?" he mumbled.

"How many vaccine boosters have you gotten?"

"What?" Thomas closed his eyes. "What are you talking about?"

"How many?"

"I don't know. I'm late on the last two. Why?" He tried to stand. "Ouch!"

Turning, Tori grabbed a black book from the box and something that looked like a phone with an antenna. "The vaccines have assembling nanotech in them. It just depends on how many you've had as to whether they can track you with them."

"Nanotech? What are you talking—"

"Let's pray yours aren't functional yet," she said, rushing to glance out the window. "Since it took them a few days to find out who helped me escape, chances are they aren't. They are here. On the street."

She dashed out of the room. Once again Thomas tried to get up. The woman wasn't making sense. Maybe this was her way of getting rid of him. He couldn't blame her. Wait. She'd tased his chip! The electrical current would fry it, wouldn't it?

She returned, a sack in hand. "Can you walk?"

Thomas could barely hear her now over the sirens. He nodded, and taking her free arm, he leaned on her as she rushed through the house and out the back door. Butch remained on the couch, gun in his lap, barely acknowledging them as they passed.

Out into the stagnant, humid air, Tori led him back through the fence, across the neighbor's yard and then through several more fences and yards. Pain coursed through him with every move, but by the time they stopped in the back of an old Publix Market, it was dissipating.

Rats crisscrossed the pavement beneath a dumpster from which the foul stench of rotten food made Thomas wish he didn't have to breathe so hard.

"Smart move, Tori," he said between heavy breaths.

She smiled and shoved strands of hair from her face. "Sorry about that. I couldn't think of anything else."

"Well, it must have worked. I don't hear the sirens anymore."

"Unless they've gone silent," she said. "But I'm pretty sure it worked. We've used it before on others."

"We?"

"The saints." A look of disgust crossed her eyes, if only for a moment.

But he knew why. How many of those "saints" had he condemned to execution?

"Come on." Turning she headed into the night. "We need to find some place to hole up, get some sleep."

"We lost him, sir." Holding the phone to his ear, Kyle ground his fist, longing to punch the wall of Vice Regent Benton's office, where he and his trackers had been combing through every scrap of Thomas's belongings, searching for any hint of where he would go.

"How the hell did you manage that, sergeant?"

Kyle held the phone away from his ear at Regent Laundry's booming voice.

"His signal was there one minute and then it completely disappeared. I assume they found a way to disable the chip."

"You think?" Landry growled. "I just can't believe it. Not of Thomas."

"The facts are irrefutable, sir. He helped her escape."

"Yes, I know. I know. But why?"

Kyle didn't know if he was supposed to answer or not, so he simply waited for Landry to continue.

"Unless..." The regent tapped his chin, the silence unnerving.

"Unless what, sir?"

He narrowed his eyes on Kyle. "Unless this is all just a ploy to find the big fish."

"Fish, sir?"

"Are you stupid, Cruz?" he exploded. "Where most of these Deviants hide, especially the leaders of the North American Region."

Kyle ground his teeth at the insult but kept his tone steady. "Ah, you mean Nyla Cruz and Calan Walker."

"Of course I mean them!" Landry yelled. "We catch them, the whole Deviant chain unravels."

"But wouldn't Vice Regent Benton have told you of his plan? Gotten your permission?"

"Not if he thought there was a Deviant spy among us."

Kyle gulped. A spy? That didn't make sense. "Why not just tell you at least?"

Several uncomfortable minutes passed, but Kyle didn't dare say another word.

"I don't know," the regent said at last. "But I do know Thomas. He's as loyal to the NWU as they come. More ambitious than I've ever seen. He would never risk all he's achieved for a silly woman Deviant. No, he has a plan, and it has to be a plan that will increase his power and position. Now, that's the Thomas I know."

"So what do you want me to do?"

"Continue to track him. His face will show up on one of the cameras eventually, especially if he wants us to find him."

"And when we *do* find him?" Kyle made sure to use when and not if. He had grown confident in his skills at finding anyone, especially a Deviant lover.

"Hang back but keep an eye on him. Whether he is on our side or not, he'll lead us right to the main Deviant hideout." A hideous smile split the regent's face. "And when he does, we'll take down the whole lot of them."

*They were stoned, they were sawn asunder, were tempted,
were slain with the sword: they wandered about in sheepskins
and goatskins; being destitute, afflicted, tormented; Of whom
the world was not worthy: they wandered in deserts, and in
mountains, and in dens and caves of the earth.*
Hebrews 11:37-38

Chapter 11

The place Tori found for them to "hole up" was a place Thomas would not have stepped a single foot inside of just ten hours ago. In fact, he wouldn't have even stopped his car outside of the dilapidated, decaying five-story structure that must have been an office building at one time.

Tori pulled a flashlight from her sack and led him to one of the offices toward the back of the building on the ground floor. A rat, joined by two cockroaches, scattered as they entered, and Thomas wondered why she'd not chosen a better place higher up, away from the bugs and vermin. But then he saw the door that led to a back courtyard, and he knew why. They needed an escape route should the NWU troops find them.

And once again, he got a taste of what this incredible woman had been through these past years.

She plopped down on what was left of a leather couch, leaned her head back, and took a deep breath.

For the first time in his life, Thomas was at a loss for words. Shock. He must be in shock. Nothing made sense anymore. His thoughts spun like a cyclone, refusing to land. His heart felt as heavy as a concrete block. He sat beside her, listening to her breathing, the patter of rats, and sirens in the distance, and hoped beyond hope this was all a nightmare and he'd wake up soon.

But the electricity still buzzing through him from the taser screamed that this was his new reality.

After a few minutes, Tori opened her sack and pulled out two strips of beef jerky, handing him one.

Beef Jerky? Thomas held up a hand. "No thanks. Not hungry."

"You should eat. We have a long way to travel tomorrow." After a few minutes, she added, "Listen, I know it's a far cry from what you're used to."

She must have sensed his disgust. Grabbing it, he ripped off a piece with his teeth and nearly choked at the taste. "What did you mean by nanotech in the vaccines?"

A few minutes passed before she responded. "There's a lot you don't know. Let's just say the vaccines aren't what you think they are."

Thomas didn't know what to make of that, but let it go. Instead, he asked, "So, that was your sister's house?"

"Yup."

"Why aren't you still living there?"

"Are you kidding me?" She huffed. "That's the first place they looked when I was labeled a Deviant Rebel."

Thomas cursed under his breath. Of course. He glanced at her, wishing he could see her face, her expression, but she kept the flashlight off. "I'm sorry."

"Are you?"

"Yes, I'm sorry that happened to you." He removed his shoes and rubbed his feet, wincing from the blisters. A stench rose, and he lowered his nose to his shirt. "I stink."

"We both do." She laughed.

"Why did you take me through the worst part of town? I've never seen such slums."

She took another bite of jerky. "That used to be a nice part of town. One of the best. My neighborhood used to be clean, upper class, respectable. That's what your NWU has done to people." Her tone was sharp, bitter.

"You can hardly blame that on the NWU. It was the war, the famine, the quakes and tsunamis, the asteroids and meteors. And all the horrible plagues those two old Jewish men unleashed. It's been a tough time for Planet Earth." When she didn't answer, he added, "The NWU has done a lot of good for people, feeding them, giving them places to live."

"Really? I'll show you one of your NWU's luxury housings tomorrow," she said matter-of-factly before finishing her jerky and pulling the phone from her sack. Rising, she moved toward the broken window and dialed a number.

"Come on…. come on, pick up. Nyla! Yes, it's me. Yes, I escaped. Praise God! But I've picked up a…."—she glanced his way—"lost puppy."

Puppy? Thomas frowned. Puppy or not, she'd hardly escaped on her own. But Nyla? Nyla Cruz? Wow. So Tori really did know the location of the largest Deviant hideout.

"Long story," Tori said. "I'll tell you later."

A female voice droned on the other end, but Thomas could not make out her words.

"Can we come?" Tori paused, listening. "Okay. Where can I meet you?" Another pause. "Got it. See you in a few weeks." She hung up the call, then remained by the window, looking out.

"Who was that?" Thomas asked.

She tsked. "As if you don't recognize her name."

"So you *do* know where Nyla Cruz is."

She faced him. "Yes, and she and Calan are the only ones who will help us now."

At her harsh tone, Thomas instantly regretted his comment. "Sorry, I'm just…Man, I could use a drink."

She released a heavy sigh. "I know you've been through a huge shock. And you're probably going to go through withdrawals now."

"Withdrawals?"

"From alcohol. You drink like a fish, Thomas." Humor laced her voice.

"Oh, man." Thomas ran a hand through his hair, the distinct scent of the mousse he'd put in it that morning conflicting with the stench of the place. She was probably right.

She headed toward him. "We should get some sleep."

The patter of rodent feet filled the room, and Thomas slipped his shoes back on, his blisters stinging. "Can we find someplace better to rest?"

"Sorry it's not the Hilton, *Vice Regent*, but you might as well get used to it." Her tone was sarcastic as she plopped down beside him.

Thomas's stomach growled. He needed food—real food. His hair was a mess. He needed a shower. He longed for his sleep number bed and his white-noise maker. But he knew he'd have neither this night.

The only good thing about today was that Tori was still by his side. The woman he nearly sent to her death had saved his life. She was stronger than he remembered, tougher, yet somehow filled with joy and peace. Which made no sense. "Thanks for not leaving me back there. You could have ditched me and ran."

"Never. You're in this mess 'cause of me."

Her words touched him. They were true, of course, but he'd rarely met anyone who had any honor or decency anymore. "Tell me about your time in that San Fran Art School."

She leaned her head back on the sofa. "Not much to tell. I loved the art. I excelled at it, actually. So much so that a graphic design company in LA offered me a job working on graphics for Disney."

Thomas whistled. "Disney? Wow. That's big time."

"Yeah, I was thrilled. At first."

"What happened?"

"Lots of bad things," she breathed out. "Lots of bad people."

"But you made it! You were at the pinnacle of success for an artist. The money must have been great. The prestige. I knew you would make something of yourself. Proud of you, Tori."

"Don't be," she mumbled. "There was a price to pay, a huge price, and it wasn't worth it."

He could tell she was falling asleep, but he wanted to know more, wanted her to keep talking, if only to get his mind off his surroundings.

"What price?" he asked.

But the only answer he received was the low hum of her snoring. He smiled. She'd always snored...light and soft, but a snore, nonetheless.

Reaching for her, he gently laid her head down in his lap and brushed hair from her face. How could anyone sleep so soundly when danger lurked all around? But that was Tori. World War IV could start up with nukes flying around them, and Tori would still sleep like a baby.

Not Thomas. He'd never slept well. Even with his prescribed sleeping pills, he tossed and turned like a ship in a storm.

And now, surrounded by rats and roaches and hunted like an animal, he knew he'd get no sleep at all.

Tori made her way across the broken asphalt that used to be an elementary school playground. Cracks lined it like an old man's face while swings waved empty in the breeze. At one time, this had been a thriving school filled with giggling children and little bodies rushing about, full of life and hope for a future. Now, the NWU taught children online with their World Education System, aka Propaganda Bullcrap.

One glance over her shoulder told her Thomas still followed. Poor guy. He looked horrible—face pale, eyes glassy, his body shaking from detox. Not only did he lose everything important to him, but he now suffered physically. Why would he put himself through this on purpose? Give up everything to live a life of suffering when he didn't even believe in God? Maybe the entire thing—her initial escape from prison, them being on the run now, was all part of his plan to capture more Deviants. And the most important Deviants—Nyla and Calan. And if true, then she was leading him straight to them.

She'd gotten up early that morning to pray, to ask God for discernment and wisdom, and an overwhelming peace cloaked her as she stared at Thomas asleep on the couch. Whether he was deceiving her or not, she was to continue on her present course, and the Lord would let her know if anything changed.

"I hope you know what you're doing, Lord," she had prayed, and she'd sensed Him smiling at her, something she'd often sensed these past years. And that, along with His love, had kept her going, moving forward, doing His work while she could.

At least Thomas had kept the hoodie over his head. Her brother-in-law's clothing fit him well, perhaps a bit tight, but she'd finally convinced him that he'd be far more comfortable in jeans, a t-shirt, and tennies, than the designer junk he'd been wearing. Tori had also been happy to exchange her shorts for a pair of her sister's jeans and her flip-flops for some running shoes. With a baseball hat shoved atop her head, she, too, did her best to avoid cameras.

Her heart took up a rapid beat as they approached the abandoned school that had housed the underground church and home for unwed mothers she had run. Hopefully, it was the last place they would look for her since they'd raided the place six months ago. Besides, she sensed in her spirit someone was still here, someone who had escaped the chaos of the raid and was waiting for her. That still, small voice had never let her down.

"What are we doing here?" Thomas came up from behind as she swung open a back door and entered the building.

"Meeting someone."

"I'm so cold," he said. "And hungry. Any food in here?"

Cold? Tori glanced outside where the rays of an angry sun heated everything to near melting. The sun had grown hotter these past years, nearly unbearable during the middle of the day.

"Sorry, no food. Follow me." She moved down a long hallway into what used to be the lunchroom, then behind the kitchen and down a set of stairs into a storage room. Each step brought back memories of her brothers and sisters who met here for worship, Bible reading, and fellowship. She could almost hear their voices singing, "Holy, holy, holy, Lord God Almighty." She smiled. Other memories surfaced, of pregnant women seeking refuge from state-mandated abortions, and babies born and nursed in this place where God's Holy Angels protected them.

Until the fateful night of the NWU raid.

She took the final step into the storage room that used to house textbooks and crayons, paper and pencils, art, science, and sports equipment, but was now covered in cushions, blankets and towels.

Thomas entered behind her and plunked down on the floor with a moan.

A footstep. A shriek. Tori swung to her left, ready to fight or run.

Brianna stepped out from the shadows, baby Callie in her arms, and Carla clinging to her pants. She smiled at Tori, tears streaming down her face.

Tori flew into her arms. "You're here! The Lord told me someone was here! I'm so happy to see you! Are you well?" Pushing back from the woman, she examined her from head to toe, then leaned to kiss the baby in her arms.

"We didn't know if you'd be here, but we heard that you escaped, and we thought…we thought you might show up." Brianna half-laughed, half-sobbed.

"Tori!" Three-year-old Carla squealed.

Kneeling, Tori swept her up in her arms, showering her with kisses. "Praise God you are all well."

Callie started to fuss, and Tori lowered Carla to the floor and took the baby, jostling her in her arms.

"Did anyone else…?" Tori could hardly even say it.

"Not that I know of. We are the only ones left." Brianna shook her head. "Wait. Except Sara. She went to NWU housing, I think."

Not Sara. Tori blew out a sigh. The young woman wouldn't do well there. She'd fall back into her old ways.

"How have you survived?" Tori asked.

Brianna gazed down at little Carla. "It's been tough, but the Lord provides."

"Well, you aren't alone anymore. You're coming with us."

Clearing his throat, Thomas struggled to rise. "What's this?" It was one thing to avoid cameras, drones, and robots with just the two of them, but with a small child and a baby?

The attractive African American woman cast a suspicious look his way.

"This is Thomas," Tori said. "He helped me escape."

"Well, then, a pleasure to meet you, Thomas." Brianna smiled.

He attempted to return her smile, but the pounding ache in his head forbid it. "I can't see how—"

"You're hurt." Cutting him off, Tori reached for a cut on the woman's forehead. "Here, let me." She looked around, and just like that, handed Thomas the baby.

Thomas didn't like babies. He wasn't a fan of children either. But his protests fell on deaf ears as Tori located a first-aid kit and bandaged up Brianna's wound.

The baby stared up at him as if he were Godzilla. Her face scrunched into a twist of fear and outrage before she opened her mouth and let out an ear-piercing wail.

Apparently, babies didn't like him much either.

Tori cast him a look of disappointment. "Here, Carla, hold this." She instructed the little girl to hold a bandage against her mother's forehead as she headed toward Thomas and took the babe. The child instantly quieted and began to coo.

His body trembled. His stomach growled, and he felt like his head would explode. If he could find one drink. Surely there was somewhere to buy a bottle of wine…anything. Didn't the NWU provide free alcohol and drugs to the masses?

The room spun. Thomas leaned against the wall and rubbed his temples

"Detox." He heard Tori explain to Brianna as she finished her nursing. Then heading toward the back of the room, she removed bricks from the wall and took something out of a hole, placing it in her sack.

Thomas hoped it was food. Better yet, alcohol.

No such luck, as finally, Tori gathered her sack and her friends and headed up the stairs.

"Where are we going?" He dragged himself after them.

Once outside, Tori smiled his way. "To show you your NWU housing and rescue my friend Sara."

Kyle always got the jitters when he was about to meet with his Tall White friend, Jura. He wasn't sure why. He'd known the alien for years and had learned so much from him. In fact, he owed his quick rise in power to Jura and his influence. But something about the man…woman…whatever it was never failed to cause Kyle's insides to squirm. Just a little. Perhaps it was merely because Jura was from another planet. That had to be it.

The guard ushered Kyle into the comfortable room at the Broward Reformation Center. The Tall White stood at the window that took up an entire wall, looking down on the prison cells where Deviants were held to be reprogrammed. He turned, smiled—that alluring sensual smile of his—and gestured for Kyle to sit.

The alien always seemed to float instead of walk, though Kyle could see his feet. His white shirt and pants blended well with his skin that was a translucent, shimmering ivory. Long silky alabaster hair hung down his back while stark blue eyes examined Kyle with an eerie interest. "You may be wondering why I've summoned you," he said.

"I assume it has something to do with the Griffin girl's escape and Thomas Benton's involvement."

"Precisely." Jura sat beside Kyle—far too close—and poured a glass of water from a crystalline decanter. He handed it to him.

Kyle took a sip, recalling that this particular water always made him feel relaxed.

"I've devised a plan to aid you in their capture," Jura said, placing his hand on Kyle's leg.

A pleasant sensation spiraled up Kyle's leg. He was not a homosexual, but something about this man did strange things to him. He cleared his throat. "I'd love to hear it."

"As you know, some of my kind can appear to be human." He waved a hand through the air. "It depends on how much of our DNA has combined with a human's." He stood, walked—or rather floated—a few steps, then pressed a finger on his chin. "I have many such types under my command."

Kyle took another sip of water, longing for Jura to touch him again. "Yes, I am aware, my liege."

Jura's blue eyes turned to ice as a seductive grin raised the corners of his thin lips. "Then why not set one of them in the path of our fugitives? To join their number and report back their location and whatever deviant activities they are involved in."

"But how will this spy find them?" Kyle scooted to the edge of his seat and set his glass on the table. "Even when he does, these Deviants aren't stupid. They may not trust a stranger."

Jura's placid smile did not hide the frustration storming from his eyes.

Kyle swallowed. He should not have contradicted him.

"You will find them. We have scanners and cameras everywhere. When you do, contact me, and I will place my spy among them." He flipped his long hair behind him. "Their weakness will be our victory, for they cannot pass up helping another human being. They will fall for it. I assure you, my son."

Pride lifted Kyle's spirits. He loved it when Jura called him son. His own father had been nothing but disappointed in Kyle. "It will be as you say." Rising, he bowed toward Jura, then made for the door.

"One more thing."

Kyle spun around.

"This will lead to your sister's arrest and execution. Are you comfortable with that?"

A question he had asked himself many times in the past year. But she had betrayed him. She had betrayed her family *and* the world. "Of course."

*And when the dragon saw that he was cast unto the earth,
he persecuted the woman which brought forth the man child.
And to the woman were given two wings of a great eagle, that
she might fly into the wilderness, into her place, where she is
nourished for a time, and times, and half a time, from the face
of the serpent.
And the serpent cast out of his mouth water as a flood
after the woman, that he might cause her to be carried away of
the flood. And the earth helped the woman, and the earth
opened her mouth, and swallowed up the flood which the
dragon cast out of his mouth.
Revelation 12:13-16*

Chapter 12

They heard the drone before they saw it. The eerie hum, accompanied by a *whisk* and *whizzing* sound sent Tori ducking behind a dumpster. Brianna and her children joined her just as Thomas rounded the corner of the empty shopping mall they'd been walking behind.

Too late. The drone lowered, heading straight for Thomas. Yanking his hood over his face, he stood frozen, unsure what to do.

"Citizen. Raise your head." The drone spoke in a lifeless metallic voice.

Thomas's heart nearly blasted through his chest. He'd seen these drones in action. It would shoot to kill if he did not comply.

The sound of electricity pulsed through the putrid air, followed by a *clank*.

The drone's gun readying to fire?

"Citizen. You will be shot on sight if you do not—"

BOOM!

Thomas instinctively dove for the ground. Heat swamped him along with the clank of metal hitting the pavement and the sizzle and spark of power.

Several seconds passed. Was he dead?

"Thomas, come on!" Tori shouted.

Peeking from beneath his hood, he saw what was left of the drone lying in a pile of metal a few yards away. Sparks shot from the broken pieces. He rose, legs trembling. Giving the hideous thing a wide berth, he approached Tori just as she shoved what looked like a gun in her pack.

"What was that?"

"A drone zapper. At least that's what we call it."

Brianna and her children emerged from behind the dumpster. "Norman was really good at tech stuff. He made a few for our church."

Carla wandered over to Thomas and slipped her hand in his. "Don't worry, Thomist. God protects us."

Her dark, curly hair bobbed in the wind while shining from her face was more peace than Thomas had felt in years.

"Come on. We need to keep moving." Pivoting, Tori started off. "I just hope that drone didn't get a good look at you," she shouted over her shoulder.

Though Thomas tried to release little Carla's hand, she only gripped him tighter and tugged him along, smiling up at him.

The NWU housing that Thomas had heard so much about turned out to be nothing but a five-story building that stretched for a block. Very few windows and no balconies decorated the front, making it look more like a prison than luxury living. No greenery surrounded it either, no parks nearby, no restaurants or stores, and certainly not the swimming pools and gardens he'd been told filled the inner courtyard.

Tori led them around back to a large garage door where no doubt supplies were loaded.

"You can't get in without a pass," Thomas said, "and if you have one, they'll spot you the minute you enter."

A sudden breeze blew a strand of her wavy hair across her face as she stared at him curiously, almost as if she pitied him. "We know. How do you think we survived all these years?"

Embarrassed once again, Thomas took a step back. In his world, he'd been in command, in charge, the one to whom people looked for answers. But this was not his world. Neither was it anything like he'd been told.

Tori knocked on the door, a specific sequence of knocks and taps that reminded Thomas of the ancient Morse code he'd read about.

They stood outside for what seemed like hours as the sun's rays speared through him, igniting his headache once again. Sweat streamed down his back. He stank. His stomach gnawed his insides. But how could he complain when the little girl beside him stood happily humming to herself?

The garage door cranked a few feet off the ground. Dropping to the pavement, Tori squeezed through. Brianna handed the baby to her and then grabbed Carla's hand and followed.

Thomas barely fit through the opening. Once inside, and after his eyes adjusted to the darkness, he saw Tori hugging a large bear of a man who spoke with her in hushed tones. He closed the door and led them through a stockroom and then into an elevator.

"Thomas, this is Bart. Bart, Thomas," Tori said. "He helped me escape."

"Then I owe you a big hug!" the man said as they exited at the fourth floor.

"No, that's…" But the man was already squeezing the life out of him. Thomas couldn't remember the last time anyone hugged him, especially a man, and with such genuine exuberance. Bart didn't smell much better than Thomas, but somehow, he didn't care. The man exuded joy.

Maybe things weren't so bad in the NWU housing, after all.

MaryLu Tyndall

Releasing him, Bart smiled, revealing several missing teeth that made him look like a pirate of old. Gesturing down the hall, he said to Tori, "Sara's in the last door to your right."

"Thanks, Bart. I owe you one."

"Naw. Anything for you." And off he went.

They passed several rooms, most with open doors. Shock and confusion raged through Thomas at what he saw. Several people inhabited each room that couldn't be any larger than his master bathroom at home. Some sat around TV screens mounted on walls, others lay passed out on the floor, while others had virtual reality goggles wrapped around their heads.

He'd been told that each family received a large suite with enough rooms to fit the number of people in their household. In addition, they were given a universal monthly income that would more than suffice for necessities, along with free internet, TV, access to the Metaverse and all the drugs and medicines they required. If anyone needed extra money, the NWU provided jobs that fit their qualifications. Of course, most of the common masses preferred not to work. Only those with higher intellect and ability received the best jobs. Capitalism had been an abject failure, creating an unfair system that spawned poverty and elevated the wealthy...or so he'd been taught.

Somewhere a baby cried. Down the hall in the opposite direction, two women shouted obscenities at each other. And the smell—the stench of too many people confined in too small a place, a mixture of urine, body odor, and rotten food—added nausea to Thomas's ailments.

They stopped before one of the rooms, and Tori rapped her knuckles on the open door.

A young woman, no older than twenty and lying on a mound of pillows, opened one eye. "Tori?" she mumbled out, and Tori rushed to kneel at her side.

"Yes, it's me, sweetie. I'm here." She placed a hand on the girl's forehead and then lifted each eyelid and checked both eyes.

Brianna slid inside, baby in her arms, while Carla pulled Thomas to sit on the only couch in the room.

As she rose, Tori's eyes glistened with tears. "She's high."

Brianna reached for her. "I'm so sorry."

"I can't leave her here."

A moan drew Thomas's attention to a cot against the far wall where a young man lay curled up in a ball, VR headset on. On the table beside the bed, pills lay scattered beside a half-empty bottle of what looked like vodka.

His heart leapt. His throat squeezed. His eyes refused to leave the precious elixir. Carla had finally released his hand and moved to cling to her mother.

"I need to sober her up," Tori was saying…and something else Thomas couldn't hear. Nor did he care. He licked his lips and started to rise.

Yet before he could take a step toward the bottle, a swath of brilliant light flashed before his eyes and landed on Tori, still talking with Brianna. Her gaze snapped to Thomas, then wandered to the bottle as if someone or something had told her his intentions.

Excusing herself, she pushed past him, grabbed the bottle and moved to a small kitchenette built into the wall beside the door.

Thomas headed for her. "No! Please! Just one sip—" But she had already poured the alcohol down the sink.

"I'm making coffee." She started opening cupboards, but Thomas no longer cared.

"How could you do that to me?" Anger churned in his empty belly. He ran a hand through his hair, tugging it until it hurt. He wouldn't even be in this situation if not for her. "I just wanted a sip."

"There is never just one sip." She poured coffee grains into the filter, added water, and turned the archaic machine on.

He stood, staring at her, furious, tired, and feeling worse than he ever had. This woman had caused him more pain in his life than he cared to admit. What the heck was he doing? He should be in his five-million-dollar mansion, back at work where he was in charge and respected. "You don't know what it feels like."

At this, she spun, pointing at him with a can of soup. "I don't? I've been to more rehab centers than you've owned homes. I've gone through detox more times than I can count—not only for alcohol but for a long list of other drugs." Her eyes burned emerald. "So don't tell me I don't know how you feel."

A sour taste rose in his throat, and he swallowed. He hadn't known any of that.

Her expression softened. "Listen, I know you don't feel well. Just go sit down. I'm getting you something to eat, and then I have to get Sara alert enough to move."

Kindness and concern filled both her tone and her gaze, surprising him and prompting him to do as she asked. Back on the couch, little Carla eased beside him and leaned her head against his arm. He didn't know what to do. Children usually hated him. She snuggled closer, nestling into his underarm, prompting him to hug her. Despite his own horrid stink and their noxious surroundings, she smelled of sunshine and wildflowers and innocence, and it filled him with a momentary sense of goodness he hadn't felt in some time.

"I'm glad Onafiel stopped you." She began humming again.

Thomas had no idea what the crazy kid was mumbling about. Still nursing his rage, he sat moping and watching Tori and Brianna try to get Sara to sit up and drink some coffee. Whatever the poor girl had taken, she was in much worse shape than him, and he doubted they'd resurrect her any time soon. She'd take a sip, mumble something, then fall back down again. He should help. With his strength, he'd be able to lift her up and get her to walk, but his head felt like it would explode, and his body shook like a leaf in the wind. If only Tori hadn't dumped out that bottle.

By now Carla had fallen asleep leaning against him. At least he didn't have to hold the baby. Brianna seemed to manage just fine with the child strapped to her chest.

Finally, they both took a break, and Tori brought him a mug of soup, smiling at Carla. "Seems you've made a friend."

The soup smelled better than a steak dinner at *Chez Paul's*. He grabbed it with his free hand. "Don't know why. Been kinda a grouch lately."

Tori arched a brow. "You? Noooo." Then turning, she went to help Brianna, who was attempting to give Sara another sip of coffee.

Jerusalem. The word coming from the reporter on the TV drew Thomas's attention, along with Tori and Brianna's.

"Thousands of Israelis are fleeing Jerusalem, some in cars, others in trains, and many on foot," the man was saying, pressing the communication device in his ear. "All because of Lord Immu Aali's command to be worshiped. His Excellency Gabriel Wolfe has created an enormous hologram in the likeness of Lord Aali, projected it before the Temple, and ordered all who pass by to bow in worship."

The scene switched to a woman reporter standing before the object in question. "Yes, and I hear he plans to place the same hologram in every major city on earth."

Wow. The hologram looked more lifelike than anything Thomas had seen. It moved, spoke and even smiled. If it weren't so tall, Thomas might think it was the Premier himself—or *Lord* as he wanted to be called now. Amazing.

Tori shared a glance with Brianna. "Just like the Scripture says."

The scene changed to a crowded freeway where cars and trucks crept along, bumper to bumper. Honking horns, loud mufflers, and shouts filled the air as they inched along. People with suitcases and backpacks slogged along the sides of the roads, some with small children in tow.

"Why are they leaving?" Thomas asked.

Tori glanced over her shoulder. "They are realizing who Aali really is, that he is the Antichrist and not their real Messiah."

Huffing, Thomas took a sip of his soup, hoping it would stay down. A longing ripped through him to be back in the game with Aali in Jerusalem, to be one of the power-players in the Global Government. Instead of sitting here with a sleeping child in the worst slums he could imagine. Starving. Miserable. With nothing to his name. *What had he done?*

The soup soured in his stomach, and he nearly vomited it back up. Setting the mug on the floor, he continued watching the TV, where torrential rains made it difficult to see the cars anymore.

The male reporter stood beneath a large umbrella. "Odd, but it was sunny just a moment ago, and now this downpour came out of nowhere. Never saw it rain this hard in Israel."

Sara moaned and Brianna knelt and placed a cool cloth on her head. "Now the flood will happen."

Tori smiled. "Yeah, but God's got this."

What the heck were they talking about? Thomas sighed and rubbed his temples, hoping to alleviate the pain.

The rain continued, and the newscasters switched to other news as Tori and Brianna attended Sara, managing this time to get her on her feet.

Thomas attempted to get up to help, but the little girl in his arms snuggled closer and his head pounded stronger. Reaching for his soup, he drank more, and then some more, his stomach finally accepting the food.

An hour or two passed, or maybe it just seemed that long. Sara was now sitting up, blinking and breathing heavily, but more alert than he'd ever seen her. Long dark hair, streaked in bright blue highlights fell past her shoulders, while a sleeve of ink decorated her entire right arm. Thomas couldn't tell what the tattoo pictured, if anything, though he wasn't a fan of so much ink on a woman's nice skin.

The same two reporters appeared on the TV again, this time at a different location, much higher up than before, and both wearing rain garb.

"Oh my God, it's a flash flood!" the woman shouted, turning from looking behind her to the camera. "It's going to swallow up all those poor people on the freeway!"

The scene was filled with the same highway as before, crowded with people and cars, but then the camera zeroed in on a giant wall of water several feet high heading straight for them.

Tori gripped Brianna's hand as they stared at the screen. Thomas thought he heard them praying.

"Nearly five inches of rain has fallen in the past hour," the male reporter said, "overflowing the Jordan and creating this rushing flood of deadly debris that will surely kill all those innocent people!"

Thomas had never seen anything like it. Did they intend to show the massacre on TV? Yet he could hardly tear his gaze away.

The reporters said nothing more as the horrifying scene filled the screen.

The water was nearly on the people now. Cars had stopped, Passengers were getting out to stare at the incoming flood. Thomas could not imagine the terror they were experiencing.

The scene shook violently back and forth for several seconds before the screen went blank. Finally, a voice, a *terrified* voice came through the speakers. "We've had an earthquake. Eitan, get the camera back on."

Muffled voices, shouting, a scream, and deep breaths emerged from the speakers.

Scenes flashed across the TV before it went dark again. After several seconds, it flicked on. The woman reporter, hair askew and with a terrified look in her eyes, held the mic to her lips. "I don't know the intensity of the quake, but it was a huge one." She pressed her ear, then glanced behind her. "Look! The people are still alive. The highway is intact, and the cars and people are still there. Pan in on where the wave was before the quake, Eitan."

The scene zoomed in on the location beside the freeway. A massive rift etched across the earth parallel to the freeway.

Steam rose from the fissure as what was left of the flood trickled over the side and disappeared.

Zarall glanced at his friend, Arithem, dressed in his military best, complete with a white robe that hung to his knees, a gold sash displaying his various medals, and a brass-plated belt into which were strapped his favorite weapons, including his red laser sword. Tall leather boots laced in gold, and a helmet bearing the insignia of the Lord of Heaven's Armies completed the ensemble. "I've never seen you look so good, Arithem."

Arithem glanced his way. "Nor *you* look so nervous."

"'Tis not every day we are summoned to the throne room." In truth, Zarall had only been called individually before the Commander once before. Shifting his shoulders, he felt uncomfortable in his dress uniform, for he normally wore his battle attire. He hated leaving his ward, especially in the dire straits in which she currently found herself. He glanced around the outer chamber of the throne room, what the Hebrews called the Court of the Gentiles. In heaven, 'twas where those with an appointment to see the King waited.

Several other angels stood behind them, friends he'd known for millennia. Redeemed saints, now blessed to be in their glorified bodies, also waited for an audience with the Lord, though He oft walked through the city to spend time with each one.

Arithem shifted his stance. "It must be of great importance, or the Commander would not have summoned us."

"Indeed." And that made Zarall ill at ease, for surely it meant more trouble for Tori. As long as she was in human form, she was capable of forsaking the Father, forsaking the Commander, and losing her soul in hell.

Two massive golden doors opened, and a herald emerged. "Arithem and Zarall, Class One Guardians of the Saints and Warriors of the Most High!"

Arithem smiled and started for the steps. "Whatever the Commander wants, we shall meet the challenge, my friend. At last we may have something to do aside from standing about and fighting off the occasional dark one."

Zarall followed, both nervous and excited. Another angel led the way and gestured where they were to stand.

Brilliant light swirled around the throne and curved over the top in a multitude of colors. The four living creatures Zarall had seen before stood beside the throne, two to the left, two to the right. Such fascinating beings with their four faces, six wings, and their wheels covered in eyes. Only the Father could create such exquisite creatures, and how blessed they were to always be by His side. The light coming from the throne was so bright Zarall blinked. The figure who sat upon it beamed like sapphire, making it hard to see His face.

Falling to their knees, the warrior angels bowed their heads.

From within the light, the Commander emerged, a human, a Son of Eve, yet also a Son of the Most High—the Father of Spirits. He was the eternal one, the Savior of all mankind, the lamb that became a lion, the Holy One, and the Commander of Heaven's Armies. His hair was white, his eyes aflame, and He wore silver armor about His torso and legs. A sword hung at His side, and He gestured for them to approach.

Zarall and Arithem stood and stepped forward.

"I have a difficult assignment for you both."

"We serve at your pleasure, my Lord," Arithem said.

The Commander smiled, but then grew serious. "A formidable enemy will infiltrate the saints you are guarding."

"Formidable?" Zarall dared to ask.

"One of the fallen ones in disguise. An enemy of high rank and great power."

"We will defeat him, my Lord," Arithem spoke boldly.

The Commander studied him. "Beware, Arithem. Too much confidence can lead to folly."

"Yes, Lord." Arithem bowed his head.

"This one is a trickster, and he brings with him a hoard of the vilest creatures. You must be on your guard at all times."

Zarall nodded but remained quiet.

"This will be a battle the likes of which neither of you have seen. You must be strong."

"We will." Arithem lifted his gaze again. "What is the enemy's plan, my Lord?"

"To prevent your wards from reaching the saints hiding in the mountains." The Commander gripped the pommel of His sword. "He will try everything in his power to stop them, even deception, if possible."

"Does he have the power to harm them physically?"

"Nay, only should the weakest of them grant him an opening."

"And what powers do you grant to us, my Lord?" Zarall dared ask.

The Commander smiled, his penetrating eyes boring into Zarall with such love and peace, he nearly fell to his knees again. "You must preserve their lives at all costs, but you cannot battle the fallen one directly unless one of them commands it."

Arithem gripped his sword. "Why not prevent this enemy from joining them? Say the word, my King, and I will do away with him."

The Commander smiled again. "Nay, I send him as a test. He must remain until your wards pass many trials. Only then can I use them to complete their missions."

They both nodded.

"It will be as you say," Arithem said.

The Commander's eyes softened. "'Tis why I have placed you with Tori and Thomas."

"If I may ask, my Lord. What is so important about these two? They seem...they seem..." Zarall suddenly wished he'd not spoken up.

The Commander laughed, a calming laughter that put Zarall at ease. "Disorganized? Confused? Weak, even?" His kind but authoritative eyes shifted between them. "I cannot work through those who are wise and strong in their own might. It is crucial that these two survive to complete their mission, for not only their souls are at stake, but also the souls of dozens more."

*He that findeth his life shall lose it: and he that loseth his
life for my sake shall find it.*
Matthew 10:39

Chapter 13

Tori sank to the dirt floor of a shack they'd found in the
middle of an abandoned orange grove. Every inch of
her body ached in exhaustion from the tips of her toes to the pain
pinching across her shoulders. Leaning her head back on the
wooden walls, she lifted a silent prayer for safety during the
night, because she doubted she could take another step.

And from the looks of the rest of them, she wasn't the only
one.

Sara curled up in a ball beside her, shaking and shivering,
though the night was warm. Brianna sat off to the side, nursing
her baby, while Carla promptly perched beside Thomas, who
lowered to sit across from Tori, yanking back his hoodie. Even
in the evening shadows, she could tell his face was pale, eyes
misty, and the color had drained from his lips. Stubble lined his
jaw, making him look like a bum. He gripped his stomach and
groaned as a tremor coursed through him. From her experience,
today and maybe tomorrow would be the worst, but after that,
he should recover nicely.

Good. She would need his strength to help Sara keep
moving. Her detox would take much longer than his.

Reaching down, she caressed the woman's sweaty
forehead. "It's going to be all right, Sara. Hang in there." Laying
her hand on the woman's shoulder she prayed, "In Jesus' name,
be healed. Remove the poison from this woman's body and fill
her with Your strength, Lord."

Sara moaned out a thank you, and Tori knew that, despite
her prayer, the poor girl would probably suffer the consequences
of her actions. God was a parent, and it would do no good to let

people off the hook for their bad choices. She only prayed God would minimize the pain. As He had done for Tori when she'd finally given up her drugs.

After they'd gotten Sara to walk with assistance, Tori had quickly ushered them out of government housing. It wasn't safe for them there, especially if that drone had gotten a good look at Thomas. Yet, walking nearly eight hours in the heat of the day certainly hadn't helped anyone. Tori kept checking in with the Lord, asking Him which way to go to avoid cameras and drones—an impossible task in these times—so, at His leading, they'd stuck to back streets, alleyways, and abandoned farmland, heading north. They'd stopped once in the shade of a tall building and shared a loaf of bread Tori had taken from Sara's apartment, along with several bottles of water. Then when the sun had begun to set, they happened upon an abandoned orange grove and set across it to find a place to sleep.

What used to be rows and rows of green bushy trees dripping with plump oranges was now nothing but blackened earth with burnt tree trunks and spindly branches lining up like Halloween ghouls waiting for candy. Tori had prayed for more food since the bread was gone and they were all hungry. And the Lord answered by leading them to a single tree in the middle of the field upon which hung five juicy oranges. It wasn't much, but it was the sweetest thing she had tasted in a long while.

Opening her eyes, she glanced around the small shack, wishing she could see the angels guarding them.

Wind blew against a door that was half off its hinges, sending a *screech* through the tiny room that was empty except for a few garden tools and a couple of empty crates. Two grimy windows looked out upon a world shrouded in darkness, evil, and deceit.

Tori closed her eyes. Who was she to lead these people to Nyla and Calan's sanctuary, UnderHisWings? It was at least a four-hundred-mile trek, and without any safe transportation, it would take them two weeks or more to get there. All with a nursing mother and her two children, a drug addict going through withdrawals, and a man she wasn't quite sure she could trust.

She glanced his way. He was staring at her but quickly shifted his gaze away. Yet even in the scattered light of a half-moon, she spotted confusion in his eyes.

"What did you think of your NWU housing?" she asked.

He huffed. "Ah...not what I expected."

"I bet."

"Not what I was told," he added more sternly. "I didn't know, Tori. They told us it was luxury living and people willingly went."

"People *did* go willingly at first. Because of the lies. Then, afterward, when the truth became known, they began to force people."

Rubbing the back of his neck, he released a heavy sigh. "What about the virtual reality goggles? That stuff is expensive, and I'm sure it provides a lot of entertainment."

"Yeah, sure. If you want to live a fake life in a fake world with fake friends and a fake job." Tori couldn't believe how naive the man was. "Not to mention, there's nothing but perversion and evil in that virtual world. People having sex with everyone and anything..."

One side of his lips quirked. "Like I said, entertaining."

"You just don't get it, do you? They give the VR goggles to people to keep them busy, keep them comatose, keep them quiet and subdued so they won't rebel against the tyranny imposed upon them."

Thomas scratched the stubble on his jaw but said nothing.

"And your universal income," Tori added. "Giving people free money and free stuff only demoralizes them, robbing them of their will to live, to work, to thrive, to create something of their own, to live as God intended."

"Tori, I mean no disrespect, but isn't it your God who wants to enslave people to do His will and obey His commands? How is that any different from what the NWU is doing?"

Frustration churned what was left of the orange in her stomach. *How do I make him see, Lord?* "God, the true God, wants to set you free, Thomas. It's your god who wishes to enslave you, get you hooked on drugs and video games that rob you of your will to live. He comes to kill, steal, and destroy, while Jesus comes to give you life, abundant life. Yes, He wants you to follow Him because He knows when you do, you'll find the joy and fulfillment He created you for."

He made no response. Instead, minutes passed before he spoke again. "So, these Jews whom God supposedly saved from the flood, is that in your Bible?"

Excited, Tori plucked her Bible from her backpack, scooted over to sit beside him, flipped the pages to Revelation 12, and read him the passage.

"First of all, where did you get that contraband?" He gestured toward the Bible.

Tori eased her hands over the fine leather. "It was my sister's."

"Secondly, a dragon? Really?" His tone was snarky. "And who is this woman it talks about?"

She forced down her annoyance. "The dragon is the devil. The woman is Israel. Come on, you have to admit it foretells exactly what happened."

He shrugged. "I don't know. Maybe."

The moonlight shifted, and she could no longer see his face, but she sensed his unbelief. Closing the holy book, she drew it to her chest, angry at herself for not being able to help him see the truth. "We should get some sleep." She scooted back to her spot across from him.

"Sleep well, Tori." His voice emerged from the shadows full of more care and love than she expected.

Thomas wanted to believe what Tori believed, but probably not for the reasons she wanted. He longed to get closer to her, to regain that bond they'd had when they were younger, both physical and emotional.

The nameless faces and figures of dozens of women he'd been with over the years paraded in his memory like so much fluff and futility. None of them had moved him, impressed him, excited him like Tori Griffin.

He watched her as she checked on Sara, covered her with her only jacket, and then promptly laid her head down on her backpack and fell fast asleep.

How she could sleep so peacefully when they were being hunted like rats for extermination, he didn't understand. Him? Sleep? Oh, how he longed for one of those sleeping pills in his cabinet.

Brianna finished her nursing and tucked little Callie safely into the makeshift sling over her shoulder, then leaned her head back against the wall with a sigh.

"So, looks like we have been unwittingly assigned night guard duty," Thomas said.

Brianna gave a sad smile as she glanced down at her sleeping girls. "I worry about them so much. It's hard to sleep sometimes."

Thomas couldn't imagine having children, or anyone he loved so much, that fear for their safety kept him up at night. For some reason, the thought made him glance at Tori, sound asleep on the dirt as if it was a down-stuffed mattress.

Brianna followed his gaze. "She's amazing, isn't she?"

He nodded, wanting to say so much more but couldn't find the words. The Tori he'd known as a teen had been flighty, fun, wild, and yet weak in many ways, insecure, incapable of facing hardships, a follower, not a leader. She'd carried around scars on her heart from a dysfunctional childhood and the abuse of a stepfather. How many nights had she cried in his arms as he comforted her?

But *this* Tori, this Tori was strong, confident, hopeful, unafraid, and definitely a leader. He wondered what had happened to change her. Not that he minded. In fact, he found his respect for her growing by the day.

He drew in a deep breath and released it. This was going to be a long night. "So, what's your story, Brianna?"

Sorrow tugged on her expression. "You really want to know?"

"Sure."

"It's not entirely pretty."

He smiled. "What did you do…for a living, I mean."

"I was CEO of Menotec Group."

Thomas flinched. "The Fortune 500 Menotec?" He whistled. "Now, *that* I was not expecting."

"Yeah, I bet." She laughed. "I had everything. Education, money, power, success. I worked hard for years to get where I was."

"Impressive."

Her brows crossed. "Not really. It's all garbage compared to knowing Jesus."

Thomas wanted to retch. "Come on, you can't tell me your God doesn't want you to be successful?"

"*My* God? Isn't He your God, too?"

"I guess Tori didn't tell you. I'm a bit of a skeptic."

"Oh…I see. Well, that's okay." Brianna patted his leg. "We were all unbelievers once."

Thomas stretched out the kink in his shoulders. "Let me put this question to you. If the world could go back to the way it was four years ago, you certainly wouldn't give up everything you achieved for this Jesus."

She smiled and shook her head as if he'd said something ludicrous. "If that's what He wanted, absolutely!"

Thomas blew out a snort. Several minutes passed as a breeze whistled around the shack and entered through the many holes. He supposed he should be thankful he was feeling a little better. Not perfect, but much better than earlier in the day. The bread and oranges helped. Still, he could not believe he was sleeping in a broken-down shack with spiders and cockroaches when just two nights ago he'd slept in his bed, surrounded by every comfort.

His gaze landed on the babe in Brianna's arms, then down to Carla lying with her head on her mother's lap. "So, you had both kids after what Tori calls the Rapture?"

"Yes. I wasn't saved then. Didn't know the world was coming to an end. We thought things would get better after the Neflams came to help."

"And they will. You'll see."

She chuckled again.

"What happened to your husband?"

Silence filled the shack with such sorrow, Thomas could almost feel it. "Never mind. I'm sorry to be so nosey."

"No, it's okay," she finally said. "A meteor struck our home. He was the only one there at the time."

"I'm sorry." Thomas remembered the asteroids and meteors that had pummeled Earth the past three years, along with the volcanic eruptions, and the contamination of both sea and fresh water. Then there had been the painful sores that had lasted for five months. Thomas never wanted to endure that kind of agony again. The Neflams said some of the disasters were due to climate change, others had been perpetrated by the two crazy Jewish men, but most were the acts of a vengeful God—the God of the Christians.

Another reason to not follow Him.

"We miss him," Brianna said, caressing Carla's forehead. "But actually, it's what brought me to the Lord."

Of course. It was always some personal tragedy that made people join cults and believe lies.

"After Menotec went bankrupt and my husband was killed, I had nothing. I had lost everything. I was pregnant and living under a bridge with a two-year-old when Tori found me."

Thomas glanced at the woman in question, a slight snore rumbling from her lips.

"She took me back to her home for orphans and unwed mothers. She took care of us, fed us, clothed us, and showed me in the Bible how everything that had happened was prophesied years ago."

Thomas withheld a laugh.

"I gave my life to Jesus then and there, and I can tell you, Thomas, I have never regretted it."

"And yet here you are on the run with two children, no food, and only the clothes on your back."

"God takes care of us, and if He doesn't, we will end up with Him in Heaven."

Heaven, another ridiculous notion, a fairy tale place where only good people went. Pure nonsense. The illusion gave hope to the weak minded and those fearful of death. Why not side with the Neflams who claimed to have technology that would transform humans into eternal beings? Now, that was something tangible Thomas could grab a hold of.

A loud, shrieking noise clamored in Thomas's mind. What the heck? He attempted to sink back into the oblivion of sleep he'd only recently fallen into, but it grew louder. Had he set his alarm? He couldn't remember. Reaching out his hand, he groped for the offending clock.

But instead of silky soft sheets, his fingers touched dirt. Instead of his digital clock, he struck a rock.

The blaring voice continued. Memories of the past few days barged into his peace like MMA fighters, knocking out all hope and joy.

Thomas opened one eye to see Tori, open Bible in her lap, head bowed in prayer.

The racket continued.

Baby Callie began to squeal.

"Citizens, the latest NWU WHO vaccine is now available. This will protect you from the Apollo Variant rampaging the world, along with a host of other contagions. All citizens must receive this vaccine. For a list of NWU Medical Centers near you, go to the NWU website for your region."

A messenger drone! And it was close. Surely it knew where they were hiding!

And he causeth all, both small and great, rich and poor, free and bond, to receive a mark in their right hand, or in their foreheads: And that no man might buy or sell, save he that had the mark, or the name of the beast, or the number of his name.
Revelation 13:16-17

Chapter 14

Thomas rose slowly and made his way to one of the windows. He couldn't remember when he'd fallen asleep, but it couldn't have been more than a few hours ago. Every inch of him ached, and the thought of having to run from some armed drone made him hurt all the more.

Tori dashed to his side.

"Don't worry, it's just a messenger drone. They don't know we are here."

She said it with such confidence, he allowed a wave of relief to sweep through him.

Brianna joined them at the window, jostling Callie in her arms. "Another vaccine? When will it stop?"

"When they implement the Mark." Tori brushed hair from her face.

"What Mark?" Thomas asked.

Callie began to fuss, and Brianna excused herself to nurse her.

"The Mark of the Beast." A ray of morning sun alighted upon Tori, causing her green eyes to sparkle with a joy he could not understand. Her black wavy hair was a mess as usual, but he'd always loved the wildness of it, like the woman herself. He'd come to believe that religion stole the freedom and fun out of someone's soul with all its rules and regulations, but Tori seemed so full of life and light even in the middle of such darkness and death.

A moment passed as their eyes met, hers searching his…and for a brief second, he saw the old Tori behind her gaze, the way she looked at him with such care and affection. Against his better judgment, he caressed her cheek with the back of his hand. She blinked, confused, but allowed his touch… before she backed away.

"You look better this morning," she said, hugging herself.

"Still have a fierce headache and the shakes, but yeah, a little." What he wouldn't give for a mirror. If he looked anything like he smelled, he wondered why Tori could tolerate his presence.

"Good. I need your help with Sara. That is, if you're staying with us."

He shrugged. "Where would I go? They want to catch me just as much as they want you. Probably more." Saying the words out loud made it more permanent, and a weight fell on him so heavy, he nearly sank to the floor. The life he knew was over. He'd do anything to get it back, to return to his position of power and wealth. But he knew the NWU. Even people they only slightly suspected of being traitors mysteriously disappeared, easily replaced by eager, ambitious, obedient upstarts.

She must have noticed his sorrow. "Listen, you don't believe like we do, and as much as I want you to, I can't force it. It must be hard to hang out with *Deviants*."

She spat the word with hostility, even as her eyes flared in anger.

He couldn't blame her. But he had nowhere to go, no friends he could rely on to hide him and not turn him in. Which was sad, actually. Still, a part of him longed to stay with Tori, no matter how wrong her beliefs.

"Trying to get rid of me?" He smiled, hoping to alleviate the tension between them. "Besides, our bet is still on, right?"

She cocked her head, studying him, suspicion etching across her eyes.

He took a step toward her, longing to take her hand in his, but didn't dare. "I will never betray you, Tori. You can trust me."

Her eyes shifted between his for a moment before she nodded. "Yes, we still have a bet that I intend to win." Then turning, she went to rouse Sara.

"What's the plan, boss?" he shouted after her.

"We get Sara up, find some food, and head north." She knelt before the young woman, who had woken and was already moaning. "And I'm not your boss."

Maybe that was true, but Thomas felt more out of place than he ever had. If he were at work, he'd be ordering others around, interrogating prisoners, making life changing decisions, and hobnobbing with elite rulers.

Brianna dashed up to him, shoving the baby in his arms. "Can you burp her? I need to take Carla out to pee."

Before he could protest, the woman disappeared out the back door.

Okay. How hard could it be? He pressed the baby against his shoulder and patted her back like he'd seen in the movies. A burp far too loud for someone so small emerged from the infant's lips.

Followed by a cascade of vomit that dripped over his shoulder and down his back.

Yup. His past life was definitely over.

When Sara rounded the corner of the building, Tori knew from her expression that she'd been unsuccessful. That and the fact she held no sacks of food. The poor girl stumbled along, perspiration beading on her neck and forehead, her arms dangling about her and her eyes in a daze.

Drones be cursed, she rushed for the girl to help her the rest of the way. Once hidden behind the empty building, she helped Sara sit.

"I'm so sorry." Sara dropped her head in her hands. "I tried."

"It's not your fault." Tori dabbed her forehead with a cloth.

"It was worth a try." Brianna smiled.

Thomas only moaned. "I don't get it. Why couldn't she get food? She's the only one who isn't on the NWU wanted list, and she has a decent Citizen Credit Score."

Sara looked up at him, at all of them, tears streaming down her face. "They told me I needed to get the new vaccine." She took a painful breath. "Without it, they wouldn't even let me in the building."

Brianna and Tori exchanged a knowing glance.

Rising, Tori studied the parking lot, empty now except for a few gas-powered cars abandoned long ago. "I thought we might have a chance to slip in before they fully implemented it." She'd hated sending Sara to the NWU food distribution center, but there'd been no other option.

"They told me I could get one for free just around the corner," Sara said, hope lifting her voice.

"You know we can't, Sara." Tori huffed.

"I'm hungry, Mommy." Carla tugged on her mom's pants.

"I know, honey. We'll eat soon."

Thomas raked back his hair. "Eat soon? Just what are we going to eat?" He began to pace, his frustration rising. "We have no food. Everything hurts. I haven't had a shower or slept in a week, and now, if they don't catch us first, we are going to starve to death and—"

"Stop!" Tori used her sternest tone. "You're scaring the children."

"Well, they should be scared. We all should be scared."

Angry, Tori pulled him out of ear reach of the others. She had no idea whether she could trust him or not, but the Lord had not told her to kick him to the curb. *Yet.* Besides, she still cared for him, still had feelings for him, evidenced by the way warmth had spiraled in her belly at his touch two mornings ago.

But enough was enough. She stabbed his chest with her finger. "You need to man up, Thomas. Man up or leave. I know you're not accustomed to discomfort, but you are the only man here and the only father figure these girls have. So, quit being a wuss and start being the man God created you to be."

Thomas watched Tori stomp away in a rage. He should be mad, furious even, for the way she spoke to him. Him? The Vice Regent of NWF North American Region. Not many had dared address him with such disrespect. But for some reason, he smiled, and a chuckle bubbled up in his throat. Maybe the hunger and pain had finally driven him crazy. Or maybe he actually deserved her beatdown. Deceived or not, she was in an impossible situation, and if he intended to stay, he needed to *man up* as she'd said.

He made his way back to the group, his proverbial tail between his legs, and mouthed an *I'm sorry* to her, which she acknowledged with a smile.

"Here, help me with Sara," she said.

Nodding, he moved toward her and together they hoisted the young girl up. Then leaning the bulk of her weight on him, he followed Tori as she headed out.

He smelled like sweat and vomit and filth, and Sara smelled no better. His stomach cried out in hunger, and his parched lips longed for a drop of whiskey, vodka, gin—he'd even settle for a beer—but he would keep those things to himself and try to assist Tori as best he could.

Who knew, maybe he still had a chance to convince her she was following the wrong God, to get her out of this cult. If so, maybe they could find their way back into the NWU's graces and live happily ever after. He did have contacts high up, people who might still trust him. It was a pipe dream, but it was all he had at the moment.

Several hours later, all of the aforementioned grievances had grown a hundred times worse. But how could he complain when neither Tori nor Brianna uttered a single word of discomfort. Baby Callie and Sara were another story. Brianna had just as hard a time quieting the babe as Thomas had in consoling Sara, who was having more difficulty detoxing than he'd had. Of course, her drugs were harder. Fentanyl, Tori had told him. The poor girl went from sweating profusely to shivering, from complaining of aches and pains to forgetting where she even was. Thomas felt for her. He knew a bit of what she was suffering, so he did his best to offer words of comfort and encouragement.

A few times when he'd been trying to encourage Sara, Tori had glanced at him over her shoulder with a smile. And that tiny gesture made it all worth it.

Either that or he was completely losing what remained of his reason.

They walked through abandoned neighborhoods, burnt fields, rusted playgrounds, deserted farmland and city back streets, avoiding cameras as much as possible and places where people congregated. How Tori knew what streets to take, what fields to cross, Thomas had no idea. She had no maps, no phone, no way to determine the best path. But she kept moving forward as if she'd taken this route a dozen times before.

They became experts at hearing the familiar buzz of an approaching drone and diving into a nearby bush or behind a structure to hide. Even little Carla did so without complaint and even *without* fear. How often did she smile up at him and giggle as if she alone knew a funny joke? How often did she slip her hand into his and grip it tight? He envied her innocence, her inability to assess the danger around her. She'd even made up an imaginary friend named Onafiel, whom she spoke to often. When she wasn't humming some joyful tune.

The sun began to set as they continued down a rather foul-smelling alleyway behind a row of brick warehouses. Halting, Tori whispered for everyone to sit and drink some water—something they'd not done enough during the long day.

Removing the sling from her shoulder, Brianna laid a sleeping Callie on her lap, and stretched her shoulders, exhaustion weighing heavy on her features. Only then did Thomas realize what a strain it must put on her to carry a baby all day, not to mention nursing her.

Tori gulped water from her bottle, then sat beside her exhausted friend. "God will provide. Don't worry. In fact, I smell something." She lifted her nose in the air. "Food. Something good."

Brianna nodded with a weary smile.

Thomas didn't smell anything except his own stink. Releasing Sara, he helped her lower to sit. Then grabbing the bottle of water Tori held out for him, he stooped and held it to her lips. After she had her fill, he finished it off.

Tori rubbed the back of her neck, rose, and began scouting the area ahead of them. Within minutes, she returned and gestured for them to start out again. Every inch of Thomas's body screamed in defiance, but, thankfully, they only walked a few blocks before she entered the back door of a building and motioned for them to follow. That's when he smelled the food— a mixture of spice and something he couldn't place. Rice? Potatoes? Whatever it was, it made his stomach lurch.

"Tori," Thomas whispered from behind her. "I'm not sure this looks safe." Even though his stomach ached for food, any food, nothing was worth dying over.

Little Carla yanked on his jeans and stared up at him. "It's okay, Thomist. The bright ones are with us."

Onafiel smiled at his ward, Carla, and she smiled back. He loved it that the innocent could see into the spirit realm, for he knew that once they became tainted by the world, their vision became clouded.

"Come, Onafiel," Arithem commanded. "Our real battle begins."

Nodding, he followed his leader, along with Zarall, Tagas, and Anahel, the protector of the mother.

Together, all four warriors took a stance around the beast. The demons surrounding him hissed at them, but backed away, for they knew 'twould do no good to battle those whose mighty skills outdid their own.

The beast, however, smirked at them, then returned to his task as if they bore no threat.

"We longed to keep her from him," Zarall said from beside Arithem.

"Aye, but 'tis the Commander's will they meet. You heard Him. And now the time has come."

"Aye, a test she must pass." Zarall heaved a sigh. "I only hope she has the strength." He glanced at the horde of slimy, shifting demons hovering behind their master. Hefting his ax, Zarall feigned a move toward them. They leapt back, and he smiled at their fear before returning his gaze to the beast. "If only we could..."

"We cannot. Not unless permission comes from the daughter of Eve."

"But how will she know? He cloaks himself in light."

Anahel nodded. "'Tis a powerful deception, the likes of which I have not seen on a fallen one."

Zarall frowned, his friend's declaration doing naught to ease his fears. "What can we do, then?"

"We watch." Arithem grabbed the pommel of his light blade. "We keep the hordes at bay. We wait for a command to battle and send this fiend to the abyss. Either from the Commander or your ward, this daughter of Eve." His eyes landed on Tori as she approached the beast.

And no marvel; for Satan himself is transformed into an angel of light.
Therefore it is no great thing if his ministers also be transformed as the ministers of righteousness; whose end shall be according to their works.
2 Corinthians 11:14-15

Chapter 15

F ollowing her nose and the flicker of light in the distance, Tori made her way through the abandoned building that must have once been a medical facility. Doctors' names and credentials decorated open doors that led to waiting and examination rooms beyond. Not much furniture remained, nor computers, instruments, or drugs. Not much of anything remained but the stink that always permeated doctors' offices— a mixture of bleach, filtered air, and sickness. Broken glass littered the floor, along with patient files scattered about like so many bad memories.

Finally, entering one particular office, Tori made her way to the farthest examination room. An older man sat on the floor, cooking over an old camping stove. He spotted her, shoved a knife out before him, and struggled to rise.

"What do you want? Leave me alone!"

Tori held up her hands. "We come in peace, mister. We are here to help."

"Help yourself to my food, more like it." Gray hair crowned his head, while his face was lined with age and gaunt from hunger. His body was, too. His shoulders bent forward, his clothing hung in rags, and he leaned on one foot.

"No." She shook her head and gestured to the man's right foot, which hung shriveled beside the other. "To help with that."

For a moment, confusion crept across his dark eyes. He stared at his injured foot and then back at her.

"And let him who thirsts, come," she said, taking a chance he was a believer. Who else would be hiding from the authorities instead of accepting free housing, food, and drugs from the NWU?

The man smiled. "Whoever desires, let him take the water of life freely."

She knew it! The Lord had led her here to help this man. He was one of them.

Lowering the knife, he began to cry. "I thought you were here to kill me and take my food. But you're an answer to prayer."

Tori gestured for Thomas, Sara, Brianna and her girls to come closer. "It's all right. The Lord wants to heal this man, and then maybe he would be so kind to share some of his food."

"Of course. I'm happy to share what I have with my brothers and sisters." Wiping his face, the man smiled, revealing a few missing teeth. "Come in. Make yourselves comfy." He glanced at the room that contained only a stripped examination table and several empty cupboards. "I'm sorry I can't offer you any chairs."

Brianna and her girls slipped inside, followed by Thomas, holding Sara up as she hobbled along.

"Ah, little ones!" The man's face brightened, and he gestured for Carla to come forward, but she shook her head and clung to her mother instead. Odd. She wasn't usually shy.

Something appeared in the man's eyes…a flash, a flicker of a shadow. It passed so fast, Tori couldn't be sure. No doubt her hunger and exhaustion were playing tricks on her. "Please sit.… Mr.—"

"Aaron. Aaron Rivas." Limping, he struggled to sit back down, then picked up a spoon and stirred a pot on the stove.

Tori made all the introductions, and Aaron seemed overjoyed to meet them all.

Even so, a shiver etched across her shoulders. Hugging herself, she scanned the room from floor to ceiling.

"What is it, Tori?" Brianna asked as she lowered to sit on a piece of cardboard, gathering her children in her lap.

"Not sure." It felt like a strong demonic presence, but whenever she had sensed an evil force in the past, she'd been able to see it...them. "I'm probably just tired."

Approaching Aaron, she knelt. "Can I pray for you?" Not that she normally had the gift of healing, but whenever she saw someone with a debilitating disease or condition, whether they were saved or not, she wanted the Lord to heal them. It's what the apostles did in the Book of Acts, and it was a great witness to the power in the name of Jesus.

"Yes, please." Setting the spoon down, he stretched out his shriveled foot.

"I bet it's been hard for you to get around with this."

He sighed and fingered his scraggly gray beard. "You have no idea." He glanced over the group as tears filled his eyes again. "I'm so happy to have company."

Tori studied his foot. There were no open wounds, but it bent inward slightly, and the skin hung on it as if no muscle remained. "What happened?"

"I was in an old, abandoned building 'bout a year ago. The NWU had targeted it for demolition, but I didn't know." He closed his eyes for a moment as if the memory were painful. "The thing came down on me so fast, I barely made it out. But my foot didn't. Broke my bones, don't know how many. Been like that ever since."

"I'm sorry."

Thomas moaned. "Why not get medical attention?"

Tori cast him a seething glance. "Christians are denied medical treatment. We are enemies of the State."

Before she saw his reaction, she faced Aaron again.

"I prayed and prayed for healing," he said. "But I just assumed the good Lord had other plans."

Tori smiled. "Maybe for you to meet us." Then laying her hand on his foot, she said, "Be healed in Jesus' name."

Thomas snorted. Moments passed. She didn't feel the normal surge of power pass through her hand, but then again, God didn't always work the same way each time.

"Now, Aaron, move your foot," she said.

He met her gaze, his eyes hopeful. Glancing down, he stretched out his leg and slowly moved his foot. It straightened from its bent position, ankle turning, toes pointing forward. The skin turned pink and plump as bone melded together and muscles grew.

Aaron gasped. So did Thomas, who took a step closer to look.

"Praise the Lord!" Brianna exclaimed.

Even Sara uttered a "Glory to God."

Tears streamed down Aaron's face as he gripped Tori's shoulders. "Thank you! Thank you!"

"No, thank Jesus, not me." She stood and held out a hand to assist him.

He rose, tentative at first, but then began hopping and dancing for several minutes, thanking them all—thanking *them* but not God. Strange.

Regardless, Tori shouted her praise to Jesus. Brianna and little Carla joined in, singing a worship song Tori had taught them. Sara lifted one hand toward heaven, but could do no more, Thomas remained standing, arms crossed over his chest, a look of shock on his face.

The atmosphere in the room changed…from one of sorrow to joy, from despair to hope. The darkness Tori had felt earlier retreated beneath the all-powerful presence of God. The Bible said God inhabited the praises of His people. Why didn't she praise Him like this more often? What joy there was in His presence! She could worship Him all night, but they were hungry and tired. Finally, Aaron ceased his dancing and sat back down to stir the soup, and she knelt beside him as he dished out the broth into plastic cups he'd collected.

"It isn't much, just some rice, beef broth, and a few carrots I found in what was left of someone's backyard garden, but everyone will get some," he said.

"Thank you, Aaron. We appreciate it." Then rising, she offered a prayer of thanks for the food and began handing out cups.

Carla giggled as Tori handed her one. "Onafiel was dancing."

"He was?" Tori exchanged a smile with Brianna. "He must have loved our praise."

She nodded, slurping down the broth.

After giving Brianna a cup, Tori filled two for Thomas and Sara and headed over to help her eat. Her fingers were too shaky to hold anything for long, but she needed to regain her strength if they were to make any progress in their journey.

"I'm not hungry." Sara pushed the cup away as Tori handed one to Thomas.

"But you *will* eat," he said. "I know you don't feel like it, but trust me. It helps."

Tori smiled. After yelling at him earlier in the day, she'd watched him closely. The old Thomas wouldn't have taken well to being insulted so harshly by a woman. Maybe the loss of everything dear to him was beginning to change his heart. He'd been nothing but kind and supportive to Sara, even though Tori knew he was suffering himself.

"He's right. Sara. Eat." She tipped the cup up to the girl's lips and made sure she swallowed some.

"How did you…how did you fix that man's foot?" Thomas asked.

Tori offered Sara another sip. "I didn't. That was all Jesus."

He seemed to be pondering her words as he finished off his broth and set down the cup. "But why would your God help an old, worthless man?"

Tori didn't know whether to be sad or angry at the question. "For one thing, no one is worthless to God. For another, the true

God, the one you think is a bully, is actually very loving, caring, and merciful."

He studied her for a moment before he gave her that half-grin of his that either meant he thought she was crazy or he was intrigued. Maybe both.

After everyone had finished their meager meal, Tori turned to Aaron. "Is it safe to stay here tonight?"

Aaron nodded. "I believe so. I've been sleeping here for a couple nights."

"Okay, then." Tori glanced over them all, suddenly feeling the weight of every life present. Not that she wasn't used to it after running a church home for unwed mothers and orphans. But they'd had a safe place, were able to buy food. Things were much more difficult now. Was she up to the task? *Why me, Lord? I'm just an artist, an ex-drug addict, a nobody.*

You are precious to Me. I am with you.

A wave of love swept over her so strong, she closed her eyes and lifted her hands again to heaven. If God was with her, who could come against her? How sweet were His words! She rarely heard them so clearly, but when she did, she wanted to bask in them.

Darkness pricked the edge of her joy, and she flung open her eyes and scanned the room. Nothing. She saw nothing. But something was here. She sensed it. Something strong and evil.

Her gaze snapped to Aaron, and she thought she saw a grin on his lips before he looked down.

"You were saying?" Thomas looked at her with concern.

"Sorry. Everyone try to get some sleep, and we'll head out in the morning."

Aaron coughed.

"You're welcome to come with us, of course," Tori said.

"Oh no." He waved a hand through the air. "I'm old and will no doubt hold you up."

"Nonsense. None of us are in good shape."

"Well, then. I'd love to!" His demeanor instantly changed, almost as if he knew she would bring him along. "Where we going?"

"To a safe haven." That's all she would tell him for now.

He smiled. "Didn't know such a place existed."

"Rest," she told him, watching him as he laid his head down on a stack of papers and closed his eyes.

He'd known the code phrase, and he seemed friendly and genuine, but something wasn't quite right. She couldn't get a strong read on him. And that bothered her most of all.

Kyle followed Regent Landry into his office at the NWF Reformation Headquarters, a much bigger and better office than he'd given Kyle.

But that would soon change. Especially when Jura arrived. A framed picture of a young man no older than sixteen sat proudly on his desk, no doubt the Regent's husband. Kyle had heard he'd married a boy after child attraction had become legal.

"So, we have him on camera." Landry waved his hand over the big screen hanging on the wall. It came to life, and he pressed various options until the video of Thomas appeared. At least they thought it was him. Hard to tell beneath the grime covering his face before he pulled his hood down.

Landry froze the scene and studied the picture for several minutes. "I wouldn't believe it if I didn't see it, but yes, that's Thomas. Never saw him in jeans and a t-shirt or with dirt and stubble on his chin, but I'd know those handsome features anywhere. Blast it!" Frowning, he sank into the chair behind his desk and leaned back. He uttered another more colorful curse. "Where was this taken?"

"Just north of St. Augustine a few days ago. They couldn't have gone much farther from there, sir."

Nodding, Landry picked up a pen and tapped it against his perfectly groomed beard. "What is he up to? That's my question." He finally acknowledged Kyle with a glance. "Do we find him and pick him up? Or will he lead us to a bigger prize? What does your Tall White say?"

Kyle had informed Jura of Thomas's location, and the Neflams spy was no doubt already being put into play. But what he hadn't done, and should have, was inform Regent Landry. He had to be cautious. Landry's pride would take a hit if he knew Kyle had gone around him. Even though the Tall Whites had great power, Landry was still his boss *and* the Regent.

"I believe Jura wishes to place a spy among their ranks to keep an eye on them and inform us of their whereabouts." Kyle smiled. "And to eventually reveal the location of this UnderHisWings hideout. *If* you agree to the plan."

Landry stared at the still picture of Thomas on the screen for several moments before he said, "Brilliant. Tell Jura I agree. Never mind." He tossed the pen to his desk. "I can tell him myself when he arrives." He looked Kyle up and down as if he were a gnat to swat away.

Kyle swallowed. He knew he was a mere sergeant, but he had a special relationship with Jura, and he wasn't about to be replaced.

"*If* he agrees to an audience with you, sir. He doesn't enjoy talking with most humans."

"We'll see about that." He rose, and Kyle stood at attention. "Good work, Cruz. Stay on task. If Thomas leads us to this Deviant hideout, it could mean a huge promotion for you, not to mention several rewards for myself."

"Yes, sir."

Three hours later, Jura arrived...or more like appeared suddenly in the middle of the control room of the Reformation Headquarters, two Tall Whites of lesser rank on either side of him. Though Kyle had seen him materialize at least a dozen times, it never failed to unnerve him.

It terrified most of the technicians, who stood frozen, staring at the alluring man...*being*...whatever he was. That the Neflams could travel inter-dimensionally was well known, but when you witnessed it in action...well, that was another thing.

"My liege, Jura." Kyle approached with a smile. "Regent Landry awaits." He gestured for Jura to follow him.

"I wish to speak to you alone first." Jura's bright blue eyes shimmered.

"Very well." Kyle led him to his office, smiling at the way the technicians in the room, both male and female, couldn't take their eyes off the Tall Whites.

He couldn't blame them. They truly were stunning creatures. One might call them the perfect humanoid—beautiful, muscular, without a single defect. Jura's escorts remained as Kyle led him to his office and shut the door.

His body reacted as it always did in Jura's presence.

The Tall White glanced at the big screen and a scene appeared. It was Tori leading a group of people through a trash-strewn alleyway. Thomas was by her side, helping a young woman walk, while an old man and a middle-aged woman with two children followed close behind.

"There they are!" Kyle exclaimed, skirting around Jura to the other side of his desk.

Jura smiled. "Our spy is in place."

Curious, Kyle stared back at the screen. "Which one?"

"The old man. She healed him. Or she thinks she did. Now he joins them."

"Excellent." Kyle sat back on his desk. "She does not sense him, then?"

"Nay. His power is great. As you will soon see."

Jura gazed at him, and a strange sensation warmed Kyle. Rising, he took a step away. "And they will lead us to the enemy hideout?"

Jura made no response, only smiled before he faced the scene once again. "The human, Thomas, is his main target."

"Because he does not follow our enemy?"

"Yes, but also because he seeks a father, an approving father. His was overbearing, always disappointed in him."

Kyle swallowed down a burst of emotion. He could relate. His eyes moistened and he looked away.

"Our spy will be a father to him," Jura continued. "He will encourage and approve of him, giving him the longings of his heart. Then he will find no need for the love of our enemy. He will find his love in our god, Lucifer."

Kyle nodded, still unable to speak. Wounds he thought long since buried in his heart rose to fester.

Jura looked at him curiously, then placed a hand on his shoulder.

A spiral of desire coursed through him.

"Your father belonged to our enemy and, as such, mistreated you, did he not?"

Kyle nodded, wanting to step away from Jura, but was somehow unable to.

"Our lord will reward you greatly for your service. He will be a father to you." He drew his face closer to Kyle's. "As I am, son."

The approval in Jura's tone, the look of care in his eyes, immediately dried Kyle's tears and sent a wave of peace through him. "Thank you, my liege."

Jura gave Kyle's shoulder a squeeze, then glanced back at the scene.

Kyle almost felt sorry for them. They looked so tired, hungry, and dirty, so discouraged and without hope. And to think that the ragged man following behind Tori was once the Vice Regent of the New World Faith North American Region. "Is there hope for Thomas?" he asked.

"Aye, he has not yet surrendered his life to the enemy. There will be a chance for him to make the right choice soon." Jura glanced around Kyle's office. "I will see Landry now. He must give you an office more suitable to your position and power."

Pride swelled in Kyle's heart, washing away the last traces of his pain. "I'm only a sergeant, your liege."

"Not for long." Jura gave him that alluring smile again. "If you continue with your obedience and good work, a grand future awaits you, my son."

Tears nearly filled Kyle's eyes again at Jura's kindness and approval. Finally, he'd found his place, his purpose, a family that accepted and loved him.

*And for this cause God shall send them strong delusion,
that they should believe a lie:
That they all might be damned who believed not the truth,
but had pleasure in unrighteousness.
2 Thessalonians 2:11-12*

Chapter 16

E ven after three days, Thomas still could not make sense of Aaron's foot being healed. He'd asked the man several times about it...whether he'd just been faking the injury or maybe it hadn't been as bad as he'd thought. At first Aaron had unequivocally stated that he'd not been able to walk on his foot for a year, and that God had healed him, but after a few days, he'd confided in Thomas that maybe his foot had been healing on its own, and Tori's touch had merely encouraged him to use it again. In fact, he still used his cane to get around.

Just as Thomas had thought.

Still, despite the fact that Aaron had drunk the God Kool-Aid like the rest of them, he liked the man. He was funny, witty, had led an interesting life, and he sort of took Thomas under his wing.

On the third day, they crossed what used to be the border of Georgia, though Tori still would not disclose the location of their final destination. Thomas got the feeling she didn't completely trust him. Which hurt a little, though he couldn't blame her. In all honesty, his respect—and *love* for her—grew by the day. He'd known many women in his past, but none with the strength, intelligence, and kindness that Tori Griffin possessed. Who knew that the flighty, live-for-the-moment teenager he'd loved so long ago would become such an incredible woman? Here she was, leading a pack of misfits to God knew where through enemy territory, hunted, hungry, and afraid. And without a complaint or even so much as a grumble.

Most women he'd dated would cry if they broke a fingernail, but Tori's concern was always for everyone else, not herself.

Sara was feeling better, walking on her own at least, though she still got the shakes now and then and had trouble keeping food down.

Not that they had any food to eat. They'd found scraps here and there, in trash dumpsters, on abandoned farms. Not much, but it was always enough to go around. And always, Tori blessed it with a prayer before they ate.

Oddly, Carla ceased holding Thomas's hand, though he didn't know why. And if he admitted it, he missed the feel of her soft little fingers and the sound of her gentle happy humming beside him. One time, he even held out his hand for her, but her gaze shifted to Aaron walking beside him and she shook her head.

Tori glanced at him over her shoulder. "There's a home up ahead where we can wait out the heat."

Thomas wiped the sweat from his forehead and nodded. It had to be well over ninety degrees out here and ninety percent humidity. Worse in the blazing sun. You'd think he'd be used to the filth, heat, and hunger after a week on the run, but in truth, he longed to go back to his mansion on the beach and pretend none of this had happened. Many mornings when he woke up after very little sleep, for a few brief, blissful seconds, he thought he was on his soft mattress about to get up and enjoy a cup of fresh-brewed coffee.

Before the realization struck him that his life was over.

Sara inched up beside him. "I never thanked you for all your help when I was…" She took a deep breath, unable to continue.

"No problem," Thomas said. "Not long before we found you, I was in the same boat, so I get it."

She gestured at Tori just a few yards ahead of them, talking with Brianna. "She's saved my life more than once."

Thomas rubbed sweat from the back of his neck. "Yeah, I'm hearing that a lot." He smiled. "How'd you get hooked?"

Despite her blue hair and the sleeve of ink on her arm, the color had returned to her skin, and her eyes were a bit clearer. She couldn't be older than twenty-two, he'd guess. "Took up with the wrong gang, especially after my parents were raptured."

Thomas withheld a snort. Aaron said nothing from his other side.

"Not that I was a good girl before then." She expelled a deep sigh. "I was a rebellious kid, caused my poor parents a lot of pain." Her eyes glistened with tears. "I was actually glad when they left. Can you believe that? I thought they'd be rehabilitated in one of those reformation centers and then come back all cool, you know?"

Thomas wanted to tell her that was still a possibility, but he kept quiet. "So, this gang you got in, they introduced you to the Fentanyl?"

"Yeah. It was all free from the NWU, along with vaccines and a universal income."

The hum of a drone filled the air, and instantly Tori pointed to the brick wall of the building they walked behind. Crouching, they flattened against it as they had so many times before like good little soldiers. Thomas flipped his hood up over his head. A siren blared in the distance. The electronic buzz grew louder, hovering over them like a vulture seeking a carcass. The *clank, clank* of metallic footsteps drew Thomas's gaze around the corner of the building. There, patrolling the street was a spiderlike machine as big as a cow with eight legs, two huge laser eyes, and two cannons for arms. He snapped his head back. He'd heard of such things—police robots—but he'd never encountered one. The thing could sense a human heartbeat at fifty yards. Why wasn't it finding them? He glanced at Tori who, with head bowed and lips moving, no doubt prayed.

Finally, the whizzing diminished, and the hum and clanks faded, and they rose and started on their way again as if the entire event was as natural as stopping to smell a rose along the roadside. Thomas smiled and shook his head at how fast his life had changed.

"We were living the life. Partying all the time," Sara continued after a few steps. "I finally thought I was free."

Thomas nodded. The NWU had done a lot for the poor, the orphans and widows. If capitalism were still in play, people like Sara would either die or have to sell themselves on the street.

Aaron moved to walk beside Tori up ahead as if bored by the conversation.

Sara hugged herself. "My friends started dying. We didn't know what from. The drugs or the vaccines? It was horrible." She hesitated as, no doubt, memories surfaced. "I ran off, and that's when Tori found me in an abandoned building, high as a kite and about to die."

His gaze found the woman in question, laughing at something Aaron said. "She's incredible."

Sara cocked her head, studying him before a teasing grin raised her lips. "You got a thing for her?"

The question shocked him, or maybe it was embarrassment that caused a sudden flush to rise on his face. "No. She's just a friend."

"Uh, ha. Sure."

Nothing more was said as they left the shelter of the building and crossed into a neighborhood, keeping as much to what remained of trees and bushes as possible, moving through backyards when they could. An eerie silence permeated each house and yard where pools and swing sets and barbecues were left abandoned. If Thomas listened hard enough, he could almost hear the voices of the people who'd once lived in these homes, their laughter, their words of love, their arguments, their lives.

But of course, they were better off now in NWU housing, weren't they?

Tori stopped, appeared to be listening to something...*or someone*... and proceeded to open a back sliding glass door and enter a home.

Once inside, everyone seemed to relax, free from the constant fear of cameras and drones.

Tori made a beeline for the kitchen, opening cupboards and the refrigerator. Sara sank to a chair in the living room. Aaron, cane in hand, hobbled to the couch, while Carla tugged on her mother's shirt.

Letting out a squeal, Tori deposited cans of soup on the counter, along with a bag of noodles and some tomato sauce. "We will feast tonight!"

Thomas looked at her in amazement. "How did you know this house was empty and had food?"

She raised one eyebrow. "The Lord told me."

He didn't care if Genghis Khan had told her. His stomach growled in yearning at the mere sight of something decent to eat.

Brianna approached Aaron on the couch. "Aaron, would you hold Callie for a moment, I need to take Carla to the bathroom." Before he could agree, she deposited the babe in his arms.

The child's ear-bursting wail made them all turn and stare. Poor Aaron seemed genuinely embarrassed, jostling Callie and trying to calm her.

Carla tugged on her mother's arm. "Mama, Callie doesn't like the bad man. Onafiel says not to let him near us."

"I'm so sorry, Aaron." Confused, Brianna quickly retrieved Callie, and after looking around, handed her to Tori. "She's not usually like that with strangers, but I'm sure it's just all the traveling. It's been hard on her, like all of us."

Aaron smiled. "Not to worry." Though Thomas noted how quickly his smile fell after Brianna walked away.

Callie cooed in Tori's arms. Something Thomas could well understand. She caught him looking at her, and confusion flickered in her gaze for a moment before she looked away. Did she know how he felt about her? Even after all these years? In a way, he hoped not, because he couldn't stand it if she rejected him again, like she'd done fifteen years ago. He'd thought he would die back then. Now, with nothing else good in his life, he probably would.

"Look, a TV." Sara grabbed a control from the couch and flipped it on.

A wide shot of the city of Jerusalem appeared before the camera zoomed in closer to a massive crowd of thousands waiting at the International Convention Center.

Tori skirted the kitchen counter and approached the TV. "Something is happening."

Lord Aali took the podium. The mob went crazy, the applause so loud and long that he couldn't speak for several minutes. Everyone loved Aali. Even Thomas. The man was not only handsome, highly intelligent, and very articulate, but most importantly of all, he cared about humanity. Standing behind him to the right was His Excellency Gabriel Wolfe, and to his left one of the Tall Whites. He wondered if Landry was there, but he didn't see him. A sudden longing to be back in the game tugged his mood into the toilet. What the heck was he doing with these Deviants?

Finally, the crowd settled, though several at the front had fainted from the excitement of being so close to the man…or god, as he proclaimed he was.

"Fellow citizens of Earth, I am here to make known to you an astonishing discovery I have withheld until now."

The mob was silent, hanging on his every word as his kind eyes scanned over them.

"I know our planet and its people have suffered greatly in recent years at the hand of our enemy, the God of the Bible."

Boos and hisses filled the center.

Tori lowered to sit, shaking her head. "He certainly isn't hiding who he is anymore." She placed Callie on her lap and bounced her up and down.

"But we will be victorious!" He raised his fist in the air, and the mob went wild again.

Thomas grew impatient. What was this great discovery?

"I'm talking about eternal life!" Aali leaned toward the crowd. "Would you like to live forever?"

Screams and shouts and words of praise answered him.

"I have developed a...well, let's call it a supernatural technology far, far above anything Earth's scientists could ever have developed. It will come with the quantum dot tattoo that bears my name. When you receive this tattoo and the vaccine that comes with it, it changes your DNA, melds Neflams technology with your human cells, and transforms you into an eternal being that will never get sick, age, or cease to exist!"

A stunned silence hovered over the mob as the meaning of his words sank into their souls. Then slowly, people began to shout, "All hail Lord Aali! Praise Lord Aali!"

Eternal life? Thomas could use some of that right now. Every muscle and joint in his body ached. But was it possible? He knew there'd been great strides in transhumanism in recent years, but this? Even so, the over-the-top response of the mob surprised him.

Aali raised his hands. The crowd grew silent. "And once we defeat our enemy and eradicate his followers from the planet, I will restore it to the perfection it once was, a true Garden of Eden, a paradise! Not a place with impossible rules set up by our enemy, but a world where we can all live free and do as we want."

Tori huffed. "The motto of Satan. Do as thou wilt."

"This is the future, the glorious future I offer all mankind," Aali continued. "What do I ask in return? That you inscribe my name, my mark upon you, bow to me, and worship me!"

Music blared. Lord Aali moved from behind the podium as half-naked men and women came onto the stage dancing erotically. He strutted back and forth, smiling, and extending his arms to the crowd. And, again to Thomas's surprise, almost the entire group of people bowed before him.

"Turn it off!" Tori shouted, and when Sara, who seemed mesmerized by the display, didn't move, Tori rose, handed Thomas the baby and snapped the control button.

"Blasphemy!" she shouted, anger flaring in her eyes.

On the contrary, Thomas had noted that Aaron seemed pleased by Aali's speech, though he now pasted on a sudden frown.

"Eternal life?" Sara said, still in awe.

Brianna returned with Carla.

Tori faced the young girl. "It's a lie, Sara. You know that. I've been over those Scriptures with you a thousand times. He will promise anything to be worshiped!" She pointed her finger at the girl. "Anyone who takes that mark of his will burn in hell forever."

Sara's eyes widened, but she nodded.

"So this is the Mark of the Beast you mentioned earlier?" Thomas asked as Carla once again slipped her hand inside his and looked up at him with a smile.

"He's offering them eternal life." Brianna took Callie from Tori. "And they can't buy or sell anything without his mark. To a nonbeliever, it would seem a good deal."

Thomas sighed. "See, this is what I'm talking about. Why would your God send someone to hell just for taking a tattoo that would enable them to survive? That seems cruel to me."

Nodding, Aaron rose and moved to the window, staring outside.

Tori exchanged a knowing glance with Brianna before she faced Thomas. "Jesus came to save humans, those made in His image. When people take Aali's mark, it changes their DNA and makes them nonhuman, and thus, not able to be saved by Jesus's sacrifice on the cross. In addition, when they take the mark, they pledge their allegiance to God's enemy, Satan."

Thomas chuckled. "So, you're saying Aali is the devil?"

"I'm saying he's possessed completely by the devil, yes."

Suppressing another laugh, Thomas studied Tori. She didn't look crazy. Her eyes were clear, her voice strong, her tone serious.

"Thomist." Carla's sweet voice drew his gaze down to her. "Onafiel says to duck."

Confused, Thomas noted Tori's body had gone rigid as she glanced around the room, then fixed her gaze out the window.

"Get down, everyone!" she whispered, sending them all cascading to the carpeted floor.

A flash of bright light brought Thomas's gaze to the window. A huge figure, brighter than the sun stood outside, a massive sword raised in his right hand.

No sooner did Arithem receive the Commander's orders, than he directed the other angels to their posts. He'd seen the enemy coming, but he'd been told to wait, to do naught. Finally, when the evil hellions were nigh upon them, the Commander had given the order to battle.

Onafiel, the only one of them with wings, spread his mighty pinions over the two children.

Anahel stood before their mother, sharp mace in his hand.

Tagas leaned over Sara, who had lain down on the couch, and Zarall, ax in hand, glanced at Arithem. "From whence does the enemy come?"

"From the sky. And quickly!" Arithem sped through the front window and stood outside.

After one glance to make sure Tori was safe, Zarall followed, wanting more information. Before he could ask, the sky turned black as the sound of a thousand wings vibrated the air.

What the humans called drones appeared, but what the sons of Adam could not see were the demons working behind them.

Arithem raised his blade. "To the battle, my friend!"

The hoard of demonic creatures sped toward them. The drones they commanded began firing into the house, their bullets penetrating stucco and brick and shattering windows.

Zarall swung his ax right and left, the blade slicing through the depraved beasts, instantly turning them into dust and sending the drone flying off into space.

Arithem did the same, shouting the Commander's name with each strike! But there were so many. They could not stop all the shots before they entered the home.

Anahel came out to help, swinging his mace before him, along with Tagas, who with spiked war hammer, pounded the enemy to dust. Among the four of them, they were finally able to stop most of the beasts from firing, and those who remained sped off, leaving vile taunts and a putrid stench behind.

Zarall's breath came hard and fast. The muscles of his arm ached as he shoved his ax back into his belt. Laughter drew his eyes to the beast standing at the broken window.

"He mocks us!" He started toward him, but Arithem held him back.

"He did this!"

"Aye, but he has been defeated."

Anahel slid his mace in a holder on his back. "I wasn't sure we would be victorious, my friends! Why did the Commander wait so long before allowing us to engage?"

Arithem glanced at the retreating swarm before answering. "The Commander wanted your ward to sense the evil, discern its origin before it arrived, but Onafiel"—he gave the winged angel a look of censure—"told the child."

Onafiel nodded. "Forgive me. I was concerned for the little ones. It won't happen again, Arithem."

"'Twould do good to remember we serve at the pleasure of our Commander, the King of Kings and Lord of Lords. We must not get too involved emotionally with our wards." Even as Arithem said that, his eyes found Thomas rising to his feet.

Zarall's sentiments exactly. 'Twas far easier said than done. He glanced at Tori. More than anything, he wished for her to succeed, to pass these tests and fulfill her mission from their Lord, for the alternative was unthinkable.

And such as do wickedly against the covenant shall he corrupt by flatteries: but the people that do know their God shall be strong, and do exploits.
Daniel 11:32

Chapter 17

Is everyone all right?" Tori swallowed a lump of terror and dread as she scanned the room. Her eyes took in each person and, upon finding them all uninjured, she allowed herself to breathe.

"What the heck was that?" Sara asked, terror streaking across her dark eyes.

"A drone attack," Thomas mumbled, but his focus remained on the shattered front window.

Callie began to scream, and Brianna drew her close. "Shh, sweetheart. It's okay. It's okay now."

Carla gripped Thomas's hand. "They protected us," she said with more confidence than any three-year-old should have after being shot at.

Only then did Tori notice the bullet holes littering the room, nicking tables, walls, doors and punching holes in pillows and chairs.

"How did they find us? And more importantly, why did they leave?" Moving to the window, she glanced up. Nothing but the usual gray haze that had replaced the blue sky in recent years.

Aaron stood off to the side, arms crossed over his chest, smiling. "They probably saw the surge of power when we turned on the TV. They monitor such things, you know. That's why they keep the electricity on."

Hmm. Of course. He might be right.

"Okay, we need to get out of here ASAP." Tori headed for the kitchen. "Go to the bathroom if you have to. I'll grab the food and bottles of water."

And once again, before they'd even had time to rest, they were on the run. Pulling a map out of her backpack, she plotted the best route. They would skirt the coast for a few miles, then head inland toward Atlanta, through Athens, and then up to what used to be the Chattahoochee National Forest, where Nyla said they'd meet her. If they kept a good pace and avoided authorities, they could make it in under two weeks. She glanced over her shoulder at Aaron as he hobbled along, then over to Sara who hugged herself, shaking, and finally to Brianna, baby strapped around her chest.

Maybe she was being too optimistic.

Lord, I don't know what I'm doing. How can I possibly keep all these people safe? She pursed her lips. Why hadn't she sensed the drone attack? She should have known it was coming and taken every precaution. They could have all been killed. What was wrong with her? Shoving back her wayward hair, she shook her head. Something was off, something was wrong. An evil presence? Maybe that's why her Godly discernment was off. No, she was being silly. Of course there was an evil presence. They were in the Tribulation.

Laughter drew her gaze to Aaron putting his hand on Thomas's shoulder. Good. Thomas needed a strong male, a father figure, and it was good that Aaron was a Godly man.

Thomas beamed at Aaron's surprise when he'd given the man his full name.

"I knew I'd seen you somewhere before," Aaron said. "So, you and that Daniel fellow were the top dogs at that huge church?"

Thomas nodded, pulling his hood up farther on his head as they crossed a street and started down a dirt path beside an old canal. "That was us. Pastored that church for several years. We had up to thirty-thousand members."

"Wow." Aaron whistled. The wrinkles at the edges of his eyes crinkled as he squinted at the sun. "Such a great accomplishment."

"Yeah, we thought so at the time."

"What happened?"

"The Neflams arrived. They took a good portion of our church for reformation." Thomas frowned. "Whoops. Sorry. I know you don't believe that, but I'm not fully convinced of this Rapture thing."

"No problem, son. We all have our beliefs. Not worth fighting over."

Thomas looked at his new friend curiously. How refreshing to find a Deviant who didn't try to force the God of the Bible down his throat. "Glad to hear it. Anyway, Daniel took the disappearance badly. His girlfriend and son were taken, and he sort of flipped out after that. The church dissolved, and I followed other pursuits."

Aaron stumbled over a rock, and Thomas reached out to steady him. "Regardless, quite some success you had. Your parents must have been so proud. Graduated from seminary, running such a huge church. That's no small feat."

A surge of pride swelled within him, along with a yearning to hear more. "My mother left my father when I was young, and my father was never proud of me. He was a deacon with a great deal of influence in the Lutheran church, and he was disappointed that I started a non-denominational church."

"Bah! Ridiculous." Aaron stomped his cane in the dirt.

"Yeah, he was pretty strict when I was growing up. I never measured up."

Halting, Aaron grabbed Thomas's arm. "Any father would be proud to have a son like you. Not only were you enormously successful in your field, but you went on to become a powerful man in the NWU."

Emotion clogged Thomas's throat as he attempted to shove back the moisture from his eyes. No one had ever said such things to him. No one had ever been proud of him. He'd spent his life trying to achieve some measure of success that proved he was worthy, that he had value. He lowered his gaze. "Thank you. That means a lot."

Aaron squeezed his arm. "I meant it. Didn't have kids of my own, but if I had a son, I'd want him to be like you."

"Even though I sent many Deviants to their death?" Thomas asked, unsure if the man knew what he had done.

"Ah." Aaron waved his cane through the air. "The past is the past, son."

Son. He called him son again.

And despite the heat, the sweat, the hunger gnawing at his belly, Thomas smiled.

They walked the rest of the day without incident, thank God. This time, Tori kept her spiritual sense alert for any trouble as she led them through suburbs and the outskirts of cities and towns, avoiding crowds as much as possible. And there *were* crowds, which was unusual. Groups of ten or more people were prohibited, except at NWU Distribution Centers, but in the late afternoon, they came across a frenzied mob outside one of the medical facilities.

A voice bellowed over a loudspeaker. "Form an orderly line, one by one, and we promise to get to each of you by the end of the day."

Halting behind the wall of a hardware store, Tori peered around the corner. The *rev* of engines and screech of tires filled the air as NWU trucks stopped in the street and soldiers in black uniforms poured out of them, guns strapped across their shoulders. They began shouting and forcing the crowd to quiet down and line up as instructed. One shabby man, out of his wits with either fear or drugs, rushed one of the armed men and was promptly rewarded with the butt end of an M16 across his skull. He fell to the ground, and the soldier ordered two others to cart him out of the way. They dumped him on the sidewalk in front of a nail salon like so much garbage.

Tori swerved back around and leaned her head against the wall. Maybe that man was the lucky one, because as soon as he took that tattoo, he would be damned forever.

Brianna dared a glance, then snapped her head back. "Whoa. There's NWU troops everywhere."

Sara sank to the ground while Thomas and Aaron took a peek.

"Look at all those people lining up for eternal life," Thomas said.

"Eternal death is more like it," Tori spat out, wondering when he was going to see the truth. And until he did, could she trust him at all?

Removing a bottle of water from her pack, she passed it around. "We can't go this way." She ran a sleeve over the sweat on her brow. "Let's head back toward the coast and find somewhere to sleep."

"Then we can eat?" Thomas asked.

"I'm hungry, Mama." Carla whined.

Sara gulped down water, then pressed a hand over her belly.

Aaron merely shrugged. "Yeah. The coast is a good idea. Probably safer there."

The buzzing sounded before Tori could react. Two drones appeared out of nowhere. Stopping above where they sat, they hovered for a few minutes, then dove straight for them. Tori's heart stopped. Would they shoot and kill them right here? No. These drones were not armed that she could see. Still, they remained for what seemed like an eternity as they zipped back and forth, stopping within inches of each one of them. Red laser eyes scanned Tori from head to toe, piercing into her very soul. She felt the evil behind these mechanical beasts—dark, malevolent, depraved.

Callie began to scream. The rest of them remained frozen in fear. Tori started to inch her hand into the pack to get her zapper. But before she could bring it out, the drones flew off toward the NWU soldiers.

"We have to get out of here!" Thomas said.

"It won't matter." Tori closed her eyes. They were done for. The drones would alert the NWU forces, and they'd be on them in seconds.

"Lord, cover us with your wings. Protect us, we pray," she said.

"Come on," Thomas urged, helping Sara to her feet.

Brianna stood by Tori, her lips moving in a silent prayer.

A minute passed, then another, and Tori dared a peek around the corner. The drones were gone, and the troops were occupied with maintaining order. Strange. Not that she didn't believe God could answer prayer and keep them safe, but such miracles were not guaranteed in the Tribulation. And why allow a fleet of drones to pummel them with bullets earlier but prevent these from reporting their location?

Either way, they were safe for now, and she uttered a "Thank you, Lord! Praise God."

"Amen." Brianna nodded.

Later that night, Tori grabbed a flashlight and a Bible and opened it to read a few Scriptures out loud before they went to sleep. They'd found an old beach house several yards from shore, gutted of all its contents, with no power or water, but it provided a roof over their heads and shelter from the rain which had started after the sun had set. A breeze whisked through the open window, bringing the slight scent of the sea, along with the sweet spice of rain, which always settled her nerves. Thomas had managed to open the cans of food with Aaron's pocketknife, and even though it was cold, the baked beans, corn, and chicken soup tasted like a gourmet meal.

She sat cross-legged on the floor and opened the Holy Scriptures to Revelation 13 and began reading about the Antichrist and False prophet.

No sooner had she started than Aaron excused himself to use the bathroom. But at least Thomas and Sara listened.

"And it was given unto him to make war with the saints, and to overcome them: and power was given him over all kindreds, and tongues, and nations.

And all that dwell upon the earth shall worship him, whose names are not written in the book of life of the Lamb slain from the foundation of the world.

If any man have an ear, let him hear.

He that leadeth into captivity shall go into captivity: he that killeth with the sword must be killed with the sword. Here is the patience and the faith of the saints."

Shivering, Sara rubbed her temples. "I know what the Scriptures say, but, man, having a healthy body that lives forever sounds really good about now."

Leaning over, Tori grabbed her hand and gave it a squeeze. "I know, sweetheart. You'll feel better soon. I promise."

"So, what can we expect next, Tori?" Brianna asked, stroking Carla's forehead as she slept with her head on her lap.

"Well, five of the seals have already been broken and five of the trumpets were blown during the first half of the Tribulation. I believe seal six and seven will happen toward the end."

"What are these seals and trumpets?" Thomas asked.

"You don't know, pastor?" Tori teased.

Thomas gave a sideways smile. "Guess I missed that class in seminary."

"You've already experienced the first five seals. One was the Antichrist arriving. That's Immu Aali. Two was World War III, three was intense famine, four was death from war, famine, and pestilence, and five was persecution and death of all Christians."

Thomas frowned. "You're telling me all of those things were predicted in the Bible?"

"Yes. I can read it for you, if you like."

He held up a hand. "No, that's okay. And the trumpets?"

"One was the meteors that destroyed a third of the trees and all the grass. Two was the asteroid that hit the sea and poisoned a third of it. The third was the meteor that struck the fresh water and poisoned a third of it. The fourth was the volcano eruptions that caused a third of the light from the sun, moon and stars to dissipate, and the fifth I'm sure you remember," She arched a brow. "That one caused the sores from the mechanical locusts that tormented all non-believers for five months."

From the shiver that coursed through him, she assumed he remembered that quite well.

"And this is all from your God." Thomas's tone was sharp. "The one you say is so good and loving."

"He wishes none to perish but all to come to repentance. He tried for over two-thousand years to get mankind to turn to Him and receive His free gift of salvation. Now, as any good parent, He is using punishment as a way to get people's attention."

Brianna gazed affectionately down at Carla. "You've obviously never had kids, Thomas. Sometimes you have to punish them to get their attention. You can't give them everything they want, or they get spoiled and complacent. God has been more than patient and generous with all of mankind."

"He's been more than patient with me," Sara added, warming Tori's heart.

Thomas snorted. "Tough love. I get it. I can't wait for the sixth trumpet."

"That would be a million-man army that will kill one-third of mankind," Tori said. "I expect that to happen toward the end as well. Not sure about the timing. It might be the Battle of Armageddon."

Brianna nodded. "And don't forget, we do still have the angels flying through the air shouting the Gospel."

"Yes." Tori smiled. "How cool is that? I'd love to hear one." She closed her Bible. "Then we have the seven bowls. But those happen at the very end. Believe me, you don't want to be here for those. It's all in here." She picked up the Bible. "I could read it to you."

Thomas attempted to pat down his unruly hair. "Naw…I sort of remember it now from seminary."

Brianna smiled at him. "I'd forgotten you used to be a pastor."

"He was a very famous, successful pastor," Aaron said as he returned, set down his cane, and lowered to sit by the window.

Tori knew God had healed him, but the man still insisted on using his cane. Odd.

Thomas scrunched his face. "Lot of good it did me."

Tori wanted to agree but kept silent. "Well, we better get some sleep." She glanced around for the softest looking spot, but without blankets or pillows, what difference did it make?

Thomas seemed to be of the same mind as he looked around and groaned. "There's nothing but hardwood floor and sand...lots of it," he complained.

"That's all we got," Tori quipped back. "You can always go outside and sleep in the dirt."

He groaned again.

"Maybe you can take Carla, sleep beside her to keep her warm?" Brianna asked Thomas. "It's all I can do to watch over Callie."

"Ah, no thanks." Thomas held up a hand. "I mean, sorry, but I'm not good with kids."

Despite his rejection, Brianna smiled. "I disagree. Carla has quite taken to you. But that's okay."

Hugging herself, Sara lay down in the corner. Aaron leaned his head back against the wall, and Brianna curled up beside her already sleeping children.

Tori's gaze met Thomas's. Even in the dim light, she could see him patting the spot beside him.

Against her better judgment, she crawled over and sat next to him.

He swung an arm over her shoulder and drew her near. She probably shouldn't be snuggling up to a nonbeliever, but his warmth and strength felt so good.

"I wanted to ask you something," he whispered, trying not to disturb the others.

"Sure." Tori closed her eyes.

"I saw something back at that house right before the drone strike."

Pushing herself to sit, she tried to read his expression in the darkness, but could hardly make it out. "What?"

"I don't know. Something…someone…big, bright, with a sword."

Smiling, Tori leaned back onto his shoulder. "An angel. That's a good sign."

"But there's no such things. And why is it good? It probably means I'm finally going nuts."

She chuckled. "It means there's hope for you yet."

Silence permeated the shack as she drifted off to sleep, but not before she felt him kiss her forehead.

Kyle knocked on Regent Landry's door and entered at his command. He'd been summoned to give a report on the whereabouts of Thomas and Tori, and he was happy to have some news.

"Come in, sergeant." The man rose from behind his desk and fingered his gray beard. "Tell me, where are the fugitives now?"

"May I?" Kyle gestured to the blank screen on the wall, and at Landry's nod, he placed the magnetic chip onto it. Instantly the scenes recorded by the drones appeared.

Thomas, Tori, the older woman and her children, the young girl and Jura's plant appeared, hiding behind a building, staring up at the drone in fear as it took the video. All except Aaron who looked bored.

"And you ordered the drones to stand down."

"Yes, sir. They did not report the fugitives to the NWU troops who were only yards away."

"Good."

"Where was this taken?"

"Just outside Savannah, sir."

"They are making their way north, then... but to where?" He twisted his lips, eyes narrowing. "Where is that Deviant hideout?"

"I suppose we'll know soon enough, sir."

"So this"—Landry pointed at Aaron—"is the Tall White's spy?"

"Yes. Which is why we no longer need to monitor drones or cameras for facial recognition. He reports to Jura frequently."

"Tell me, sergeant, what does Jura's plant say about Thomas? Is he one of them, or is he merely playing them for fools in order to find their location?"

"Aaron has not determined that yet, sir, though he does say that Thomas does not believe as they do, and he makes that quite clear."

Landry nodded, smiling. "Good. I still have hope for him. Excellent work, sergeant. Finding and dismantling this Deviant hideout, which is the only one left in the North American Region, is Lord Aali's top priority."

Kyle gulped. "Lord Aali?"

"You heard correctly." Landry sat on the edge of his desk and gave Kyle a pointed stare. "He is intent on finding all Deviants and bringing them to justice. Only then can the Earth heal and his plans for a Utopian paradise succeed. That is why"—he pointed at Kyle—"your work with this Tall White is vital, and you can bet on a huge promotion and raise when you are successful. For us both."

Kyle couldn't help but smile. "Thank you, sir. I won't let you down."

"Then be about it." He waved him off, and Kyle left, feeling like he floated on air. If his parents could see him now... his sister...he was no longer the black sheep of the family, no longer the screw-up. He was going to have more power and money than they ever dreamed of.

*When the enemy shall come in like a flood, the Spirit of the
Lord shall lift up a standard against him.*
Isaiah 59:19

Chapter 18

A wall of water rose out of the sea, higher and higher,
its white, foaming crest curling like a fishhook seeking
prey. Demons, dark and slithering, danced on top,
laughing...mocking... spitting.

Wake up! Wake up!

Tori jerked awake and sat with a start.

Thomas rubbed his eyes and stared at her. "What's wrong?"

Oh my, she'd slept in his arms! But that didn't matter now.
What mattered was the sense of doom, the heavy darkness
descending upon them.

And fast...

Her gaze took in the others. Everyone was still asleep,
except Aaron who stood at the open window staring toward the
sea. A shadow hung over him like a cloak. She blinked and when
she looked again, it was gone.

Lord? She asked the source of truth. *Is it coming for us?*

Yes. Leave now, my daughter.

Tori jumped to her feet. "Everyone, wake up! We have to
leave! Fast!"

To his credit, Thomas didn't question her. He just stood and
helped Brianna with the children, then rushed over to Sara, who
seemed confused. Callie began to scream.

Carla rushed to Sara's side. "Onafiel says we have to run.
Come on, Sara. Onafiel says to get up."

Tori smiled. Whoever this imaginary friend was, he seemed
to know what he was doing. With Thomas pulling on one arm
and Carla on the other, they finally got Sara to stand and grab
her things.

Swinging her backpack over her shoulder, Tori gestured for them all to hurry.

Aaron remained at the window.

"Aaron, come on!" she shouted, but he wouldn't move.

Darting to the window, she grabbed his arm, but not before she glanced outside. The beach had grown. No, not grown. The tide had gone out, exposing yards and yards of wet sand full of seaweed, shells, and a few flopping fish. No normal tide did that.

"Come on!" She took Aaron's cane and handed it to him. "We don't have much time."

Nodding, he finally hobbled after her.

Out the door they dashed, down the sandy pathway to the street—well, as fast as any of them could dash. A hazy glow from the morning sun settled over them as they waded through puddles and slogged through mud left by last night's rain, past homes, electric car stations, and restaurants long since abandoned. Homeless littered the street. Drug addicts wandered about in a daze. A chill etched up her legs from her soaked shoes and jeans, even as they weighed down her every step.

Shadows encompassed them. Where were the rays from the rising sun? Something was blocking them.

Faster! Tori sensed the Spirit say. *Higher!*

"What's goin' on?" Thomas huffed beside her.

"Tsunami," was all she had time to say before they approached a high-rise apartment building, at least twelve stories tall.

A sound filled the air, an eerie sound, a powerful sound—the sound of rushing water, combined with thumping and crashing, and muffled screams.

Halting, she glanced over her shoulder. And wished she hadn't. A foamy wall of debris-laden water at least ten feet high reached for them around buildings and trees like the hungry claws of an ancient dragon.

"Take Sara and get to the top floor!" Tori ordered Thomas, and after casting a look behind him, he complied without saying a word.

"Brianna, take the girls."—Tori all but pushed them through the door—"and follow Thomas as fast as you can."

Halting, Aaron stared up at the tall building. "I'm not so good on stairs. You go ahead."

"If you stay here, you'll die!" Was he so deaf, he couldn't hear the water? Yet still he remained in place, a strange…*almost sinister*…look on his face.

"Come on!" Taking his arm, she swung it over her shoulder, bearing the bulk of his weight, and charged into the building and up the stairs.

The man was dead weight, dragging his feet up each tread, hanging onto her like he had no strength at all.

They weren't going to make it.

Heart thumping so loud, she could hear it over the roar of the water, Tori did all she could do. She prayed. "Lord Almighty. I need Your strength. And Your speed, now more than ever."

"There! Finally, she prays!" Zarall shouted, thrilled that his ward called out to the Father for the help she needed. "Can I save her?" He glanced up at Arithem, who had ensured Thomas was out of danger and was now descending the stairs.

The mighty warrior nodded. "Aye, 'tis the Commander's will this time. You aid them, and I shall delay the sea."

Zarall shoved his ax back into this belt and spread his arms over Tori's back, lifting her off the ground and taking the weight of her body onto himself. Rushing up the many flights of stairs, he ignored the beast beside her who turned slit-like eyes toward him and hissed out a series of foul curses and blasphemies.

"Be muzzled, you viper of hell!" Zarall commanded and the creature instantly silenced.

Zarall deposited the daughter of Eve on the twelfth floor, where Onafiel, Anahel, and Tagas remained on guard. Nodding, he went to help Arithem.

The mighty commander angel stood before the wall of the sea, arms spread wide across the advancing water, face pinched, muscles bulging from the strain. Upon seeing Zarall, he released the flood and flew into the air to join him.

The sea struck the building with such force, it shook and began to crumble at the base. Zarall and Arithem plunged into the water and wrapped their arms around the structure, using their bodies as shields against the force of the sea.

Zarall was surprised at the enormous power punching his back. But no sooner had it started, than the pounding dissipated, the sea moved on, and finally quieted into a swish and gurgle.

Turning, he and Arithem gripped each other's forearm in victory.

"Well done, my friend," Arithem said.

Zarall wiped water from his face and glanced upward. "She noticed. She sensed the evil."

"Aye. She is learning. This is good."

Zarall drew a deep breath and frowned. "But she still does not sense the beast."

"Never fear, my friend." Arithem squeezed water from his tunic and nodded for them to join the others. "She will."

Zarall followed him upward, hoping beyond hope he was right.

After making sure Aaron was settled, Tori raced for the window where everyone else was standing. She had no idea how she'd made it up the stairs so fast. One minute she was on the first flight, knowing she probably wouldn't make it, and the next, she was in an apartment on the twelfth floor.

A massive flood of water, filled with broken pieces of furniture, mud, and all manner of plastic and sharp utensils raced toward them. They were out of its reach, but Tori had no idea if the building would hold.

"Oh my God," Thomas said, clinging to the window ledge. "What is that?"

Brianna clung to Callie. Tori picked up Carla and held her close.

Sara began to weep.

The water struck them with the force of a racing semi-truck.

"Hang on!" Thomas shouted, reaching out to draw Tori close.

The building shook. Steel and iron screamed in defiance. Stone cracked and crushed. The floor beneath them shifted.

Closing her eyes, Tori lifted another prayer.

The thunderous roar of the water softened. The building stopped quaking. Thomas's grip around her shoulder loosened.

She glanced out the window. The sea bubbled and churned beneath them, reaching past the second floor, but the tsunami had passed.

Brianna blew out a sigh. "Praise the Lord!"

"Amen!" Tori added.

Carla giggled and pointed at something in the vacant apartment, but when Tori looked, nothing was there. "What's so funny, sweetheart?"

"They are celebrating and dancing." She smiled.

Thomas continued to stare out the window. Poor guy. Without the Lord and the comfort of His presence, how could anyone endure these times?

Pain radiated up her right arm, and lowering Carla to the floor, Tori noticed red blisters had formed along the underside of her arm. Strange.

She glanced at Aaron, sitting in a chair where she'd left him, completely unfazed, it would seem, by the tsunami. He smiled her way.

She smiled back, but her attention returned to her arm. Odd. Wasn't that exactly where she'd touched the old man as she helped him up the stairs?

Thomas had never been happier to finally sit down and remove his shoes. After the waters subsided, leaving behind piles of scattered debris, they'd emerged from the high-rise unscathed in body, but unnerved in spirit. Anxious to get away from the sea, Tori led them inland toward Atlanta, keeping to small towns, and even then, to alleyways, parking lots, and fields.

No one seemed in a talkative mood after their near-death experience. None but Aaron, who moved from person to person, spending time getting to know everyone and making them laugh at some silly joke he told. What a kind man. Thomas had even heard him apologizing to Tori for not being fast enough as they'd raced up the stairs that morning. Like he could help it. He'd also befriended Sara, offering her words of comfort and encouragement, telling her she was brave and strong and would make it. But whenever he approached Brianna, Callie would cry, and Carla would shrink away from him. Brianna profusely apologized, and Aaron said he understood that many children were frightened by the way the elderly looked. What an understanding man. Much more than Thomas would be. In fact, Aaron was like a gentle father figure to them all, especially to Thomas, whom he spent the most time with. Thomas had never met anyone like him. He rarely talked about himself, like most people did. Rather he wanted to know more about Thomas, his dreams, ideas, accomplishments. And he never failed to show his approval of the things Thomas told him.

Thomas hadn't realized up to this point how much he needed an older and wiser man's approval. But Aaron was a Deviant and that troubled Thomas…troubled him and also made him begin to wonder if there wasn't something to this God of theirs. Especially after what he'd seen earlier.

"So, what's for dinner?" He smiled playfully at Tori as she settled Sara on the floor of an old closed-down diner, one of those fifties remake places, complete with jukeboxes and soda fountains. None of which worked anymore.

They'd found an empty room in the back next to the kitchen that must have been used as an office but had been stripped of all its furniture.

She smiled, placing her hand on her hip. "I don't know. How about a burger, fries, and a milkshake?"

"I could go for that." Brianna laughed as she grabbed a few pieces of used carpet and formed a bed for Callie and Carla.

"I second that," Sara added in a weak voice, while Aaron nodded his enthusiasm.

"Well, let me go see what I can scrounge up."

"Wait." Thomas put his shoes back on, wincing at the blisters. "Let me help." He might not be a real part of the group, a Deviant, but he should at least act like a man, a leader, and help her out.

"But you just took off your..." Before she could finish her sentence, he was by her side. Her smile was worth the ache in his legs and pinch in his shoes.

They searched the kitchen, in cupboards, pantries, even the stove for a scrap of anything. The massive walk-in freezer was as dead and hot as a tomb.

"Now what?" he asked, staring at her in the fading shadows. She was truly beautiful, even with her messy hair and dirt streaked across her cheek. Even with her torn, stained shirt and muddy jeans—jeans that molded perfectly to a figure that had filled out nicely since he'd been familiar with it years ago. *Very* familiar. A spray of black lashes surrounded eyes the color of a lush forest, eyes looking at him now with a mixture of confusion and...care?

"We pray. God will provide." She said the words so matter-of-factly that he almost believed them himself.

But four hours later when darkness invaded and most everyone had fallen asleep, Thomas's stomach shouted in revolt and his minuscule faith dwindled.

Tori still wandered about, checking on everyone and looking outside to make sure no NWU troops were about.

"May the Lord shelter us beneath His wings this night," she whispered as she sank to the carpeted floor beside Thomas.

He'd been hoping she'd join him again, so he ignored the foolish prayer. "Come for more cuddling?" he teased.

"I wasn't..." Rising, she started to leave, but Thomas grabbed her hand before she could. "Sorry. Didn't mean to embarrass you. I enjoy it when you're near."

Releasing a deep sigh, she sank back down. "Sorry. I'm just edgy, I guess. And I don't want people getting the wrong idea."

"What idea would that be?"

"That we are...an item...intimate."

He wanted to ask her why that would be a bad thing, but instead simply said, "God forbid."

She sat up, staring at him, though he couldn't quite make out her features. "Yes, He does. You're a nonbeliever, and worse than that, your job is to kill people like me." She swatted hair from her face. "Even worse, you already broke my heart once. I'm not letting you do it again."

"Whoa. That's a ton of *worse* things." He smiled.

She leaned back against the wall with a huff. "You're impossible."

"I'll attest to that. And to the nonbeliever thing. But my job isn't to kill anyone anymore, and it was *you* who broke *my* heart."

She half-laughed, half-snorted. "I wanted you to come to San Fran with me, but you went off to seminary instead."

"If you had stayed in Florida, I could have seen you most weekends."

"Whatever. It doesn't matter now."

If that was true, why did she keep bringing it up? More importantly, he longed to know more about their time apart. Fifteen years can change a person, and it certainly had in her case. "What happened to you over there? In San Fran and then LA?"

Several minutes passed. A siren screamed in the distance, accompanied by Brianna's deep breathing.

"Hollywood is a dangerous place," she finally said. "People don't realize how evil things are there. If you want to be anyone, if you want to be famous and successful, you have to sell your soul to the devil." She hesitated. "And I mean literally...Satan himself. Who I guess is your *god*," she spat out with disdain.

"If you mean Lucifer, no. I don't worship him. He's the NWU god. I serve no one."

"Everyone serves someone," she said with finality. "Anyway, I got caught up in it. The parties, drugs, the wickedness. I saw things no one should ever see...the depravity..." She gulped. "The poor children."

Thomas had no idea what she meant by *the poor children,* and he wasn't sure he wanted to know.

She hugged herself. "Thank God the Rapture happened, and my sister and family disappeared, or I wouldn't have come home. I might have stayed and gotten in too deep...gone too far to ever come out."

Thomas longed to put an arm around her and draw her close, but he didn't want to stop her from sharing. "Weird that your sister was so strong a Deviant."

Crossing her legs, she sat forward and shoved a hand through her tangled hair. "You would call her a very dangerous Deviant." She laughed. "But yes. She loved Jesus with all her heart, tried to convert me over and over. Stupid me. I wouldn't listen. I loved her so much, but I thought all the chaos of our childhood must have caused her to cling to the myth of a God who loved her." She glanced at Thomas. "I turned to evil, and she turned to good."

"Her husband and kid were taken too." Only then did Thomas begin to understand how hard it must have been when the Neflams came and took people to reformation camps, split up families, and tore away loved ones.

"Yes. My niece."

"I'm sorry."

She blew out a sigh. "I'm not. It was the only thing that made me open my eyes. She left a ton of information for me: CDs, videos, books, Bibles, letters, and emergency supplies."

Thomas rubbed the stubble on his chin. "Wow."

"Yeah. I spent two months absorbing all the information. I didn't sleep, hardly ate, and went through a miserable detox." A shiver ran through her.

Thomas rubbed her back, not knowing what else to do.

"But at the end of it all, I got on my knees, submitted myself to Jesus, and determined in my heart to do everything I could for as long as I remained alive to serve Him, to bring as many people to Him as possible and try to make up for all evil I had done."

"I'm sure you weren't *that* bad."

"I was." She leaned back against the wall and blew out a long breath. "No more."

Thomas frowned. "You see, that's what is wrong with your God. He demands obedience. He demands that you follow rules. If you screw up, He sends you to hell."

She shook her head. "You're so wrong about that, Thomas. That's exactly what your god wants people to believe, yet the opposite is true. Yes, God wants us to live righteously and avoid sin, but only because that's how He created the world. Sin causes pain and suffering. Doing good causes happiness and blessings. He is a Father and wants the best for us. Besides, if Jesus had not died on the cross and paid the price for everyone's sin, all of us would end up in hell. But once we follow Him and trust Him for our salvation, He forgives every bad thing we do, and if we continue in Him, we go to live with Him forever."

She sat up again and looked at him, though he couldn't see her face. "Once you know Jesus, you love Him, and once you love Him, you want to serve Him."

The woman was passionate about this God of hers, that much was obvious. She'd been willing to die for Him, be crucified…without so much as batting an eye. Thomas could never understand that kind of love and loyalty.

"Okay, I hear you. But what about all the times your God commanded the Jews to slaughter thousands of innocent people, even women and children, and animals! How can you defend that?"

"Things aren't always what they seem. Those people God wanted killed had mixed their blood with Fallen Angels. Their DNA had been corrupted, and yes, even the animals. If the Hebrews hadn't destroyed them, they would have eventually intermarried with them and the pure bloodline that would bring forth Jesus would have been contaminated."

"You've got an answer for everything, don't you?"

"No, but God docs."

Afraid she would leave after hearing what he said next, he grabbed her hand and held on tight. "Lucifer requires nothing of his followers. We can do whatever we want. There are no rules, no restrictions, and he is now offering eternal life as well. He has brought the entire world together in harmony and peace. He doesn't order the massacre of thousands. He truly cares for mankind. It seems to me that he is the god who should be followed."

"Oh, really?" She laughed. "No restrictions? How about that you have to get his quantum stamp and worship him, or you can't buy or sell anything? Or what about his law that you can't believe in Jesus or you'll be arrested and killed? Sounds like restrictions to me."

She had a point there, he supposed. "He is trying to create a world free of disease, poverty, climate change, war, and discord. Sacrifices must be made."

"Ah, I see." She huffed. "Well, I guess time will tell which one of us is right."

Thomas didn't want to fight. He wanted quite the opposite. "Truce?" He squeezed her hand.

"Truce." She squeezed it back. "For now."

"I guess we'd better get some sleep. You're welcome to lean on me again." He swung an arm around her and attempted to draw her close, but she resisted. "Come on. I don't bite."

"I don't know about that," she teased. "I seem to remember you had quite a dangerous bite in the past."

"Dangerous? Or Enjoyable?"

"Both," she said, but even so, she fell against him and laid her head on his shoulder. And after a few sighs and huffs and snuggles, she fell fast asleep.

As usual. While Thomas sat awake for hours.

Still, it gave him time to ponder their discussion. She'd made some good points, but then again, so had he. Regardless of which god was better, in their present circumstances, the choice was easy. Follow Lucifer and live or follow this Jesus and die. And Thomas was not ready to die. Not after he'd finally found Tori again. Now, all he had to do was convince her that allegiance to the NWU and Lucifer was the only logical choice.

*Therefore take no thought, saying, What shall we eat? or,
What shall we drink? or, Wherewithal shall we be clothed?
For after all these things do the Gentiles seek: for your
heavenly Father knoweth that ye have need of all these things.
But seek ye first the kingdom of God, and his righteousness;
and all these things shall be added unto you.*
Matthew 6:31-33

Chapter 19

Tori woke up with Thomas gently stroking her forehead as he used to do when they'd spent the night together so many years ago. All those glorious sensations instantly flooded her, warming every inch of her body right down to her toes. She gave a moan of pleasure before she realized where she was.

And leapt from his arms.

His brows shot up as a sparkle of humor filled his blue eyes.

She wanted to be angry—at herself for feeling things she ought not. But the man before her looked nothing like Thomas Benton, Vice Regent of the NWF North American Region she'd met weeks ago. His normally perfect, slicked-back hair stuck out in all directions. Dark stubble lined his chin, while a streak of mud spread across his face from forehead to cheek. His shirt was torn and stained, his jeans caked in mud, and he smelled like a dumpster left out in the hot sun for weeks.

She giggled.

"What's so funny?" His brows crossed, joining two smudges of dirt between his eyes.

Dabbing her thumb on her tongue, she attempted to wipe some of the mud away, but he grabbed her hand. "What are you…? Ah, I'm a mess, and I stink." He lowered his nose to his armpit and cringed. "This is all your fault, you know."

She smiled. "You've changed. You used to be obsessed with your appearance."

He huffed. "It's not like I have a choice anymore."

"I like it." She held a hand to her nose. "Except for the smell, of course. But the grungy, scruffy look suits you."

He rubbed the stubble on his jaw and quirked his lips to the side in that sexy smile of his. "It does?"

She slapped his arm. "Don't get a big head about it." Yet suddenly she felt self-conscious of her own appearance. *And* her smell, a foul smell she wasn't sure belonged solely to Thomas. "I guess we both could use a shower."

Rising, she dusted off her jeans and glanced out the window, where the gray of dawn pierced the darkness, then back at the rest of them, fast asleep—Callie and Carla cuddled up to their mother, Sara curled up in a corner, and Aaron, back leaning against the wall, chin on his chest. She hated to wake them, but they had a long day of walking ahead. If only they could find a car that worked, but that would only expose them further.

"I'm going to go pray," she whispered to Thomas. "Let them sleep a few minutes longer."

Nodding, he smiled up at her, and in that smile a thousand memories resurfaced, and with them, feelings she'd long since buried. He'd been her first love, and if she were honest, her only real love. Even as a teen, he'd been so caring, so adoring, gentle. How many times had he listened to her as she rambled on about her abusive stepfather and then held her for hours while she'd cried her eyes out?

Jerking her gaze away, she headed out the door into the front of the restaurant. No time for memories. No time for sentimental feelings. And especially no time for romance. Not with a nonbeliever.

"Oh, Lord." Tori knelt before one of the booths and folded her hands. "I need you. I need Your guidance, Your wisdom, Your protection. I don't know what I'm doing. These people look to me to keep them safe, to feed them, to guide them to a place where they are protected. But who am I?" Tears began to fall, and she dropped her head to the sticky booth. "I'm a nobody. A woman who didn't even have the common sense not to get involved in all the evil of this world. Please help me."

I am with you, daughter, until the end of the age.

Although she wasn't sure she was only remembering a Bible verse or hearing directly from the Lord, she hoped desperately for the latter. "I know, Father," she murmured. "But I feel so lost."

You are my precious one whom I have chosen for this task. Trust in Me.

Raising her head, she wiped her eyes and looked up through the grimy window. "Me? Chosen?"

No answer came, just a blanket of peace and love that wrapped around her, chasing away her doubts and fears. After several minutes, during which she worshiped her King, Tori returned to find everyone awake.

Thomas was helping Sara to her feet, Brianna breast-fed Callie in the corner, and Aaron slurped down water from a bottle. Carla approached Tori. "I'm hungry."

Tori knelt. "I know, sweetheart. God will provide." Though she said the words with finality, she wasn't completely sure of them anymore. Quietly repenting, she rose. "Let's get ready to go. Use the bathroom if you need to, and let's fill up those water bottles from the sink."

With moans and groans, everyone did as they were told, leaving Tori alone in the room. Or so she thought. A tug on her shirt brought her gaze down to Carla.

"Onafiel says to look outside."

Tori chuckled. "Oh, he does, does he? Well, we'll be out there soon enough." Saying a silent prayer for food, she took the little girl's hand and, after checking to ensure the coast was clear, led the others out the back door of the restaurant.

Spread across a small patch of grass were tiny specks of something that sparkled in the morning sun.

"Food!" Tugging her hand free, Carla ran toward the odd sight.

"Wait!" Brianna dashed after her, but the little girl had already picked up whatever it was and shoved it in her mouth.

The group circled around her, staring in horror.

"Yummy!" she exclaimed and reached for more, but her mother grabbed her hand before she could. "Don't! We don't know what this is."

Carla looked up at her with glee. "It's angel food, Mama."

Stooping, Tori lifted a piece from the grass to her nose. The scent of fresh-baked bread filled her nostrils. Her mouth watered. She placed it on her tongue, and her tastebuds exploded with a taste similar to donuts, but much, much better.

Manna, the word drifted through her mind.

"It's manna," she said with excitement. "God has provided!" Grabbing a cluster of the sweet bread, she held it up to heaven. "Thank you, Father, for this food. Bless it to our bodies!"

"Amen. Praise God!" Brianna gave the nod for Carla to keep eating as she brought piece after piece of the heavenly wafers to her own mouth.

Thomas stood staring at them all as if they were nuts.

Tori looked up at him in between bites. "Try some. It's good."

"But where did it come from?" he asked.

Aaron stood by his side, looking equally puzzled, but at least Sara had dropped to her knees and was enjoying the meal.

"It's from heaven. From God," Tori said. "You know your Bible, *pastor*. Remember the manna God provided for the Israelites in the desert?"

"Yeah, but that was just a fable."

"Really? Well, come have a bite of a fable." She smiled. "And you too, Aaron. This may be our only meal for today."

Onafiel fluttered his wings in joy, hoisting the sack of manna over his shoulder. "I love it when the Father provides!"

Zarall smiled. "And you had the privilege to transfer it into their dimension, my friend. Well done."

Onafiel smiled.

Arithem crossed arms over his chest and watched the sons and daughters of the Most High enjoy the divine treats. Too much heartache, pain, and loss had followed them of late. 'Twas good to see them enjoy a moment of heaven.

Anahel gestured to the beast. "He does not partake."

"Nay, he cannot," Arithem said. "'Twould burn his insides and expose him for what he is, a spawn of hell."

The fiend in question glanced their way, fully able to hear their conversation. His eyes turned fiery red as he hissed out a blasphemy.

Ignoring him, Arithem glanced at his ward, kneeling beside Tori, enjoying the heavenly food. "The beast has grown closer to Thomas. The deception is strong."

"Aye." Zarall grabbed the handle of his ax, wishing he could toss it at the vile fiend. "He seeks to keep him from the Father."

"And he seeks to murder these precious saints before they can complete their task," Arithem added.

Anahel stared at his ward, Brianna. "'Tis why we are here."

"But we cannot act without their permission," Onafiel said.

Arithem nodded. "And we won't gain their permission unless they recognize the spiritual threat."

Zarall studied Tori as she leaned back and patted her full belly, laughing. "She must pass her tests. She must learn what the Father teaches her. Or all will be lost."

Four days later, Thomas still could not figure out where the donut-like substance had come from—or continued to come from, for it had appeared each morning since. No matter what filthy rat-infested hovel they spent the night in, no matter that dozens of birds, squirrels and other creatures should have eaten it up before they woke, it was there, splayed across whatever patch of dead grass was available, glistening like dew in the sun.

"See, God isn't such a bully now, is he?" Tori had said with a grin. "He feeds His people because He loves us."

Aaron's muffled grunt had been almost indistinguishable, but Thomas had heard it, nonetheless, making him wonder at the man's true beliefs. Regardless, he was a kind old soul who went about listening and caring and cheering everyone up. The past few days he'd been spending more time with Sara, extending a comforting hand and a listening ear. The young girl seemed to perk up in his presence. Thomas couldn't blame her. She, no doubt, needed a good father figure as much as he did.

Another thing Thomas could not figure out was the vision he'd had from the window of that high-rise apartment as the tsunami struck—a huge glowing creature wearing armor and bearing all manner of weapons, holding back the force of the water. Then as quickly as he had appeared, the bright being was gone. An angel? But no, that couldn't be true. Angels weren't any more real than Santa Claus or the Easter Bunny. Just silly myths intended to bring joy and comfort to children and weak-minded adults. Which was why he hadn't told anyone. Thomas needed to be in control of his mind. It was all he had left.

The days and nights blurred together, uneventful for the most part. They trudged onward, dodging cameras and drones and any cars on the road. Occasionally, one of the new NWU Cyborg Units Thomas had only heard about walked down the street in civilian clothing. Unlike the Spider drones, these robots looked completely human, walked like humans, and even had facial expressions and human sweat. If not for Tori, Thomas would have ignored them and gone on his way and would probably have been caught, but she sensed them somehow and quickly found places to hide.

Tori seemed to know a lot of things ahead of time. Where to hide, what streets were safe to take, when to duck into a building even before NWU troops appeared, where to find water, and what places were safe havens for sleep. Was she that adept at dodging danger at every turn, or was she hearing from this God of hers?

Thomas didn't want to know.

Hence, they avoided crowds, NWU Medical and Distribution centers, Reformation Centers and NWU housing. They also skirted around homeless camps and anywhere people congregated for fear of violent attacks, which were common these days. Due to the scorching heat, the drought that had ravaged the Earth, and the poisoned meteors, the water in many rivers and lakes was either contaminated or very low. But Tori always managed to find an untainted source. If not for that and the morning manna, they'd all have died from starvation.

Yet, what baffled Thomas even more than the heavenly food were the horrid conditions of every city, town, byway, highway and suburb they passed through. He'd been told that the NWU's primary goal, aside from world peace and prosperity, was to provide pristine living conditions for all people, no matter their race, education, or upbringing. Everyone would be assigned a job, an income, a place to live, and all the food and medicines they needed. In addition, the NWU would clean up the cities, rebuild roads, build more climate friendly structures using the advanced technology of the Neflams, and eradicate crime and homelessness.

But what Thomas had witnessed these past twelve days was quite the opposite. Each NWU housing center seemed worse than the last. Streets, along with abandoned buildings, were left in disrepair, garbage and sewage littered the landscape, and every park or underpass housed homeless camps filled with wandering vagrants. He'd not seen one new building, not one cleaned-up park, nothing but mayhem and destruction. Certainly not the utopia they'd been promised.

Despite his inability to sleep well, nights became Thomas's favorite times. Tori would always snuggle up beside him, and they'd end up talking for a few moments before she inevitably fell fast asleep. He didn't mind. Her closeness brought back memories of happier times, and he needed to focus on those, rather than on his current predicament.

By late afternoon, they reached the outskirts of Madison, about a day's walk from Atlanta. The scabs on Thomas's feet from old blisters had been rubbed raw, every inch of his legs ached, his filthy hair matted to his head, and the sun had seared the skin on his bare arms pink. Other than that, he felt great! In truth, he'd caught a glimpse of himself in a passing store window and what he saw in his reflection made him cringe. Three weeks ago, if he passed someone on the street who looked like him, he'd run as far as he could in the other direction. Times had certainly changed. He still suffered from moments of despair at the direction his life had taken, his mighty fall from power and wealth. He wasn't even sure where he belonged anymore. He couldn't go back, couldn't be a part of the NWU or he'd be executed. And yet, he didn't completely fit in with these Deviants either.

He glanced at Tori up ahead as she conversed with Sara and continued leading them through the back parking lot of a boarded-up strip mall.

Carla's tiny hand slid into his, and Thomas couldn't help but smile. He'd never liked kids. They were so…so… needy and messy and annoying. But this particular one was definitely worming her way into his heart. "And how are you today, Miss Carla?"

She smiled up at him. "My feet hurt Thomist, but I know everyone's do."

"Here." Leaning over, Thomas swept her in his arms. "I'll carry you for a while, how's that?"

Her tiny arms circled his neck, and she squeezed him, giggling.

Brianna slipped beside them. "You don't have to carry her, Thomas."

"I know. But she's not very heavy, and it has to be hard for her little legs to walk all this way."

Brianna reached up to caress her daughter's cheek. "She's my tough girl."

Carla perked up. "I am brave and strong, one of the Father's special children." She grinned. "At least that's what Onafiel says."

"Well, Onafiel is right," Brianna said.

Thomas's gaze dropped to Callie beginning to fuss in her mother's arms. He couldn't imagine how difficult it was to care for little ones in such dangerous times. If Brianna wasn't a Deviant, and with her education and skills, she wouldn't have to worry at all. Yet here she was, putting her kids through a nightmare. For what?

"You know the NWU would help you. Give you money and a place to stay if you couldn't find work," he said.

"You think that's why I'm here?" She laughed, her beautiful dark skin glistening in the sun. "I'd have no trouble finding work with my skills." Callie started to whine, and she held the baby out to Thomas. "Hold her a sec, will you?"

"Sorry, precious." Thomas set Carla on the ground and then took the babe from Brianna. Fumbling the wee thing for a moment, he drew her close, hoping she wouldn't barf on him again.

Brianna adjusted the straps of her holder. "Their eternal future is far more important than their comfort in this life."

Thomas frowned. "*If*, and that's a big if, what you believe is true."

"Would I be going through this if it wasn't? Like I said, I live in terror for my kids. I'd do anything for them. But following my Savior, knowing Him is worth it all."

Thomas shook his head. "I guess I'll never understand your allegiance to this God who would allow you to suffer so much. I mean, what if we are caught and you are tossed into a reformation camp, separated from your kids, or this weird manna stops coming and your kids starve?"

Brianna's dark eyes searched his, and he saw pity in them. "Yes, in truth, those things terrify me, keep me up at night. I would rather boil in oil than have anything bad happen to my girls." Tears pooled in her eyes as she retrieved Callie and placed her back in her holder, and Thomas felt bad he'd said anything. "Tori says I need to trust God, and that's what I'm trying to do. It's not always easy, I admit that, but my faith is growing. I can never turn back now."

Thomas nodded, though he still didn't understand.

Halting beside the back of a store, Tori pulled out her map, studied it for a minute, then faced them. "We need to avoid Atlanta, so we go north, weave around Athens and then it should only be two or three days from there."

"No, Miss Tori." Carla dashed to her side and looked up. "Onafiel says we have to go to Atlanta."

Tori brushed the dark curls from Carla's face. "Well, this time your friend is wrong. Atlanta is a very dangerous place for us right now."

Aaron leaned on his cane and nodded. "I agree. North we go!"

"Sounds good to me," Sara added.

Thomas rubbed the back of his neck and stared up at the sun high in the sky. How it could be so hot through all the haze was beyond him. Hot and dry. Unfortunately, they still had at least five hours of daylight. But avoiding a major city was a good idea. "Let's do it," he added.

Tori stared at him, yet not really *at* him. She closed her eyes, then opened them and looked around as if she'd heard something no one else had. "Wait." She glanced at her map again, then walked a few yards away and stood, staring at the pavement. Finally, after what seemed an eternity, but was only ten minutes or so, she returned, a determined look in her eyes.

"We head toward Atlanta. I don't know why or how near the city we will get, but this is the what the Lord wants."

A wave of shock drifted over the group, keeping them silent. Thomas was the first to speak up. "Do you think that's wise? The NWU troops will be all over the city."

Tori released a deep sigh. "I'm sure they will, but I must do as the Lord says."

"Are you sure you heard from Him?" Thomas pressed, an unavoidable skepticism in his voice.

"Yes."

Brianna flattened her lips but nodded in agreement.

Sara shrugged as if she didn't care

But Aaron seemed to grow agitated, even angry. "This is insane. If we go near Atlanta, we'll be caught and killed."

Tori folded up her map and slipped it into her back pocket. "If that is God's will, then that is God's will. You can join us or not."

Aaron pointed his cane at her, fury flaring from his eyes. "How do you know you're hearing from God? I'm a Christian too, and I sense He is saying to avoid Atlanta!"

But Tori would not be moved. "Like I said, you can join us or not."

"She's going to get us all killed," Aaron mumbled as they headed out.

Thomas agreed. It seemed this God of theirs was leading them straight to the guillotine.

*For as many as are led by the Spirit of God, they are the
sons of God.
For ye have not received the spirit of bondage again to
fear; but ye have received the Spirit of adoption, whereby we
cry, Abba, Father.
Romans 8:14-15*

Chapter 20

L ord, are you sure about this? The closer they got to
Atlanta, the more demons Tori saw. They were
everywhere—congregating near homeless camps, hovering
around NWU housing facilities, sitting on top of nightclubs and
walking amongst the crowds lining up to get their food
allotment. She'd expected to see more of the vile creatures near
highly populated places, but so many? Their stench and the
oppressive weight of darkness was overwhelming. Even so, she
knew the Lord was with them—saw scattered glimpses of the
angels guarding them, a flash of light here, a beam of brilliance
there. More than that, she felt their mighty presence. And she
thanked the Lord for their protection every day.

They needed the heavenly warriors now more than ever,
especially as they made their way through Decatur, a suburb of
Atlanta. It was one thing to avoid drones and cameras in rural
areas but near a large city where every cockroach was surveilled,
well, that was another thing entirely.

She glanced up at one such camera mounted on top of 6G
dispersion equipment high on a pole. Leading the group around
the back of it, she hoped to avoid being seen, but it swung in
their direction.

Lord, help us, she prayed as she did each time they'd been
unable to avoid other cameras. Either the Lord was truly making
them invisible, or something else was going on. By all accounts,
they should have been recognized long ago by the surveillance

AI and surrounded by a dozen NWU police. The thought settled uncomfortably in her mind, like an annoying gnat, nibbling bit by bit at her reason.

They passed in front of an old 7-11 with broken windows boarded up by sheets of wood—a relic of days gone by when you could drive up and get a Coke Slurpy or cup of hot coffee. A time of innocence, or at least *perceived* innocence. Tori had since learned that the Satanists had actually been running the planet from behind closed doors for hundreds of years. Much of the history of the US and the world they'd been taught in school were lies. But what did it matter now?

Laughter brought her gaze back to Sara who was smiling at something Aaron said. It was good to see the young girl laugh, but that niggling sensation rose within her again whenever she looked at the old man. Something wasn't right, but Tori couldn't put her finger on it. Beyond them, Thomas carried Carla while Brianna fidgeted with a whining Callie. Maybe they should all stop for a rest.

Sunlight disappeared and Tori glanced up to see a series of roiling black clouds forming across the sky. A raindrop splattered on her forehead.

"Come on!" she shouted, making a dash for the underside of a freeway on-ramp ahead. By the time they all ran beneath, the skies unleashed a torrent of rain, more rain, in fact, than Tori had seen in quite some time due to the global drought.

Unfortunately, they were not alone. Several homeless tents snuggled against the concrete wall just yards away. Thomas saw them too, and they exchanged a glance of concern.

"Let's sit down for a minute and rest our legs until it passes." Tori wanted to talk with Sara, anyway, and maybe the homeless would leave them alone.

The sweet scent of rain filled the air, and Tori drew in a deep breath, a simple pleasure in the middle of so much pain. *Thank you, Lord.*

"I'll grab everyone's bottles and collect the rain," Thomas said with a smile.

"Good idea."

The man was becoming more useful than she would have ever expected.

Hugging herself, Sara sank down against the concrete wall and closed her eyes.

"You feeling okay?" Tori knelt beside her, wiping a strand of hair from her face.

"Yeah. I just want to get better, you know?" She swallowed. "I'm sick. I feel like crap. I have a killer headache that won't go away. I can hardly keep down any of that manna everyone's eating, and I can't sleep. Look at me." She glanced at her body. "I'm wasting away." Tears filled her eyes. "Even in rehab, they give people drugs to get by. I just need...I just need... a little, you know? Just to keep me going." A tear slid down her cheek, and she batted it away.

Tori's heart sank. "I know it's super hard."

"No, you don't!" Sara's eyes flared.

Tori bit her lip. "Okay. Maybe not exactly what you are feeling, but I also was in rehab. You know that."

"But they help you." Sara's eyes drifted to Aaron assisting Thomas with the bottles. "He says he can get me something to help."

Shocked, Tori looked at the man. "Oh, he does, does he?" She huffed, then faced Sara again. "You're almost done. You're at the end now. Don't quit on me." Leaning over, Tori hugged her, squeezing her hard. "I love you, girl," she whispered in her ear. "We are going to make it."

When she pulled back, tears streamed down Sara's face. "Thank you. I'm just so hungry, so tired. I'm not strong like you."

"I'm not strong, Sara. It's God who is strong. Lean on Him. Okay?"

She nodded. "Aaron says maybe God doesn't want to heal me. Maybe He won't forgive me."

Fury bubbled in Tori's gut. "That's a lie and you know it."

A loud rumble of thunder shook the ground beneath them. Settling her racing heart, Tori stood and fixed her gaze on Aaron. He capped the last of the bottles, then shook the rain from his hair, laughing with Thomas. How dare he offer any kind of drug to Sara!

She marched toward him, but he moved to hand Brianna her full bottle of water. Carla shrank behind her mom while Brianna handed Callie to Aaron. "Can you hold her a sec while I give Carla some water?"

Before Aaron could grab the baby, Callie shrieked so loud, the drugged homeless peeked out of their tents.

Horrified, Brianna withdrew the child. "I'm so sorry. Must be the storm. I was sure she would be used to you by now."

"Not a problem." Aaron smiled, but when he turned away his face seemed to change—if only for a second—into something hideous, dark and reptilian.

Lightning flashed, coating everything in eerie silver.

A shiver etched down Tori's back. A wisp of darkness slunk around the man.

Until he looked up and saw her staring at him.

A wide smile lit his face as he approached. "Tori, I was thinking with everyone so discouraged that we should all hold hands and pray together. Maybe sing a praise song to chase away these demons of despair."

Tori searched his eyes for any deception but found none. Maybe she was just tired, seeing things out of her exhaustion. Surely an evil man or demon would not suggest such a thing. "That sounds like a great idea, Aaron. But I need to discuss something with you."

"Sure." He leaned on his cane and winced.

"I'm glad you've made friends with Sara, but under no circumstances are you to offer her any drugs. And please do not speak for God to her. God loves her, wants to heal her, and forgives her. That's what His Word says. To tell her otherwise is a lie and highly discouraging."

His gray eyebrows crossed even as his bottom lip twitched slightly. "I never said such things, Tori." He glanced over his shoulder at Sara. "I don't know why she would tell you that. Could be hallucinations from the detox."

Tori cocked her head, studying his expressions, his tone. He seemed sincere, but her gut was telling her otherwise. Maybe it was that everyone looked to him as some kind of father figure. Her real father had abandoned her at age ten, and the only father she'd known after that had abused her sexually and emotionally. So she supposed she had an issue with "fathers."

"Okay, then. Maybe you're right. Let's get to that prayer."

After gathering everyone in a circle, Tori asked Aaron to lead them. She had not heard him pray yet, and this would be a good test. A devil in disguise would not be able to pray in Jesus' name.

But he didn't pray in Jesus' name. He prayed to God, yes, the God of the ages, he called him. He prayed for protection, food, healing, and guidance to their hideout. Then he proceeded to offer words of worship to God.

Tori took over with a song of praise to Jesus. Brianna, Sara, and Carla raised their voices high, the sweet sound echoing off the concrete and melding with the *tap-tap* of rainfall.

Thomas didn't join in, but she didn't expect him to. But Aaron? He mouthed the song, but his stance, his expression lacked any zeal. Odd

Tori didn't have time to consider it when voices from behind her shouted, "Give us your food, water, and clothes, you stinkin' Deviants!"

Before Tori could respond, Thomas grabbed a large stick from the ground, rushed forward, and pushed her and the others behind him.

"Back off! We want no trouble!" he shouted.

If they weren't smack in the middle of the worst seven years of human history, it could be a scene out of a romance novel, complete with a brave hero rescuing his lady. The thought made Tori smile, despite the circumstances.

Three men approached—filthy, dressed in rags, and with a stench that overwhelmed even the sweet scent of rain. One of them held a knife.

Thunder bellowed, adding emphasis to Thomas's threat.

"You got one stick, an old man, and women and children," the leader with the knife said. "Just hand it over or we'll gut the lot of you." A drug-induced glaze covered his eyes, almost making him look zombie-like. In fact, all three looked as though they were the walking dead.

Callie screamed. Sara slid behind Brianna. Oddly Carla seemed completely unafraid as she stood beside her mother, staring at something off to the side.

Aaron merely narrowed his eyes at the men.

"We mean it, mister!" The knife-man charged forward.

Plucking his ax from his belt, Zarall charged forward, his intent to battle the hoard of demons inhabiting the man with the knife. If one could call him a man, for 'twas obvious his DNA had been altered so much, he was no longer fully a son of Adam.

"Wait!" Arithem ordered, mighty hand in the air. "Let us see how he handles this threat."

"Alas," Anahel protested as he hovered over Brianna, "he does not know 'tis spirits he battles and not flesh."

Arithem nodded. "But his male heroics will do much to unite he and Tori, for united they must be to complete the Commander's plan."

"Ah, these foolish humans with their romantic notions," Tagas added, standing beside Sara.

Zarall huffed. "Indeed. And 'twas such notions which destroyed a third of our kind after they were cast from heaven."

Thomas shoved the man's knife away with a bat of his stick, then swept down and clubbed his attacker across the knees.

The half-human screamed and fell to the ground, dropping his knife. One of the others grabbed it and slashed Thomas across the arm. A line of blood appeared.

"Protect your charges!" Arithem shouted.

Hefting his sword, Arithem started forward, but Thomas leapt out of the way of the next attack, kicked the man in the gut before he could regroup, and then pounded him across the back. The knife flew from his hand and Thomas caught it.

The third man fled. Struggling to rise, his two friends followed.

Arithem smiled at his friends. "See? I did not have to do a thing," he said proudly.

"Aye." Zarall sheathed his ax. "But now she must deal with the storm." He nodded to the torrent of rain around them. "Will she realize the source before it does them harm?"

Onafiel fluttered his wings as he gazed down at Callie in her mother's arms. "'Twould that it will not come to that."

Anahel drew his spiked mace and glared at Aaron. "Your time will come, spawn of hell!"

Aaron grinned, which only infuriated them all.

"Never fear." Arithem crossed arms over his chest and nodded at Tori. "She senses the evil. She is close to passing this test."

"I pray you are right, my friend," Zarall said with a sigh. "For if she doesn't, many souls will be lost."

"You're bleeding." Tori pressed an old rag over Thomas's arm.

"It's nothing." He looked behind him where more people emerged from tents and were heading their way. "We need to leave."

She agreed.

"Way to go, son!" Aaron slapped him on the back. "I would have joined you if I was twenty years younger."

Thomas smiled, and Tori could tell that the old man's praise meant a lot to him.

She headed over to help Brianna with Callie. Covering themselves with jackets and backpacks, they dashed out into the deluge.

To say Tori was impressed with Thomas would be an understatement. How many times had he risked his life for her? Too many to count, starting with many times in their teens, to helping her escape from certain death at his Reformation Headquarters, and now to protecting her from drugged vagrants. In fact, if not for his heroics, he'd still be Vice Regent of New World Faith North American Region, living in his luxurious beach mansion and hobnobbing with the ruling elite. She glanced his way as he helped Brianna settle a blanket over Callie to shield her from the pouring rain. His torn shirt clung to a muscular body, the sight of which sent a swirl of warmth through her, despite the storm. His saturated hair matted to his head, dirt slid down his skin in rivulets as the rain washed it away, and he limped slightly from the blisters on his feet.

She'd smile if he didn't look like a mere shadow of his former self. Guilt pinched her. She'd done this to him. Yet…in the long run, his soul was better off with them. At least he had a chance to make the right choice for eternity. *Lord, please help him to see.*

Facing forward, she bent her head and pressed onward. One good thing about the storm was that it sent people into shelter, leaving their small, bedraggled group sloshing forward on empty streets. At first the rain felt good, like a cleansing shower, wiping away all the dirt and grime of the past weeks, but soon it turned their clothing into dead weight, making it difficult to move. Puddles formed all around them as bellows of thunder never failed to make her heart lurch.

More than once she thought about seeking shelter until the tempest passed, but it gave no indication of letting up at all. And she wanted so desperately to get to Nyla and Calan's haven. Once there, she could rest and relinquish the responsibility for these precious people. There, she could find the strength of fellowship with other believers stronger than her. There, they would be safe, at least as much as was possible in the Tribulation.

Thunder roared again from the dark skies above them, followed by a streak of white lightning that cast an eerie glow over their surroundings—a scene out of an apocalyptic movie, destruction devoid of all color.

Sara shivered beside her, and Tori swung an arm around her, drawing her close.

"I'm soooo coooold," she muttered.

"It'll be okay. Hang in there. It's almost dark, and we'll find a place to sleep."

"I don't knoooow if I'll make it."

"You can, girl. You will."

Aaron appeared beside them, slapping his cane in the puddles and looking like a saturated garden gnome. "Seems the storm is only around Atlanta." Lifting his cane, he pointed to the northeast. "Perfectly clear over there. Maybe we should change plans?"

Frustration churned in Tori's gut, even as she glanced where he pointed. Clear blue skies beckoned in the distance. But...*she sought the Lord's voice within*...no, regardless of the storm, they were to head toward Atlanta.

She shook her head. "I know it sounds crazy, but we are supposed to go to Atlanta!" she shouted over the pounding rain.

Wiping the water from his eyes, he leaned toward her. "Did God really say that? Or are you only imagining it?"

Angry, she studied him, searching his eyes for his motive. Maybe his concern was purely for their safety. Still, he sounded an awful lot like the snake in the garden who tempted Eve by questioning the Word of God. And that unnerved her more than the storm. "We go to Atlanta," she said with finality before turning her attention forward again.

After another hour, Tori led them under the awning of an office building and pulled out her map. They were a mere hour outside the outskirts of Atlanta. They could make it by nightfall, find a place to rest, and then enter the city in the morning. She still had no idea why the Lord wanted them to go there, but she continued to feel the Spirit's strong leading, and He never led her astray.

"We'll rest here for a moment," she announced as everyone did their best to shake off the water, wring out their clothing, and plop to the ground to give their weary legs a break. Brianna curled up with her kids while Thomas helped Sara settle down on a rare dry spot. Aaron stood off to the side, leaning on his cane.

The clamor of the rain lessened. Droplets slowed from pounding to tapping the cobblestones in front of the building. Perhaps the storm was passing. Good.

A vision struck her hard in the gut.

A tornado—a massive dark funnel cloud larger than life. It gobbled up everything in its path, moving with lightning speed. Demonic faces leapt at her from within the funnel, grinning, cackling like witches, mocking, threatening. The tornado raced toward them. Tori's heart seized.

The scene changed.

Callie's tiny, frail body lay in the mud.

The vision disappeared. Pulse racing, Tori gripped her stomach and bent over.

Thomas rushed to her. "Are you okay?"

A wall of ice struck her right side. Penetrating, creating a chill that sent trembling waves through her. She glanced up and saw Aaron grinning at her with the most evil look in his eyes. Instantly, a kind smile returned to his lips.

"Tori?" Thomas pressed.

"Yes, I'm fine. Sorry. I had a vision, a terrible vision." She looked over at Callie sleeping in her mother's arms. *Lord, no. Not Callie.*

It does not have to be.

Tori pursed her lips, hoping beyond hope that was the Lord she heard.

"A vision. I don't get it." Thomas raked back his wet hair and studied her with curiosity.

"It's okay."

"The rain stopped!" Aaron proclaimed, approaching her. "What can I do to help? You carry a huge burden for us all."

Tori searched his eyes yet again for any hint of wickedness and deceit. But she saw nothing. Just an emptiness, a vacuum, which was weird. Shouldn't she see the light of the Lord? *Why can I not discern whether this man is good or evil, Lord?*

"No, thank you, Aaron. We should start walking again and take advantage of this break in the storm."

Yet no sooner did they all head out, than the storm picked up again, only this time, a strong wind beat on them, turning raindrops into pellets that struck them from all directions.

They slogged forward for almost an hour. In the distance, skyscrapers poked into the dark clouds. Atlanta. They were nearly there. Tori gestured to an old parking garage devoid of cars. "We can sleep there."

Before she could even turn and head that way, an enormous roar bellowed across the sky, like the sound of an approaching train, a *giant* train.

"God help us," Thomas said from beside her.

She followed his gaze. A massive funnel cloud took up nearly the entire western horizon, spinning and churning, black and ominous—a furious monster sucking up everything in its path and spitting out the bones.

Shock held Tori in place.

It was exactly like her vision.

And they had nowhere to run and hide.

For we wrestle not against flesh and blood, but against principalities, against powers, against the rulers of the darkness of this world, against spiritual wickedness in high places.
Ephesians 6:12

Chapter 21

Grabbing Tori's arm, Thomas scanned their surroundings. Nothing but a parking garage, an office building with glass windows, a small dog park, a movie theater and a strip mall. He'd never faced a tornado before, but he knew none of those buildings would protect them from a direct hit. They needed somewhere below ground. Trouble was, there wasn't anything.

His heart vaulted into his throat. The wind slammed him. He stumbled and nearly fell.

Tori was saying something, but he could no longer hear her.

The black funnel was heading straight for them. Fast. They could never outrun it.

A large piece of wood flew at them, and he shoved Tori down. It sped over their heads, just inches away. The others crouched behind them, clinging to each other. The wind pounded them from all directions. Thomas couldn't move. It tore the breath from his lungs. He gasped for air. Debris struck them... slicing, bruising.

Was this to be their fate? After all they'd endured? If he was a praying man, he'd plead with this mean, vengeful God of theirs, but why would He listen to Thomas?

The roar was deafening now, so loud, it vibrated every cell in Thomas's body. He tried to search for a place to hide, but he could barely turn his head, barely see anything through the wind and rubble.

Were they inside the tornado? He could no longer see the funnel, only a thick blackness. A thousand knives sliced his body, making him feel like a sailor running the gauntlet for some offense.

Brianna screamed. He barely heard her above the noise, but the terror in her voice was unmistakable. Still, he could not move.

Tugging from his grip, Tori did the absolute last thing he expected—she shoved her body upward and lifted her arms to heaven. Bracing her feet apart, she struggled to remain upright against the buffeting wind. But how? He tried to join her but could barely lift his head.

She shouted something he could not make out.

"Yes!" Zarall pounded his fist in the air. "At last. She recognizes what the storm is!"

"Aye!" Arithem joined in his zeal and motioned the others to battle.

Onafiel, Anahel, and Tagas, weapons drawn, rushed forward, and together all five warrior angels charged the demons that caused the massive funnel cloud.

The vile beasts would not go down without a fight. Zarall flung his ax toward a particularly corpulent brute with beady red eyes. It struck with precision in the monster's belly, releasing a sludge of greasy fat. Retrieving his ax, Zarall spun to find two hideous brutes rushing toward him, mouths open, hefting spiked clubs. Meeting the first one, he swept his ax down, chopping his club in half. Anahel struck the other one from behind with his mace.

Zarall nodded his thanks before taking on the next filthy hellion.

Arithem swung his glowing blade across the necks of two demons, severing both their heads with one sweep. Instantly their bodies turned to dark ash and floated away on the breeze, their hideous shrieks fading in the distance.

Tagas crashed his spiked hammer onto the head of a short, squat freak covered in a slimy stench that made even Zarall's nose curl. Pain sliced his leg. Spinning about, he swung his ax before him. Three demons leapt back, growling.

Onafiel flew above them, holding a bucket. "Move Zarall," he shouted.

Zarall barely had time to get out of the way before Onafiel poured a river of burning lava on their heads. They melted to the ground in pools of black sludge.

"Thank you."

Nodding, Onafiel flew off to help Arithem. But the mighty angel quickly dispatched the last depraved spirit, sheathed his blade, and nodded in victory toward his companions.

"These were strong ones," Zarall said, shoving his ax back in his belt.

"Aye, the beast who summoned them is powerful." Arithem nodded toward the fallen one disguised as the old man.

Anahel approached, his breath coming hard. "You should be proud, Zarall. Your ward discerned from whence the storm hailed."

He smiled. "Aye, and she used the authority granted her from the Commander."

Arithem glanced at Tori. "She has passed this test."

"Why does the beast wish them not to go to Atlanta?" Tagas stared at his ward, Sara, who was shivering and hugging herself.

"I know not yet, but I sense there are things there which Thomas must see," Arithem said.

"Oh, my!" Onafiel flew to where the small babe lie in the mud. "Alas, I was so distracted by the fight, I didn't see…"

"'Tis alright, Onafiel." Arithem approached. "Fear not. 'Tis part of the Father's plan." Folding arms over his chest he glanced at Zarall and then at the daughter of Eve, Tori. "Let us watch and see what she does."

The funnel cloud dissipated. The rain stopped. The wind ceased. Rays of golden sunlight speared through the remaining dark clouds.

With the power of the Holy Spirit still buzzing through her, Tori dashed over to Callie, who lay still on the muddy ground at least five yards from where they all had huddled.

No! No! No, Lord! Her insides screamed, dragging claws of terror over her soul. *Not Callie, Lord!*

Brianna dropped to the ground beside her baby and gently picked her up. Callie didn't move. The despondent mother let out a scream so full of horror and sorrow that it leeched all hope from Tori. Desperately searching for wounds, Brianna listened for breathing, even gently shook her baby, all the while every one of her agonizing wails stabbed Tori in the gut.

Thomas and Sara stood at a distance, shock and horror on their faces. Aaron approached, his expression unreadable.

Carla slipped beside her mother and placed a hand on her shoulder. "It will be all right, Mama. Don't worry."

Holding Callie tightly to her chest, Brianna leaned over her and released another torturous howl.

And Tori remembered her vision. The tornado had been a spiritual attack. She'd finally sensed that, albeit a little too late. But she'd commanded it to cease in Jesus' name. And it had. Just like that. Perhaps Callie's death was also part of the same attack.

Kneeling beside Brianna, she held out her hands. "May I?"

Brianna looked at her curiously, eyes red and puffy, tears streaming down her cheeks. She seemed unwilling to release her precious child, to *ever* release her.

"Please," Tori pleaded.

Brianna reluctantly handed her the child, sobbing.

Tori held the lifeless baby tight and closed her eyes. *Lord, is this Your will? Will You grant me Your power?*

Yes. The voice was barely audible, but firm, and Tori knew what she had to do.

Opening her eyes, she stared down at the silent baby. "Wake up. Arise, my precious babe. In Jesus' name."

Nothing. Not a single movement, nor the wisp of a breath.

"Ridiculous," Aaron said from behind her.

Ignoring him, she brushed dark locks of Callie's hair from her forehead. "Awake, little one, in Jesus' name."

Thomas fought back tears. Poor Callie. The tornado must have ripped her from her mother's arms. At least it had not taken her too far away before the winds ceased. But this?

He swallowed down a burst of emotion, wanting to do something, but knowing he couldn't. What kind of God would take the life of such an innocent baby? He sank to his knees in despair. Sara joined him, sobbing as if it was her own child. Aaron stood to the side, watching in unbelief.

Tori took the babe from Brianna and uttered nonsensical words, something about the child waking up. Had she gone mad? How cruel! Rising, he started toward her. Her words would only cause more pain for Brianna. It was best to let the mother mourn, and afterward, they could find a place to bury the babe in peace. Even thinking such a thing brought more tears to his eyes.

He swatted them away.

Callie looked so small and frail in Tori's arms. She spoke more nonsense over the child, breaking Brianna's heart further.

"Tori, maybe it's best to stop—" Thomas started.

Callie gasped. A small breath at first, but finally her chest began to rise and fall, softly at first, barely noticeable. But then she opened her eyes and stared up at Tori. Reaching up, she put her chubby little fingers in Tori's mouth and giggled as if she'd just awoken from an afternoon nap.

Squealing, Brianna took Callie from Tori's arms. "Thank you! Thank you!" More tears poured down her cheeks.

Carla giggled and hugged her mom.

"Don't thank me," Tori said, wiping her face. "All God's doing."

"I can't believe it!" Brianna exclaimed, laughing and bouncing Callie up and down with glee.

Neither did Thomas. "She must have just been knocked out when she hit the ground."

Brianna gazed up at him, her dark eyes sparkling, her face a puffy mess, but her expression one of sheer happiness. "No. She was dead, Thomas. She had no breath in her." She glanced back at her baby. "The Lord brought her back."

Grunting, Aaron hobbled over to them, but Sara remained where she was, staring at the scene as if she were watching a movie.

Thomas couldn't blame her. He'd seen many strange things in his life, but someone rising from the dead? Couldn't be. "People don't just come back to life." *Unless they were gods, like Aali.*

"Onafiel told me she would." Carla knelt and caressed her sister's cheek. "I told you not to worry, Mama."

Tori rose and smiled at him. "Not without Jesus, they don't. You should know that from the Bible. He raised several people from the dead, not to mention Himself."

"Those are just fables." Yet Thomas couldn't take his eyes off Callie cooing in her mother's arms.

"Apparently not." Tori winked at him then glanced up at the sky, a hazy blue now with no signs there'd been a storm only moments before. Everything dripped around them, a symphony of musical taps that seemed oddly soothing.

Lifting her hands toward heaven Tori praised the living God. What a sodden mess she was, a wonderfully beautiful sodden mess, and he longed to take her in his arms. Despite the fact she was certifiably crazy. Rising from the dead. Bah.

Yet… he'd been sure the child was dead.

And they overcame him by the blood of the Lamb, and by
the word of their testimony; and they loved not their lives unto
the death.
Revelation 12:11

Chapter 22

N ot only had the rain stopped and the skies cleared, but
the next day as they approached the outskirts of
downtown Atlanta, there was no indication a tornado had passed
through the city at all. No flattened buildings, no cars
overturned, no piles of rubble. Thomas could make no sense of
it. A tornado that size would have left an unfathomable trail of
destruction. When he'd asked Tori about it, she'd simply
replied, "It was a spiritual storm, not a physical one." At that,
he'd laughed and said that for a spiritual storm, he'd sure felt the
wind and rain.

She had faced him with a grin. "Sometimes the spiritual
manifests in the natural, particularly as we approach the end."

"The end of what?" he had asked.

"The end of the age and return of Jesus," she had said with
assured confidence. Shielding her eyes from the sun, she
glanced at him. "You should know these things, *Pastor.*"

He shook his head. "I'm no pastor. Never really was."
Although he'd studied Scripture in seminary, he couldn't
remember learning anything about the Tribulation or the book
of Revelation. And especially not anything about angels or
whatever the glowing beings were that he kept seeing. Even
during the madness of the tornado, even with all the debris flying
about, Thomas had seen flashes of glowing metal, an ax, and
even something that looked like a medieval mace. Crazy stuff.
Maybe the Deviant insanity was rubbing off on him.

Now, as they made their way down a back alleyway, he glanced at Callie, fast asleep in her mother's arms, and smiled. Ahead, little Carla held Tori's hand as she walked beside Sara.

Aaron slipped beside Thomas, hobbling along, and smiled at him.

"I don't know how you keep up, Aaron," Thomas said, "but you're pretty spry for an old guy."

"Got no choice." Aaron coughed and nodded toward Tori. "She's a tough leader."

"She is that." Thomas could hardly keep his eyes off her. He'd been the strong one when they were teens. He'd been the one urging her not to give up, to keep going, to look to the future when she'd be free of her stepfather. How she had changed. This God of hers, bully or not, had been good for her.

Aaron leaned closer. "Do you really think she raised that baby from the dead?"

Thomas swallowed, ignoring a rising pain from a new blister on his foot. "I don't know what to think. You're the Deviant. Can your God do such things? And, if so, why would He be concerned with one little baby?"

Aaron scratched his gray beard. "Not sure." He stumbled over a rock, and Thomas grabbed his arm to help. "God is distant these days. He's busy pouring out His wrath on all sinners."

Confusion swamped Thomas at both the man's words and his bitter tone. That wasn't the God Tori spoke of. She told of a loving God, a God who died to save mankind. "Sounds like you're not a fan."

Aaron shook his head. "Oh...oh... yeah, I'm a fan...just repeating what the Bible says. I mean, did God really say He'd heal the sick and raise the dead? Sure, it happened in the early church, but miracles like that haven't happened for thousands of years."

"Hmm. True. Maybe you're right." Yet for some reason the thought stole the spark of hope that had lit within Thomas that maybe...just maybe...he'd been wrong about God.

A few hours later, Tori led them to the back of an abandoned house surrounded by burnt trees that looked like the charred arms of the dead reaching from the grave. Thomas shivered at the thought.

Pulling out some crusty bread, she broke off a piece and passed the loaf around as everyone took out their water bottles. "We should be downtown soon," she said between bites, though Thomas could sense the apprehension in her voice.

Aaron lowered to sit between her and Sara. "Shouldn't we avoid downtown? Makes no sense to go where NWU troops are swarming, not to mention cameras and drones everywhere." He shook his head. "Just makes no sense."

Carla tore a piece of bread and handed the loaf to her mother. "Onafiel says we must go."

Tori shared a glance with Thomas, and he saw the hesitancy in her eyes. Yet, when she faced the group, she said with confidence, "I sense that, too, Carla. So, we go."

Aaron huffed. "You're going to listen to some kid's imaginary friend?" He looked over them all. "We're going to get captured and killed. This is nuts!"

Beside him, Sara hugged herself and let out a whimper. "Yeah, maybe he's right, Tori."

Thomas quite agreed, but he didn't say anything. He'd learned that when Tori made up her mind, she'd made it up, especially when she thought she'd heard from this God of hers.

Aaron put an arm around Sara and drew her close. "It'll be all right. Shh now."

Brianna moistened a small piece of bread on her tongue, then slipped it inside Callie's mouth. "I'm with you, Tori. Whatever you decide."

Tori closed her eyes, feeling the weight of the world on her shoulders. The safety, the lives of these precious people depended on her hearing the words of the Lord correctly. How many times had she thought she'd heard from Him, only to discover later that it had only been her own wishful desires? Surely, she'd matured in her faith since then, but it hadn't been that long ago.

Rising to her feet, she moved away from the group, needing to be alone with the Lord, desperate to hear His voice. In the distance, sirens blared, drones buzzed, and something mechanical clanked and clinked. A woman's scream echoed on the wind, bringing with it the scent of rotting garbage and pain— the sounds and odors of the Tribulation.

Lord, do I proceed to Atlanta?

The noise grew louder, attempting to drown out that still, small voice. She focused on the Holy Spirit within her, picturing the Lord sitting on his throne. The vision came to life. He smiled at her and reached out his hand as if to caress her cheek. *Go as far as I tell you.* That was all he said.

She bowed her head. "I will, Lord. I trust You."

With the exception of Brianna, the group was none too happy when Tori returned and announced they would continue into the big city. Doubts began to rise again as they started on their way, but Tori did her best to shove them aside. There must be something in Atlanta the Lord wanted them to do or see, something so life-changing that the enemy had sent a tornado to keep them away.

She glanced over her shoulder at Aaron, talking with Sara. The old man was becoming a nuisance. Instead of supporting Tori, instead of praying along with her for God's will, he was contradicting her every move, introducing doubt among them. Yet…even now as he looked up and smiled, she saw no malice, no subterfuge surrounding him. She had a gift. She could see evil in the spirit realm, but for some reason when it came to Aaron, if he was on the enemy's side, she was blind to it.

Or maybe she was just too paranoid.

Could be due to the thousands of demons she spotted every day lurking around buildings, sitting on rooftops, swirling around and through the people she saw. Only her constant prayer seemed to keep them at bay. That, along with an angelic escort she could not see but sensed was with them. The thought made her smile.

By mid-afternoon, the sweltering heat drained every last bit of their energy. Sara was struggling, Aaron's hobble was more pronounced, and Callie whined more frequently.

The eerie hum of a drone, no, *three* drones, filled the air. The crafts swept in before Tori could dive for cover, hovering over them like vultures, the demonic red light of their cameras… staring, analyzing, mocking. Having grown accustomed to the mechanical monsters, they all froze. If the drones decided to shoot them, there was nowhere to run anyway.

But once again, the flying freaks took off as if they weren't worth their time.

Which made Tori all the more nervous. It made no sense. She and Thomas had to be on the top of the NWU's hit list. Yet none of the cameras, drones, or surveillance cyborgs had reported them.

Something was wrong. Terribly wrong.

That's when she saw them. At first they looked like old telephone poles or windmills lined up beside the road in the distance. But the closer they got, the more her stomach dropped and her heart shrank. Finally, her breath caught in her throat.

Crosses extended as far as the eye could see.

With people hanging on them, crucified.

"Wait!" Thomas shouted after Tori as she marched toward the horrid scene. She'd instructed everyone to head down one of the side streets to their left while she went on to investigate. But what was there to investigate? Nothing but agony and death.

He'd done his best to usher the others away from the scene, but he couldn't allow Tori to witness the sight alone. Yet now as he caught up to her and she stopped before the first cross, Thomas had a hard time keeping the bread in his stomach.

A man, or what was left of him, hung lifeless on the cross, nails piercing his hands and feet while ropes tied about them kept him upright. Wounds covered his emaciated body—gashes, open sores, and bruises. His head hung down to his chest, strands of hair covering his face, which was probably a good thing. Written on a sign nailed above his head were the words:

Deviant. *Follower of the false God, Jesus*.

Sinking to her knees, Tori dropped her head into her hands and sobbed. Since they started on this trip, he'd rarely seen her cry. No doubt she wanted to be strong for the rest of them. Yet now, all her fears and sorrows spilled out onto the dirt before this man's cross.

Forcing down his own horror and nausea, he knelt by her side, swept an arm over her shoulder, and held her while she cried uncontrollably. He didn't know what to say, what to do, so he just held her, like he'd done so many times before. This time, the abomination before them was so much worse than anything that had happened in her past.

In truth, Thomas was having a hard time with it, himself. How could an NWU that spoke of peace, reconciliation, and reformation perpetrate such a loathsome punishment against another human being? Sure, the Deviants were troublemakers who held back society. Sure, they needed to be caught and reconditioned, and those who couldn't be reprogrammed had to be eliminated. He'd come to grips with that long ago. There was no swifter and painless death than by the guillotine. But this? This was beyond barbaric, beyond anything that resembled human decency.

More importantly, how could he have worked for and with people who could do this to a fellow human?

He scanned the line of crosses extending so far into the distance there seemed no end to them. There had to be hundreds, maybe thousands, a warning to all who entered the city.

Tori cried for what seemed like an hour, alternating between leaning forward with her palms in the dirt and hugging herself. Finally, her wails reduced to sobs and she sat upright, trying to catch her breath. Leaning her head on Thomas's shoulder, she let out a final cry and said, "It's just so hard, Thomas. It's so hard. I don't know how to go on."

"But you *will* go on." He rubbed her arm. "You will. Because you're strong, Tori. You always have been. You just never knew it."

She half-laughed, half-cried and looked up at him. Sunlight sparkled in her moist eyes. He ran a thumb over her cheek, wiping away her tears. "I'm sorry, Tori. I.... " He swallowed. "Had no idea the NWU committed such atrocities."

She nodded, starting to glance back up at the man, then must have thought better of it. Instead, she scanned the row of similar crosses stretching into the distance. "I know, Thomas. It's okay. These people are in heaven now, receiving a crown and many rewards for their sacrifice. They did not love their lives to the death..."

Thomas withheld a huff of disbelief. What kind of God required such a sacrifice in order to be rewarded?

"Come on. Let's get back to the others." He helped her stand, and when she fell against him, he turned her away from the cross and hugged her tighter than he had in a long while. They stood there for several minutes. Honestly, Thomas could hold her like that all day. It felt right. It felt good. He loved that she leaned on him now, that he could be of some help.

Finally, she pushed from him, and he eased a lock of hair from her face and kissed her forehead. Then turning, they headed back.

Surely now, Tori would decide to not proceed any further into Atlanta.

That's when they saw Sara, standing just yards away, staring at the crucified man, a look of abject horror on her face.

*And he had power to give life unto the image of the beast,
that the image of the beast should both speak, and cause that
as many as would not worship the image of the beast should be
killed.
And he causeth all, both small and great, rich and poor,
free and bond, to receive a mark in their right hand, or in their
foreheads: And that no man might buy or sell, save he that had
the mark, or the name of the beast, or the number of his name.
Revelation 13:15-17*

Chapter 23

Tori did her best to console Sara, but the girl was beyond any human comfort. So, she prayed for her, over her, laying hands on the poor woman, doing all she could to eject the spirit of fear and allow God's comfort to flood her. Finally, her trembling ceased, her lip stopped quivering, and her tears stopped flowing.

"I can't...I can't..." she kept saying. "They'll do that to us."

Tori wished she could assure the girl that wouldn't happen, but in the Tribulation many of God's saints would die for their faith. The book of Revelation described countless multitudes who'd been beheaded standing before the throne, demanding justice.

"Whatever happens, Sara." Tori grabbed her hand and gave it a squeeze. "God will be with us. He will never leave us, and He will see us through. Any momentary pain will soon be forgotten in light of the joys of heaven."

The girl nodded, but tears started to flow again nonetheless, making Tori doubt about going further into Atlanta.

Yet, at the Holy Spirit's leading, onward she went, feeling like a shepherd leading the sheep to the slaughter.

Aaron took over comforting Sara while Brianna walked beside Tori. Behind them, Thomas held Carla's hand or rather,

Carla held his hand as she happily strolled along, humming praise songs, and completely oblivious to any danger at all. Ah, to be an innocent child again.

The deeper they went into the city, the noisier and dirtier things became. Human excrement littered the streets. Garbage mounded in piles or drifted about on the wind. And the stench. Like nothing Tori had every smelled. It wasn't just the odor of sewage, garbage, and human sweat, but there was an added stink of rotten eggs, almost like sulfur.

The spiritual scent of evil.

The people who walked about barely glanced their way, and when they did, it was with hatred. Tori couldn't help but notice that their movements seemed almost robotic, their eyes devoid of life.

More than once, she wanted to turn back.

More than once, she asked the Lord if she was on the right track.

Up ahead, skyscrapers came into view, reaching toward the gray sky as if seeking some meaning to the madness below.

"What the heck is that?" Brianna gestured to one of the buildings…*no, not a building*. It moved. It spoke. A giant?

Heart scizing, Tori inched forward, edging around a tall office complex to their right.

She halted. Terror fired across every nerve.

There, standing at least a mile away was a giant Immu Aali. He rose far above all of Atlanta's skyscrapers as he gazed down upon the people and smiled.

Smiled?

Sara screamed.

Brianna grabbed Carla and drew her close.

With arms outstretched, the giant statue—or was it a hologram?—spoke in a voice that thundered so loud, it shook the ground beneath them.

"Be at peace, my children. I am your savior. I am your god. Bow to me and receive my mark, and you will live forever!"

Tori wanted to shout, *Blasphemy*! Instead, she pressed a hand over her stomach and bent over as a burst of nausea churned in her belly.

Rushing to her, Thomas gripped her hand. "Are you all right?"

"Yes." She rose, forcing down her fear, her disgust.

Thomas looked up at the statue. "It's Aali," he said with wonder. "Or a hologram of him, just like the one in Jerusalem." He blew out a whistle and shook his head. "Looks much more ominous in person."

"It's so real…" Brianna added. "He looks so real."

Aaron merely stared at it, not an ounce of emotion tainting his expression.

"It's the statue everyone must bow to," Tori said. "From the book of Revelation."

Which made her want to run as far away from it as possible. *Go a little farther…*

Against everything within her, Tori obeyed.

Brianna grabbed her arm, stopping her. "Shouldn't we stay away from it?"

"I agree!" Aaron held onto Sara, who seemed to be having trouble standing. "This is insane."

Even Thomas looked at her with skepticism.

"Just a bit closer," Tori said, her eyes fixed on Sara, who seemed calm, almost euphoric from only moments before. "What's wrong with her?"

Aaron continued to hold her up. "She's fine. Better now."

"What did you do?" Tori started for him, anger simmering in her gut, but the statue of Aali spoke again, this time drowning out her thoughts and stealing her breath.

"Come, children. Taste and see what I offer is good. Eternal life!"

Thomas stood in her way. "Come on, Tori. Let's get this over with. Go have your look and then let's ditch this city. I have a bad feeling about this."

"Oh, really? A bad feeling?" She hated the sarcasm in her voice, but her anger got the best of her. "This is your world government's plan to enslave mankind and send them all to hell. And you call it a bad feeling?"

Jerking from his touch, she forged down Peachtree Street, crowded with cars and people, drones and cyborgs, finally turning another corner, where they had a clearer vision of the monstrosity.

Mobs of people congregated at the foot of the statue around an NWU Medical Processing Center. Bands of troops assisted each person who came forward to bow before the statue. As soon as they did, they were led to stand in another line that entered the medical center where they would, no doubt, receive the Mark of the Beast. Of course they didn't know it was the Mark of the Beast. They thought it was a vaccine/Quantum tattoo that would not only cure all their diseases but give them eternal life. Not to mention enable them to buy and sell so they wouldn't starve.

What an evil, evil deception! She wanted to shout, to warn the crowd about to make the worst decision of their lives. Unavoidable tears spilled down her cheeks. There were so many of them…so many willingly lining up to receive something that would sentence them to hell for all eternity.

A loud clap of thunder rumbled, causing everyone to look up. A bright flash sped across the sky from east to west—like lightning, but slower and much, much brighter—even as a voice shouted so loudly Tori covered her ears.

"If any man worship the Beast and his image, and receive his mark in his forehead, or in his hand, the same shall drink of the wine of the wrath of God, which is poured out without mixture into the cup of his indignation; and he shall be tormented with fire and brimstone in the presence of the holy angels, and in the presence of the Lamb: And the smoke of their torment ascendeth up for ever and ever: and they have no rest day nor night, who worship the Beast and his image, and whosoever receiveth the mark of his name."

The voice ceased, leaving behind an ominous echo as everyone continued to stare above in silence. One man broke from one of the lines in and raced away. The troops were on him in seconds, dragging him to a separate building beside the medical one.

"They'll kill him," Tori mumbled, still stunned by the voice from heaven.

The statue of Aali raised his fist in the air. "Pay no attention to our enemy. He causes fear. He wants you dead. Look what happened to that poor soul who listened to him." He gestured to the building where the man had been dragged. But soon, a smile—a malignant smile—wiped away the hologram's rage. "Now, who wishes to live forever?"

And just like that, the mob cheered, ignoring God's warning.

The line started moving again.

"I don't get it," Thomas said. "This is in your book?"

"Yep. Including the angel shouting his warning above us."

"Angel, eh?" Thomas glanced up again.

Leave now, daughter.

The words were clear and strong.

Rising, Tori flung her pack over her shoulder. "Let's get out of here."

"Finally," Aaron said.

"Wait." She fixed a pointed gaze at the old man. "Where's Sara?"

He shrugged and looked around. "Dunno."

Brianna screamed, pointing at something over Tori's shoulder.

Sara! She was moving forward in a line of people about to bow before the statue.

"No! No!" Tagas drew his spiked hammer and marched after Sara.

Arithem leapt in front of him and placed a hand on his chest, holding him back. "Nay, my friend. There's naught you can do. She has made her choice."

Tagas knew he was right. Knew he had no permission to fight the demons escorting Sara to her death. Still, it took everything in him to not take them both on and send them to the pit before their time. He gripped his hammer so tight, pain spiked across his fingers.

"'Twas not her choice!" He gestured to the beast behind them. "He gave her sorcery which dulls her mind."

"Aye, and she chose that, as well." Arithem glanced over his shoulder at the young girl now bowing before the statue. The sight brought unusual sorrow to his soul, and he could only hope his own ward would not make the same horrible mistake.

Zarall approached and gripped Tagas' shoulder. "I'm sorry. None of our wards are assured they will make it to the end. 'Tis the Father's gift of free will which allows them to fall."

Tearing his gaze from Sara, Tagas spun about, hefted his hammer toward the beast, and growled.

Ducking, the old man grimaced, his dark eyes sparkling with malevolent spite, taunting Tagas to attack, for he knew that doing so would be a defiance of the Commander's orders.

"Ignore him," Onafiel said. "His time is short, and his end is in the lake of fire."

At that, the beast spat a clump of black slime onto the street.

Tori's wail brought their attention back to their wards. Zarall moved to stand by her side as she attempted to run after Sara.

Thankfully, Thomas stopped her and held her tight.

She fell against him, then dropped to her knees in agony.

"Will she overcome this tragedy?" Zarall asked Arithem. "'Tis almost too much to bear. She feels responsible for them all."

"She is strong." Arithem nodded at her. "She must make it. She must overcome."

Anahel gripped the handle of his mace and growled at the demons surrounding them. He and Onafiel were doing their best to keep the evil horde away from their wards. "Why does she not see the beast for who he is?"

"She will," Zarall said. "She has to."

"And when she does." Arithem's penetrating gaze pierced the old man. "Her command will send us to battle."

Zarall agreed. "It cannot come soon enough."

The next two days passed in a blur. Tori could not get the vision of Sara entering the Medical Center to receive the *Mark* out of her mind. It replayed over and over, like some loathsome nightmare. And each time, she couldn't help but think it was all her fault. She should have been more attentive, more understanding. She should have kept a closer eye on her. She should have run after her, yanked her from the line, and dragged her back.

But Thomas had forcibly kept her from doing so.

At first, she hated him for it, but inwardly she knew he most likely had saved her life. The center was swarming with NWU troops, and they would never allow anyone to stop what had to be their strict orders to get everyone injected with the Seal of Satan.

Sara had stopped at the threshold of the NWU Medical facility. Just for a second. She'd glanced over her shoulder as if she wasn't sure about what she was doing. But before Tori could even wave or yell, the darkness inside the building reached out for her and swallowed her up. Since then, Tori had been unable to go an hour without crying. Sara was lost. Hopelessly lost, and she would spend eternity in hell. The thought was so overwhelmingly torturous, Tori lost the will to go on, the will to eat, the will to do much of anything, even the will to pray.

Honestly, she was mad at God. He'd purposely brought them to that place…to that very spot where people bowed before the Beast. Why? A test for Sara? A recovering addict suffering from detox? A weak, new believer? Why would God give her such an impossible temptation?

Thomas had repeatedly tried to console her, but she ignored him. Brianna remained quiet, just as upset as Tori was. Yet now, as they plodded along in an open field outside the small town of Dawsonville, she glanced at Aaron hobbling along with his cane to her right. She was sure he'd given Sara something, some drug to help with her detox, but he'd repeatedly denied it. He was lying. She knew it. But why? Who was he really? Doubts crowded her mind about the old man. She needed to ask the Lord to reveal the truth to her, but she was mad at Him at the moment.

"I don't know how to help her," Thomas said to Brianna walking beside him.

Brianna sighed and shifted Callie to her other hip. "Give her time." She brushed a tear from her eye. "Losing Sara…" She shook her head, gathering her own emotions. "Well, it's just too much. She's seen too much pain. We all have."

Thomas wasn't sure if getting this *Mark* was an eternal death sentence like they said, but he, too, was sad to see Sara go. The girl had been making progress, growing stronger each day. Well, until she'd witnessed the crucifixion. That may have been the final straw that pushed her over the edge.

It nearly pushed him over the edge, too. He could hardly believe the NWU he'd once served could perform such barbarism. Sure, he knew they crucified some Deviants, those they wanted to make an example of. But he'd never witnessed a crucifixion, never really considered how brutal and cruel it was. No, the NWU was certainly not the kind, benevolent, world government he'd once believed in. In all the cities and towns they'd traveled through, he'd witnessed none of the advancements they claimed to be enacting, not even a hint. In fact, he'd seen nothing but destruction, devastation, crime, filth, garbage, hunger, and disease.

"But she won't even eat." He ran an arm over the sweat on his brow. "She hardly says a word."

Aaron hobbled up on Thomas's other side. "Give her time, son. It was a shock, and she cared a great deal for the girl. I did too." He muttered out a sob that seemed devoid of real sorrow.

What was Thomas thinking? Aaron had been a great comfort and help to Sara. Of course he cared about her. They were all in mourning.

Even Carla, walking beside her mother was not her cheerful self.

"You were a great help to her, Aaron," Thomas smiled at his friend. "I'm sure you're feeling the loss too."

"I am." Aaron gripped Thomas's shoulder and gave it a squeeze. "I am, son."

Excusing himself, Thomas moved to walk beside Tori. "You really should eat something."

She flashed the glimmer of a smile his way but said nothing. It was the first smile he'd seen on her lips in days, and he'd take what he could get.

"We close?" he asked.

She nodded. "Almost to the outskirts of the Chattahoochee National Forest. Then I'll try to contact Nyla."

He gripped her hand and squeezed it. "Then your job will be done."

"My job will never be done in the Tribulation," she shot back harshly, jerking back her hand. After several seconds, she added, "I'm sorry. Yes, you're right. I won't be totally responsible for anyone's life anymore."

A hawk squawked overhead as they reached the edge of the field and stepped onto a dirt road.

"It isn't your fault, you know," he said.

"So you told me." She halted, shielding her eyes from the sun. "What is that?"

"What?" He followed her gaze where a dark line, or maybe a road? cut across the landscape.

"It looks like a huge crater." Tori pulled out her map and studied it. "It's not on the map."

"Hmm. Maybe it's not too deep," Thomas offered.

But after they walked another mile and halted at the edge, it might as well have been the Grand Canyon. At least a hundred feet deep and a mile across, it stretched as far as the eye could see to both their right and their left.

Tori sank to her knees. "This isn't supposed to be here. It will take us weeks to find a way around it. Nyla may not wait for us."

"Why? Where else could she go?"

"She gave me only two weeks to get here before they planned on going deeper into the forest." She ran a hand through her mass of black hair and looked up at him. "And it's already been two weeks. We're never going to make it."

*Wherefore God also hath highly exalted him, and given
him a name which is above every name: That at the name of
Jesus every knee should bow, of things in heaven, and things in
earth, and things under the earth; And that every tongue
should confess that Jesus Christ is Lord, to the glory of God
the Father.*
Philippians 2:9-11

Chapter 24

Tori stood and tucked the map back inside her pack. Hot
wind whipped up from the canyon and blasted over
them as they stared dumbfounded at the obstacle before them.
She wanted to cry, but she had no tears left. Instead she just
stood there, longing to pray, but not even sure how to do that
anymore.

The sun sank lower in the western sky as dark clouds rolled
in above them. Callie began to fuss, and Brianna slipped away
to feed her.

Aaron shook his head. "Guess we need to go back and find
shelter for the night."

No! She didn't want to go back. She didn't want to retreat.
They'd come too far.

Father, help! Finally, she cried out to the only One who'd
always been there for her.

Precious daughter…

The comforting greeting eased through her like sweet
molasses, shoving aside all her anger and misgivings.

I'm sorry, Father. I'm sorry I was angry.

Open your eyes, was the only response.

She spun around to find Aaron waving his cane over the
field they'd just passed through. Odd.

A fork of white-hot lightning shot from the clouds and
struck the field. Instantly, the dry grass burst into flames.

What the heck?

A gust of wind swirled around them, passing over the field and tossing embers through the air in every direction. Other parts of the field soon ignited. Tori could only stare at what quickly became a wall of fire.

"What the.... ?" Pivoting, Thomas uttered a curse word.

Brianna drew her children close and exchanged a frightened glance with Tori.

She turned to the right, seeking a path of escape, but a blazing tree had already fallen across the dirt, blocking their way.

"This way!" She started toward the left, but in the distance, a field of blazing brush ran right up to the canyon.

A gust of smoke nearly suffocated Tori as she stormed toward Aaron. "What did you do?"

Backing away, the old man stumbled over his cane. "What?"

Halting before him, she poked his chest with her finger. "I saw you. Waving your cane over the field. What did you do?" She seethed, glaring at him. "*What* are you?"

"Tori!" Grabbing her arm, Thomas yanked her back, coughing. "Stop it. He's just an old man."

"No, he's not." The voice came from Carla, who moved to stand between Thomas and Tori. Everyone's gazes latched onto the little girl.

"He doesn't have an angel," she said.

Aaron laughed uncomfortably.

Thomas joined him.

But both Tori and Brianna stared at the little girl, blinking.

Tori knelt before her. "Carla, can you tell me what Onafiel looks like."

The girl nodded, her curls bouncing in the wind. "He's kinda short, about the size of Thomist." She gazed up at him then back down again. "He's gold and bright light. And he has wings."

Tori shook her head as the realization hit her. Onafiel wasn't some imaginary friend. He was an angel! "And you're sure Aaron doesn't have an angel with him?"

"This is ridiculous!" Aaron shouted.

The little girl shook her head. "No angel."

Rising to her feet, Tori faced Aaron. "Now, I know exactly what to do with you."

"Finally!" Zarall exclaimed, drawing his throwing ax. "She sees!"

Arithem continued to watch. "Not yet, my friend, but she is well on her way."

The beast sneered at the Holy Angels, then feigned a look of innocence at the humans.

"What are you talking about? This is insanity." He gestured toward little Carla. "You listen to the imaginings of a three-year-old!"

"No." Tori spoke with authority, making Zarall beam with pride. "I speak on the authority of the Most High."

"Ah ha!" Zarall shouted.

Onafiel hovered over Carla and Callie, lest the beast unleash a curse upon them, while Anahel stood before Brianna, brandishing his mace.

Thomas slipped between Tori and the hellion. "Come on now, Tori. We are all upset about Sara, but Aaron—"

"This isn't about Sara," she snapped, whipping a strand of hair from her face yet never loosening her gaze upon the beast. Light penetrated her mind, visible light in the spirit realm, light that chased away the darkness of deception.

"She is figuring it out now," Arithem said to Zarall.

Pushing past Thomas, Tori approached the beast. "It was you. *You* called in that drone attack that nearly killed us all, you generated that tsunami, you created that tornado!"

The beast pointed his cane at her to keep her from advancing further. "Preposterous! How could I have done such things?"

"You," Tori continued, "gave Sara something to dull her senses, soften her fears, so—" Tori gulped down emotion, shaking off her rage. "So she would more easily receive the Mark of the Beast."

The fallen one tsked. "You're nuts! The girl was petrified after she saw those people crucified. I tried to console her as best I could." He shifted his eyes over the group. "I told her not to go to Atlanta, didn't I?"

"Tori," Thomas said. "This is crazy. He did try to talk you out of going to Atlanta. He's one of you, for God's sake!"

"No, he is not," she responded, keeping her eyes on the beast.

Arithem drew his golden blade. "Wait for my command," he told the other angels.

Zarall could hear his own breath, feel his muscles contract in anticipation.

"One thing I can't figure out," Tori said, hands on her hips. "Is why you didn't want us to go to Atlanta so bad. Seems it worked out in your favor in the end."

The beast's gaze swung to Thomas ever so briefly before returning to Tori.

She glanced at Thomas, the light inside of her growing brighter and brighter. "Ah… you didn't want him to see the evil your boss is perpetrating, is that it?"

Thomas huffed and moved to stand beside the vile creature. "What are you talking about, Tori? Aaron has been like a father to all of us. He's been a huge help."

Arithem frowned. "Still, he does not see."

The son of Adam might have expected his friend to smile at him for his defense, but instead the beast stared at the four mighty angels, weapons drawn, surrounding him.

"Get away from him, Thomas," Tori commanded.

"Why?"

But Tori was already speaking.

"In the name of Jesus, the Holy One of Israel, the true Messiah, the Son of the Living God, the Commander of Heaven's Armies," Tori began, and with each title, the facade cloaking the beast began to fade. Like old paint peeling off a wall, bit by bit his appearance transformed—skin into scales, gray hair to black, exposing the fallen one beneath. He rose to his full height, nearly as tall as Arithem. Massive muscles bulged on his arms and thighs. Long black strands of slimy hair hung to his waist. His dark eyes became pools of sludge. Bronze armor covered his chest and torso. His skin, which once reflected the glory of God, now sizzled and smoked like day old coals. Opening his mouth, he let out a growl so loud, Tori's hair flew behind her.

"You will all die anyway!" he shouted.

Thomas leapt away from him.

Brianna began to pray in tongues.

Tori continued. "I rebuke you in the name of Jesus. You have no authority here. Be gone at once!"

"Now we fight!" Arithem gave the charge.

The mighty angels rushed the fallen one, slicing and hacking and pummeling him so hard, he could barely fight back. Arithem sliced the beast's arm nearly in two, Zarall tossed his ax into the angel's gut, Anahel struck him repeatedly with his mace, and Onafiel stabbed him with his long knife. Still the beast managed to cut Arithem's leg and toss him aside before he slammed the hilt of his blade across Zarall's skull, knocking him to the ground. All the while, he bragged of his superiority over them.

Quickly recovering, Arithem and Zarall joined Anahel and Onafiel and continued to fight, amazed at the beast's power. Finally, limping and injured, and knowing he stood no chance if he continued, the mighty fallen one took flight, shouting blasphemies at them in a cackling tone before he disappeared into the clouds.

Breath heaving, the warrior angels nodded at each other in approval of the fight.

"He was one of our enemy's strongest generals. We did well," Zarall said.

"Aye." Arithem glanced at his ward, who stood in shock at what he had seen. "Maybe now, he will open his eyes to the truth."

But Zarall's gaze was on Tori. "She has one last test to pass. And I fear 'twill be her biggest yet."

Something wasn't right. At his desk in his new plush office, Kyle flipped through the latest reports on his laptop—videos, photos, drone captures, and information Jura had given him from the spy he'd planted in Thomas's group. He'd never seen so many tragedies befall so small a band of Deviants. A drone strike, tsunami, a tornado, and most recently, a brush fire that seemed to hem them in. He'd add starvation to the list, but somehow Thomas and his friends found food every day. An impossible task without a good NWU Social Credit Score and Lord Aali's new quantum mark. Regardless, over the past three weeks, Kyle had enjoyed watching Thomas, the once arrogant, sophisticated, wealthy snob transform into a filthy, bedraggled emaciated version of himself. Why, the man looked worse than some of the Deviants they had in lockup.

So what was bugging him? He sat back in his chair and stared at the screen where the latest satellite footage captured the group traipsing across a barren field, stopping suddenly, and then turning to see the field catch ablaze by lightning. His eyes focused on the old man Jura said was the spy. If his sole purpose was to get the group to this UnderHisWings hideout as quickly as possible, why did it seem every tragedy possible occurred to prevent just that? Jura had said the spy was a Neflams, even better, a father of the Neflams. Shouldn't he then be powerful enough to either avoid or stop such tragedies altogether?

He clicked on the Update button. No new information. The same thing it had said an hour ago and an hour before that.

Unacceptable. Perhaps he should send in some drones for a closer look.

Wait.

Minimizing the current tab, he clicked on a search engine and hunted for the tsunami that had struck the coast of Georgia two weeks ago. Nothing came up.

He looked for the tornado outside of Atlanta. From all accounts, no such event had occurred.

Anger flared in his belly. Why? Who was trying to stop Thomas and his friends from reaching the Deviant hideout?

There was only one person...or rather, one *being*...who knew.

Two hours later, Kyle knocked on Jura's chamber, located in the tunnels beneath the New World Faith Reformation Headquarters, angry that the Tall White would not see him before now.

His anger dissipated once he entered the room, or rooms. He'd been here once before when Jura had summoned him to convey the progress of his spy, but he hadn't recalled how opulent it was. Everything was white, from the walls to the couches and tables, and even Jura's desk. All except the floor, which was a checkerboard of white and black.

Turning from his desk, where he stood looking at something, Jura smiled at Kyle, that approving, yet seductive smile that seemed to erase all his misgivings.

The smile quickly faded as he gestured for Kyle to sit and approached with a look of apprehension on his face. In fact, Kyle had never seen the Tall White so unsettled. He'd always been the perfect example of peace, always full of assurance and comfort. And praise. Oh, how Kyle needed the praise.

"What is it you desire, Kyle?" Jura sat across from him and poured steaming liquid into two cups.

"You seem upset," Kyle asked. "Has something happened?"

Jura passed him a cup. "Nothing to concern you."

The mug began to quiver in his hands, and Kyle set it down. "I've been wondering." He drew a deep breath to calm his nerves. "It seems the spy you placed with Thomas has been trying to keep them from their destination."

A moment passed in which Jura studied him. "Why say such a thing?"

"I checked on all the tragedies that have happened to them, and none of them actually occurred. Seems they were somehow generated or maybe part of an interdimensional event."

"Hmm." Jura curled both arms over the back of the couch. His lips twisted slightly, and Kyle gulped. Had he upset him?

"Is your spy trying to keep them from UnderHisWings?" Kyle pressed.

Cocking his head, he gave Kyle a sideways grin. "You are a very clever lad, aren't you?"

Yet this time, the words didn't seem like a compliment. "So, it's true. But why?"

Jura leaned forward and took a sip from his cup, ever so calmly, before he looked up at Kyle. "It is better Thomas and the Deviants die before they reach this UnderHisWings." He spat out the last word with more disdain than Kyle remembered hearing from him.

"What?" Kyle stood. "UnderHisWings is the top Deviant hideout in the North American Region. How could finding its location be a bad thing?"

"Sit!" Jura spoke with commanding authority, his eyes blue icicles.

Kyle lowered to the couch, suddenly fearful of this creature before him.

"Do you dare question my decisions, Kyle?" Gone was the affection and pride from Jura's voice.

"No." Kyle stared at the floor. "I just don't understand."

"Then know this, young human, should Tori and Thomas make it to UnderHisWings safely, their power increases tenfold. We may never be able to defeat them."

Kyle dared to look up at Jura. "What power?"

"The power of their God." Jura's lips twisted as if he tasted something sour. And for a brief second, the Tall White's eyes turned a deep black.

"But if we know where they are, surely we—"

"Nay!" Jura's shout sent Kyle's heart thumping so loudly, he was sure Jura could hear it.

"It won't matter." Jura waved his long fingernails through the air. "They must die before they reach it."

"Then why doesn't your spy just kill them?"

Jura's eyes flared. "Because he cannot! He cannot touch them until they willfully step away from our enemy's protection." Smoke emerged from his lips even as he smiled. "Like young Sara."

Kyle folded his hands together. He could care less about Sara. What he *did* care about was his promotion—a promotion he wouldn't get if he didn't find the Deviant hideout. "Killing a few Deviants is nothing compared to finding UnderHisWings."

"Stop saying that word!" Jura pressed hands over his ears and walked to his desk.

When he spun back around, he wore that alluring smile of his. "We all must make sacrifices in this war."

It was at that very moment that Kyle realized Jura had used him, lied to him, told him what he'd wanted to hear in order to get what he wanted.

He'd been betrayed, just like his parents had done when they'd left him, and Nyla, his sister, who had abandoned him as well.

Standing, Kyle asked for the latest report from the spy, not that it would do any good. But Jura shifted his feet and looked away, finally saying, "He is no longer in play."

"Then how—"

"I am making other plans," Jura said.

After nodding and exiting the room, Kyle took the elevator to the floors above. *Yeah, well, I'm making plans of my own.*

If ye have faith as a grain of mustard seed, ye shall say
unto this mountain, Remove hence to yonder place; and it shall
remove; and nothing shall be impossible unto you.
Matthew 17:20

Chapter 25

Thomas had no time to absorb what had just happened, not the freakish vision of Aaron turning into some devilish monster, nor the gleaming bright blades hefted by shimmering men fighting him off, and especially not the moment he disappeared, leaving behind a puff of sulfurous smoke.

He had no time because the fire moved quickly toward them, filling the air with smoke and searing their skin with the heat.

Tori spun around and dashed for the chasm, then glanced back at the fire. "We're trapped."

Hoisting Carla in his arms, he moved to stand beside her as Brianna came up on his left.

He glanced below. No cliffs, no rock jettisons they could lower down onto. Nothing but sheer rock as smooth as butter.

He hugged Carla close and looked back at the fire. There was no way out. They were all going to burn alive.

Mind, soul, and *spirit* still buzzing after rebuking and casting Aaron away, or whoever he was, Tori once again felt her heart sink to the depths at their present predicament. *Lord? Please, Lord?* She pleaded with the Almighty for an answer. Anything. After all they'd been through, all they'd endured, this could not be God's will.

"Carla?" She moved a lock of curls from the little girl's face as Thomas held her close. "Where are the angels now?"

Lifting her head from Thomas's shoulders, she glanced about and coughed. "They are here. Onafiel smiled at me."

"Did he say anything?"

She shook her head, plopped her thumb back in her mouth and leaned back on Thomas's shoulder.

Nothing. Could the mighty warriors not help them? It made no sense.

Closing her eyes, she lowered her head. *What do I do? What do I do, Lord?*

A vision of the drone attack appeared, followed by the tsunami, then the tornado, and finally the fire. *Why are you showing me this, Lord?* Yet… all those tragedies had happened when Aaron was with them. Had he conjured them up like she assumed? Spiritual events, not physical. And if that were true, then she must battle in the spirit and not in the flesh.

Emboldened, she faced the fire and stretched forth her hand. "Be gone in the name of Jesus!" she shouted over the crackling flames. After everything that had occurred, she fully expected them to dissipate, even disappear completely.

But the blazing fire remained. Bright orange and yellow flames leapt for the dark sky higher and higher and getting closer and closer.

Coughing, Tori covered her mouth and backed away.

Thomas shouted something to her, but she couldn't hear over the roar of the fire. The heat seared her skin. Callie screamed.

Spinning around, she faced the canyon once again, heart in her throat. This doesn't make sense. *It doesn't make sense. Lord!*

Wait. Perhaps the fire was natural, instigated by Aaron, yes, but started from an actual lightning strike.

That would mean…that *must* mean that the canyon was not real.

Walk, my precious one.

Thomas had resolved in his mind that he and his friends would burn to death. He only hoped that the smoke knocked them all out before the flames struck. At least they would go in peace and not in agonizing pain. On his right, Brianna held a screaming Callie close, trying to console her, while he clung tightly to Carla, who wasn't making a sound, not a whimper or cry. In fact, her body was not tight with fright at all.

To his right, Tori smiled at him. Smiled? No, he was probably seeing things through the smoky haze.

But what happened next, he knew was real.

She touched his arm, gave him a squeeze, and nodded at him in a way that said everything would be all right.

Then she squared her shoulders and stepped into thin air over the canyon.

"No!" Thomas screamed. Had she chosen falling to her death over being burned alive?

He reached for her, but his hand struck air. Slamming his eyes shut, he refused to watch the woman he loved fall to her death.

But there was no scream. No cry of despair from Brianna. Nothing. He opened his eyes.

Tori stood a yard from the edge of the cliff on nothing but air.

It was the fire, the terror. It was all driving him mad. There was no other explanation.

Smoke enveloped him, and he coughed it away, staring at the strange sight, but not believing his eyes.

Tori took another step and turned. A wide smile brightened her face. Cupping her hands, she yelled something, but Thomas couldn't make it out. He couldn't think, couldn't breathe.

"It's not real!" He finally heard her shout.

She held out a hand and gestured for him and Brianna to follow her.

Laughing beside him, Brianna took a tentative first step, then another and another until she stood beside Tori.

Flames scorched Thomas's back. He only had minutes before he and Carla would burn alive. Death at his back. Death at his front. What did it matter? He'd take a freefall over being burnt to a crisp.

Here goes nothing...and everything.

Sucking in as much air as he could, he stepped over the cliff's edge.

And the air transformed into dirt, solid and strong, beneath their feet.

"She passed! She did it. Did you see that?" Zarall asked his friends as he leapt up and down for joy.

Arithem gripped his shoulder and smiled. "Indeed, my friend. She has passed the Father's tests. 'Tis great news!"

Onafiel hovered in the air over the children. "And they are all safe!"

Anahel nodded. "The beast is gone, and they soon will be at UnderHisWings."

Then why did sorrow weigh upon Arithem? He studied Thomas as he followed Tori down the dirt road. "Alas, even after all he has seen, he still has not submitted to the Commander."

Zarall sighed. "He is in shock. Give him time."

"He doesn't have much time." Arithem frowned. "Soon the Father will allow his biggest temptation, and in truth, I am not sure what this son of Adam will choose."

Thomas barely noticed the dramatic change in landscape as they entered what used to be called the Chattahoochee National Forest, according to Tori. They went from a flat country road surrounded by dry fields to a hilly landscape thick with trees. Or rather what used to be trees. Most were nothing but charred trunks devoid of leaves, although there were patches of green springing up here and there, a testimony to the stubbornness of life.

Which led him back to the one thing he'd been avoiding thinking about. Eternal life. Offered by both Lucifer and the God of the Bible. One was evil, one was good. One lied. One spoke the truth. Both had power, extraordinary power. But which one led to life, *real* life?

Tori and the Deviants said the God of the Bible was the real God, and that He was good and holy and loving.

The Neflams said it was Lucifer who wanted the best for mankind, a good god who gave mankind freedom to live as they desired, who wanted to free people from the demanding restrictions and vengeful wrath of God.

Thomas had chosen to believe the latter because it made sense with what he knew of the God of the Bible and all His rules and regulations. Tori's God really did seem like a bully, like an angry God ready to unleash judgment on poor mankind.

But what Thomas had witnessed in the past three weeks threw all of his beliefs into a chaotic whirlwind. He didn't know what to think anymore. So he chose not to think at all.

Especially not about Aaron, whom he'd come to respect and care for, whom he'd looked at as a father figure. Obviously, he wasn't human. Maybe a Neflams of some kind? A spy. A liar. Was anything he'd said to Thomas true?

Dejected, he plodded along, following these ever-cheerful Deviants to a hideout where he doubted he'd fit in. Tori and Brianna never ceased to talk about the recent miracles of their God—as they called them—and Carla had resumed her constant singing.

And although it was nice to be around happy people, and he'd grown to care for them all, Thomas battled a war within himself as memories of his prior life rose to taunt him. Oh, how he longed for a shower, a shave, some decent, clean clothes, and his soft mattress. Even more, he longed to regain his position, power, and prestige, to be valued for his opinion by those above him. To be close to the people who made all the decisions.

Yet here he was, exhausted beyond belief, muscles aching, stomach growling, filthy, smelly, and in charge of nothing at all. In fact, he was being led around like a sick puppy by a woman who had broken his heart. He glanced at Tori talking on her SAT phone up ahead before she slammed the antenna down and slipped it back in her pack.

She was a mess, her wild hair hanging in wavy strings, her jeans ripped, her skin smudged with dirt. What a beautiful, strong, remarkable woman. When she looked his way and smiled, he couldn't help the leap of his heart. He loved her. He wondered if he'd ever stopped.

Apparently not, since he'd given up everything to save her and continued to follow her even now.

But would it be enough? For her *and* for him?

"Nyla and Calan are meeting us tomorrow morning just five miles from here," she said excitedly, then glanced upward. "It's getting dark. Let's crash for the night."

Once again, Thomas settled down to enjoy his favorite time of each day. After partaking of stale bread and handfuls of wild blackberries Carla had found, they all sank onto beds of leaves under a dark sky, devoid of light. Either there were clouds above them, or the sky was too hazy for any stars to poke through. And without a fire, the night quickly became pitch black.

Tori lowered beside him and laid her head on his shoulder. "Crazy day, huh?"

"That's an understatement." He snorted. "First my friend turns into a grotesque monster and flies away and then we walk over thin air that instantly turns into solid ground. Yeah, I'd say it was a crazy day."

She laughed. "Nobody ever said God was boring."

Thomas raked back his filthy hair. "I still don't get what happened."

"Aaron was our enemy all along, trying to kill us and stop us from getting to UnderHisWings. I should have seen it. I should have sensed it."

Thomas shook his head. "You aren't psychic. Give yourself a break."

"No, but I have a prophetic gift from God. There's no excuse."

Thomas swung an arm around her. "You take way too much on yourself, Tori. You've done a great job keeping us safe, getting us here."

She sighed. "Not Sara."

A night warbler sounded from far away, even as a breeze stirred the leaves on the ground.

"So, tell me," Thomas asked. "What was Aaron? Not human, I'm guessing." He chuckled. "And how did you get rid of him?"

"Not sure what he was. Maybe a fallen angel. He was pretty powerful." She drew a deep breath. "And I didn't get rid of him. God did. The name of Jesus, the most powerful name ever. You know, it's like the story in the Bible when Moses' snakes ate up Pharaoh's snakes."

"Say what?"

"Man, for a pastor, you sure don't know your Bible."

He shrugged.

"Moses went to Pharaoh in Egypt to demand he let the Israelites go. But Pharaoh's magicians got their power from Satan, and they turned their staffs into snakes. So Moses threw down his rod, and God turned it into a snake that ate up the magician's snakes."

"Hmm. Sounds a bit fantastic."

She raised her head to look at him, but he couldn't see her eyes. "Don't you see? God is always more powerful than Satan. God is the Creator. Satan is a created being. Oh, sorry, guess that's your god."

"No. Not sure about that."

"Really?"

Thomas reached up, seeking her face, and upon finding her cheek, he brushed his hands over it. "I've seen too much to deny that your God is not only powerful but good."

"There's hope for you yet, Thomas Benton."

He sensed her smiling

"You're one special lady, Tori. How did I ever let you go all those years ago?"

She huffed. "I've been wondering that myself, but—"

Thomas couldn't stand it another minute. Reaching around her head, he pulled her lips to his.

Ah, sweet nectar! He thought she'd jerk away or slap him, but instead, she sank into the kiss, deepening it, caressing, loving. Her taste—that sweet yet spicy taste of her. Oh, how he'd missed it. His passion grew. He could tell hers did too. It was like the fifteen years between them instantly vanished.

Until she withdrew and sat up, breath coming hard.

"You okay?" he asked.

"No," she responded in a playful tone. "Don't do that again."

"Seemed like you enjoyed it."

"Well, of course I did. I'm not dead." She moved away. "I should go sleep somewhere else."

"No don't." He reached for her. "I promise to be good. Just lie here with me, okay?"

She huffed out a sigh, but finally, she laid her head back on his shoulder and snuggled beside him.

Thomas caressed her forehead ever so slightly, and within minutes her body relaxed, and he knew she'd fallen asleep.

"I love you," he whispered.

The only response he got was her gentle snores.

Crouching behind a patch of burnt shrubbery, Kyle clicked on his tablet and brought into focus a map of the old Chattahoochee National Forest. One of his men had just given him the coordinates where he'd last seen Thomas and Tori. There. He pointed to the exact spot on the map. Just two miles to the northwest. They were close. So close.

After speaking with Jura, Kyle had gained an audience with Regent Landry, explained the situation, and got permission to conduct his own search for the Deviants. Landry still held hope that Thomas was working undercover to expose the location of the infamous hideout. Kyle wasn't sure. But he'd soon know the truth.

He'd put boots on the ground, men skilled in tracking, at the very spot where the fire had broken out in the field, and they'd been following the Deviants ever since, making sure to keep far enough away so as not to be discovered.

"Sergeant Cruz." A voice came over his comms.

Kyle pressed the object in his ear. "Yes."

"I believe the girl just made contact with the other Deviants. They've altered course and are heading northwest."

"Good work. Keep following," Kyle commanded, then turned to Branson, who stood beside him. "Take five men and flank them on the right."

"Yes, sir." The man headed out as Kyle ordered Lampin to do the same on the left.

Then putting his tablet back in his pack, he swung it over his shoulder and gestured for the remaining men to follow him.

He smiled. Soon the Deviants would lead them straight to their hideaway, and by then, Kyle would have them surrounded. He, alone, would be responsible for not only locating the most important Deviant hideout, but for bringing to justice the most notorious Deviants in the North American Region.

He could only imagine the rewards and promotions that awaited him.

For He shall give His angels charge over you, to keep you in all your ways. In their hands they shall bear you up, lest you dash your foot against a stone. Psalm 91:11-12

Chapter 26

Tori could hardly contain her excitement. So much so, she ran through the forest, shoving aside spindly branches and kicking up dry leaves as she went. In the distance, something moved. She halted, peering through the brush. *Wait.* An arm, a face appeared!

Nyla!

Dashing toward her, Tori caught a glimpse of Calan as she flew into Nyla's arms...before she bounced off something around the lady's belly.

Backing away, her gaze dropped to the bump in question. "Oh, my goodness, you're pregnant!"

Nyla grinned and exchanged a glance with Calan. "So it would seem."

"Praise God!" Tori could not help the tears flowing down her cheeks. "You have no idea how happy I am to see you!" She embraced her more gently this time, breathing in the scent of her, all spice and forest.

Calan joined his wife. "We *can* imagine. You look like hell"—he looked behind Tori— "you all do."

Brianna, Callie slung about her chest, along with Thomas and Carla entered the small clearing.

Tori made the introductions as Nyla went to embrace Brianna, then knelt to kiss Carla on the cheek. The little girl giggled.

Calan shook Thomas's hand. "I hear you rescued our Tori from certain death."

Thomas nodded sheepishly and raked back his hair. "Guess you could say that."

"Well, we owe you. And thanks for getting everyone here safe."

"I can't take credit for that." Thomas glanced at Tori. "That was all her doing."

Tori approached. "It was all God's doing." She embraced Calan and stood back. "You guys look great. A little rough around the edges but great."

Nyla's long dark hair hung in waves to her waist, and aside from a few shadows beneath her eyes, she looked as beautiful as ever. Calan, who'd once been a Navy SEAL, had not lost his muscular physique. His hair had gotten a bit longer than his usual military cut and there was more scruff on his jaw, but he beamed at his wife as if she were the most precious thing in the world.

"It's not always been easy, but God takes care of us." Calan glanced around. "Speaking of, it's not safe to be out here." He jerked his head toward Thomas. "Is he with us?"

Frowning, Tori shook her head. "I don't think so."

Thomas huffed. "Standing right here, you know. And, of course, I'm with you!"

"Are you a believer in Jesus or not?" Nyla narrowed her eyes at him. "We can't risk taking a Vice Regent of the New World Faith to our hideout."

Growling, Thomas kicked the dirt, then blew out a frustrated sigh.

He didn't have to say anything for them all to know his answer.

"So, let me get this straight," he began in a sharp, angry tone. "After all I've been through, after all I've done to help your friends get here, you're going to leave me alone in the middle of the forest?"

Tori gulped, her heart suddenly shriveling.

Calan stared at Thomas, his expression sorrowful yet dogmatic. "I'm sorry, man, but we can't risk it." He no sooner said the words, then he suddenly stiffened and looked around.

"What is it?" Tori asked.

Birds chirped, wind rustled through leaves and whistled around burnt trunks, and squirrels scavenged for food. Nothing unusual.

"Evil lurks close by," Calan responded, still peering into the forest.

Tori followed his gaze, searching for signs of demons, but saw none.

Nyla slipped her hand into her husband's. "Calan is rarely wrong about these things."

Tori sought the Spirit within. *Danger.* She sensed it now. But from where? Kneeling before Carla, she moved a curl from the girl's face. "Do you see the angels?"

The little girl nodded. "Onafiel says to run."

Thomas could only stand by and watch as Calan issued orders for them to split up and run in different directions. He whispered something to Tori—no doubt a location where they could meet up again—before he grabbed Nyla's hand and disappeared into the shrubbery.

"I'll go this way," Tori said, pointing to her left. "You go that way," she thumbed to her right. "I'll find you guys later. Don't worry."

Clutching her children, Brianna headed off, gesturing for Thomas to follow.

He shook his head.

She hesitated a moment, fear sparking in her eyes, before she took off, dragging Carla behind her.

Leaving Thomas all alone.

Maybe that was their plan all along, a way to leave him without just walking away.

He heard nothing unusual. Saw nothing unusual, especially not angels or demons. Frowning, he lowered to sit on a nearby boulder to rest his weary feet, battling a vicious mire of emotions, and all the while wondering how it had come to this?

Then he heard it… the softest of sounds, the snap of a twig, the crunch of a leaf, the brief static of a communication device.

Someone was coming.

Leaping upright, he darted after Brianna and the girls, but they were long gone.

Minutes passed, maybe an hour? He lost track of time. In fact, it was *him* who was now lost. Everywhere he turned, everywhere he ran, everything looked the same—burnt trees, shrubs, fallen logs, dead leaves and an occasional squirrel. Why was he running anyway? More importantly, who was he running from? He'd lost Tori and Brianna. Maybe he'd never find them again.

The thought sliced a gaping wound across his heart.

Sweat beaded on his forehead, arms, and neck. Thirsty. He was so thirsty. Yet he kept running. Grabbing his backpack, he attempted to pluck out his water bottle. His foot caught on a fallen branch. Down he went. He tucked his shoulder just before he hit the dirt, hoping to avoid a broken hand. Instead, excruciating pain shot from his ankle.

"Ugh!" Pushing from the ground he sat and pulled his leg toward him, then slowly turned his foot to the right and left.

"Ouch!"

Struggling to rise, he tried to put weight on it, but it hurt like hell. Sprained, at least. Not broken. Either way, he wasn't going to get very far.

Reaching in his pack, he finally got that drink of water, gulping it down and cursing himself for being so clumsy. Some hero he was.

More leaves crunched in the distance, followed by the faintest echo of a human voice.

Grabbing a nearby stick, he rose and hobbled in the other direction, ignoring the pain. Whoever these people were, they probably weren't friendly.

Leaves crackled. Footsteps padded.

Thomas stopped, preparing himself to be caught.

But it was Calan who stepped out of the brush. His breath was heavy, sweat glistened on his forehead, and his wary gaze looked this way and that. "Thomas, what happened?"

"Tripped. Sprained, I think."

"Come on, then." Calan shoved his shoulder beneath Thomas's armpit and swung an arm around his waist. "Let's get you to safety."

They'd only made it a few yards when the sound of someone approaching crackled in the air.

Thomas stopped. "Go. I'm slowing you down."

"No." Calan continued walking, holding Thomas up.

"They'll catch you." Thomas yanked from his grip. "I'll be okay." He didn't know why, but the last thing he wanted was for this Deviant to be caught.

"I'm not leaving you here alone." The ex-Navy SEAL's tone gave no room for argument.

They started on their way.

"Stop or I'll shoot!" The command came from behind them.

Thomas turned to see two NWO troops pointing guns straight at them.

Uttering a growl of frustration, Kyle followed it up with some choice cuss words. "They know we're here. But how?" No time to figure it out, he began spouting orders, sending his men this way and that. "I want them all caught. Alive!" he yelled, before gesturing for his second in command to follow him and rushing into the brush.

Pulling his Glock from its holster, he charged ahead, eyes focused for any movement. He cussed again. The only way he'd be able to discover the location of UnderHisWings now would be to capture and torture one of them into telling him. No problem. They had methods that would make a man order his own mother's execution. This was only a temporary kink in his plans.

With Smitty, his second in command by his side, Kyle swatted away branches and tree limbs as they made their way quietly through the thick forest. He had to catch at least one of these Deviants. Failure was not an option. Not if he wanted to advance in the NWU Reformation Security Forces. It would take much more than his alliance with Jura or any of the Tall Whites. He had to either provide intelligence that would lead to the arrest of many Deviants, or he had to perform those arrests himself, preferably both.

But finding any of them in this forest was like searching for a gnat on a tiger.

Wait.

A female voice drifted to him from up ahead, ever so hushed, but there, nonetheless.

Gesturing with his head in that direction, he led Smitty forward. Careful not to step on any twigs, they approached a small clearing where three women and a child could be made out through the web of leaves surrounding them.

They had no weapons that he could see as they huddled together and shared water from an old canteen.

Nyla! His sister rose from the group and looked around. Her stomach rounded into a ball in front of her. Pregnant?

Kyle dove behind a shrub, Smitty following.

She looked good, strong, even carrying a baby. But then again, she always was the strong one. And he'd been the weak druggie, the black sheep of the family. Pain pricked his heart. He had loved her once, and she him.

Until she had betrayed him.

One of the other women looked his way. Tori Griffin! Ha! Catching her would be a huge feather in his cap.

She *continued* looking his way, as if she could see right through the foliage into his eyes.

Kyle shifted uncomfortably.

Tori whispered something to Nyla, and she nodded, motioning for the other woman to stand.

Slowly the black lady rose, gripped the hand of a child beside her, and dashed into the brush, Tori by her side. Nyla disappeared into the forest on her right.

Somehow, they knew Kyle was there. Cursing, he leapt from behind the bush. "Go after Tori and the black woman," he ordered Smitty, while he darted after his sister.

"Onafiel, Anahel, Zarall, after your wards!" Ranoss shouted as he charged after Nyla. With Arithem and Anisian gone, Ranoss had been left in charge. Though he really had no need to order the angels to protect their wards. 'Twas their assignment from the Almighty. But Nyla! She had been through so much. Had he been able to protect her thus far only for her to be captured now? And by her own brother?

Oh, Commander, let it not be so!

Drawing their weapons—Anahel, his mace, Onafiel, his long blade, and Zarall, his ax—the three warrior angels surrounded Brianna, Tori, and the children as they raced through the minefield of trees and fallen branches, thorns, and rocks. Encumbered by the children and their own exhaustion, the humans moved too slowly.

The soldier chasing them would have no trouble catching them.

In truth, he was nearly upon them now, a hoard of demons surrounding, spurring him on.

But the angels could do naught until the daughters of Eve commanded.

Zarall grew impatient.

Drawing his weapon, the soldier slapped aside a branch and shouted. "Stop right there, or I'll put a bullet in the child!"

The demons cackled and snorted as if they'd already won.

The women halted. The angels growled in frustration. Why did they not use the power the Commander had given them?

Slowly, Tori turned and stared at the possessed human. "I command you to stop and return from whence you came in the mighty name of Jesus."

"That's my girl!" Zarall shouted. "Onafiel, shield them from his eyes! Anahel, with me!" The two angels swooped down upon the mob of hideous spirits swarming about the man.

No sooner had Tori issued the command than the NWU soldier halted, blinked, and stared at them in wonder. The weapon wavered in his hand as he reached with his other hand to rub his eyes. When he opened them again, he uttered a sigh of unbelief and glanced across the clearing and into the surrounding woods...

As if he could no longer see them.

She would laugh, jump for joy, lift her hands in praise if she weren't so frightened. Yet, as her heartbeat returned to normal, she saw the demons swooping up and down and all around the soldier. They sliced right through him, whispered in his ear, and uttered such dreadful sounds, she wanted to plug her ears.

Brianna gripped her hand and eased beside Tori, trembling.

Carla, however, clapped in glee. "Onafiel made us invisible, Mommy!"

Tori glanced at Brianna and smiled. "She's right."

"And the other angels are fighting the black dots," the little girl exclaimed.

Tori's gaze landed back on the man, who swatted the air around his head as if he were being attacked by a swarm of bees.

The demons disappeared one by one, uttering shrieks of pain and cries of defeat. And each time, a glimpse of a glowing weapon, a golden ax, a shimmering hammer appeared flying through the air.

Finally, when the vile spirits had left the soldier, he turned and dashed back the way he had come.

Carla began to dance, twirling and hopping about, singing *Jesus loves me, this I know*. Overcome with joy, Brianna chuckled.

Sinking to her knees, Tori raised her hand in praise and thanked the Lord for His protection and His mighty angels. Carla and Brianna joined her, and together they praised God and prayed that He would protect Nyla, Calan, and Thomas as well.

*By this shall all men know that ye are my disciples, if ye
have love one to another.
John 13:35*

Chapter 27

Nyla knew this forest. Knew it as well as she'd known Fort Lauderdale when she'd been stationed there as an NWU Florida Peace Keeper. So it was easy to navigate around trees, boulders, even creeks—all familiar landmarks—to evade capture. She was at the top of the NWU Deviant Kill list. They wanted her and Calan more than any other Deviant in the North American Region. Which is why she'd sent Tori, Brianna, and the kids in the opposite direction. Now, if she could only lure them away from them while not getting captured herself. Of course that was easier said than done with her being seven months pregnant. She'd kept herself strong and healthy, but still, running with this extra weight wore her down. Not to mention was maybe hurting her precious child.

Weaving around a group of trees, she balanced carefully down a steep incline, then took off at a slow sprint over a flat area filled with underbrush. Sweat dampened her shirt and jeans. Her breath came fast and hard, and several small cuts sliced her arms where she'd swiped thorn bushes. Though she was a trained warrior, she hated being without Calan, but they'd decided long ago that should they run into NWU troops, they should separate. Best they didn't both get caught, for who would run UnderHisWings?

She lifted up a prayer for his safety, for all their safeties. Even though she knew that in the Tribulation, most saints would lose their heads. It was a fact they lived with on a daily basis— a fact they had come to accept. Yet before they possibly faced that end, Nyla had vowed to save and shelter as many saints as she and Calan could. And UnderHisWings had been born, a safe haven where Tribulation saints could find rest, fellowship, protection, and food. Best of all, their numbers grew daily as many people finally woke up and turned to Jesus for salvation.

Nyla thought on these things as she rushed through the forest, praying that God would allow her a little more time to help save more people. Halting before a wide stream, she wiped sweat from her brow and chuckled. It wasn't too long ago she'd been the one arresting "Deviants" and sending them to their deaths. Oh, how the Lord had changed her!

Catching her breath, she glanced over the creek, at least twenty yards wide and filled with huge boulders that, if one was careful, could be used as a bridge to the other side. Water dashed against and between them, tossing white foam in the air and forming little waterfalls.

The sound of the rushing creek washed over her, soothing her as she rubbed her belly, praying for the safety of her child. It wasn't the best time to bring a babe into the world—and they certainly hadn't expected *or* planned it—but God's will be done.

She glanced over her shoulder. If the soldier was good, he'd not be far behind. But he couldn't track her over this creek. Carefully stepping on the first boulder, she leapt to the next one and the next, avoiding any wet spots that would be slippery. One fall would either crack her skull on a rock or send her tumbling down the river in the mad rush of cold water. No thanks.

Finally, she made it to the other side and was about to turn and disappear into the forest when she heard a familiar voice.

A *very* familiar voice.

"Stop right there!"

On the other side of the creek stood her brother, pointing a gun at her chest.

Kyle! He looked good, older, more muscular, and quite handsome in his uniform. She wanted to smile. She wanted to hug him. She hadn't realized how much she'd missed him until that moment.

"You going to shoot me, Kyle?" she shouted back.

"Come back over here so I don't have to." He gestured with his Glock for her to cross the creek again.

"Can't do that." She shook her head, knowing she should run, but desperate to look at him awhile longer.

He fired.

The bullet whizzed past her ear. Close. Too close. Her heart shriveled. Did he miss on purpose or were they too far apart?

Kyle must have thought the latter because he started across the creek, leaping from boulder to boulder.

Turning, Nyla ran as fast as her belly would allow.

Ranoss waited for her command, anything that would grant him permission to protect her.

Alternatively, Zhaviel also waited, but somberly, for said command would cause him to do harm to his own ward.

From on shore, Ranoss nodded at his friend as he walked beside Kyle on the boulders. "I know 'tis hard for you, Zhaviel. He does not yet believe."

Zhaviel's gaze was fixed upon Kyle. "I do oft wonder why the Commander has me remain with him. Will he ever believe? His soul bears many wounds from his past, wounds he hopes this world and our enemy will heal."

"But only the Father of Spirits, the Almighty God can bring such peace and joy."

"Aye." Zhaviel nodded, gripping his spiked club in hand, waiting to do the unthinkable for a Guardian Warrior Angel— harm to one's ward.

Nyla looked at her brother, a pained look on her face.

"She loves him," Ranoss said, just as she turned and dashed into the forest. After one last glance at Zhaviel, Ranoss followed.

Clearly conflicted, Nyla struggled forward around trees and shrubs, tears flowing down her cheeks. "Do him no harm, Father, but please prevent him from following me or catching any of us."

There! Finally, the prayer they'd been seeking.

A shriek of pain echoed through the forest. Nyla halted, breath heaving, and spun around.

Another yelp.

"Kyle!" Quickly retracing her steps, Nyla emerged beside the creek to find Kyle had slipped and fallen into the water. His foot was stuck between two large boulders as water crashed over him, pushing his face below the surface. Struggling to stay afloat, he gasped for air, but the cold water blasted over his nose and mouth.

Zhaviel stood beside him, feet in the creek, burlap robe soaked, and club in hand. He cast a look of sorrow at Ranoss.

"She asked that no harm be done him," Ranoss shouted at his friend.

Zhaviel snorted. "Aye, and for that, I thank the Almighty, for I merely gave him a shove. Hence, his foot is only sprained, and he will live."

Ranoss smiled. "Hopefully long enough to give his life to the Commander."

"Indeed." Zhaviel shoved his club back in his leather belt.

Ranoss glanced at Nyla. "Now, let us see what she does."

"Kyle!" Nyla wasted no time navigating the boulders to where her brother was trapped. Kneeling on the closest one, she crammed one foot between two sturdy rocks and stretched a hand out to Kyle. "Grab hold!"

Water blasted so hard over his face, he could not answer, yet the confusion and terror in his eyes was unmistakable. His head fell beneath the water for a moment before he forced it back up again and gasped for air. He could not continue this way. Sooner or later, exhaustion would win and he'd drown.

"Kyle!" Nyla shouted over the mad rush of water. "Grab my hand!"

Finally, he let out a loud groan and thrust his hand into hers.

Bracing her weight against the boulder beside her, Nyla leaned forward and gripped his arm with both hands. Icy water soaked her jeans and dampened her belly as it dipped into the creek. With all her might, she pulled, yanking him from the force of the waterfall. He reached around her waist and clung to her like a lifeline. His gasps filled her ears. His wet clothing soaked through hers to her skin.

She embraced him, happy to hold her little brother again. "It's all right, Kyle. It's all right. Now, I need you to wiggle your foot, see if you can free it from the boulders." She wasn't sure whether that would work or how stuck it was, but at the moment, she could think of nothing else to do. She couldn't let go of him to help or he'd fall back into the water, and one small move of her own might send them both tumbling into the creek. Still clinging tightly to her, he moved his foot and let out a scream of pain. He jiggled it again, groaning. Finally, his body tightened, and he jerked his leg. "Uhggg!"

The foot came free. He fell backward. Nyla gripped him again, but he thrust his good foot into the dashing water and shoved her away. Then placing both hands on the boulder beside them, he leapt onto it. At first, he lay there on his stomach, breathing so hard, Nyla could hear it over the torrent.

She, too, freed her foot and climbed onto the boulder beside his. Now what? Should she run? She searched for his Glock, but it must have fallen into the creek. Still, he was her enemy, or rather, the demons who controlled him were. But he was also her brother and always would be. Oh, how she wished, how she *prayed*, he'd come to the Lord before it was too late.

Pushing against the boulder, he turned to face her. Water dripped from his dark hair onto a ripped NWU Reformation Security uniform, decorated with several pins and patches. A gash across his forehead oozed blood. His dark eyes searched hers as if he hardly recognized her.

"You've done well for yourself in the NWU, sergeant." She gestured toward his insignia.

He swallowed hard. "Yeah, they've been good to me." He hesitated, still catching his breath. "Why?"

Bringing her hair over her shoulder, Nyla wrung it out. "How do I know why they've been good to you? Probably 'cause you've killed a lot of *Deviants*," she spat out, though instantly regretted her tone. Now was not the time to argue.

He snorted, his lips flattening. "No. I meant why did you save me?" He glanced at the rushing water. "You could have left me to drown and gone free."

"You're my brother."

"Am I? Is that why you betrayed me?"

"I didn't—"

"I'm bringing you in." He pressed the compiece in his ear, then cussed.

Nyla smiled. Waterlogged. Good. He couldn't call for help. In fact, with what might be a sprained foot and no weapon, Nyla doubted he'd be bringing her anywhere. "Whatever, Kyle. Let me look at your foot first. Take off your boot."

Confusion twisted his expression, but he did as she requested, moaning with each pull of the tall leather boot.

Once his foot was freed, Nyla gently moved it back and forth, ignoring his moans. "Quit being a baby. It's only sprained." She smiled up at him. "But we'll have to stop that bleeding." She nodded to the gash on his forehead.

Kyle reached up to touch it, unaware of his injury until that moment.

Nyla struggled to rise.

He gripped her arm. Tight. "Where you going?"

"To get something for your wound," she shot back. "What are you going to do, keep us both here in the middle of the creek until we die of starvation?"

At that, he frowned, but released her anyway.

She wasted no time retreating over the boulders back to shore where she gathered a handful of goldenseal leaves she'd spotted earlier. She crushed them into small pieces with a rock, ripped a long piece off her shirt with her knife, then returned to her brother.

He had not moved. Instead, he 'd been watching her, a look of bewilderment on his face.

Please save him, Lord Jesus. Please save my brother. Nyla silently prayed as she knelt before him, washed his gash, and covered it with the moist leaves. Then, wrapping the cloth around his head, she tied it in the back.

"There, that should do it. Now, let's get you up and back to shore." Rising, she reached out her hand, and this time he gripped it.

Placing his weight on his good foot, he started to teeter, but Nyla leapt beside him and grabbed him around the waist. It took them several minutes, but finally they made it to solid ground, where Kyle tested his bad foot. Only sprained as she'd thought.

He barely uttered a word as she proceeded to locate a stick tall and strong enough to use as a crutch. Instead, he leaned against a tree trunk and followed her every movement.

She handed him the stick and smiled, cherishing this time with her brother. They'd never really gotten along as kids, and after their parents were raptured, he'd been nothing but a spoiled drug addict mooching off her. But she'd missed him. Loved him more than she could say.

He raked back his wet hair and took the stick. "Thanks."

Tears pooled in her eyes. "Any time." Wiping them away, she retreated a step. "You should be able to hobble back to wherever the other troops are."

"They are my troops. I'm in command." He raised his chin.

She smiled. "Like I said, you've done well in the NWU."

He reached for her, but she leapt out of his way. Anger flared in his eyes, a vile hatred that shocked her. A demon lunged from within him, fangs barred and dripping in blood, reminding her that the battle was not with Kyle, but with the evil spirits that controlled him.

"Kyle, turn to Jesus, the real God, who loves you more than you could ever know. Eternal life only exists through Him. Everything else is a lie, a counterfeit."

More demons appeared, churning around him in a vicious brew.

He spat on the ground. "Spare me your Deviant crap, sis."

Another cut to her heart. "I wish you well, Kyle. I'm sure you'll make it to your people." She hiked onto the first boulder, then turned one last time. Kyle stood leaning on the stick, a bloody bandage about his head and his eyes full of hate. Would she ever see him again? *Lord, be with him.*

She smiled. "You know I love you, Kyle. I always will." Then spinning around, she made her way across the creek and into the forest, heart breaking.

He that dwelleth in the secret place of the Most High shall abide under the shadow of the Almighty. I will say of the Lord, He is my refuge and my fortress: my God; in him will I trust. Surely he shall deliver thee from the snare of the fowler, and from the noisome pestilence. He shall cover thee with his feathers, and under his wings shalt thou trust: his truth shall be thy shield and buckler.
Psalm 91:1-4

Chapter 28

Thomas nodded at the guard, then turned and ran his hand over the front door of his house. Nothing. *Oh, yeah, that's right.* Sighing, he fished in his pocket for the temporary device they'd given him that would unlock his home, car, and work and grant him access to a host of other things and areas—exactly what the chip in his hand had once done.

Until Tori had zapped him.

He waved it over the door, and it clicked open. Once inside, he tossed it onto the table and, using his crutch, limped through the lavish entryway into his living room. Everything was the same—the *exact* same as when he'd left it on that fateful day when he and Tori were chased by NWU troops. How long had it been? Three weeks? It might as well have been three years for how different he felt.

He glanced around at the luxurious black and white couch, the marble floor, the immaculate quartz kitchen countertops, the pool outside the glass windows, and the bar fully stocked with his favorite liquors. Oddly, he felt no yearning to pour himself a drink. No yearning at all! Instead, the only thoughts going through his head were how lavish and expensive it all was. Such incredible waste for only one person.

In truth, he no longer felt as though he belonged here.

Plopping down on the couch, he leaned forward and ran fingers through his hair. Still dirty and sticky! Regent Landry had sent him home for a bath, a shave, and a good night's sleep. He could use all three, but for some reason, he felt guilty enjoying such luxuries when Tori and the others were still out there somewhere, hungry and dirty.

All except Calan, who'd been caught along with him. As soon as Sergeant Cruz and his men returned with them, Calan went to lock up and he'd gone to see Regent Landry.

In all honesty, Thomas thought he'd be executed on the spot. He'd prepared himself for that, as much as any man could. But instead, Landry had asked him if the entire thing had been part of Thomas's plan to infiltrate UnderHisWings.

When he'd answered yes, Landry had shouted, "I knew it! I knew I could trust you." Which made Thomas feel all the more guilty and worthless. Still, Landry had ordered medical to examine his foot and then sent him home to rest. "We'll discuss both your insubordinate actions"—he'd leveled a scrutinizing eye upon him—"and what you found out in the morning." He'd patted Thomas on the back, gave him the chip device, and sent him on his way.

Of course, it didn't surprise Thomas that the man still put a guard both in front and back of his house. Trust didn't come easy for men in high positions.

And Landry had good reason not to trust him. The main one being, he'd lied. He'd not orchestrated any plan to infiltrate the Deviant hideout. What a genius plan that would be, and one that a man in his position should have thought of. But everything he'd done had been to protect Tori, to keep her safe, to watch over her.

Then what the heck was he doing here?

He leaned back, heart aching more than it should. All he had to do was play the game, lie through his teeth, and he could have everything back he'd worked so hard to achieve, his power, position, future, respect, plenty of good food, women, a mansion on the beach, and a Mercedes.

Then why, since he'd been back, were all his thoughts focused solely on Tori. Was she safe? Did she have enough to eat? A place to sleep? Who would watch over her now?

"You are a foolish man, Thomas Benton," he said. "A very foolish man."

Tori shivered. Darkness transformed the forest into spooky shadows—spindly branches reaching for them, clumps of thorny bushes, an obstacle course of fallen trees, dark ditches, and cascading ravines. With their arms around each other, she and Brianna brought the children close between them, trying to keep them warm.

Leaves crunched. Tori's heart picked up a beat. She glanced through the foliage for any movement. After a few minutes, a person emerged from the shadows, but it was too dark to tell who it was. Thomas, maybe? She had no idea what had happened to him. The last time they spoke, he was told he couldn't join them in UnderHisWings. He had looked so disappointed, even hurt. It had broken her heart.

"Tori, Brianna," a female voice whispered.

"Nyla!" Rising, Tori ran to her and hugged her, careful not to harm the baby. "You're wet! You must be freezing. What happened?"

"Long story." Nyla greeted Brianna and the girls as they crawled out of their hiding place.

"Did you see Thomas?" Tori asked.

Nyla shook her head. "Calan?"

"No. It's just been us here."

Hanging her head, Nyla released a long sigh. "Let's go then. The sooner we get to UnderHisWings, the safer we'll be."

"What?" Tori grabbed her arm. "We can't just leave Thomas and Calan out here!"

Taking her hand, Nyla removed it from her arm and squeezed it. "If Calan is not here, it's because he's been captured." Sorrow filled her tone, and she hesitated before continuing. "Thomas was probably caught too."

Tori's insides crumbled. "But he didn't know where we were to meet."

"No, but I saw Calan run after him. Either way, we can't stay out here all night. If Calan found him and they are hiding, they'll make it to UnderHisWings soon."

"Or maybe he's already there," Brianna added with hope.

A hope that quickly dwindled after another hour of traipsing through the forest—thankfully with Nyla in the lead or they'd be hopelessly lost. How she knew where to go in the darkness when everything looked the same, Tori could not fathom. Yet, onward they went, climbing up and down steep hills, traversing treacherous creeks, and squeezing their way through patches of trees so close together, it was difficult to breathe. Finally, they scrunched their way between two boulders and a copse of trees and entered a cave, hidden from view.

Moonlight rained down through holes above, revealing a small empty cavern.

Nyla picked up a stick and rapped a sequence of taps on the wall, then said, "Jesus Christ is Lord!"

People came running from every crevice, corner, and passageway, startling Tori. Gripping Brianna's hand, she backed away, but after Nyla introduced them to everyone and they offered kind greetings and hugs, her heart settled.

The joy of the moment soon dwindled when Nyla told them Calan had most likely been captured.

"We will pray for him," one older man said.

"Yes, we will, Mitch. But for now, let's get these dear sisters in Christ some food and rest. They've been on a long journey."

Nodding, Mitch led the way through a maze of tunnels deeper into the cave, finally ending up in a large enclosure. A hole in the roof above let out the smoke from several small fires, while providing fresh air for those below. Scattered across the cave floor were blankets, sleeping bags, pots, pans, medical equipment, laundry hanging on lines, and even an old stuffed chair.

At least fifteen more people ran to welcome them, drilling Nyla with questions, bringing the total number of saints to twenty-five. Men and women of all ages and races, living together, helping each other, meeting all needs. It reminded Tori of the Book of Acts and the early Christians. She smiled.

The scent of unwashed humans melded with the savory scent of food cooking, and her stomach lurched even as her mouth watered. *Food. Real food.*

"You must be starving." Nyla led Tori and Brianna to sit by one of the fires and within minutes, an older woman named Mary brought them bowls of stew. A crowd gathered around them as they ate, curious about the newcomers.

Tori gulped down the delicious feast, trying to answer their questions as best she could.

What is it like out in the world now? What things did they see? Had they seen the images of the Beast? What about the Mark? How did they evade capture?

Between her and Brianna, they did their best to convey the events of their harrowing journey, including the crucifixions, the Neflams spy, and how they'd lost Sara. Callie slept through the entire thing, but Carla entertained everyone with stories of the angels who'd accompanied them, angels who were still with them, she announced. A fact Nyla confirmed with a smile.

Yet, the memory of Sara, along with the loss of Thomas, pressed heavy on Tori. She found it difficult to rejoice for any of their victories, even to find peace in this incredible sanctuary. She'd failed. Yes, she'd brought Brianna and her children to safety, but what about Sara and Thomas? And now Calan had been caught because of her.

"Let's pray," Nyla said, reaching one hand toward Tori and one to the person on her other side. Soon, the entire group formed one big circle, hand in hand, and each took turns both praising God and praying for Calan and Thomas and for the saints across the world to keep the faith and their testimony and not to love their lives to the death.

Tori had never heard such heartfelt prayers delivered with both laughter and tears. When it came to her turn, the Holy Spirit seemed to take over, offering up a plea with such passion and eloquence, she knew it had not come from her. After her prayer, someone spoke in tongues and another interpreted.

"Be encouraged, saints. Stay strong in the power of My Might, for the days ahead will be difficult, but your reward will be great! Even now, all of heaven cheers you on. Keep the faith, do not deny My Name. Endure all things and soon you will enter your rest, a glorious eternal future so wonderful, you cannot imagine. I love you with an everlasting love."

After the Words were spoken, silence drifted over the crowd. Tears filled Tori's eyes, and she fell to her knees before the one, true living God. Others followed and soon songs of praise and worship echoed through the cavern as the saints lifted hands in the air.

"The angels are dancing!" Carla exclaimed as she began to twirl and hop around the cave. Two other children joined her, giggling.

Tori had never been with so many saints in one place. Nor had she felt the power of the Holy Spirit so strongly. Love, joy, and peace flooded her heart, temporarily pushing out the sorrow and pain. Perhaps this was but a glimpse of the joy of heaven, of being with Jesus.

The worship went on for at least an hour, but soon with yawns and stretched arms, people retreated to their sleeping bags. Nyla led Tori and Brianna and the girls to an empty corner of the cave and gave them pillows and blankets.

But Tori couldn't sleep.

With the praise of God on her lips, Brianna quickly drifted off, both her children snuggled beside her. Soon light snoring filled the cave, along with the sizzle of coals and somewhere the *drip-drip* of water.

Still, Tori couldn't sleep. Shoving aside her blanket, she sat and glanced around. Movement caught her eye, and she saw Nyla sitting by one of the fires, staring at the flames.

"Can't sleep either?" Tori said as she gestured to a spot beside Nyla. "May I?"

Nyla smiled. "Sure."

Lowering to sit, Tori drew her knees up to her chest and sighed. "Thinking about Calan?" she asked, then suddenly felt stupid. Of course the woman was. He was her husband, the father of her child.

Nyla caressed her large belly. "Yes. We haven't been apart for over a year now." She wiped a tear from her eye. "I guess I feel a bit lost without him." She glanced around the cave. "By the grace of God, we started this place together with only five people. Look what the Lord has done."

Tori's heart grew heavy. "I'm so sorry, Nyla. It's all my fault. I led the troops here."

"What?" She huffed. "No way."

"If you hadn't come out to meet us, Calan would—"

"Stop thinking like that right now." Nyla's tone bore the authority she'd no doubt used when she'd been an NWU Peace Keeper.

Tori ran her fingers over the course dirt covering the bottom of the cave. "But it's true."

Nyla shook her head. "Do you think God didn't know what would happen? Do you think He's worried about this kink in His plan?" She laughed. "Calan is in God's capable hands, and His will be done."

"But what if he never comes…" Tori gulped.

Nyla gripped her hand. "Then I'll see him in heaven."

A tear slipped down Tori's cheek. "I don't know how you can be so strong."

"I'm really not." She gazed back at the fire. "Why do you think I'm here praying instead of sleeping?"

"And I've disturbed you." Tori started to rise, but Nyla held her back.

"No, I need the company. Tell me about Thomas. It was obvious from the looks you were giving each other that something is going on between you."

Against her will, warmth spiraled through her. "That obvious, huh?" She sighed. "You know the story. I told you before."

"Yes, but there seems to be a new chapter."

Memories of their time together the past month pranced through Tori's mind—the private conversations they'd had at night when everyone was asleep, the way he caressed her cheeks and was so gentle with her, how he took care of her, protected her, kissed her—all fond memories, despite their dire situation. "Yeah, we've grown close. Even though he's an arrogant, pretentious, entitled jerk, he came through for us during our journey. Not sure I would have made it without him."

Nyla tossed another log in the fire, shooting up sparks into the air. "Wow. Hard to believe, seeing as he was something like what, number three in the New World Faith?"

"Yeah. Pretty high up there. He interrogated me." Tori laughed.

Nyla joined her. "*That* I would like to have seen."

A sudden grief stole Tori's joy. "But he's gone now. Probably been executed. Or worse."

"We don't know that. We must keep up hope. So, he never…" Nyla hesitated. "Gave his life to Jesus?"

"No. He was so resistant, even after everything he saw, the miracles, the angels, the evil his NWU perpetrates."

"He's been brainwashed, like most people."

Tori dropped her head in her hands. "I feel like such a failure. God tasked me with bringing five people to UnderHisWings. One took the mark and is now eternally damned. The other…"—she shook her head—"never saw the truth." She swallowed down the burning in her throat.

"But you saved three."

"Is it enough?"

"Enough? For what?"

"For God. I owe Him so much, Nyla. I owe Him everything after what I've done."

Nyla stared at her strangely. "Oh, you mean your past. So, what? You got into drugs, fame, fortune. You slept around and you dabbled in the occult. So what?"

"What do you mean, so what? I hurt myself and tons of other people. I even had an abortion." There. She'd said it. She'd told someone. Surely now Nyla would be disgusted.

Instead, Nyla put her hand on Tori's arm. "I didn't know that. I'm so sorry."

"I murdered my child!" Tears poured down her cheeks and dropped onto her lap. "I deserve hell for that."

"Yes, you do," Nyla said.

Though Nyla's words were not what she expected, Tori batted her tears away. At least someone understood.

"In fact," Nyla added, "we all deserve hell for the bad things we've done. Don't think you're so special that your sin is worse than anyone else's."

Tori snorted. "I don't think I'm special. I think I'm scum."

"Welcome to the club." Nyla raised her hand to shake Tori's, but Tori only stared at her.

"Jesus paid our debts on the cross. He wiped away all our sins with His sacrifice. Once you believe in Him and follow Him, those things you did before? They are gone. God doesn't even remember them."

"Wish I didn't," Tori huffed.

"So, you think you have to somehow work off your debt with God? Make up for what you did?"

Though Tori hadn't thought of it that way, it sounded about right. "He saved me in every way possible, from hell, from a life of misery and emptiness, and from my own failings. How can I not want to do everything I can to further His Kingdom?"

"Oh, you sweet thing." Nyla swung an arm around her shoulder and drew her close. "First of all, we should all want to do everything to serve our King. That should be the desire of every saint, but we don't do it out of obligation or as some payment plan for God's gift of salvation. What He offers is completely free, no ties, no restrictions. He only wants our love and a relationship with us."

Tori bit her lip. Yeah, she knew that. But somehow, she never felt worthy of such a lavish gift. "You don't know what I've done."

"I know what you told me, and I have an inkling of the rest. But look at what I've done! I put many saints in reformation camps where some were killed. How do you think I live with that?"

Tori shifted her gaze to Nyla. "I didn't know that."

"God can even use our horrid pasts to serve Him."

"Really? How?"

"Think of it. You got involved in the occult, so you know how evil spirits work. Didn't you tell me that you see demons on occasion?"

Tori nodded.

"So, God used your knowledge of the occult to help you understand our enemy and how he operates. That's huge."

Tori blew out a sigh. "Yeah, but I didn't spot Aaron, didn't see he was evil until he'd done a lot of damage."

"But you *did* spot him eventually. And you passed the other tests."

"Tests?"

"Yeah. You told me about the drones, the tsunami, the tornado, and the cliff. You knew they were spiritual attacks. Most people wouldn't have been able to figure that out. So you see, God chose you for that exact purpose. No one else but you could have brought Brianna and her girls to safety. And now, I have a feeling He's got other plans for you here at UnderHisWings."

"You think?"

"Yeah. I do. I sense it deep in my spirit."

Tori smiled. She'd never considered that God could use her evil past to help others. She'd not even looked at all the disasters they'd encountered as tests. And more importantly, she'd never really felt worthy of God's forgiveness.

"God loves you, Tori. So much. Stop trying to make up for your past, and just allow the Holy Spirit to guide your future."

A sense of peace blanketed her, caressing away her fears and sorrows. Joy burst within her, followed by an overwhelming love so strong, she could not fathom it. She began to laugh, to giggle, to shake her head at her own stupidity.

"Your angel is smiling." Nyla gestured behind Tori, and she glanced back, but saw nothing.

"He is?"

"Yup. And many others are rejoicing."

Tori wiped tears from her cheeks. "Don't tell Carla, or she'll get up and start dancing."

They both laughed.

"But what about Thomas?" Tori asked when they both settled down. "I feel like I should at least go and see if he's alive, maybe rescue him?"

"Ah, so little you against the entire NWU?"

"I guess that sounds stupid."

"If the Holy Spirit leads you to go, then go. God will be with you. Otherwise..."

"I need to stop trying to do things on my own and trust God."

"Exactly."

Tori nodded. "I'll have to get used to this resting on God stuff."

Nyla smiled and drew her close again. "You will. But for now, both our men are safe in His mighty hands."

The coming of the lawless one is according to the working of Satan, with all power, signs, and lying wonders, and with all unrighteous deception among those who perish, because they did not receive the love of the truth, that they might be saved. And for this reason God will send them strong delusion, that they should believe the lie, that they all may be condemned who did not believe the truth but had pleasure in unrighteousness.
2 Thessalonians 2:9-12 (NKJV)

Chapter 29

Kyle leaned his crutch against the wall, then hobbled to sit at the sterile gray table across from the infamous Calan Walker.

He stared at him for several minutes, a tactic of interrogation that was intended to cause discomfort to the criminal. Instead, Calan merely stared back, a calm expression on his face, and a look in his eyes that said, *can we just get this over with?*

Impressive. The man had once been a Navy SEAL and no doubt had been trained in handling interrogation.

"So, we meet again, Nyla's brother," he said before Kyle had a chance to speak.

"I'll be the one asking the questions," Kyle returned.

"Fine." Calan held up both hands. "It's just that you look more like her than I remember...same eyes... hair."

At the mention of his sister, images flooded his mind of their time at the creek, how she'd saved his life at the risk of her own, thoughts he'd been unable to squelch since he'd located his troops in the forest and returned to St. Augustine. He rubbed his eyes. In fact, the visions had kept him up all night, tossing and turning on a bed of guilt and confusion.

"Rough night?" Calan asked.

"Where's your Deviant hideout?"

Chuckling, Calan raked back his hair. "What? No small talk first?"

Struggling to rise, Kyle slammed his fist on the table. "Think you're funny, don't you?"

Calan didn't wince, didn't flinch. Instead, he smiled. "You also have her temper."

Kyle sank back to his chair, ignoring the throb in his foot. "This is no joke, Mr. Walker. If you don't provide some useful information, then you will be useless to us. And you know what that means."

Calan sliced his thumb across his neck and made a swooshing sound. "Yeah. I'm aware." Yet no fear, no apprehension sounded in his tone.

He was good at this.

Kyle leaned back in his chair, studying him. If he could break Calan and discover the location of the Deviant hideout, Regent Landry promised a huge promotion, maybe even the leader of the North American Reformation Security forces.

Then he wouldn't need his association with Jura to advance. He wouldn't need the Tall White. It was good the creature had left before Kyle returned, because he had no desire to see him. Not after he'd lied to Kyle about his spy's true purpose. Kyle had foolishly thought Jura liked him, had his best interest at heart, but he was just as much a liar as Kyle's father, as Nyla. Both only cared about themselves. Both had betrayed him. And now, both had abandoned him.

"I have the power to end your life today if I want."

One side of Calan's lips rose as if Kyle had said something amusing. "Actually, that's true. You do. But only because God has granted you that power. Besides,"—he shrugged—"you'd be doing me a favor."

Kyle snickered. "Are all you Deviants this crazy?"

"I suppose." Calan cocked his head. "You know Nyla loves you. She prays for you every night."

Kyle snorted. "Oh, is that why she betrayed me?"

"Betrayed you how?" Calan's brows lifted. "By becoming a Deviant? By wanting you to find the same joy and peace she has found? By wanting you desperately to join her in eternity and not spend it in the lake of fire."

"Enough!" Kyle shouted. "The God you serve is a bully and a liar. Lucifer is the real god who offers us eternal life."

"It's all in the Bible, Kyle…you know, that banned Book that's been around for thousands of years. Use your head, son. Look around you. Who really is the evil god?"

Kyle didn't want to look around. He wanted a promotion and the money and power that went with it. He wanted to prove to his parents, his sister, and everyone that he wasn't some snot-nosed brat hooked on drugs who couldn't do anything right.

"Where is the Deviant hideout?" he hissed between clenched teeth. "Where is my sister?"

"I can't tell you that. I *won't* tell you. But I will tell you this. All you need to do is repent of the evil you've done, give your life to Jesus, and follow Him. Then you'll live forever in a paradise you can't imagine." Calan hesitated, staring at Kyle, who looked stunned. "Oh," he continued, "don't take the new tattoo Aali requires. If you do, you'll be damned forever. Listen to me, Kyle." He reached his hand across the table, the chains on his wrists jangling. "Just ask the God of the Bible if He's real. Just ask Him and be open for His answer."

Why Kyle listened to all of that, he couldn't say, but the look in Calan's eyes had him mesmerized. It was a look of pity, sorrow, and such love he'd never seen before. It was as if some other person had taken over Calan, a person who loved Kyle more than anything and who wanted to save him.

It was a look he could hardly turn away from.

Don't be a fool! A whisper filled his ears. *Lucifer has saved you, given you everything you want. And there's so much more he can give you. This man is a liar.*

Tearing his gaze from Calan, Kyle rose to his feet, hobbled to his crutch, shoved it under his shoulder, and opened the door.

He turned to face Calan. "I'll give you an hour to think about it. Then you get one more chance to answer my questions or you'll be executed immediately."

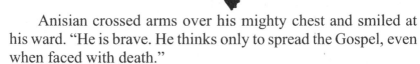

Anisian crossed arms over his mighty chest and smiled at his ward. "He is brave. He thinks only to spread the Gospel, even when faced with death."

Zhaviel nodded, his gaze following Kyle as he hobbled out of the room. "I fear for mine. His desire for earthly rewards is great, even obscuring the truth from his eyes."

Anisian gripped his friend's shoulder. "There is still hope, my friend. Did you not tell me his sleep was greatly disturbed last night?"

"Aye, more than I have seen." Zhaviel started after Kyle.

"Then the Father of Spirits lures him, calls to him. Be patient and let us see how the Almighty works a miracle in his heart. After all, many prayers have gone up to the throne for this one." Anisian nodded toward Kyle.

Zhaviel smiled. "Indeed. 'Tis true. Thank you, my friend. I will see you soon." And off he went, following close behind his ward, leaving Anisian alone with a rather slimy-looking dark spirit who just appeared behind Calan.

"Begone, vile one!" Anisian commanded, but the spirit merely grinned his way and waved a hand full of sharpened black fingernails through the air.

"He does not want me gone," he hissed.

Anisian studied his ward. Elbows on the table, Calan dropped his head in his hands and gripped his hair.

"Oh, Lord, am I never to see my child be born? Am I never to see my precious Nyla this side of heaven?" His tone ached with sorrow, regret, and pain.

And with each word of doubt, the hideous demon grew larger and larger.

Anisian drew his long blade and took a step toward him, hoping his ward would overcome this test and call upon the Almighty.

The demon leered at him, revealing two yellowed fangs. His foul scent curled Anisian's nose.

Huffing, Calan lifted his head and leaned back in his chair. He sat there quietly for several minutes, a pained expression on his face. The dark spirit spun a cyclone of doubt and fear around his head, and Anisian feared Calan would not be able to resist his last and greatest test.

Yet, what could he do?

Naught without permission.

Finally, Calan raised his hands to heaven and smiled. "Not my will, but Yours be done, my King."

Before the last words had emerged from Calan's mouth, Anisian swept his blade through the air and severed the demon in two. His shriek faded into silence even as his dark body turned to ash.

Sheathing his sword, Anisian took up a stance by his ward, a huge grin on his face.

Leaning on his cane, Thomas stood before Regent Landry's office and knocked on the door. No sooner had he entered the NWF Reformation Headquarters than his assistant, along with several others, greeted him kindly, all proclaiming how good it was to see him and have him back. He wondered at their sincerity, especially since several gave him wary looks—especially his assistant Rodney, who took him aside and in an anxious tone told him Landry wished to see him immediately. It was bad enough he'd been escorted to work by two guards, but did everyone in the office suspect him of treason?

He laughed at his own thoughts. He *had* committed treason. But what good would it do now to admit it? It wasn't like he could run back and find Tori. She was no doubt safely at UnderHisWings—at least he hoped so—wherever that was.

In the end, after all he'd done, they had not trusted him. Tori had not trusted him.

So, if Landry and the New World Union thought he'd infiltrated the Deviants as a spy, so be it. At least he could resume his powerful position and return to his normal life. That's what he wanted, what he'd dreamed about while wandering around with the Deviants, hungry, exhausted, filthy, and in pain.

Wasn't it?

Still, the fact that Landry had assigned guards to watch over him meant they did not fully trust him, something Thomas hoped to rectify today. He also wanted to find out what happened to Calan. The man wouldn't be here if not for Thomas.

"Enter!" the shout came from within the office, and opening the door, Thomas hobbled inside.

"How's the ankle?" Landry said from behind his oversized desk.

"Sore," Thomas responded with a smile.

"Have a seat, Tom. I must say you look a lot better than yesterday."

"Thank you, sir." He had felt a whole lot better, too, after a hot shower, shave, and a hearty breakfast of eggs, ham, and toast. Carefully, he lowered to sit in the plush leather chair. "And thank you for sending the food over."

Landry smiled. "Figured you wouldn't have anything in your fridge."

The only thing left in his fridge had been something Tori had bought. Which, of course reminded him of her. Not that he needed reminding. She'd been on his mind all night as he wrestled with his sheets.

She'd left him with a broken heart once, and now he'd allowed her to do it again. What a fool!

"When can I resume my duties, sir?" Thomas dared to ask.

"Not so fast, Tom." Landry rose, poured two glasses of bourbon from the wet bar against the wall, and handed one to Thomas.

He lifted a hand. "No thanks."

Landry's brow arched. "Thomas Benton turning down a drink? You *have* changed."

More than he knew.

Sipping his drink. Landry sat on the edge of his desk and gave Thomas a pointed stare. "I need to know. Why didn't you inform me of your plans to infiltrate the Deviant group?" His tone had transformed from a friendly superior to one of judge.

Thomas swallowed. "Honestly, sir"—he cringed at the coming lie— "I didn't plan it at all."

"What?" Anger simmered in the man's narrowed eyes.

"Wait, wait. Hear me out," Thomas said. "Yes, I broke Tori out. Yes, I took her home, but it was only to get the information we needed from her. I knew you wouldn't approve of assigning her into my custody, and I had to make her believe I was on her side." The lies kept coming, flying off his tongue like feathers on a wind of deceit.

Landry listened intently.

Thomas shifted in his seat. "Because of our close past, I knew I could get her to talk, but I had to get her in a place where she felt safe and trusted me."

"Hmm." Landry fingered his stylish beard. "Makes sense."

"But then somehow you or Sergeant Cruz found out I had helped her escape and you sent troops to my house. I had to make a quick decision. Go with her and keep up the ruse or allow her to be captured and ruin any chance she would talk to me in the future." Sighing, Thomas shrugged. "So I ran. I knew you could track me, but then she zapped me with a taser and fried my chip."

"Ah…that's why we lost your signal." Landry nodded.

Thomas smiled. Landry believed him. Good grief, he almost believed himself.

"A bold move, Tom. Very bold." Landry rose and circled behind his desk. "I knew you hadn't betrayed us. I just knew it."

Thomas's ankle ached and he shifted it slightly. "Thank you for believing in me, sir. I'm only sorry I went to all that trouble for nothing."

"That depends on what you know, what you can tell us." Excitement flared across the man's eyes. "You spent a month with them. Surely you discovered something that would help us."

I discovered that they are kind, brave, resourceful and loving people, and that their God protects and feeds them. Thomas shoved aside the thought. "Not much, sir. We were almost at their hideout when Sergeant Cruz and his men chased us down."

"Yeah. That was a mistake. His men were highly trained in stealth surveillance. They had orders not to make their presence known until you were at the Deviant hideout. How did you discover them?"

Thomas ran a hand through his hair. Calan had sensed they were there, probably from his God, but Thomas couldn't very well tell Landry that. "We heard them. The Deviants are very sensitive to any unusual noises."

"Hmm. So you have nothing to tell me? No intel at all?"

"All we did was travel from Florida, through Georgia, and up to that national forest. We did a lot of walking, very little talking, and when we found shelter each night, we crashed."

"But surely you talked with Tori. She trusted you by then. Were you able to get anything out of her?"

"I tried, but she wouldn't tell me the location of any underground churches or hideouts. She said most were all shut down anyway. And whenever I asked about UnderHisWings, she refused to answer."

Landry blew out a sigh, followed by a curse. "I suppose these Deviants have learned to trust no one. What a waste. You could have died, and for what?"

"Well, I'm back now. And I'm sorry I ran off without your permission."

"Your intentions were good." Landry finished off his drink and sank back into his chair, studying Thomas for any hint of deception. But Thomas had learned long ago how to hide his emotions behind a veneer of compliance.

Smiling, Landry slapped his desk. "Much has happened in your absence. Have you seen what Aali has been doing?"

Only his creepy giant holograms and forced tattoos. "No, we didn't have access to news."

Landry nearly leapt from his seat. Unusual wonder and awe filled his eyes. "He really is god!" He shook his head as if the thought were beyond belief. "You should see the miracles His Excellency Gabriel Wolfe is doing in Lord Aali's name."

Lord, eh? "What sort of miracles?"

"Raising the dead! Feeding multitudes of hungry people with only a basket of food, healing the sick, causing rain to fall from heaven, stopping violent storms. He's even cleaning up our environment. It's amazing!"

Thomas knew his Bible well enough to know that Jesus had done those same things, at least if the Scriptures were true. "Wow," he exclaimed with less enthusiasm than he intended. Still, he would believe it when he saw it. "Sounds like he's doing a lot of good."

Grabbing Thomas's drink, Landry powered it down. "Tons of good. He's the savior of the world. And now he offers us eternal life."

"You mean the statue and the quantum dot tattoo he's making people get?"

"How did you know about that?"

"We saw one in Atlanta." Memories rose of Sara entering the NWU Medical building and Tori collapsing to the ground in a heap of agony, of the loud voices from heaven warning people not to take the Mark as they called it. Bile rose in his throat.

"Aren't they magnificent?"

Eerie and disturbing was more like it. "Yeah."

Shifting his hand over the black screen on the wall, Landry switched it on, then grabbed a remote and began flipping through scene after scene of people being raised from the dead in various morgues throughout the world, the paralyzed leaping from their wheel chairs, patients fleeing an entire wing of a hospital as Aali walked through healing them, the hungry and homeless with full plates of food, and finally crowds of people numbering in the hundreds of thousands cheering Aali and bowing to worship him.

As impressive as the images were, Thomas couldn't help but compare them to the misery, poverty, filth, and repression he'd witnessed when traveling with Tori. Quite the contrast. A contrast he didn't wish to think about at the moment. He couldn't go back. He could only go forward, and to survive, he had to put those memories behind him.

"So, when can I get back to work?"

Shutting off the screen, Landry frowned. "Well, here's the thing. You see, I believe your story, I do, but His Excellency Gabriel Wolfe and Lord Aali want proof of your loyalty before they trust you again."

Thomas's gut twisted. "What proof?"

"First, you must interrogate Calan Walker, and if he doesn't talk, carry out his execution, and secondly, you must bow before Lord Aali himself and receive his mark of allegiance on your right hand or forehead."

Have an audience with Aali Immu himself? Wasn't that what Thomas had always wanted? Yet for some reason, the thought disturbed him. Greatly. Everything within him wanted to scream. Instead he smiled and nodded.

"You can speak with Mr. Walker today if you wish, and I'll go ahead and make the arrangements for your virtual meeting with Lord Aali tomorrow."

*I charge thee therefore before God, and the Lord Jesus
Christ, who shall judge the quick and the dead at his
appearing and his kingdom; Preach the word; be instant in
season, out of season; reprove, rebuke, exhort with all long
suffering and doctrine. For the time will come when they will
not endure sound doctrine; but after their own lusts shall they
heap to themselves teachers, having itching ears;*
2 Timothy 4:1-3

Chapter 30

So, you think you can just come back here and resume your position like nothing happened?" Kyle slipped beside Thomas as he limped down the hall from Landry's office.

"Good morning to you, sergeant," Thomas responded, not even granting Kyle enough respect to stop and speak with him. "And that's Vice Regent Benton to you."

Thomas stopped at his office, entered, and attempted to shove the door shut.

Catching it with his crutch, Kyle followed him inside and stopped before his desk.

Thomas speared him with a sharp gaze before setting aside his cane and lowering to sit. "I would be careful if I were you on how you address your superior."

"So, Landry didn't fire you."

Thomas's blue eyes turned to ice. "That's Regent Landry to you, and no, but I can certainly put in a recommendation for your dismissal."

Anger boiled in Kyle's gut. "I know you're lying about your loyalties."

"And how do you know that?"

"Aaron was quite plain in his reports to Jura."

"Ah, that makes sense. He was your Tall White's spy." Thomas flattened his lips as the slightest hint of unease flashed across his expression. "So, he gave you reports on us?"

Kyle blew out a snort. "The fact that you say 'us' implicates you."

Thomas leaned back in his chair. "You have no proof of your accusations. Nor do I need to explain my actions to you."

"Aaron told us how close you were with Tori, how you'd snuggle each night and whisper to each other, how you went out of your way to protect her, and how you made friends with the others."

Thomas squirmed in his seat, ever so slightly, but Kyle had been trained to notice such things. "It's what undercover spies do. Get close to their enemies. Or didn't you learn that in *guard* school. That is what you are, after all, just a guard who won favors with a Tall White."

Kyle ground his teeth together until they ached. How he'd like to punch that smirk off Thomas's face. "A guard who not only caught you, but caught the great Calan Walker," he retorted.

Again Thomas winced. *Why?*

"Listen, sergeant." Leaning forward, Thomas folded fingers on top of his desk and offered Kyle a rare look of kindness. "We are not so different, you and I." He glanced at Kyle's crutch and chuckled. "And I don't mean that we both sprained our ankles. I mean that we both are ambitious men, and from what I know, abandoned by parents and betrayed by friends."

Now it was Kyle's turn to squirm. The man was good. He knew how to fire a shot straight into the gut.

"It's not easy for us to trust," Thomas continued. "It's probably why we've achieved what we have." He smiled. "So, how about a truce?"

Kyle stood there for a moment, leaning on his crutch and staring deep into the eyes of this man he was sure was a traitor. No, he would not fall for his fake kindness. He didn't get to where he was by being gullible.

"I will prove my suspicions, sir," he said with scorn. "Just like I proved you helped Tori escape. And when I do, I'm going to take you down."

Stomach tied in a million knots, Thomas shuffled into the interrogation room where Calan was being held. Talking to the man who had risked everything to save Thomas, getting him to betray his friends, his pregnant wife, and if not, send him to be executed, was the last thing Thomas wanted to do. Ever.

But here he was at Landry's request as a condition of his own freedom. In fact, he could hardly look at the man as he shut the door and took his seat. *What a complete jerk I am!*

"You clean up nice, Thomas," Calan said with a smile as he pointed to Thomas's expensive business suit and polished Italian loafers.

Oddly, that morning, Thomas found he actually preferred jeans and a t-shirt, but if he was to convince everyone of his loyalty, he had to dress the part. One glance at the camera in the corner reminded him that he had to choose his words carefully.

"Listen Calan, they…*we* are going to kill you, even torture you, if you don't tell us the location of UnderHisWings." He might as well start out strong. No sense in playing good cop with a man who knew he'd betrayed them.

"You knew Daniel Cain well, didn't you? Weren't you his assistant pastor?" Calan asked as if they were having coffee at a local shop.

Thomas blinked. At the mention of Daniel, all his harsh questions flew out the window. "He was my best friend growing up. We went to seminary together. Started a church that grew to be one of the largest in Fort Lauderdale." For some reason the memory made his shoulders rise a little higher. Those were good times, happy times. "Wait, you knew him, too." Of course he had. Calan had been part of Daniel's first underground church.

"I was his bodyguard for a time," Calan answered. "After the Rapture."

"The disappearance, you mean."

Calan shifted his feet, jangling the chains around his ankles. "What was he like before…?"

"Daniel?" Thomas smiled. "Strong-willed, passionate, driven, honest to a fault."

"Yeah. He was pretty amazing, even more so after he got truly saved."

He betrayed you. He abandoned you. A voice slithered through Thomas's thoughts. He frowned. "He wasn't who I thought he was," he shot back. "As soon as his girlfriend and son were taken, he started preaching nonsense. We lost the church, all the money and fame we worked so hard to achieve. After the NWU formed and they arrested Deviants, he started an underground church. Wanted me to join him, begged me." Thomas could still see the pain in his friend's eyes as he pleaded with him to become a Deviant. And when Thomas refused, Daniel had just walked away, out of his life forever.

"I know that must have hurt," Calan said.

"Don't patronize me." Thomas seethed, trying to control his temper. "I'm not here to talk about Daniel Cain."

"Fine. What do you want to talk about? Tori?"

At the sound of her name, Thomas's heart wilted. "Why would I want to talk about a woman who also betrayed me? No, we are here to talk about your impending execution. *If* you don't talk."

"I could tell she loves you."

"Enough!" Growling inwardly, Thomas stood and shoved his face just inches from Calan's. "Do you want to see your wife and child again?"

Despite Thomas's outburst, Calan remained calm, unflinching. "I will see them again. And Daniel too." He smiled. "I know your father was rough on you, Thomas. He was high up in the Lutheran church, right? Strict, unloving, demanding?"

Thomas sank back down, stunned at the man's knowledge of him. But of course, he must have heard it from Daniel.

"I know you felt abandoned by him," he continued, "then by Daniel, and by others since, even Tori. But I'm here to tell you that Jesus will never abandon you. People let us down, but God never will. He loves you with an everlasting, overwhelming love."

Thomas knew he should put a halt to this garbage right away, knew Landry and others watching would be furious at him for allowing this man to spew his Deviant crap. But the look of love in Calan's eyes was like nothing Thomas had every witnessed. Pure concern...for him! No one, except Tori, had ever looked at him like that. No one.

"You came to my rescue in the forest even when it meant you would get caught, too. Why?"

Calan shrugged. "Because that's what we saints do. We lay down our lives for each other and for God."

Confusion spun through Thomas. "But I'm not a sain—Deviant."

Calan smiled. "Not yet."

Not ever. Don't listen to him! The voices started up again. *Do you wish to die alongside him?*

"Don't listen to them," Calan said.

"Who?"

"The demons speaking to you right now."

Thomas shifted in his seat. *How did he know?*

"Tom, what the hell are you doing?" Regent Landry's voice blared over the compiece in his ear. "Drag the information out of him, or I'll send in someone who will!"

"Okay, I'm done with you, Calan. Either tell me where UnderHisWings is, or I'll have no choice but to order your execution."

Calan smiled. "Do what you must, Thomas. I've done what the Lord asked of me. I've finished my race. Now I'm ready to die for my King."

And I saw thrones, and they sat upon them, and judgment was given unto them. And I saw the souls of them that were beheaded for the witness of Jesus and for the word of God, and which had not worshiped the beast, neither his image, neither had received his mark upon their foreheads or in their hands. And they lived and reigned with Christ for a thousand years.
Revelation 20:4

Chapter 31

Thomas could hardly believe he was, once again, witnessing the brutal execution of a friend. Not that Calan was a good friend, but he was a friend of Tori's and a man who had risked himself for Thomas, a good man by all observations.

So, with a heart as heavy as a brick, he limped into the observation room and was not at all surprised to find Sergeant Cruz there, along with Regent Landry. They both had advocated to crucify Calan, make a spectacle of him for other Deviant leaders to witness, but Thomas had been able to talk them down from such an agonizing death. From his experience, it only emboldened the Deviants, impassioned them to continue with their cultish beliefs in order to make the martyr's death count for something. Or so he argued.

Thankfully, though Sergeant Cruz protested, Landry had agreed, and now Calan was to be beheaded. At least it would be quick and painless.

Yet when Thomas turned toward the one-way window and saw Calan enter the room held up by two guards, he realized the painless part was only a dream. One of Calan's eyes was swollen shut, a gash slashed his left cheek, blood dripped from a wound on his head and from several deep cuts on his arms, and the nails had been ripped from his fingers. In addition, he limped and pressed a hand over his stomach as if he'd been punched. Several times.

Thomas faced Landry. "Who ordered this?"

Sergeant Cruz chuckled. "Told you he cared about this Deviant."

Landry leveled a hardened gaze at Cruz, silencing the lad, before he turned to Thomas. "I did. His arrogance needed crushing, and I wanted one last chance to get some information out of him. Even gave him some drugs to make him talk. Nothing worked." He huffed. "He's a strong one." He faced the window again. "Your time with the Deviants has made you soft."

Tightening his jaw, Thomas withheld a growl. He had to be careful, or he'd be the next one led to the guillotine.

Calan glanced up at the window, knowing he was being watched. A slight smile curved his bloodied, swollen lips as the guards shoved him forward. He fell to his knees, crying out in pain.

Thomas clenched his fists.

Yanking him to his feet, the guards positioned him before the guillotine as the executioner read Calan's list of crimes— treasons against the NWU, spreading lies and insurrection, belonging to an illegal cult. Thomas had heard it all before. Many times, in fact, for the many Deviants he'd sent to their deaths.

Through the reading, Calan merely stood, calmly, serenely, as if he were waiting in line for coffee.

Just like Daniel had done.

"I give you one last chance to save your life," the executioner said. "Reveal the location of the Deviant hideout, deny Jesus, submit to Lord Aali, and take his mark of allegiance."

Calan chuckled, or at least it sounded like a chuckle as a mixture of spit and blood dribbled from his mouth. Thomas moved a little to the left for a better look at his expression.

He *was* smiling! *Just like Daniel had been.*

"Can't do that," Calan said. "Jesus is the one true God, the only way to eternal life. Why would I trade that for a Mark that leads to hell?"

Frowning, the executioner shook his head in disgust. "You are all alike. Fools!" He nodded for the guards to force him back to his knees and place his head in the guillotine block.

"I forgive you!" Calan shouted. "I forgive you, Thomas and Kyle, and all of you!"

The guards laughed. The executioner snorted.

Landry shook his head. "Good riddance to this Deviant."

Grinning, Kyle crossed arms over his chest.

A sour taste rose in Thomas's throat. Along with a suffocating clump of confusion and horror.

"Receive my spirit, Lord Jesus," Calan said. "I am coming home."

The blade dropped.

Thomas looked away.

Anisian stood tall beside Calan as his ward refused to deny the Commander, refused to bow to the enemy, refused to submit, even as he stared at the sharp blade above him, splattered in blood.

Zhaviel clapped Anisian on the back. "How wonderful for you, my friend. 'Tis the moment you have waited for."

"Aye," Arithem spoke from his other side. "You have protected him since birth, mourned when he drifted from the truth, endured when he defied the Almighty's laws and suffered the consequences, and then celebrated when he repented and returned to follow our Lord."

Indeed. Every memory was deeply embedded in Anisian's heart. His eyes blurred with moisture, and he quickly wiped it away. 'Twouldn't look good for a mighty warrior of the Most High to cry. "And now, I rejoice at his homecoming!" he shouted in victory. "He has finished his race. He has won the prize."

Arithem glanced up to where Thomas watched the proceedings. "He does not approve. In truth, he mourns this barbarous death."

"'Tis a huge step for him," Zhaviel said. "Be encouraged. There is still time." But Zhaviel's eyes were focused on Kyle, gloating over Calan's death. He released a heavy sigh. "I do not know why the Commander keeps me with this one. He is far from the light."

"Have faith," Anisian said as the two guards forced Calan's head into the holder. "Our God is mighty to save!"

"Indeed." Zhaviel nodded. "You are right."

Anisian took a step forward, ready to escort Calan to his heavenly home. "He forgives them. What joy it is to see these sons of Adam become like their Savior!"

"We will miss you, Anisian," Arithem said.

"We will meet again, my friends."

The blade dropped.

Calan's spirit-body rose out of his earthly one, a huge grin on his face when he saw the angels.

"I am Anisian, your guardian." He held out his hand.

Calan grabbed it. "Where is my King?"

"He is most excited to see you. I will take you to Him."

Thomas slammed the door of his house on the guard, tossed his key device onto a table, and stomped as fast as his cane would allow into the living room toward his wet bar. He needed a drink, and he needed one bad. Grabbing the bottle of aged bourbon, he poured a glass and picked it up. The pungent odor drifted to his nose, causing a yearning in him that was almost impossible to resist. He needed to numb the emotions raging within. He needed to silence the voices. He needed to squash the guilt. And the only way he knew to do that was by deadening all three with alcohol.

Drink, drink your fill, and you'll feel much better.

His lips touched the rim of his glass. His heart took up a rapid beat. A vision of Tori staring at him with love and approval filled his mind. She had said alcohol opened doors for the demonic. Even if that wasn't true, he knew from experience that the euphoria it produced never lasted. And it always came with a price. *No!* He couldn't. He wouldn't. Setting the glass down, he grabbed his cane and hobbled to the kitchen. His gaze landed on Tori's drawings stuck to the fridge with magnets. Two of her best—one of him and one of the sea. He swallowed down a burst of sorrow. He'd never see her again.

Moving to the living room, he spotted more of her drawings strewn across tables and chairs where she'd left them. He grabbed one of them from the coffee table, one he'd not seen before. It was of him sitting on the sand, staring at a bright light coming from the ocean. Strange. He tossed it down and swiped a rebellious tear from his cheek.

The sun set, luring shadows out from the corners and crevices of the house—moving, undulating, breathing shadows. They slithered over his couch, across the floor, around tables and up the wall. A chill crept over him. He trembled and then laughed at himself. Was he a child to be afraid of the dark?

Or were demons real?

"Lights on," he commanded.

Nothing. Instead, the shadows grew darker. Had they removed his voice commands too?

Cursing, he limped to the sliding glass door and flung it open, then made his way past the pool and gardens and onto the sand. His cane dug into the soft silt, making it harder to walk. Pain radiated up his leg, and he finally gave up and plopped down.

Tori loved the beach. He remembered the day he'd found her here praying. She'd said the sea reminded her of God's glorious power and beauty. A moon rose over the dark waters, sprinkling silver light on select waves even as a few stars could be seen through the normal hazy sky. The sand felt warm and soft beneath him, and he drew a handful and allowed it to sift through his fingers. A light breeze tickled his face, bringing the slightest scent of the sea beneath all the normal foul smells. Yet it was still there, and it brought back memories of better days growing up surfing in South Florida. When life had been normal and filled with hope.

Calan was dead.

And Thomas had killed him. Maybe not directly, but he had not fought to stop it, had not tried to help him escape like he had Tori. But how could he have? It would have been a death sentence for him as well.

Yet the look on Calan's face as he approached his own death! Such peace and joy. Joy! At being executed, at being tortured! And his confident words, his statement of faith in Jesus, and his forgiveness of all of them. The scene mimicked Daniel's execution, along with so many others Thomas had witnessed.

What was it about these Deviants that gave them such faith, such assurance of their life after death? Sure, their God could do miracles. Thomas had witnessed that. But He was a bully, a God full of anger and wrath who thought nothing of murdering thousands who didn't obey Him. Those stories were in their precious Bible, after all! And they played out in all the current disasters He'd unleashed on the world. So, why would they trust Him to be kind to them after death?

No, it was better to trust Lucifer, the light bearer, the one who had more than proven he loved mankind by not putting any rules and restrictions on them, by working to create a utopia here on earth, and by also offering them eternal life. Not some pie in the sky dream of it, but the real thing with this new quantum tattoo of his. Or his son, Immu Aali's tattoo, for that is what Aali was calling himself now—Lucifer's son.

Yet...those loud angelic voices thundering down from the skies above Atlanta, warning people not to take the Mark or they'd end up in the lake of fire.

Why would a bully God give such a warning? Why not just let everyone be destroyed?

Thomas raked back his hair, unclipped his gold cufflinks from his shirt, tossed them to the sand, and rolled up his sleeves. For some reason, he no longer cared whether he got sand on his expensive suits, no longer cared that his hair wasn't perfect, and his nails were dirty, and he needed a shower. Maybe Landry was right. He *had* changed. But soft? No. If anything, Thomas had grown strong.

Tori. He missed her so. Even though she had betrayed him in the end. Just like his father, whom he could never please, and Daniel who abandoned him. And Aaron. Though the man turned out being evil, he'd left a gaping wound on Thomas's heart. Perhaps *because* he was evil. Thomas had thought him good, a father figure who understood Thomas and praised his accomplishments.

Yet now all those accomplishments seemed rather empty.

Down the beach to his left, the *clink* of glass, laughter, and music told him a party ensued. The powerful wealthy enjoying the fruits of their obedience to the NWU. Yet not all who obeyed the NWU had privileges, like he'd once believed. Most lived in insufferable conditions.

He cursed. Had those Deviants brainwashed him? Everything he'd ever wanted was finally within his grasp. He'd not only been reinstated in his position of power and wealth, but Landry had assured him he could eventually become part of Aali's personal spirit guides. He would have all the power and money and women he wanted.

Except the only woman he wanted was Tori.

You will forget her soon enough. She betrayed you. You deserve better. There are many women far more beautiful, far more pleasing than she.

The thoughts came from outside him, but they rang true. How could he ever trust her again? Besides, she was at this hideout now, and he had no way to contact her.

Then why was he so confused? There were two gods, Lucifer and the God of the Bible. Which one was the real God?

Thomas had a feeling that the answer to that question was the most important thing he could ever know.

Arithem stood, blade drawn, staring at the dark spirits circling around Thomas. He could not touch them until Thomas called upon the name of the Lord. And, of course, they knew that as they sneered, leered, and hissed at him, mocking the warrior of the Most High.

But they would have their day.

Arithem would remind them of that, except at the moment, he was more concerned for his ward. Thomas was clearly troubled, clearly distraught, not only at what had happened to Calan, but at everything he'd witnessed.

Now was the moment of decision—the moment every minute in his life up until this time had led him to. Would he choose to follow the light or the darkness?

Arithem now understood what humans went through when they stood helpless watching a loved one make a life-threatening decision. He almost wished the Father of Spirits had not granted angels emotions, for then he'd merely be standing guard, calmly awaiting orders.

Not feeling every inch of him strung tight in anticipation. And fear.

He'd had other wards before this one. Some had chosen well, others had not. Yet, for some reason, he'd grown attached to this particular son of Adam, something for which the Commander would surely chastise him.

Yet Thomas had suffered much, had come close to the light more than once, only to believe the enemy's lies and retreat again. This time, however, Arithem sensed he was closer to the light than he'd ever been.

Hence, he stood, waiting, hoping, watching as more demons crowded around Thomas, choking him with their lies.

He glanced above, beyond the starry skies, sensing that all of heaven awaited in great anticipation for this one son of Adam's choice.

For whosoever shall call upon the name of the Lord shall be saved.
Romans 10:13

Chapter 32

A strong wind blasted over Thomas, stirring the sand at his feet and rustling through his hair. Darkness settled thick on the beach with only a half-moon and a few visible stars to offer their light. Even so, the shadows from his home seemed to have followed him, moving about him in mists of black even darker than the sky.

Demons, Tori had called them. She saw them everywhere. Or so she said.

He rubbed his eyes. He was just imagining things.

Yet, memories of their journey refused to vacate his mind. If Lucifer was Aali in the flesh, and he was ruling the world, why was there so much misery, pain, disease, and famine? Even people in the NWU housing centers barely survived. Sure, they had food, but what quality? Fake meat, lab-created vegetables? Whatever they ate, it couldn't be very healthy since everyone looked sickly. They owned nothing of their own. They took no pride in their work, if they even had jobs, and most of them lay around self-medicated, living in a virtual world. Was this the utopia Aali had promised?

Free food, medicine and housing for all. That's what he'd said. Thomas snorted. And that's exactly what he'd given them. Yet, most people, along with Thomas, had a different picture in their minds.

The cities and small towns they'd passed through were nothing but wastelands, the citizens wandering around in squalor, filth and disease. Most looked like freakish zombies. Many were violent. Even the farmland was either abandoned or burned up by one of the recent meteors.

And yet, the rich and powerful lived in luxury with plenty of healthy good food, fancy homes, and cars. Sounded more like communism to him than the social and economic equality the NWU touted.

Then there was this tattoo of Aali's, the *Mark*. If Aali was all about freedom, why were people killed for not taking it? Many were worse than killed, but tortured and crucified in a monstrous death. Why so brutal? A shudder ran through him even now as the scene of those people hanging on crosses blazed in his mind. Sure, the Mark was supposed to eradicate disease and make everyone immortal, but why not just allow those who didn't take it to live out their lives and die naturally? Why the rush to execute them?

Aali wants the best for everyone. He must get rid of those who keep humanity from evolving into the gods he has proclaimed they can be.

Again, the voices. Not from Thomas. Odd. True, Aali had told everyone that humans could become gods of their own. Sounded wonderful. Immortality. No more sickness or disease. Think of what the human race could accomplish!

But what about the Deviants? He'd been told they were crazy, mentally unstable, backward, ignorant, authoritarian, determined to stop humanity from evolving. Yet Thomas had found the opposite to be true. Tori, Brianna, and Sara had treated him with nothing but kindness. Even though he didn't believe as they did, they'd welcomed him, befriended him, cared for him. And the God they served was just like them. Everything He did, the miracles, the food He provided, the protection from disasters, how He'd raised little Callie from the dead—everything He did was for their good.

In fact, if Aaron really was working for Lucifer, everything he threw at them—the drones, the tsunami, the tornado, and finally the cliff—had been defeated by the name of Jesus. Even the cliff. Thomas chuckled, remembering how they had walked out onto nothing but air.

Then there were the glimpses of huge bright beings with swords. Thomas could not deny he'd seen them on more than one occasion.

Tori and little Carla had said they were angels.

Carla. What a sweet, beautiful child, full of such light and love. He missed her, missed the feel of her tiny hand slipping in his.

Whatever the shimmering beings were, they had protected them. Just like the Bible said.

They are wicked! They seek to deceive you to not believe in Lucifer! It is he who cares for you, who wishes to prosper you and grant you freedom and happiness.

Thunder rumbled in the distance, and Thomas dropped his head in his hands, willing the voices to stop. But they continued, nonetheless.

If you choose the false god you will die. You will lose everything.

If you choose Me, you will find life, and find it more abundantly.

Thomas lifted his head. The second voice was different from the others, clearer, more pure, filled with hope. *God?* Hadn't Calan told him to call out to God, to ask Him to reveal Himself?

"NO!" the largest demon, the one with the goat horns and red flaming eyes, screamed. "Circle him! Whisper more lies," he commanded the other vile spirits.

"Not so fast!" Arithem moved to stand between the horde and Thomas. "He has called the Almighty."

One of the smaller demons, a squat, slimy creature, hissed at Arithem. "He has but said the name, naught more."

Thomas bowed his head. "God, if you're real…if you are the true God, please reveal Yourself to me."

"Ah ha!" Raising his blade in the air, Arithem brought it down upon the dark ones, slashing this way and that. The weaker ones turned into dust immediately. The stronger ones came at Arithem with all manner of crude weapons. One struck him in the thigh. Pain radiated up his side.

A long knife came out of nowhere and hacked the demon. Anisian appeared beside him. "The Commander said you needed help."

Arithem smiled. "Indeed."

Together the mighty warrior angels battled their opponents, stabbing, striking, punching and kicking them. The demons put up a fight. More collapsed into a heap of dark ash. Finally, the few who remained ran away, uttering hideous blasphemies as they went.

Arithem grabbed his friend's fist and nodded. "Thank you."

Anisian smiled then faced Thomas. "Now, let us see if our efforts were worth it."

Thomas waited, feeling suddenly foolish talking to a God who probably couldn't hear him. Or maybe didn't want to. Thomas had done nothing but shun Him, ignore His Word, and kill His followers. Why would He give Thomas the time of day?

A speck of light formed on the horizon far out at sea. Not the reflection of the moon, but something much brighter, something golden. It grew larger and larger, coming closer and closer.

A UFO? One of the Neflams' ships?

No. He'd seen their ships, and this was much brighter...faster.

Should he get up and run back to his house? Thomas's heart nearly crashed through his chest.

Still, he sat, mesmerized, unable to move. This was just like Tori's drawing!

By the time the light hit the shore, it was the size of a man, a shimmering man who stepped from the water onto the sand and moved toward Thomas.

He squinted at the bright light. Pulse racing and mind spinning, he lowered his gaze to the sand, unsure what to do.

Was this God? If so, would He incinerate Thomas on the spot for all his sins?

Two golden boots, engraved with Hebrew words, appeared in his vision as light enveloped him.

"Thomas," a voice said, though not like any voice Thomas had ever heard. It sounded like the mad rush of a river, deep, abiding, loving.

A hand appeared. A hole punctured the wrist right through to the other side. Fingers pressed beneath Thomas's chin and raised his gaze upward.

The figure of a man blazed behind the dazzling light. A smile formed on his lips. *Such love!* Such love beamed from his eyes, Thomas could not tear his gaze away.

"Who are you?" Thomas asked.

"I am Jesus, the One who died for you. Receive me and live."

And then He was gone.

Darkness surrounded Thomas. He rubbed his eyes, where the vision of the man remained. A sweet scent showered over him like nothing he'd ever smelled before.

He hung his head. Tears came hard and fast, dropping onto the sand. *Jesus is real!* The God of the Bible was real. He was not a bully. He was pure love. The love Thomas had been searching for his entire life, unconditional, abundant, overwhelming love.

"How can you love me after all I've done?" Thomas sobbed.

I have always loved you. Repent and I will wash away all your sins.

The bright flash of a sword swept across the darkness, and Thomas dropped his elbows to the sand.

"I repent. I'm so sorry. I'm so sorry. I've been so stubborn, so stupid, so arrogant." More tears came, choking his voice. "I submit to you, Jesus, my King and my God."

Before he even finished his words, joy like he'd never known bubbled up in his heart, rising to his throat and emerging in laughter, beautiful, joyous laughter.

Sitting up, he wiped his eyes as a cloak of immeasurable love settled on his shoulders. He sat there for what surely was half the night, thanking and praising God.

Finally, when the first hint of dawn turned the horizon gray, Thomas grabbed his cane and hoisted himself to stand. He drew one last breath of the sea air, then turned to face his home, shoulders back, mind and heart settled.

He knew exactly what he had to do.

*That if thou shalt confess with thy mouth the Lord Jesus,
and shalt believe in thine heart that God hath raised him from
the dead, thou shalt be saved.*
Romans 10:9

Chapter 33

Halting before the Communications Room at NWF Reformation Headquarters, Thomas closed his eyes. *Lord, if you're really with me, I need Your strength now more than ever.*

No voice came, no blanket of warmth and assurance, but deep inside, a sense of purpose, truth, power, and, yes, love stirred and grew to fill his soul. The Holy Spirit lived within him, the proof of the living God and assurance of salvation, giving him strength to endure whatever came.

Smiling, he opened the door and hobbled inside the dark room used for virtual communication with those far away. Thomas suspected who he'd be conversing with, and one look at Landry's grin confirmed it.

What Thomas had not expected was Sergeant Cruz's presence, along with two NWF guards standing at attention on either side of the hologram projection pedestal. One of them held a medical bag in his hand.

Landry approached. His eyes held the usual approval and pride—a sentiment Thomas had craved for so long to fill his feelings of unworthiness, his need for a father.

But he had a Father now, the best one.

"This is a momentous occasion, Tom. Not many people are privileged enough to meet with Lord Aali one-on-one. Or at least the closest thing to it." He clapped Thomas on the back.

Cruz, who stood beside one of the guards, frowned. Or was it more a sneer?

Thomas released a sigh. "I'm surprised he would take the time for me."

"Why wouldn't he? You are only two steps removed from being one of his personal spiritual advisers." Landry nodded at the technician sitting behind an instrument panel. "Besides, he requested an audience, said he wanted to witness your loyalty for himself. I don't have to tell you how important this meeting is, Tom. His Lordship's impression of you could skyrocket your career immediately."

Thomas swallowed, mind and emotions spinning.

Yes...you can finally have everything you want, the slippery voice whispered in his ear.

"Lord Aali is ready," the technician announced.

Landry waved a hand for him to proceed.

A vertical beam of light appeared on the pedestal and instantly expanded into the image of Lord Aali. He looked much the same as the few times Thomas had seen him in person. Yet, he seemed taller, his eyes more narrow, and his clothing more refined. Jewels glittered around the fringe of his coat and across his fingers, and he stood with an almost palpable arrogance that had been absent before.

"Hello, Thomas," he said. "I have granted you a great privilege and opportunity today." His voice was deep and carried an echo that made it sound otherworldly and ominous.

"Thank you for the audience," Thomas said.

Landry leaned in to whisper in his ear. "My Lord."

Ignoring him, Thomas hoped Aali wouldn't notice his omission.

Aali cocked his head, studying Thomas with piercing, dark eyes that reminded him of black holes, sucking in all the light around him.

"Regent Landry speaks well of you, but if you are to continue in my service, I wish to witness your loyalty for myself." Aali smiled. Not a friendly smile or a kind smile, but one that sent a barbed chill through Thomas.

If he was supposed to respond, he failed again. His mind spun in a thousand directions even as his eyes landed once again on the medical bag in the guard's hands.

They intended to give him the mark!

Aali's jaws tightened at Thomas's silence. He cleared his throat, staring at him, his penetrating gaze slicing deep into Thomas's soul. "You must bow before me, Thomas Benton, swear your allegiance to me as your leader and your god," he said, almost in a pleading tone. Odd. "Then receive my stamp on your hand. Follow me and you will live forever!"

Thomas's gaze shifted from Aali to Landry to Cruz and finally to the medical bag. *Eternal life, power, and pleasures*! a voice swirled in the air around Thomas with the stench of death and decay.

His heart thundered. A tingling traversed his spine and down his arms. He could have everything he'd ever wanted right here and now. *Or* he could give it all up and be executed.

Arithem stood, arms crossed over his mighty chest, helplessly watching to see what Thomas would do. Aye, Arithem had seen the demons whispering lies in his ward's ears, knew Thomas recognized their voices, but he had not rebuked them yet.

And this concerned Arithem most of all.

"He will make the right choice," Zhaviel said from beside him, glancing up at Arithem, who stood at least two feet taller. "He has encountered the Commander."

Arithem sighed. "Indeed. 'Twas so merciful of our Lord to reveal Himself to Thomas in so powerful a way. He received Him, His spirit was born anew. Behold the light within him!" He gestured toward Thomas's chest where evidence of the Holy Spirit shone brightly. "Yet he hesitates. Why?"

Zhaviel gripped the handle of his club. "He is a babe in the faith. Our enemy offers him everything he has dreamed of." He glanced at Kyle and sighed. "And my ward salivates to kill him."

"Wait." Arithem lifted his chin and listened. "Someone prays for Thomas. Prayers are going up to the throne for him! Do you not smell the sweet incense?"

Zhaviel drew a deep breath. "I do, my friend. 'Tis great news. Ah, behold the light within him glows. The Father of Spirits gives him strength!"

"Such power He grants His children, the power to petition the throne! If they would but use it more often." Hope returned to Arithem as he continued to watch.

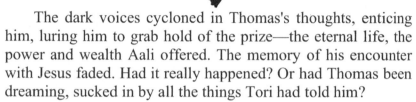

The dark voices cycloned in Thomas's thoughts, enticing him, luring him to grab hold of the prize—the eternal life, the power and wealth Aali offered. The memory of his encounter with Jesus faded. Had it really happened? Or had Thomas been dreaming, sucked in by all the things Tori had told him?

Just a dream. Not real.

Something shifted inside him. The slightest sensation.

"Thomas?" Landry's voice turned sharp, his eyes even sharper. "Lord Aali is waiting."

A kaleidoscope of images passed through his mind—glowing beings with swords, rescues from certain death, fresh bread every morning, Callie opening her little eyes as breath came back into her, the love shared between the Deviants, and the image of Jesus on the beach with the hole in his wrist.

I will never leave you or forsake you. The promise grew within him, filling every crevice of his soul.

Thomas faced Aali. "I will never bow to you or take your stamp. I bow only to the King of Kings and Lord of Lords. His name is Jesus."

Several things happened all at once. At the name of Jesus, Aali covered his ears and let out an ear-piercing scream, the dark voices that had been haunting Thomas disappeared, Kyle snorted in disgust, and Landry stared at Thomas as if he'd sprouted wings and hovered in the air.

He grabbed his arm. Tight. "What are you saying?"

Thomas yanked from his grasp. "I thought I was quite plain."

"Told you he was one of them." Kyle nodded for the guards to grab him.

"I want him dead!" Aali shouted. "Crucified for all to see!"

Landry bowed before him. "It will be done, my Lord."

A spark of fear burst within Thomas, but he pushed it down. Whatever kind of death he endured, he'd not do it alone, and it would be worth it in the end. He knew that now.

"How dare you waste my time with this charade, Landry!" Aali cursed, his face twisted in rage. The hologram disappeared.

Landry's eyes flared red. "Look what you have done!" He pointed a finger at Thomas. "You fool!"

Thomas smiled as the guards gripped both his arms. "No, sir. I have finally come to my senses."

"Take him away!" Landry shouted, the pain in his eyes evident behind his anger. "Lock him up until I can make the appropriate arrangements." He faced Thomas again. "You love this Jesus so much, then you will suffer and die just like He did."

Kyle should be thrilled to watch the great Thomas Benton fall. And at first he was. After all, he'd been right about the Vice Regent's loyalties from the beginning, and he reminded Landry of just that after Thomas had been dragged away.

But now, alone in his luxurious NWF apartment, his thoughts and emotions flipped this way and that on a roller coaster of confusion and anguish. Sure, he'd suspected Thomas all along, but watching him actually turn down a huge promotion, tons of money and power, *and* eternal life for this God of the Bible completely and utterly baffled him. Especially when it meant certain death. And a very long, torturous death at that.

Then there was Calan. Kyle had seen the same look in his eyes that he'd seen in Thomas'—a look of peace, confidence, joy. Even as Calan was about to have his head chopped off, even then, he'd not shown an ounce of fear or regret. In fact, quite the opposite.

Calan's words kept repeating over and over in Kyle's mind, no matter how hard he'd tried to evict them.

Use your head, son. Look around you. Who really is the evil god?

All you need to do is repent of the evil you've done, give your life to Jesus, and follow Him, and you'll live forever in a paradise you can't imagine.

Just ask the God of the Bible if He's real. Just ask Him and be open for His answer.

Could Kyle be on the wrong side?

He also couldn't shake Lord Aali's reaction to the name of Jesus. Aali had always been in control, confident, sophisticated, never overreacting to any situation. It was one of the reasons Kyle admired him. He knew what he was doing and could be trusted. His temper tantrum today shocked Kyle and revealed a very angry, demanding tyrant, not the loving, caring leader Kyle believed he was.

Pure evil and hatred had burned in the man's eyes. Or *god,* as he claimed to be. What sort of god would order the crucifixion of a man, a good man by all accounts, simply for not bowing to him? Seemed rather arrogant to Kyle. So what if people refused to bow or take the stamp? They'd soon die of starvation anyway since they'd not be able to buy food. Why not leave them be? Let them fend for themselves. Though even that seemed cruel, but at least they'd be free. Yes, the stamp offered immunity from disease too, and those who refused it would be carriers, but only amongst themselves. What harm was that to the rest of the world?

Kyle was not too young to remember that the country of his birth, the United States of America, had once valued freedom—freedom of speech, freedom of religion, freedom to pursue happiness in whatever form you desired. Precisely what Aali had promised when the Neflams arrived and appointed him leader. After all the wars, asteroids, meteors, pestilences, and famines, the world had been ready to unite under one wise, benevolent ruler who promised a utopia of freedom, plenty and peace.

Plopping on his couch, he dropped his head in his hands. He'd not really given the bowing and the Mark much thought before. He'd just figured Lord Aali would not demand something that didn't benefit mankind. In fact, if Kyle hadn't been so busy chasing Thomas and Tori, he would have already gotten it.

But that evil look in his eyes...Kyle could not shake.

Nor could he shake the love in Nyla's eyes. Or Calan's and now Thomas's. Not just love for a friend or family, but love for an enemy, love for someone who wanted them dead. That's a love that made no sense to Kyle.

Aali's love, if he possessed any, was conditional. He knew that now. Obey or die. Those were the words of a tyrant—the exact thing he accused the God of the Bible of being. Jura's love had also been conditional, as was Kyle's father's. At least he'd thought so at the time.

But this God, this Jesus, He taught His followers to love even their enemies. If this God loved His enemies, then how much more would He love those who followed Him?

He is a fraud, a bully! Voices filled Kyle's thoughts. *He will steal all your joy, your power, your money. He demands worship and then He will get you killed.*

Maybe that was true. Following this Deviant God would cost Kyle everything. He blew out a sigh and stared at the bottle of pills on the table. More than one shrink had labeled him an empath, highly emotional, with an anxiety disorder. The pills calmed him down, leveled the mountains of confusion and disorder in his mind.

Grabbing the bottle, he snapped the lid and shook two pills into his hand.

That's right. Take them. They always make you feel better.

But did Kyle really want to feel better? Or did he simply want to know the truth?

Thomas had said they were alike. That much was true. Which made it all the harder to understand his decision. Perhaps he was the only one to help Kyle make sense of it all.

Sliding the pills back in the bottle, Kyle capped it and set it aside. Then rising, he grabbed his coat and headed out the door, locking it with his wrist.

He had to talk to Thomas. This might be his last chance.

For to me to live is Christ, and to die is gain.
Philippians 1:21

Chapter 34

"I'll take it from here," Kyle told the guard who escorted him to Thomas's cell.

"Are you sure, sergeant? The ones that are going to be crucified can get pretty violent."

Kyle smiled at the man who was near his own age. "I'll be fine, corporal. Now back to your post."

"Yes, sir." The young man pointed to the cell ahead. "You can talk to him from the outside if you change your mind. The button's right there."

"I know." Kyle grew impatient. "Good night."

Saluting, the man marched away.

Kyle wasn't sure what to expect when he approached the one-way mirror that made up the front wall of Thomas's cell. Maybe a man weeping, trembling, or pacing at the thought of his horrifying death in just a few hours, maybe even on his knees praying to his God for mercy and rescue. But what he saw instead was a man with upraised hands, smile on his face, tears pouring down his cheeks, singing. *Singing?*

Leaning on his crutch, Kyle pressed the button that allowed him to hear into the soundproof room.

"Praise the name of Jesus! Praise the name of Jesus. You're my rock. You're my fortress. You're my deliverer. In You do I trust!"

Kyle snapped the sound off, more baffled than he'd ever been. For several minutes, he could only stand and stare dumbfounded at the man who faced an agonizing death praising the God who was allowing it, who caused it! He should walk away. The fear had obviously driven Thomas mad, and there was no sense in talking to a crazy man.

But something kept him there, moved his hand over the door lock and even pushed him inside. *Something*, because Kyle didn't remember making a conscious decision to do any of those things.

"Sergeant Cruz!" Thomas lowered his hands and swiped the moisture from his face. "What a nice surprise."

No sarcasm, no snarkiness infiltrated his tone, but a genuine joy at seeing Kyle.

Crazy. Yup. The man was nuts.

The door clanked shut, echoing through the tiny room that consisted of a cot, a blanket, and a toilet.

"Why are you singing?" Kyle asked.

Thomas smiled. "Because I'm free. I'm saved, and I'm going home." He waved his arms around as if he were in a palace not a prison.

Kyle snorted. "I hate to break it to you, but you're not going home. You're going to the grave."

"Exactly." Thomas gestured toward his cot. "It's not much, but it's all I can offer you to sit on."

"Why?" Kyle asked.

Thomas raised his brows. "I don't suppose you're asking about the cot, right?" He laughed, then grew serious, studying Kyle. "You want to know why I wouldn't bow to Aali and take his mark. Why I purposely signed my own death warrant. Is that it?"

Kyle nodded. "I just don't get it. You said we both want the same things, but you're throwing all those things away. And for what? Some bully God."

"He's not a bully, Kyle. He's everything!" He raised his hands again and lifted his face to the ceiling. "He's our Creator, our Friend, our Father, our Companion, our Protector, Provider, and most of all, Savior."

Kyle narrowed his eyes. "They brainwashed you. Tori and the rest."

"No. They led me to the truth. Don't you see?" Excitement flared in Thomas's eyes. "I was the one brainwashed... by the world, the culture, Aali, and all our leaders, by religion, by our enemy Lucifer. He is the author of lies, confusion, pain, and death. He is the evil one, Kyle. He wants to drag us to hell."

"Hell." Kyle huffed. "Like there is such a place."

"There is. And there's a heaven too. And that's why I'm singing. Because I know where I'm going. My Savior died for me so that I could be there with Him." Thomas took a step toward him. "And you can too, Kyle."

Arithem could hardly contain his joy. "Behold, he is but a babe in our Lord, and yet already he is a fisher of men!"

"And he fishes for my ward! God be praised!" Zhaviel thrust his club in the air.

Arithem drew his blade just in case. "Still, see how he listens to the demons, he entertains their lies."

"Aye," Zhaviel sighed. "He sits upon the edge of eternity, and there is naught we can do to push him in the right direction."

"Nay, but be on the alert. Thomas uses the weapons the Almighty has given him, the Word of God and the name of the Commander." Arithem nodded proudly, then glanced back at Thomas. "He sees us. Observe how he smiles our way."

Limping backward, Kyle gripped the handle of the Glock he'd stuffed in his belt.

"Do you think I would hurt you?" Thomas laughed. "I'm trying to save you." He retreated, staring and smiling at something on his left.

Maybe he *was* truly crazy. "What are you looking at?"

Thomas leaned on his cane. "You wouldn't believe me if I told you."

"Try me." Kyle had no idea why he remained listening to this fool. Thomas had obviously lost it. Or had he? There was something in his eyes, some force, some power he'd not seen before. Not the glazed look of a madman at all. It was love. It spilled out of every pore, radiated over his skin, beamed from his smile. Overwhelming love. For Kyle? He'd done nothing but hunt Thomas down, doubt him at every turn, and gloat over his soon coming execution. Yet was it Thomas's love Kyle felt, or did it come from Someone else?

"Okay." Thomas sighed. "I'm looking at two very mighty warrior angels standing here with us." He said the words so matter-of-factly, so calmly, and with such confidence, it was hard for Kyle to disagree.

"Angels, eh?" He huffed.

Thomas shrugged. "You asked. And they have pretty cool weapons too."

Now Kyle laughed.

Why are you still here? This guy is a lunatic and a liar.

Kyle could not deny that. Maybe he *should* leave. Maybe there was no answer to his question. Maybe Thomas had just gone crazy, and that was all there was to it. Placing his crutch under his arm, he turned toward the door.

"I rebuke you demons. I muzzle you in the name of Jesus! Be silent."

Halting at Thomas's strange words, Kyle faced him. He couldn't say why, but a sudden weight seemed to lift off him, as if someone removed a heavy blanket from his shoulders, an oppressive blanket. The whispers urging him to leave vanished.

"God is a good God, Kyle," Thomas appealed. "He is pure love. What other God would send His only Son to be tortured and murdered for a bunch of losers like us? When Jesus rose again, He conquered our enemy and opened the way for us to live forever with Him. Amazing grace!"

A flash of brilliant gold swept across Kyle's vision, drawing his gaze to two beings standing to his right. One had a sword, the other a club. Both wore armor.

Both smiled at him.

His knees gave out.

Lunging for him, Thomas caught him, and helped him to sit on the cot.

Buzzing filled Kyle's head as breath fled his lungs. "I saw them."

"The angels?"

Kyle looked up, but they were gone. "Yes."

Thomas laughed. "Told ya."

"What the…" Kyle blinked and stared at Thomas. "It's all true… everything you said."

Smiling, Thomas nodded.

"All this time, I've been wrong and my sister was right." He bent over, struggling to breathe.

Thomas sat beside him. "It's a lot to take in, isn't it?"

Kyle rubbed his eyes, his thoughts and emotions jumbling in shock. Could this be true? Could this really be true? "I hated Nyla when she joined the Deviants. I wouldn't listen to her or my Tata, my grandmother. I wanted to be powerful and wealthy and feel like I was somebody."

"It's the same trap I fell into. But you *are* someone. Someone very important to Jesus! You are precious, worth dying for."

Tears filled Kyle's eyes as an overwhelming sense of peace cloaked him, a peace he'd never felt before. "I want to follow Him."

"I have to ask you something, Kyle." Thomas grew serious. "Have you taken Aali's quantum stamp?"

Kyle wiped moisture from his face. "No. I've been too busy tracking you." He chuckled.

Thomas smiled. "Good. Then if you truly want to become a follower of Jesus, repent of your sins, believe in Him, and submit your life to Him."

"That's it?"

"Yup." Thomas grinned. "But following Him will be hard. Don't make the decision lightly. You know better than others what you're getting into."

Hard was an understatement. Kyle would lose everything and be hunted the rest of his life. Possibly die a horrific death. But how could he deny the overpowering sense of goodness, love, and joy that surrounded him? "I'm ready."

Thomas led Kyle in a very simple prayer, but even before he uttered the words, he felt a light burst within him, deep down, as if something was born, something good and holy. The love that he'd seen in Thomas's eyes became real to him, filling him, soothing away all the wounds of his past.

And for the first time in his life, Kyle felt loved and valued.

They sat there for several minutes, crying and thanking God.

Finally, Kyle grabbed his crutch and struggled to rise. "I've got to get you out of here!"

"What?" Thomas said with a bewildered look on his face.

"I just know it. I'm supposed to help you escape."

*Come, my people, enter thou into thy chambers, and shut
thy doors about thee: hide thyself as it were for a little moment,
until the indignation be overpast. For, behold, the Lord cometh
out of his place to punish the inhabitants of the earth for their
iniquity: the earth also shall disclose her blood, and shall no
more cover her slain.*
Isaiah 26:20-21

Chapter 35

Two months later

Tori had no idea what she was doing. Who was she to deliver a baby? Not only had she never had one herself, but she'd not even witnessed childbirth. At least Brianna had given birth to two healthy children, and Jane, a young woman helping them, had been a nurse before the Tribulation, albeit in the dermatology department.

Nyla let out an ear-piercing scream, only made more chilling by the way it echoed in a thrumming shriek throughout the cave.

Lord, please help me. Tori prayed. Please bring this baby into the world healthy and strong. And keep Nyla safe too! She didn't know what else to pray. Should she rebuke the enemy's plans? No time for that as Nyla screamed again, squeezing Tori's hand so tight, she was sure one of her bones would break.

Tori glanced at Brianna, who looked as petrified as she was.

Returning her attention to Nyla, she dabbed a cloth over her forehead. "It's okay, Nyla. We're here, and God is with us."

Nyla nodded as the pains subsided.

And Tori's hand gained its feeling.

They'd moved her to a private alcove beside the main room where several people held hands and prayed for the birth.

Smiling at Brianna and Jane, Tori was grateful for the support. Ever since Nyla's labor began, Tori's prayers had been scattered and full of more fear than she knew she should have.

They'd gathered blankets, warm water and soap, a sterilized knife, and a needle and thread for sewing the umbilical cord. But how do you gather skill at birthing... along with courage?

Exhaustion weighed on Tori's eyelids. Poor Nyla had been in labor for twelve long hours. The hardest part was seeing her in such pain and not being able to alleviate it.

Nyla's entire body tensed again. She closed her eyes and squeezed Tori's hand.

"I'm never having another baby!" she screamed at the top of her lungs.

Tori and Brianna shared a smile. In her agonizing delirium, Nyla had been shouting many such declarations.

The pains were coming faster now. Harder. Tori had no idea how to check for dilation or whatever doctors did. "Lord, you're going to have to deliver this precious child in one piece," she whispered.

"I feel like pushing," Nyla ground out through clenched teeth.

"Then go for it," Tori said. *God help us.* Dilated or not, here the baby came.

Twenty minutes later, Tori handed Nyla her new son wrapped in a blanket. The birth was amazing, stunning, beautiful to watch a new life come into the world. What a miracle! And he was so small, so fragile, and yet so perfectly made.

Jane had clipped the cord and tied it off and was now helping deliver the afterbirth.

Tears streamed down Tori's cheeks as Nyla held her son close and got her first look at his face.

"He's beautiful. Just like his father," she said and kissed him on the forehead. "How can I ever thank you two?" She glanced up at Tori and Jane.

"It wasn't us." Tori began gathering bloody cloths. "You did all the work, with the Lord's help. We were just here to catch the little guy. What will you name him?"

Now it was Nyla's turn to cry as she stared at her son. "If it was a boy, Calan wanted him named Daniel."

"Good name." Tori wiped her own tears. "After a good, Godly man."

"And Calan's mentor." Nyla gave a sad smile, and Tori knew she missed her husband. Terribly. Just like Tori missed Thomas.

"Do you think we'll ever see them again?" Tori asked.

Two weeks later

The forest was beautiful this time of day. Tori drew a deep breath of fresh air—at least as fresh as it could get in this world—and sat on a boulder perched before the entrance to the cave. She came out here every evening as the sun set, her special time alone with the Lord, to pray, to praise, to enjoy the birds chirping and watch the setting sun paint red and orange on leaves and tree trunks before it left for the day.

Since Thomas and Calan had been caught, the days blurred together in a mishmash of the work and activities required to care for and feed God's people. Unfortunately—and against both Tori and Nyla's warnings—a few of them had traveled into the nearest city, hoping for news of lost loved ones. They never returned. Most likely captured by the NWU. Now, their group was down to a mere twenty-two souls, most of whom were either too weak, old, or young to fend for themselves. Nyla and Calan had done a great job running things, but in his absence, Tori had stepped up. And even more so now that Nyla was a new mother.

Yet there were days when Tori strained under the burden placed upon her. Not just the physical burden of providing food and protection, but the spiritual one. Who was she but an ex-druggie who didn't have sense enough not to get involved in the occult?

Sure, with Nyla's counsel, Tori realized she'd been forgiven, that she didn't have to earn God's love and approval. But still...

Lord, are you sure You have the right person for the job?

A brown bird with red feathers on his head landed on a branch above her and sang such a happy tune, she couldn't help but smile.

Yes, dear one. I am sending help.

Wait, did she hear that right? Help?

A vision sprinted so fast through her mind, she barely saw it, barely recognized Thomas and.... Kyle?... walking through the forest.

Leaping to her feet, she scanned the trees and shrubs. She turned her ear to listen for any unusual sound. Nothing.

Still, she *had* seen them. She knew it.

Diving back into the cave, she hurried to get Nyla. It took some convincing, but the new mother reluctantly handed Daniel to Brianna for safe keeping and followed Tori into the forest.

"Are you sure, Tor?" she asked.

Tori brushed aside a branch and forged ahead. "I'm sure. It's them. I saw it."

"You saw Kyle?"

"Yes." She smiled at her friend over her shoulder. "Can you believe it?"

"No," Nyla said. "Listen, if it's them and they are close, shouldn't we be more cautious? Neither of them were saved last time we saw them. They could be hunting us."

Halting, Tori spun to face her friend. "Good point. But... I don't know. When the vision came, I sensed joy, peace, not anger or fear. It didn't even occur to me that they could be our enemies. They were happy, smiling." *Crud.* Tori drew a deep breath and frowned. Aaron had tricked her, had deceived her for so long. She had not seen him for what he was. Was she making another mistake?

Nyla gripped her hand. "I know you're thinking of Aaron, but you have grown since then. You learned from that experience, and you're stronger for it."

"Am I?" Tori wasn't so sure.

"Trust God. He will lead you. What are you sensing?"

Tori closed her eyes. *Lord, tell me what to do. Don't let me make another mistake.* She heard nothing, sensed nothing but a strong peace that flooded her spirit. She opened her eyes. "That we should find them."

"Okay, let's go then. But be careful."

Tori's visions from the Lord had never let her down. In fact, even now, the Holy Spirit was leading her, giving her a sense of which way to turn, what hill to climb, what creek to cross. Surely, He would not be doing that if it weren't His will.

After several more minutes, she heard something. Ever so slight, but there. A chuckle. A male chuckle. A familiar male chuckle. One that made her heart skip a beat.

Inching ahead, Tori swept aside branches and leaves, her heart swelling with excitement, her pulse racing in anticipation. Could it be? *Could it really be him, Lord?* She sensed no fear, no warning, but only a warmth that swept down to her toes.

Kneeling behind a thick shrub, she eased a clump of leaves aside.

There, beside a pile of wood, sat Thomas and Kyle, smiling and joking as they attempted to light a fire.

Their clothes were mere rags, their hair long and unkempt, their beards full, and they'd both lost weight. But it was them. Tori's heart swelled at the sight of the man she still loved.

Nyla knelt beside her and let out a gasp at the sight of Kyle, the same questions Tori was asking written on her face. If they were hunting the Deviants, why did they look so ragged and unfed? And why were they smiling and joking around?

"Ask the Lord," Nyla whispered.

Nodding, Tori closed her eyes and sought the Lord's still small voice. *Should we trust them, Lord?*

Yes.

Grinning, Tori rose and after gesturing for Nyla to follow her, brushed aside the foliage, and burst into the clearing.

Thomas stared at the one person he'd been dreaming about for two months. The one person he'd longed to see more than anyone—besides the Lord, of course. He must be hallucinating...from hunger, exhaustion, fear. But there she stood, gorgeous as ever with her crazy hair and stunning green eyes, smiling at him. *Smiling?*

He said nothing. Only jumped to his feet, ran toward her, and took her in his arms.

"Tori! Tori!" He dove his face into her hair and drew in a deep breath of her unique smell. Then cupping her cheeks, he smiled at her, tears pouring down both their faces. "It's you! I knew it." He planted kisses all over her face, ending up on her lips.

Nyla suddenly appeared beside them, clearing her throat and separating them. Her gaze landed on Kyle. She hesitated, studying him.

But Kyle didn't hesitate. Barreling toward his sister, he flew into her arms, embracing her tightly. They both laughed and cried at the same time.

"I told ya," Thomas said to Kyle, then glanced at Tori. "Told ya she'd know we were here."

Pushing back from her brother, Nyla wiped her eyes. "How did you find us? Why are you here?"

Kyle nodded at Thomas. "Thomas said he had no clue where your hideout was but that Tori would know when we arrived."

Thomas gripped Tori's hand and squeezed. "And she did."

She shook her head. "I still don't understand. What happened?"

Drawing a deep breath, Thomas shoved back his messy hair. "Long story."

Nyla slapped her brother. "Last time I saw you, you tried to kill me."

Kyle kicked the dirt, grinning. "Yeah, sorry about that, sis. I was wrong." He glanced at Thomas. "About so much."

"Are you?" Nyla took a step toward him and stared into his eyes. "You are! You've given your life to Jesus!"

Kyle nodded and Nyla flew into his arms again.

Tori spun Thomas to face her. "And you, mister? Have you come to your senses, too?"

"What do you think?" He eased a lock of her hair behind her ear.

Tori gave him a sideways grin. "It took you getting caught to convince you?"

"It was Calan."

At the mention of his name, Nyla faced Thomas.

He lowered his chin. How in the world could he tell her the bad news?

"I already know, Thomas," she said. "I could feel it when he left."

"I'm so sorry."

Kyle looped an arm around his sister's waist. "His words to us, to both of us, and the way he died, he helped us see the truth."

"His death was not in vain then." Nyla wiped a tear.

"No, and you'll see him again." Kyle drew her close.

"Do you believe that now, Kyle?" she asked him.

"I do. I'm so sorry for… everything." Swallowing hard, he stared at the dirt.

"It doesn't matter now."

"Praise be to God!" Tori said. "He does answer prayers, even for the most hard-headed. We were praying for you two every day."

Thomas shared a glance with Kyle. "We felt your prayers. God strengthened us, helped us see the truth. And he sent angels too!"

"You saw them?" Tori asked

"I did too!" Kyle exclaimed.

Thomas flung his arms out. "They are around us now!"

"Are they?" Everyone looked over the small clearing, but apparently only Thomas could see them.

"Well, I for one, am glad you had an angelic escort." Tori studied them both. "God knows what you'd look like if you hadn't."

"Yeah, you guys look horrible," Nyla added.

Thomas chuckled. "We've been through quite a lot these past months."

"Months?"

Kyle shook his head. "It wasn't easy coming here. The entire NWU and NWF are looking for us."

"But enduring those weeks with you," Thomas glanced at Tori, "taught me much."

She smiled.

A chilled breeze swept over them, stirring leaves at their feet.

Kyle glanced above where the faintest stars began to twinkle in the darkening sky. "So, we going to stand out here all night?"

"No," Nyla said, "Let's head back to UnderHisWings."

"And then what?" Thomas asked.

"We hide." Tori said. "The worst is yet to come. We hide and we pray and we wait for Jesus to return."

"There's no guarantee any of us will survive," Nyla added. "But either way, we will be with the Lord!"

Arithem, Zhaviel, Zarall, and Ranoss danced all the way back to UnderHisWings as they escorted their wards. How could they do otherwise? 'Twas a joyous day when finally those whom the Commander assigned to their watch made it into the Kingdom!

"I cannot stop leaping for joy!" Ranoss shouted, skipping over a fallen log.

Arithem chuckled. "Neither can I! How we have longed for this day, my friends! To see our wards saved for eternity!"

"Ah." Zarall shook his head with a smile. "The struggles and trials we have seen them through!"

Zhaviel nodded, glancing at Kyle. "In truth, there were many days I ne'er thought to see him saved."

"But the Lord of Hosts is Mighty to Save!" Arithem hefted his sword in the air.

"He is the King of Kings! The Lord of Lords!" They all shouted in unison.

The angels broke out in a song as they continued to escort the saints to their hideout.

"What do we do now, Arithem?" Zarall asked. "Have you heard from the Commander?"

"Aye. We are to protect the saints who remain at UnderHisWings. They must stay hidden there or they will be killed. That is all I have heard."

Ranoss, Zhaviel, and Zarall nodded. "Then that is what we will do."

And I heard a great voice out of the temple saying to the seven angels, Go your ways, and pour out the vials of the wrath of God upon the earth.
Revelation 16:1

Chapter 36

The next three years passed in agonizing slowness for the saints at UnderHisWings. They received very little news of what was happening outside their cavern hideout. Perhaps that was for the best. The world was enduring the worst time in its history and many people were being slaughtered by the Antichrist, while others endured the wrath of a mighty God.

The saints heard the sixth trumpet bellow, the sound penetrating deep into their woods, and they knew from Scripture that the four angels bound at the river Euphrates had been released to kill a third of mankind through a two-hundred-million-man army.

They prayed for the lost to repent and turn to God before it was too late. But thankfully the war never reached their forest haven.

So they spent their days in prayer and praise, hunting for food, and taking care of each other. God always provided what they needed not far from their cave, and more than once, many had seen the angels who protected them.

Some days it was hard to imagine the horrors happening in the world around them. Especially as they watched Daniel, Callie, Carla and the other children grow bigger and stronger each day and laugh and play like innocent children. In truth, the sight of them helped everyone cling to the hope that their lives would someday go beyond the moist dark walls of these caves and into a glorious eternity when Jesus returned.

There were other small joys along the way. The birth of another baby from one of the married couples. And a wedding! One of the saints had been a Justice of the Peace before the Tribulation, and he was happy to perform the ceremony that united Tori and Thomas in marriage. Tori almost felt guilty experiencing such joy when the world suffered such agony.

God sent other blessings as well. He led hungry, persecuted saints from all over the North American Region into the forest near UnderHisWings to join their number. Tori's gift of spiritual discernment became crucial to weed out the true believers from the pretenders and NWU spies. In the end, the band of Tribulation saints had grown to nearly one hundred. Taking care of them and helping them grow in the Lord became a full-time task for Tori and Thomas, but with God's help, they knew they'd been called for that exact purpose.

Sometime in the final year, Tori sensed that the Lord was about to pour out His seven bowls of wrath. In the evening Thomas would read the passages from Revelation describing these events. The first bowl brought a horrible sore upon those who had taken the Mark of the Beast. The second bowl turned the entire sea into blood.

The saints were not affected until the third bowl turned every river to blood. Only by the grace of God were they able to find safe drinking water around their cave, and when they couldn't, Nyla prayed over the bloody liquid they'd drawn from the creek, and it instantly turned into clear, fresh water.

They knew exactly when the fourth bowl was poured. The temperature in the forest rose so high, it was nearly impossible to venture out for food or water. The sun's rays seared their bare skin and even sizzled their hair. Inside the cave, the heat drained them of all their energy, making it impossible to move about, lest they overheat and die. During that time, the saints prayed and praised, and God provided the same manna at the entrance to the cave each morning that He had provided for Tori and Thomas on their journey.

The fifth bowl brought a darkness so thick and heavy it saturated everything and cloaked the forest in black. Even the fires they kept burning inside the cave could not dispel it or shove it away. During this time, the saints huddled together, singing and praying and comforting one another with the promises of God found in Scripture.

Tori sensed when the sixth bowl was poured, and they all knew that the Euphrates had dried up and the Antichrist was assembling an army from the kings of the east and from each world leader, drawing them to the Battle of Armageddon in order to fight the King of Kings.

Which meant only one thing. Jesus would soon return to take them home!

And I beheld when he had opened the sixth seal, and, lo, there was a great earthquake; and the sun became black as sackcloth of hair, and the moon became as blood;
And the stars of heaven fell unto the earth, even as a fig tree casteth her untimely figs, when she is shaken of a mighty wind.
And the heaven departed as a scroll when it is rolled together; and every mountain and island were moved out of their places.
And the kings of the earth, and the great men, and the rich men, and the chief captains, and the mighty men, and every bondman, and every free man, hid themselves in the dens and in the rocks of the mountains;
And said to the mountains and rocks, Fall on us, and hide us from the face of him that sitteth on the throne, and from the wrath of the Lamb:
For the great day of his wrath is come; and who shall be able to stand?
Revelation 6:12-17

"It's starting!" Tori shouted, her voice echoing through the cave.

The dear saints—all the precious people she'd come to love—stared at her with exhausted looks.

"What is it?" Nyla hoisted three-year-old Daniel into her arms.

"Don't you feel it?" Tori gestured for everyone to follow her.

The ground shook beneath them, gently at first, but soon it began to shift and slide violently.

"Outside, everyone!" Thomas yelled.

Chunks of rock loosened from the walls and ceilings and fell upon them as the saints scrambled to leave the cave they'd lived in for so long.

Once outside, Thomas and Tori counted everyone to make sure they had all made it just as a deep voice boomed above them in the sky.

"The kingdoms of this world have become the kingdoms of our Lord and of His Christ, and He shall reign forever and ever!"

Everyone looked up with wonder.

"What is it?" Brianna asked, one hand gripping Callie's and the other one Carla's.

"It's the final trumpets and seals!" Nyla shouted over a loud clap of thunder.

Lightning flashed, coating the remaining trees in metallic silver.

"Get ready, everyone!" Tori shouted, gripping Thomas's hand in hers. "We are about to leave this place!"

She could hardly believe it. Her heart nearly crashed through her chest. Could this really be the moment they'd get out of here and see Jesus, see their loved ones? Could this nightmare finally be over?

She and Thomas had done their best to keep the saints alive and encouraged. And they'd not lost any except one young woman who went in search of her husband. They'd begged her not to go, but she wouldn't listen. Though her husband was lost and had taken the mark, she missed him. She never returned.

A stomping sound penetrated the forest. Hail began to fall. Small at first, then larger and larger, leaving imprints in the dirt that spit clouds of dust.

They had nowhere to run!

"Lord, protect us!" Tori shouted over the noise.

Angels materialized and formed a circle around the group, covering them with their mighty hands and forming a solid shelter above them.

"Praise God!" Thomas shouted.

The quake grew stronger. The saints fell to the dirt and embraced each other. The hail stones splintered huge trees, crushed branches into wood shavings, and flattened boulders. Yet not one of the massive ice rocks struck the saints.

Everything went black as if someone flipped a switch and turned off the sun. A red moon appeared above them, turning everything the ominous color of blood. Flaming meteors zipped across the sky.

Though she was terrified, Tori rose and gazed upward. Thomas appeared beside her and grabbed her hand. To her left Brianna and her children huddled together, and on her right Kyle and Nyla clung to each other.

The sky began to slowly disappear like a curtain disintegrating from old age. Much to Tori's amazement, a brilliant golden city appeared and standing before it was a shimmering throne.

And the one who sat on it was the Ancient of Days.

"Hold on!" Tori said, smiling. "We're going home!"

And then they were gone.

And I saw heaven opened, and behold a white horse; and he that sat upon him was called Faithful and True, and in righteousness he doth judge and make war.

*His eyes were as a flame of fire, and on his head were
many crowns; and he had a name written, that no man knew,
but he himself.
And he was clothed with a vesture dipped in blood: and
his name is called The Word of God.
And the armies which were in heaven followed him upon
white horses, clothed in fine linen, white and clean.
And out of his mouth goeth a sharp sword, that with it he
should smite the nations: and he shall rule them with a rod of
iron: and he treadeth the winepress of the fierceness and wrath
of Almighty God.
And he hath on his vesture and on his thigh a name
written, King Of Kings, And Lord Of Lords.
Revelation 19:11-16*

One minute Thomas was standing in a forest pummeled by
hail and lightning, staring at a sky full of meteors that was
disintegrating before his eyes, and the next he was standing in a
field of flowers, blown gently by a wind that was filled with the
sweetest music he'd ever heard.

Several large warrior angels—for that is what they had to
be—stood before them, fully armored, bearing swords and all
manner of weaponry. He recognized several of them.

The snort of a horse drew his gaze to his left where
thousands, maybe tens of thousands of white horses lined up as
far as he could see, grunting and pawing the ground. Upon them
perched people of all shapes, sizes, and colors, dressed in white
and wearing breastplates and shields of gold.

Beyond them, a massive golden city perched on a hill, its
mighty ivory towers and spires reaching into a rainbow-colored
sky.

"Whoa!" Kyle exclaimed. "Are we in heaven?"

"I think so." Nyla laughed and glanced back at the rest of
the saints.

Thomas followed her gaze. The UnderHisWings saints
looked as astounded as he was. Yet the older ones were young

again, the weak looked strong, all exhaustion and pain erased from their faces.

In fact, now that he looked at Tori, she was more beautiful than he'd ever seen her. He stretched his shoulders, noting that the perpetual ache was gone. He pressed hands down his torso and gripped his thighs. He was strong, firm, and full of more energy than he ever remembered. This must be his new body!

Bubbling laughter rose in his throat, uncontainable, joyous, laughter. Turning he embraced Tori, then grabbed Nyla and Brianna and the rest, and they hugged, laughed, and cried for joy.

"We made it! We made it!"

"Was there any doubt?"

That voice. That remarkable, indistinguishable voice. Tugging from the saints, Thomas turned, blinked a few times, then found himself unable to move.

Daniel. Daniel Cain stood before him, stronger, younger, happier. Beside him stood Angel, or "Smokes," as they had called her, looking more like her name than ever. Isaac, their son, now a young man, studied Thomas with curiosity.

"Daniel." Thomas's voice cracked. "I'm so sorry."

Daniel opened his arms and Thomas flew into them. "I'm so sorry. I'm so sorry."

"It doesn't matter." Daniel nudged him back. "It's all right now. I forgive you. It's done. You made it!"

Thomas hung his head. "I was so wrong." He glanced at Angel, who was smiling his way. "I tried to have you killed!"

She laughed, her eyes sparkling with so much life and love, tears once again streamed down his cheeks.

"I forgive you, Thomas. Welcome to heaven!" She drew him close and embraced him tightly.

A squeal turned him around, In fact several squeals and cries of joy.

Two people and a child surrounded Tori, embracing her with love and happy tears—her sister's family, no doubt.

Beside her, Nyla and Kyle hugged what must be their parents and the woman she called Tata, her grandmother.

A crowd also formed around Brianna and her two little ones, everyone laughing and hugging and crying at the same time. Grabbing Callie's hand, Carla dashed toward one of the angels—the only one with wings—and they began twirling and dancing and singing in celebration. More children ran toward them as the other angels joined in.

Thomas couldn't help but smile at the mighty warriors leaping and skipping for joy right alongside the children as they praised the God of all Creation.

Separating from her family, Nyla searched the enormous field, then scanned the many horses lined up in perfect formation, and Thomas knew who she was looking for.

Her eyes lit and he followed her gaze to see a man walking toward her, emerging from among the horses. Calan! A huge smile beamed on his face. He looked strong, healthy, not at all like the last time Thomas had seen him all beat up with his head on the guillotine block.

Clutching young Daniel, Nyla ran toward him. What a scene it was! Thomas couldn't tear his gaze away as the couple flew into each other's arms, hugging and crying and kissing. More tears blurred Thomas's vision as he watched Calan see his son for the first time. Hoisting the young lad up, he flung him around, then kissed and embraced him so much, Thomas was worried the young Daniel might protest. But the boy only grinned and giggled and cried out "Daddy, Daddy!" over and over again.

Wiping his eyes, Thomas watched as all the saints who'd just arrived were reunited with family and friends. Beyond their little group, more people Thomas had never seen before were also greeting their loved ones.

"Your number is small."

Turning at the voice, Thomas looked up at an angel standing before him. "What number?"

"The saints who made it through the Tribulation without dying," the large warrior said.

Nodding, Thomas studied him. "I've seen you before."

"Aye, I am Arithem. I was assigned to protect you."

"To protect me?" Thomas was stunned. "Thank you."

"Thank the Commander." He nodded toward a bright light beyond the horses.

The other saints moved beside Thomas, wanting to hear what the angel told him. Even as they did so, other angels joined them, and Thomas knew that these mighty warriors had been their guardians from birth. He shook his head in awe. To think that God valued them so much that He assigned such incredible beings to watch over them. If Thomas had known that on earth, *really* known it, he never would have been afraid.

Yet instead of saying anything further, the angels began singing and praising God Almighty, rejoicing that the saints they'd guarded had made it into the kingdom.

Thomas could only stare in wonder at the emotions they expressed, the heartfelt praise, the joy, the way they unabashedly worshiped and adored Jesus.

Looking beyond them, Thomas wondered if any of his family had made it, but he saw no one heading his way. Instead, Tori slipped beside him, her smile brighter then he'd ever seen as she introduced him to her family.

A child headed toward them, around eight years old, with gorgeous black hair and green eyes and the brightest, most joy-filled expression on her face. She halted before Tori and gazed up at her.

For a moment, Tori only stared at her with a confused look on her face. Finally, trembling, she knelt before the child. "Are you...?"

The girl nodded, smiling.

Tori swallowed her up in her arms, clinging to the child so tightly, Thomas thought she'd squeeze the life from her. If such a thing was possible in heaven. Who was this child? He longed to ask but couldn't bring himself to interrupt the heartfelt reunion.

Finally, Tori released the girl. Tears spilling down her cheeks, she ran her hand over the girl's hair, face, her arms. "You're so beautiful! What is your name?"

"What were you going to call me?"

Tori drew the child close again.

Confusion raked through Thomas.

"Gabriella." Was all Tori said. "I'm so sorry. I'm so very sorry."

"It's all right, Mama. It's all right. I've been waiting for you."

Mama?

Tori glanced up at Thomas, her eyes glistening. "This is my daughter, Gabriella. Gabriella, this is your stepfather, Thomas."

Before Thomas could even process what he'd just been told, the girl fell against him and wrapped her little arms tightly around his waist. Overcome with a hundred emotions, Thomas returned her embrace while his own eyes filled with tears of joy. A ready-made family? Could things get any better? But yes, they could! There was only one more Person Thomas wished to see above all else.

Ceasing his dancing, Arithem moved to stand before them. "You wish to see the Commander?"

"More than anything!" Tori said.

"He will be here soon."

The other angels grew silent, almost solemn, as they stared at the heavenly city in the distance.

"Pour the final bowl," a thunderous voice echoed from the throne, and an angel holding a golden bowl flew past them, descending to Earth.

Thomas knew from Scripture what would happen. The biggest quake ever to strike the planet would level mountains, sink islands, and split Jerusalem into three parts. Every major city would fall, and hailstones even larger than what they had experienced in the forest would pummel the earth.

"It is done!" A deafening voice from the throne bellowed.

A trumpet sounded, loud and clear, and the lines of horses began to part in the middle. A brilliant light passed between them. Above the heads of the people on the horses, the top of a golden crown appeared, moving slowly to the front.

It must be the Lord! Thomas wanted to race toward him, bow at his feet, look into his eyes!

But Arithem held out an arm. "Not yet." The angel turned to address them all. "You have come at a momentous time. The Commander returns to Earth to destroy His enemies and rule and reign for a thousand years. He will not be able to greet you properly at this time."

The head of a white horse emerged from the front line, mighty and strong. Fire snorted from its nostrils as wind whipped its golden mane. Its muscular body appeared, strapped with a golden bridle and stirrups engraved with royal insignia.

And sitting on top of him was Jesus.

He wore a white robe that fell down upon armored boots made of brass. A golden breastplate sat upon his chest and a two-edged sword was in his hand. His hair was white, his eyes a flame of fire, and atop his head he wore many crowns. A name was written across his chest that no man could read, but on his robe and on his thigh were written the words

King of Kings and
Lord of Lords

Thomas fell to the ground and bowed before Him, as did all the saints.

He looked their way and gestured for them to rise. His eyes sought out Thomas and remained there long enough for Thomas to become saturated with His overwhelming love. He did the same for each saint who had just arrived, saying nothing, but not needing to.

"Welcome, my children." His voice was confident, strong, as deep as the ocean, and Thomas resisted the urge to fall to the ground again. "Welcome, my good and faithful servants. Mount up and join us in this final battle."

Though Tori didn't want to leave Gabriella's side, Arithem and the other angels took the children into safekeeping, then led Thomas and his friends to horses reserved just for them. After assisting them in putting on their armor, they helped them mount and gave them nods of approval. Thomas had never ridden a horse, but somehow, he knew how to sit comfortably in the saddle.

Hardly able to contain his excitement, he glanced at Tori on her horse beside him and saw the same thrill in her eyes as he felt. Beyond her, Calan, Nyla, Daniel, Angel, Isaac, and Brianna sat regally upon their steeds.

Far ahead of them, the Lord hefted His mighty sword high in the air and uttered a booming shout. "Come, saints, let us defeat our enemies and restore Earth to its former glory. Then you will rule and reign with me forever! It is finished. I am the Alpha and the Omega, the Beginning and the End, and I will give of the fountain of the water of life freely to him who thirsts."

Raising their swords in the air, the saints uttered an ominous roar that seemed to shame the very heavens beneath them.

And before Thomas knew it, the horses took flight and descended to Earth.

About the Author

AWARD WINNING AND BEST-SELLING AUTHOR, MARYLU TYNDALL dreamt of pirates and sea-faring adventures during her childhood days on Florida's Coast. With more than twenty-nine books published, she makes no excuses for the deep spiritual themes embedded within her romantic adventures. Her hope is that readers will not only be entertained but will be brought closer to the Creator who loves them beyond measure. In a culture that accepts the occult, wizards, zombies, and vampires without batting an eye, MaryLu hopes to show the awesome present and powerful acts of God in a dying world. A Christy and Maggie award nominee and two-time winner of the RWA Inspy Reader's Choice Award, MaryLu makes her home with her husband, six children, four grandchildren, and several stray cats on the California coast.

For a peek the characters and scenes from the book, visit my When Angels Rejoice Pinterest Page!

If you enjoyed this book, one of the nicest ways to say "thank you" to an author and help them be able to continue writing is to leave a favorable review on Amazon! Barnes and Noble, Goodreads, Bookbub (And elsewhere, too!) I would appreciate it if you would take a moment to do so. Thanks so much!

Comments? Questions? I love hearing from my readers, so feel free to contact me via my website:

https://crossandcutlass.blogspot.com

Or email me at: marylu_tyndall@yahoo.com

Follow me on:
BLOG: http://crossandcutlass.blogspot.com/
PINTEREST: http://www.pinterest.com/mltyndall/
BOOKBUB:https://www.bookbub.com/authors/marylu-tyndall
AMAZON: https://www.amazon.com/MaryLu-Tyndall/e/B002BOG7JG

To hear news about special prices and new releases sign up for my newsletter on my website Or follow me on Bookbub!
https://crossandcutlass.blogspot.com
https://www.bookbub.com/authors/marylu-tyndall

Other Books by MaryLu Tyndall

THE REDEMPTION
THE RELIANCE
THE RESTITUTION
THE RANSOM
THE RECKONING
THE RECKLESS
THE FALCON AND THE SPARROW
THE RED SIREN
THE BLUE ENCHANTRESS
THE RAVEN SAINT
CHARITY'S CROSS
SURRENDER THE HEART
SURRENDER THE NIGHT
SURRENDER THE DAWN
FORSAKEN DREAMS
ELUSIVE HOPE
ABANDONED MEMORIES
ESCAPE TO PARADISE TRILOGY
SHE WALKS IN POWER
SHE WALKS IN LOVE
SHE WALKS IN MAJESTY
VEIL OF PEARLS
WHEN ANGELS CRY
WHEN ANGELS BATTLE
TEARS OF THE SEA
TIMELESS TREASURE
WRITING FROM THE TRENCHES

Made in the USA
Las Vegas, NV
25 January 2023

66251650R00187